Counterfeit Legacy

a novel by
Kay Moser

Seton St. Clare

Seton St. Clare Books, a division of Seton St. Clare Communications
P.O. Box 8543, Waco, Texas 76714-8543
4906 Lake Englewood, Waco, Texas 76710
Printed in the United States of America
by Davis Brothers Publishing Co., Inc. of Waco, Texas

Cover art by Don Magid of Waco, Texas
Interior design by Cyndi Wendt Sykora

Library of Congress Cataloging-in-Publication Data

Moser, Kay
    Counterfeit Legacy / by Kay Moser.—1st ed.
        p.   cm.
    ISBN 1-890236-38-1
    1. Contemporary Texas—Fiction. 2. 19th Century Southern
States—Fiction
    I. Title.
    1997   97-66262
                                                            CIP

To Mary

Thank you for saying yes.

Chapter 1

Caroline Forrest Randolph did not notice the ominous, gray-green clouds moving over her house as she sat at her antique writing table responding to social invitations, but the angry, impatient storm would wait no longer for her attention. Crack! Boom! Caroline jumped from her chair when she heard the ear-splitting sounds of the lightning and thunder. She whirled around and stared out the French doors. The sudden, violent thunderstorm that surrounded her restored 19th century home was typical of an early spring deluge in Dallas, Texas. Such a volatile storm would spare no one's house—not even the home of Caroline's husband, David Morgan Randolph, the owner of Randolph Industries International.

A second flash of lightning crackled across the late afternoon sky. Caroline covered her eyes with her hands and then swiftly moved her hands to her ears as the second boom of thunder shook the house. The angry cloud released its torrents of rain. A great gust of wind toppled a piece of statuary in the garden and convinced Caroline that this storm promised danger to more than the manicured shrubbery.

Caroline fled to the main hall and crouched under a heavy walnut table that stood next to the stately staircase. All thoughts of her normally well-ordered, secure, elegant life fled from her mind. The vicious clouds tore the sky with their jagged lightning and filled the air with howling wind and booming thunder. "A tornado!" Caroline exclaimed. "This has to be a tornado. What's going to happen to me? Will the house blow away or fall in? I must—" A ferocious gust of wind blew the heavy front door open, and Caroline felt the sting of hail on her bare legs and arms. She screamed and covered her head as the front door banged wildly and the hail tore at her skin. Just as the sound of her scream of terror died away, she heard a deafening crash in the drawing room and felt the floor shake under her.

Suddenly the violence was over.

Caroline's brain struggled to understand that the front door was no longer banging against the wall, that the hall was littered with hail, but the sharp pieces of ice were no longer attacking her skin. The thunder now sounded more distant, and the flashes of lightning were no longer so close that they were blinding. All that was left of the storm was a torrential rain streaming straight down to the ground—and whatever damage the storm had left in the drawing room.

Caroline crawled out from under the walnut table and stood up. She was trembling uncontrollably. She stumbled to the front door and closed it. As she turned around, she looked in dismay at the hail that covered the center hallway of the elegant old house which she had so carefully restored. Strength began to surge back through her legs as her mind cleared and as she realized that the upsetting experience of the last few moments had not seriously harmed her. Her thoughts turned to the drawing room and the horrendous crash she had heard in there. Nauseating fear rose in her as she slowly walked toward the double doors of the drawing room. She turned the elegant brass handles, so carefully polished that morning by her housekeeper, but she could not make herself fling open the doors.

"I have to face this eventually. Whatever has happened is only becoming worse as I stand here quivering," she tried to reproach herself into acting. "Open the doors, Caroline!" She pushed her weight against the doors, and they flew open. Her eyes surveyed the room quickly, spotting the valuable, precious things she had placed there, checking them as if they were her children. A remarkable number of things were in place. The two ends of the long rectangular room had not been touched by any kind of permanently damaging force, but in the middle of the room, there was a tangled mass of wet tree limbs. Quickly her eyes traveled down the length of the tree, following its trunk past the broken drawing room window as far as she could see. Immediately she understood what had happened. This tree was the venerable, old oak that had grown across the street in her neighbor's yard. It had been the pride of the block, but now it had fallen and crashed through the large central window of her magnificent drawing room.

Because it was planted so far from her house, only the very top of the tree had actually landed in her drawing room. The uppermost branches had swept down the wall directly across from the window, leaving great scars on the plaster and ripping the various portraits and other decorations off the wall. Caroline knew that those precious decorations lay in a broken mass under the branches. The sight of smashed chairs, a crumpled love seat, and broken mahogany tables turned her into a stone of immobilized despair. She had chosen every piece in this room to create an impressive but welcoming atmosphere. Suddenly Caroline's mind flew to the single, most treasured item in her house. It was preserved in a shadowbox frame that had hung on the now scraped wall. "Oh no!" she cried as she came to life again. "I must find it. Oh, it just can't be destroyed. It just can't!"

She scrambled to the tree and picked her way through small branches, peering down carefully at the items that were smashed beneath her feet. They were beyond hope. Finally she saw the back of a large, framed item. She drew in her breath quickly as she recognized the shadowbox frame that held the most precious heirloom she possessed. "It's ruined!" she cried, but as tears filled her eyes, she pushed aside several more wet branches and reached down for the shadowbox. She pulled it from the branches and turned it over, as broken glass flew around her hands. She felt the sting of a cut on her left hand, but she ignored it momentarily in her anguish to discover if the heirloom could possibly be saved. She stepped back out of the branches of the tree and stared down at the shadowbox. The glass that had protected it for decades was gone, but her great-great-grandfather's silk vest, her most prized possession, seemed to be undamaged by the smashing of its frame or the water that had come into the room when the wet tree fell.

Aware now that her left hand was bleeding, her most pressing fear was that she would get blood on this precious vest. She wrapped the hem of her skirt around her bleeding left hand before carefully pulling the vest from its frame with her right hand. She hurried out of the room and into her sitting room, where she laid the vest on her desk. She continued on to the downstairs bathroom to care for her hand. As she stood before the vanity, she caught a glimpse of herself in the mirror for the first time since the storm had struck. Her normally well-groomed, deep auburn hair was wet and tangled around her face. Her grayish-blue eyes looked bloodshot, and her face was wet with a mixture of her tears and rain. She was shocked by her appearance and the fright in her eyes. Her left hand began to throb, and she remembered that she had come to bandage the cut. She reached for a fresh white towel with her right hand. Then she cradled her left, bleeding hand in the white towel and stared at it.

"Will I ever be able to look at my hand again and not see blood on it—if I do this thing?" The unbidden, unwelcome question forced itself to the front of her mind and out of her mouth.

Swiftly she covered her left, bleeding hand with the towel as she scolded herself. "What absurd nonsense! This is a cut on your hand which is bleeding. That's all it is, Caroline. It has nothing to do with—with—with that! Don't let your fertile imagination run away with you."

She uncovered her left hand and saw that it continued to bleed. She felt unnerved by the sight of the blood, so she jerked her head up and stared angrily at herself in the mirror.

"I tell you this has nothing to do with—with—nothing to do with anything in the past or in the future!" She spoke the words forcibly, determined that they should become her truth, but her eyes betrayed her; they did not believe her words.

She dragged her eyes away from her own image in the mirror, turned on the cold water faucet, and stuck her bleeding hand under the cold water. "You should be more concerned about whether you need stitches in this hand. You've made your decision about the other matter."

Another voice deep inside her disagreed. "No, you haven't. You're not at all sure you can do it, Caroline."

She brought her hand closer to her face and stared at it in the dim light from the window. Suddenly she realized that she had turned on no light, but when she reached for the switch, no amount of frustrated flipping of it would produce electric light. "The storm," she muttered. "Of course, the storm has knocked out the electricity. I wonder how bad the damage to the neighborhood is? How bad is the damage to the city? How long will it be before someone comes to help? What can I do about a tree in my drawing room and no electricity?" Panic began to rise in her, but she fought it down. "I'm not hurt, not really," she reassured herself, "but how many people around me are hurt? What should I do? What can I do?"

Every question she asked herself increased her anxiety, until she finally snapped at herself, "Stop it, Caroline! No doubt the officials have control of the situation. You must be sensible. Think about the neighbors. Can you see anything from the front porch?"

She wrapped her cut hand in a guest towel and hurried back to the main hall, pulled open the front door, and stepped out onto the porch. She gasped. The street was littered with uprooted trees and downed power lines. She strained to see through the driving rain. The houses were all standing, but they looked damaged.

"Is anyone in your house injured?" a man shouted from the street. She could see his bright yellow rain coat and helmet and knew he was a fireman or a disaster relief worker.

"No, I'm okay," she yelled back, "but my neighbors—"

"Go back inside!" he commanded. "The streets are too dangerous. We're checking every house for injured people."

"But what do I do?" she shouted.

"Just stay put!" he called back as he continued down the block.

She went back inside the house and closed the heavy door. She felt terrifyingly alone, as if the last person on earth had abandoned her. "Oh, I wish David were here," she cried, "or that Hannah hadn't left for her night off." A quiver of fear ran through her. "No, it's stupid to wish such things. If they had been here, they might have been hurt. I've got to take hold of myself. I can't just stand here shaking," she scolded herself. "I'd better check the rest of the house for damage." Quickly she went upstairs and hurried from room to room. She found only a few window panes broken. When she returned to the foot of the staircase, anxiety enshrouded her again.

"You simply have to wait," she told herself. "Do something to get your mind off the storm." Resolutely she returned to the bathroom and fumbled in the cabinet, found some gauze and tape, and bandaged her hand. She continued talking to herself as she walked back to her sitting room. "Everything looks fine in here. The main hall was not disturbed except for the hail that blew in. The damage in the drawing room seems to be quite contained in a single area right in the middle. The wind's not blowing, the rain's coming straight down, so the water damage isn't getting too much worse. The tree, of course, is lying in my drawing room, but there's nothing I can do about that. I wonder how long it will take to get the electricity back on. I should mop up the water off the wooden floor in the hall. That'll take a little time and get my mind off other worries."

She went back into the kitchen, found a mop and pail in the closet and came back to the hallway. After mopping up the melted hail, carefully protecting her cut hand as she worked, she found herself alone again in the battered house as evening approached. Impatiently she went back into her sitting room and jerked up the telephone. It was dead. She paced around the room, then stared out the window. The rain was still pouring, the clouds were low and dark, but there was no wind. She saw several bright flashlights and could vaguely see the people holding them. There was nothing to do but wait in the increasing darkness for the city employees to come deal with the tree in the drawing room.

Panic began to rise in her as she looked around the sitting room and realized how dark it had become.

"I've got to have some light," she told herself firmly, "and I must concentrate on something. Otherwise this waiting will drive me crazy. The street is absolutely littered with downed trees. I'm sure the clean-up crews will come as quickly as possible, but, of course, the first priority must be finding those who are injured. In the meantime I must keep myself calm."

She walked to the dining room and brought back a candelabrum which she placed on the mahogany table next to her favorite chair. After she had lighted the five candles, she aimlessly picked up the vest and sat down. Carefully she removed the remaining glass fragments. "I've never even seen this vest up close," she said. "As long as I can remember, it's been behind glass in its frame. I remember staring up at it on the wall in Grandmother's drawing room. How important it seemed to be as Grandmother told me all those marvelous stories about her wealthy, powerful grandfather. By the time I was twelve, I would shiver with excitement when she promised me that the vest would be mine some day. I never thought she would give it up while she lived, but she did. Of all the wedding presents David and I received, this vest was the one I treasured most. Oh, thank goodness it's safe!"

She began to examine the ivory-colored, silk vest. Even though it was a man's vest, it was covered with intricate embroidery, crafted in tiny stitches of silk thread. The major motif of the design was a delicate vine which trailed across the vest with a leaf or tiny flower growing here and there from the vine. "Such a design would be considered feminine now," Caroline murmured, "but men of wealth wore embroidered vests for centuries. What beautiful needlework this is!"

"Thank goodness James Bradford's vest is safe. I could bear to lose all the antiques and family pieces in the whole house if I had to, but never this vest. To think that James Bradford, my great-great-grandfather wore this! This vest is my connection to the great Bradford legacy I've always treasured. Oh! If it had been destroyed, I would have had to tell Grandmother it was gone. I believe it would have killed her. How lucky she was to have actually known him! I have always wished I could have. Well, if there's anything good about this storm, it's the opportunity it has given me to actually touch James Bradford's vest, to feel a little closer to him."

She began to trace the intricate tendrils and tiny leaves of the vine and to place an appreciative finger on the little flowers that the seamstress had embroidered so many years ago. There were several stains. She considered their possible sources, as if she were handling the vest to prepare it for a museum presentation.

"This is undoubtedly a tea stain. This one is darker. Perhaps it is coffee." She ran her finger over the stain. "And this one," she came to the third, gasped, and quickly drew her finger back. "This one looks like— No! It's not—it is red wine," she decided instantly. "A very dark red wine, a burgundy, no doubt." Hastily she moved her attention to the hand-crafted button holes and the beautiful buttons. She examined the pockets of the vest and contemplated the type of gold watch that had undoubtedly been housed there. She owned a portrait of her great-great-grandfather, a small one her grandmother had given her. She imagined him wearing this vest and pulling his large, gold watch out of the pocket on his left to check the time. She stuck her own fingers into the left-side pocket and felt a strange, rough stitching at the bottom of the pocket. "That's odd," she murmured. She pulled out the lining of the pocket and realized that the heavy watch her great-great-grandfather had tucked there had worn through the lining. Someone had meticulously hand-sewn the bottom of the lining back together. Caroline studied the darning stitches used for the repair and then stuffed the lining back into the pocket. She turned the vest inside out and admired the careful, even stitches that connected the lining of the vest to the ornately-decorated outer shell. Slowly, methodically she ran her finger along the edge of the neck of the vest, admiring each tiny stitch some unknown seamstress had made over 125 years ago.

Suddenly her fingers hit a crisp place in an otherwise pliable fabric, and at the same time her ears heard the slightest crackle. She was startled. "There's something between the vest lining and the outer shell," she exclaimed to the empty room where she waited. "Something is sewn into the vest. What is it and who would do such a thing?" Once again she ran her fingers over the area and listened intently. She heard the same crackling noise and felt something stiff under the fabric. She bent the area between her fingers and heard the crackling noise again. "It's undoubtedly a piece of paper," her excitement rose, "not a very large piece of paper, perhaps two or three inches square. What on earth is it? Why is it here?" Slowly she began to work the paper down from the neck area of the vest across the chest, back toward the pocket. It took a long time to edge the piece of paper down to the pocket, and as she diligently worked at it, the candlelight flickered in the darkness, casting a circle of light around her chair.

"There!" she exclaimed when she had achieved her goal. "If I want to, I can open the stitches where this pocket lining has been repaired and read what is on this piece of paper. I wonder how long it has been here. I could never bring myself to rip open any stitches that are original to the vest, but this repair in the pocket lining would make no difference." Unable to resist the temptation, she hurried to her desk drawer and came back with tiny needlepoint scissors. Leaning over the vest, she pulled out the pocket lining once again and carefully snipped just a few stitches, just enough to open the lining two inches. Then she put the scissors down on the table and looked at the opening. The five candles cast strange, dancing shadows across the silk she had unstitched. All thoughts of the storm and the tree that had crashed into her drawing room were erased from Caroline's mind. "If I want to, I can reach into the past by reaching through that opening and pulling out that piece of paper. I can reach back into the 19th century and know something. But what? Will I be disappointed? Will it be a perfectly commonplace piece of paper, some meaningless list, some scrap of a business document?" She made no movement to retrieve the paper. She was mysteriously drawn to it, but she was afraid it would disappoint her. "What do I want to find? What do I seek, sitting here in 1996, facing the most important decision of my life, a decision I can't force myself to make?" She peered into the hole.

"What do I *want* to find?" she asked herself again. And

instantly she knew the answer. "I want to find the solution to my present dilemma. I want to find a way out of this horrible thing I must do."

No storm, no damaged heirloom vest had been able to divert her mind completely from her dilemma. No matter how many times she had told herself, "I won't think about that now"—she was always thinking about it. For some insane reason, she now believed the answer to her dilemma was on this piece of paper and had been there for 125 years.

"Well," she said aloud, with more bravado than she felt, "whatever it is, I must know."

Gently she thrust two fingers into the opening she had made and clasped the piece of paper and pulled it forth. It had ragged edges and was folded in half. Obviously someone had hastily torn it off of a larger sheet of paper, folded it, and given it to her great-great-grandfather. She stared at it unopened, petrified that it would not bring her what she needed. Finally she took a deep breath and opened the piece of paper. In faded brown ink, written in a spidery, feminine handwriting, she read, "He knows nothing. Meet me at midnight." There was no signature.

Caroline was so startled by what she read that she could not absorb the words. She blinked her eyes, held the paper closer to the candlelight, and read it again. It was not addressed to anyone, but it was obviously meant for her great-great-grandfather because it had been put into his pocket. "He knows nothing. Meet me at midnight." She was disappointed. This piece of paper did nothing for her life. It did not move her one inch closer to a solution of her problem. Anger rose in her, and she was tempted to crush the paper in her hand, but she could not release the notion that there was a reason she had found it. "My great-great-grandfather must have put a note in his pocket, a note which went through the hole in the bottom of his pocket. Someone repaired the hole without knowing the paper was there, stuck between the lining and the outer vest. But why didn't the seamstress who repaired the pocket notice the floating piece of paper? Apparently no one has noticed it, or no one has been interested enough—or desperate enough—to retrieve it. It is here for me. I know it is! But what does it mean?"

She read it again. "He knows nothing. Meet me at midnight." Her imagination leapt into action. "A woman wrote it, apparently handed it to my great-great-grandfather, but she refers to some 'he.' Whoever this 'he' was, it was important that he didn't know something. It was important enough to her to cause her to write it down and give it to my great-great-grandfather. But what woman would he be meeting at midnight? What difference does it make to me? What possible difference can it make over 125 years later to anyone, much less to me?"

Chapter 2

Loud pounding on the front door startled Caroline. Carefully she laid the vest and the note on her desk and hurried to the door. When she opened it, she found two men wearing bright yellow raincoats.

"Are you all right?" the first man asked. "I'm Tom Bennett from the City Emergency Services. This block is quite a mess. Is anybody injured in your house?"

"No," Caroline replied quickly. "Thank God, I'm fine, and there was no one else in the house when the storm hit. As you can see, however, a tree crashed through the window of the drawing room."

"Yes ma'am," the second man spoke up. "That tree's causing us a lot of problems. I'm from the electric company. We've gotta move that tree because it's blocking the street, and it pulled down every wire on this block."

"How long do you think it will be before you can repair all this?" Caroline asked anxiously.

"We won't be able to make much difference tonight," Tom Bennett spoke up. "That tree was a very large, old oak. It's gonna be a major job to remove it from the street, and that seems to be the most pressing need, so we can get the power back on in this area."

"Are any of my neighbors hurt?" Caroline asked

"Nothing serious," Bennett responded. "We have pretty much canvassed the area. There are a lot of people with bruises and cuts. I believe we have three or four people with broken bones, but basically the storm touched down in only an eight-block area, and there's very little human injury. We've transported a few people to the hospital, but mostly they're elderly people who are frightened and have health conditions that need to be monitored. It simply wouldn't be safe to leave them in their houses."

"Thank goodness," Caroline said. "It could have been a great deal worse."

"Yes ma'am," Bennett spoke up again. "It certainly could have been."

"Was it a tornado?" Caroline asked.

"As best as we can tell, ma'am, it was a tornado, but it only stayed on the ground for a few seconds, and it seems to have centered right here on your block. There's more than one tree down. There are a good number of roofs ripped off. You're very fortunate that the only damage you have is this one tree in your living room."

"That's all I've found," Caroline answered. "I've checked the house. There are some windowpanes out on the upper floors, but there doesn't seem to be any structural damage. There's been no leaking, in spite of this torrential rain, so I assume the roof must be in fairly good condition. Of course, I can't really tell without going up into the attic—"

"No, don't do that; it's not safe for you to go up there. Come tomorrow morning, you'll want to have someone take a look at everything," the man said. "You'll need to have the chimneys checked, the roof checked, have a contractor come check for basic structural problems. As for tonight, ma'am, you're gonna have to spend the night somewhere else."

"Oh, but I can't leave my house," Caroline protested. "After all, the front of it is totally torn open. Anyone could walk right in."

"Well, that's true enough, ma'am, but we do have a heavy police guard in this area, so we don't expect any looting or anything. Only workmen and the few residents who insist on staying are gonna be here through the night."

"I'm one of those residents who insist on staying," Caroline informed him. "I spent a great deal of time and money restoring this house, and I plan to stay and take care of it."

"Well, now, as I understand it, you're here alone. I don't like the idea of a woman alone tonight in this kind of situation. Is there someone we can call to come stay with you?"

"But if you're going to have policemen patrolling, I can't see why you're concerned. And as for calling anyone, well, there are some people I would like to contact but only to let them know that I'm safe. There's really no need for anyone to come stay. It's not likely I'll get any sleep anyway."

"Well, ma'am, you're a citizen and a taxpayer and have a right to make your own decisions, but if you were my wife, I would insist you leave." He hesitated, obviously hoping Caroline would change her mind.

"I'll be fine," she said firmly.

"Okay, if you insist." Bennett gave up the argument. "As soon as dawn comes, there'll be trucks and workers with chain saws here to remove the trees from the road."

"And we'll get those electric wires back up, ma'am," the electric company man added.

"Is it too much trouble for you to call a member of my family?" Caroline asked. "I do have an elderly grandmother not too far away, and I'm afraid she'll worry. If someone could just call her, then she will call my mother and father and anyone else who might be concerned."

"Well, I'm sure we can handle that, ma'am, if you'll just give me a phone number and a name," Bennett agreed.

Caroline invited them into the foyer, but they declined after glancing down at their heavy, wet boots. She hurried to her sitting room, and when she returned to the foyer, she gave Bennett a piece of paper with her grandmother's name and telephone number on it. "If you will please call this number, either my grandmother or her housekeeper will answer. Just tell her that I'm safe and that I'm staying here tonight but that the phone is not working. She will spread the word, I'm sure."

"Okay, ma'am," Bennett took the piece of paper. "I'll have one of the girls back at the office call her. You sure you want to stay here by yourself?"

"Yes, I'm quite sure," Caroline said confidently, although she felt a little shaky. "I'll be just fine."

"Well, if you have any kind of problem at all, just come out on your porch and shout for help. There'll be an officer close by. Whatever you do, don't leave the porch and go out into your yard. I don't want you accidentally electrocuted."

"Thank you very much," Caroline said as she tried to smile bravely. "I promise to stay put." They nodded and turned away, and she closed the door.

"There really isn't anything for me to be scared of," she told herself. "It's just this wretched situation I've gotten myself into. I've been unnerved for weeks now, unnerved in general, and now this blasted tree has to come falling into the drawing room. But I suppose I should be grateful that I haven't been hurt and that no one else has been harmed very seriously.

"Listen to me, talking to myself again! Well, I don't care. It makes me feel better, and there's no one here to hear me anyway. I can't imagine that I'll be able to sleep tonight. I think the best thing for me to do is to lie down on the couch in my sitting room where I can hear anything that happens. Thank goodness I have plenty of candles, but it's going to be a long night, so I better get the flashlight from the kitchen and bring some more candles to my sitting room. I should try to eat something, but I don't think I could keep food down."

After returning to the sitting room, Caroline built a fire in the fireplace and sat down on the sofa. David, of course, is abroad, she thought bitterly. How many days of our marriage has he been abroad? And how does it happen that those days always seem to coincide with the catastrophes of our lives? Well, I'll just have to manage. If the city officials don't get that tree out of the drawing room first thing in the morning, I'll have to try to hire some men to come take it away. Then I'll have to find carpenters to board up the front of the house until I can make plans to rebuild that section, but I'd rather worry about all of that in the light of day. I can't listen to the radio or the stereo to get my mind off things. If only there were enough light to read by. If I can't read, what am I going to do all night?

Perhaps I should have left, but no, if I left the house, I would feel like I was abandoning my own child. Tears sprang to her eyes as the thought of a child passed through her mind, but she quickly scolded herself. Don't think about that either. Think about that later. Oh, if only David were here. If only I could tell him the truth. But I can't. He'd never forgive me. How could I have done such a stupid thing? How could I have even thought of deceiving him—tricking him? Nothing is as important as our relationship; I must protect it no matter what the cost. I love David so much. I loved him the first time I ever saw him, even though I didn't know I loved him, not consciously anyway. Somewhere deep inside of me I felt I had come home. I knew that my life had changed in an instant.

"Don't start daydreaming about the past, Caroline," she scolded herself. "You need to solve your current problems." She stood up, determined to take action, but when she realized there was nothing she could do, she plopped back down, sighed and said, "I can't do anything but wait. I might as well remember the good times."

Just six years before in 1990, D. Morgan Randolph had been no more than a name to Caroline, a name which appeared periodically on large donation checks to restore Randolph House. Randolph House was Caroline's first position as the senior curator of a major restoration project. She was only 28 years old, only four years out of graduate school, and yet the year before, she had landed the directorship of the major Texas restoration project of the year. What a coup that had been!

She was far too clever not to communicate as personally as she could with D. Morgan Randolph, the donor of thousands of dollars to the project that would undoubtedly make or break her reputation as a preservationist. So she never sent an ordinary letter thanking D. Morgan Randolph for the thousands he contributed. She always responded to his gifts with an extensive, hand-written account of how his donation would be used, thanked him for his generosity and deplored the fact that he was unable to serve on the board of directors. Mr. Randolph resided abroad most of the year because of his position in Randolph Industries International. Yet his interest in Randolph House was very personal, for it had been the ancestral home of his father's family, and it had been he who had decided, after the deaths of his parents, to give the property to the National Trust and open the property to the public.

And oh, what a beautiful example of early 19th century architecture Randolph House was! Since it had once been the focal point of a plantation, it sat on the outskirts of the city, surrounded by 5 acres of the original plantation land. Those acres had been turned into a beautiful garden in the 1920's by D. Morgan Randolph's grandmother. What a perfect museum home for Dallas, Texas. It was in excellent condition structurally, for it had been loved its entire life; but it had, of course, been updated, remodeled, and decorated quite a few times. Caroline had her heart set on returning it to the way it looked the day it was finished in 1875. Of course, that desire meant that she had to raise tremendous amounts of money as well as spend months with specialists as they scraped through layers of paint, looking for the original colors, and as they explored every nook and cranny looking for bits of wallpaper to reproduce. Caroline pored over old family account books and journals looking for any information that would make it possible for her to know for certain what the house had looked like in 1875.

Even though he was in Europe, D. Morgan Randolph was a great help because he shared all the family records, as well as a good bit of his money. It took almost a full year of intense activity, but finally by Christmas of 1990 Caroline had managed to restore the double parlors, the main hall that ran the full depth of the house, the elegant staircase, and the dining room. There was a great deal more to restore, but she knew that she needed to raise money to go further; and to secure more donations, she needed to show the patrons the results of their support.

"Besides," Caroline told her staff, "this house was donated as a gift to the people of Texas and to Americans in general. It's time to throw open the doors of Randolph House to all those who have supported the beginnings of the restoration and to the public. We'll plan a gala evening, a formal, Christmas reception, by invitation only, for the patrons who have contributed to the restoration. After they have the first look at the completed rooms, we'll open the house to the public for the Christmas season." Her fund-raising plan produced a frenzied fall that was full of last-minute details of the restoration, as well as the gargantuan effort of planning the reception and decorating the rooms for Christmas in the fashion of a plantation house in 1875.

The restored rooms were magnificent when they were decorated, but her success had created a tug of war in her heart. Part of Caroline ached to have the whole house restored, but another part of her never wanted to finish the whole house because then she would have to move on to a new project. Most of all she felt proud of her accomplishment, excited and happy.

However, on the afternoon of the reception around four o'clock, she was not feeling proud and happy. She was feeling utter frustration as she stormed up a ladder in the front parlor and tried to re-attach the cedar swag that kept falling down from its place high over the mantel. "Four hours from now," she muttered, "this house will be filled with elegantly dressed patrons who will want to see the results of their investments, and I cannot keep this blasted swag in place!" It was a tall ladder she stood on, but she had swallowed hard, climbed it bravely and had tried one more time to staple the swag in place. "There!" she proclaimed triumphantly when she won the battle with the swag. As she started backing down the ladder, her eyes on the conquered swag, the greenery suddenly fell down again. She was so startled and infuriated that she turned loose of the ladder for just an instant and began to fall backwards. Terror seized her heart as she felt herself free-floating down toward the hardwood floor, but just as she expected to hit and land with a thud, she felt strong hands snatching at her. She was confused, disoriented, and frightened half out of her wits, but she did have enough sense left to understand that she was not going to hit the floor, that someone had caught her.

"You're okay, you're just fine," a deep masculine voice insisted. "You just lost your balance, but you're not hurt. You're okay." There was a quiet firmness combined with great gentleness in that voice. She looked up into the face of her rescuer and realized he was a total stranger.

"Thank you," she gasped. "I believe you've kept me from breaking my neck. How can I ever thank you?"

"Delighted to be of service," he said rather saucily.

She stared into his blue eyes for half a minute before she realized that her face was only a foot or so from his and that he was still holding her in his arms like a child. There was something distinctly unsettling about having this remarkably handsome, older man holding her in his strong arms.

"Um, would you mind putting me down?" she asked, trying to regain her composure.

"Certainly." Gently he placed her on her feet and steadied her by holding her arms for a few seconds.

"I'm okay," she told him as she smiled up at him.

"But you nearly weren't," he said a little severely. "Whatever possessed you to climb such a high ladder and try to arrange a piece of a tree fourteen feet above this floor?"

"Well, as a matter of fact, that's my job. There will be several hundred distinguished guests here in four hours, and that blasted swag will not stay up. In fact, I'm going to have to go back up that ladder and fix it again."

"No, you're not going to go back up that ladder," the man informed her.

Caroline stared at him in amazement. "I beg your pardon," she said as calmly as she could manage. "I really have no choice. You see, I'm the curator of this museum house, and that swag has to be fixed, and there's no one left on the premises to fix it."

"I'm here," he said.

"Well, thank you very much," she replied "for what I assume is an offer of your services. But I really can't ask you to go up that ladder and do my work."

"It's as much my house as it is yours," he informed her gently.

"Oh really! Is it indeed?" she asked with a definite hint of sarcasm.

"In fact, technically, it's more my house than yours."

"I'm afraid I don't understand," she shook her head impatiently, "and I'm also afraid I don't have time for small talk. Who are you?"

"I'm D. Morgan Randolph," the man smiled at her.

Caroline was stunned. All she could think of was her appearance. She had on a pair of dirty jeans and an old sweatshirt from her alma mater. Her long auburn hair was in a ponytail, a good bit of it dragging across her face because it had slipped loose from the barrette that was supposed to be holding it. She wore no makeup and actually had dirt under her fingernails because she had worked so long and hard that day.

She gasped. "D. Morgan Randolph. Oh no!"

"Oh yes," he laughed, "and I assume that you must be Caroline Forrest."

"I wish I weren't." She hung her head and looked at the tops of her old, worn-out tennis shoes. Both of her big toes were visible through frayed tears in the canvas. "Or at least I wish this whole event could be erased. I wish I could just meet you this evening. I assure you that I don't normally look like this."

"I'm sorry to hear that," he murmured. "I rather like your ponytail—and the toes are a nice touch."

There was laughter in his voice, but it wasn't ridicule.

"Well, if you like this ponytail," she informed him as she raised her head and stared into his eyes, "you would have loved the one I had when I was ten years old."

"I'm sure I would have," he agreed. "Now, Miss Forrest, the

house looks lovely. You've done a marvelous job of restoring it. Mother would be overwhelmed with pride if she could see it. And it's obvious you've worked yourself to the bone to decorate the house for this evening. I want you to go home now and be kind to yourself for a few hours, so that you can greet your guests feeling a little bit better than you feel right now."

"Oh, but I can't leave," she exclaimed. "I can't possibly let the guests arrive and see that swag hanging all the way down to the mantel."

"I'll take care of fixing the swag," he assured her.

"Oh no, I couldn't ask you to do that."

"I won't allow you to go back up that ladder," he informed her.

She stared at him for a moment. Generally when someone said she wasn't allowed to do something, she responded in anger, but this time she felt very special for some reason she couldn't explain.

"Caroline!" another masculine voice yelled from the main hall. She recognized it as Taylor's voice.

"In here," she called, "in the front parlor."

Quickly Taylor popped in, glanced around the room and declared, "Looks great. You did a fantastic job. No surprise to me, of course." He stalked across the room, threw his arms across her shoulders and planted a kiss on her cheek. "Your usual tasteful, elegant performance," he gestured briefly toward the room.

"Except for this swag," she stepped forward to escape Taylor's half embrace and pointed to the swag.

"Oh." Taylor looked at it.

Suddenly she remembered her manners and the importance of Mr. Randolph. "Oh, Taylor, this is Mr. Morgan Randolph, the owner of Randolph House—at least, the former owner. Mr. Randolph, may I introduce my friend Taylor Wilkinson to you?"

"How do you do," both men said as they shook hands in a very formal fashion.

"What are you going to do about the swag?" Taylor demanded of Caroline.

"I'm going to fix it, of course."

"No," Mr. Randolph objected. "You're not going to fix it. You're going to go home and rest and come back this evening."

Taylor stared at him but said nothing.

"You are Miss Forrest's friend, I believe?" Mr. Randolph asked with a special emphasis on the word "friend."

"That's right," Taylor answered.

"Then perhaps you could escort her home and see to it that she takes care of herself. I'll take care of the swag. Excuse me." Without another word he turned and steadied the ladder. Taylor and Caroline stared at him nervously as he agilely scurried up to take a closer look at the problem. He appeared to be in his early forties, but in many ways he acted younger than Taylor, who was thirty. In a few seconds he returned to the floor.

"No staple gun is going to hold that swag up, Miss Forrest," he declared. "I'll need a hammer and some nails and wire. I'm sure you have that kind of thing around here."

"Well yes, yes, we do," she stammered. "We have a workshop out in the carriage house, but the carpenter is gone."

"I don't need a carpenter," Mr. Randolph smiled. "Believe it or not, I do know how to drive a nail. You go on home, rest and relax, dress for this evening, come back and be the belle of the reception—a position you have certainly earned."

"But Mr. Randolph, I couldn't possibly allow—"

"I'm afraid, Miss Forrest," he took her by the arm and started guiding her toward the door, "you couldn't possibly stop me. Taylor," he looked back over his shoulder at the younger man, "why don't you see your lady friend home?" His words to Taylor sounded like a question but carried the impact of a command.

By this time all three of them had arrived in the main hall, and he was encouraging Caroline out the front door.

"The next time I see you," he said gently, "I want to see you all dressed up to receive your guests."

Somehow she couldn't argue with this man, so she nodded and murmured, "Thank you."

By the time she reached her car, Taylor, who had said nothing, suddenly spoke up. "You don't really need me to see you home. You know the way home."

"Of course," Caroline said impatiently.

"Well, I believe I'd better get in there and help that fellow out. He's not as young as he used to be, no matter what he thinks," Taylor confided to her.

She looked at the premature, middle-aged spread on Taylor's mid-section and remembered the trim waistline of D. Morgan Randolph, but she said nothing.

"It isn't safe for him to be up on that ladder," Taylor continued. "I better go back and help."

There was a definite tone of rivalry in Taylor's voice.

"Do as you like," Caroline said, her exhaustion suddenly overwhelming her. "I'm too tired to care. Nothing but a bubble bath and a hot cup of tea could make me care about anything."

She threw herself into her car and drove off as Taylor strode hurriedly back to Randolph House.

Back at her condominium Caroline went straight upstairs and turned on the faucet in the whirlpool bathtub. In a matter of minutes she was able to slip her weary body down into the churning warm water that was scented with roses from the bubble bath she had added to it. For five minutes she let her mind drift as the water moved around her, massaging her body. Then she turned off the whirlpool and just lay there, relaxing. Her mind stopped drifting and, as quickly and definitively as a laser beam, settled on the subject of D. Morgan Randolph. She relived the moment of falling and being caught in his arms and looking up into his face. He was a very handsome man. Dark hair that was graying, gentle blue eyes, a definite quality of refinement, combined with unmistakable masculinity. It was a rare combination. He was dressed impeccably in the kind of gray, tailored suit that one can only buy in London. A conservative white shirt, dark tie. Yes, he was quite handsome and quite special. Then she remembered her own appearance and groaned. She turned her head and looked at the heap of filthy jeans and sweatshirt and tennis shoes on the floor of the bathroom. "Good grief," she muttered. "I've waited a solid year to meet this man, and, of course, I would be looking like that!" She kicked up the foamy water, then lay there for a full minute feeling depressed. Finally her mind turned to the coming evening. "I won't look like a wreck this evening," she smiled coyly. "No, indeed, I won't! Mr. Randolph won't even recognize me."

Caroline Forrest stood before the twelve-foot-tall pier mirror at one end of the front parlor of Randolph House and stared at her reflection. She looked like a magnolia that had miraculously bloomed at Christmas time. Her dark-green velvet dress was a copy of a 19th century ball gown. It left her shoulders bare, then gracefully followed her curves to her tiny waist and finally flowed luxuriantly to the floor in a full skirt. The ivory tone of her face and neck flowed into the creamy softness of her shoulders and arms like the petals of the magnolia bloom poised above its dark green leaves. She had arranged her deep auburn hair on top of her head in a mass of loosely organized curls. The dancing light in her blue-gray eyes was the natural result of excitement from many sources: her debut as the curator of an historic property, the charm of the Christmas season with the beautiful decorations that glittered around her, and more than she wanted to admit—her anticipation of seeing D. Morgan Randolph again.

As she paused in front of the mirror a few seconds longer, she allowed herself the thrill of thinking of the tall, dark stranger who had entered her life only a few hours earlier. She had dated Taylor for five years, during which time there had been a slow, seemingly inevitable progression toward some kind of commitment between them. They were not engaged, but by the standards of judgment of their social class, they were considered a perfect match. They had similar backgrounds, the same goals, and were almost the same age. Still, this stranger, D. Morgan Randolph, whom Caroline had just met, was the cause of the beautiful blush on her face—not Taylor. Caroline tried to chastise herself and feel wicked for even thinking of another man, but all she could feel was joy and excitement. Finally she laughed at her reflection in the mirror, shrugged her shoulders, and whispered, "Why not? Just for tonight. Why not?"

A loud, clattering sound at the front door forced her to move away from the mirror and think once again of her duties as the hostess for the evening. She started toward the double doors that opened into the hall, but the doors were flung open, and she was suddenly confronted by Taylor whose face was beaming. He thrust a small package wrapped in gold foil and shining green ribbon at her.

"Merry Christmas!" he boomed. "I know it's too early to give you your Christmas present, but I want you to wear it tonight, so here it is."

Mechanically she took the package and stared down at the gold foil, as she struggled to draw her thoughts away from D. Morgan Randolph.

"Oh Taylor, thank—thank you," she stammered. "I'm totally surprised. I—I never expected—I don't have—"

"No, no," he interrupted loudly. "Of course you didn't expect this. I've been planning it for months. After all, what better night to give you this particular gift than tonight? Open it, and you'll see what I mean." He dragged her across the room to one of the 19th century love seats and gently pushed her down. "Open it," he commanded. "You'll understand when you see it."

She tore open the wrappings and quickly exposed a box from a well-known jewelry store. Her heart thumped wildly with fear until she realized that the box was too large for a ring. "Taylor, I have a feeling you've done something you shouldn't have done."

"Nonsense," he proclaimed, as he stood over her and excitedly rubbed his hands together. "Open the lid."

She looked up at him. He looked like a child about to spring a great surprise on a favorite friend. She looked back down and opened the lid; a stunning bracelet of emeralds and diamonds glittered on the black velvet interior of the box.

"Taylor!" she cried. "I can't accept this."

"Why not?" he demanded.

"It's obviously very expensive. Too expensive."

"I can afford it," he said proudly.

"It's not a question of whether you can afford it, Taylor. It's a question of whether you should afford it, whether I should allow you to afford it, whether it's even—well—you know, a proper gift, considering—"

"Considering what?" he demanded.

"Well, considering that it's very expensive, Taylor, and it's not like we're—"

"Engaged?" he questioned.

"Right," Caroline responded. "Engaged or—or—for something this expensive—married."

"Oh, Caroline, sometimes you have the most ridiculous ideas. This is not the Victorian Age. A man can give a woman whatever he wants to give her, whatever he can afford."

"But Taylor, a gift of jewelry, a gift of this expense—"

"Nonsense," he insisted. "It's the perfect gift for the perfect moment. I ordered it months ago when you told me you were going to wear green velvet. It's absolutely perfect for tonight. It's a tribute to your beauty, Caroline. It's a tribute to your accomplishments. I want you to have it. It's your Christmas present. You can't refuse it."

Again she gazed up into his face and saw the shiny eagerness in it. "I don't know," she hesitated.

"Well, wear it!" Taylor reached down, snatched the bracelet from the box, took her left wrist in his hand, and quickly clasped the bracelet on it. "Wear it for the evening, and then I know you'll want to keep it."

"Taylor, I have a lot of reservations—"

"Caroline!" a woman's voice called from the hall. "Caroline, we're here."

Caroline recognized the voice of her assistant and knew that no matter how glamorous the evening might feel, she was here to work. Business hours had just begun for her. She stood up quickly and gave Taylor a stern look, "I'm not accepting this, you understand," she said quietly.

"Just wear it," he insisted. "Then we'll see how you feel."

She laughed, gave him a quick kiss, thrust the torn wrapping paper into his hands, and turned herself into a professional curator. "Get rid of that paper," she pleaded, "before the guests arrive. But don't throw away the box. You may be returning this bracelet."

He smiled cockily at her as she turned and hurried to the hall and to her duties.

An hour later Caroline was standing in the hall at the foot of the graceful staircase welcoming more patrons to the already packed historic home. More than one hundred people had arrived in elegant Christmas gowns and handsome tuxedos. The rooms were aglow with candlelight which worked its inimitable magic on the intricately carved moldings and mantels. The large, multi-paned windows, catching that glow, turned into gold-washed mirrors that reflected the light and colors of the room back at the guests. Caroline reveled in the beauty of the old-fashioned Christmas decorations and the glitter of the fashionable, wealthy people, who had come to marvel at her accomplishments. Still, every time the front door opened, she gazed hopefully at it, but so far the right person had not arrived.

Half an hour later Caroline was deep in conversation with the

Cuthberts, an elderly couple who had contributed a great deal of money to the restoration, and the woman was bombarding her with loud compliments on the excellence of her work. Caroline saw that the front door was opening again, and her pulse quickened as hope rose in her. Trying not to appear rude to the woman, she nodded at the lady's last comment, but she quickly turned her head to see who had entered. Finally she found the eyes she had been hungering to see. His eyes met hers and communicated quite emphatically, "I only came to see you."

"Really, darling Caroline, I just can't say enough about how marvelously you have done your work here," the lady exclaimed as she took Caroline's hand and forced her to return her attention to the lady's face.

"Thank you," Caroline murmured for the thousandth time that night. "We do so appreciate your support, and without it, none of this would have been possible," she repeated the words that had become something of a chant because she had spoken them so frequently in the last hour.

The lady launched into a new stream of compliments, and Caroline's heart sank as she realized that she was trapped with this couple with no hope of escape until this woman was through with her.

Then a saving voice invaded the conversation. "Good evening, Dr. Cuthbert, good evening, Mrs. Cuthbert."

The lady stopped in mid-sentence and stared up at the handsome man at her side. "Why, Morgan Randolph!" she exclaimed. "I haven't seen you in ages."

"Been abroad, no doubt," Dr. Cuthbert added.

"Yes, sir," Morgan responded. "Been abroad."

Dr. Cuthbert shook his head and laughed. "Well, there are at least two of us men in this social set who are silly enough to work when we don't need to—you and me."

Morgan smiled, "I confess I like to work, sir." Then he turned to Caroline, "Miss Forrest, I wonder if I could talk to you about a private matter for a moment."

"Of course," Caroline said quickly. "Will you excuse me?" she asked the Cuthberts.

"Oh, you'd better go talk to him," Mrs. Cuthbert laughed. "After all, he's Morgan Randolph, and it's his family's house that you're restoring." She patted Caroline on the shoulder and smiled at Morgan. "We'll just go and see what the refreshment table has to offer. Come along, dear." She took the arm of Dr. Cuthbert, who winked at Caroline and Morgan after his wife's back was turned. Caroline felt a flush of rose rise to her cheeks, and she suddenly found herself unable to meet Morgan Randolph's eyes.

"You look beautiful tonight," he said quietly. "I should come up with a much better adjective than 'beautiful,' but I don't think there's one in my vocabulary that would do justice to you."

"Thank you," Caroline murmured as she shyly lifted her eyes to his.

"You've done a magnificent job with the house."

"Thank you," Caroline murmured again. "None of this would have been possible without your—"

"You don't need to give me that speech," he said as he laughed quietly. "I'm sure you've said it a few times tonight."

His laughter broke the tension in Caroline, and she also laughed softly. How marvelous, she thought, and how strange. He seems so close, so dear to me. Even in the midst of this noisy crowd I feel such intimacy with this man.

Those were her thoughts, but her words were conventional. "I'm beginning to feel like a very broken record," she confessed.

"It's not terribly cold out. Would you spend a minute alone with me on the front verandah?" he asked. Caroline's hopes sailed to the ceiling as she guessed that he was feeling something similar to her own emotions.

"I really shouldn't leave," she gazed around at the throng of people.

"Well, there's no doubt you're the most important person here," Morgan conceded. "But there are so many people here, I don't think you'll be missed for just a few minutes."

Caroline felt like a young school girl suddenly, very shy but very eager too. The eagerness won the battle.

"Fresh air sounds wonderful," she admitted. "But not the front verandah. Perhaps the side verandah."

"Yes," he agreed eagerly. "The front verandah would give us no privacy at all."

He took her arm and ushered her out the front door and around the corner of the house to the side verandah. They stood at the base of one of the large, white pillars, and she gratefully leaned against it for a few moments.

"This is wonderful," she sighed. "I didn't realize how stuffy it was getting in there."

"It's more than wonderful; it's magnificent," he insisted. "If I were an artist, I would paint you just the way you look right now."

She turned her surprised eyes to his. "I beg your pardon?"

"There's moonlight streaming down to whiten your skin, but the candlelight from the house is flowing through the window and turning your beautiful hair to the color of glowing coals."

Caroline blushed deeply.

"I'm sorry," he said. "I didn't mean to embarrass you. No, that's not true. I'm not sorry. I'm glad I said it."

"Well, thank you for the compliment," she said hurriedly. "It was good of nature to give us a full moon tonight, wasn't it?"

"Yes," he agreed. "And before the evening's over, I hope you can get far enough away from the house to see how beautiful it looks, all lighted up by the Christmas candles, and the moonlight—well, it adds a special touch. What I'm trying to say is, it's a wonderful evening. A very special evening for you—and for me."

Caroline loved Morgan Randolph for at least trying to be poetic, for trying to put his feelings into words. Her own emotions were running so high, she barely trusted herself to speak. "Well, Christmas does give one a chance to make a house special," she said lamely.

"I brought you a small gift," he changed the subject abruptly.

"Oh, you shouldn't have," she said.

"It's only a token of my appreciation for what you've done for my ancestors here at Randolph House."

He handed her a small, extremely light-weight box. It was a plain white florist box with a pink ribbon tied around it in a simple bow. She pulled the end of the ribbon, and when it fell free from the box, she opened the lid. There she found a single, exquisite, blush pink blossom, surrounded by dark glossy leaves and a circle of lace.

"It's exquisite," she whispered breathlessly. "I've never seen anything like it. What is it?"

"Not terribly Christmasy, I confess, or elegant enough for such an occassion as this, but it seemed to me to fit you. It's an heirloom rose that mother loved. She brought the first bush with her when she married my father and came to Dallas from East

Texas. Here in Dallas, Mother's roses had always quit blooming by Christmas time, but Dad was able to call East Texas and have someone send a perfect blossom for Mother to wear at their Christmas reception."

"How kind of you," Caroline began, falling back on her finishing-school manners to cover the depth of the delight she felt. "How very kind of you to think of this, and what a wonderful tradition. This is just what my dress needs. A lovely corsage."

"Oh, it isn't a corsage," he corrected her quietly. "Actually it's a very old form of giving a lady flowers. It's a wristlet. In the 19th century when a lady attended a ball, she often wore a flower on her wrist." He removed the flower from the box, then took the box from her hands and laid it on a wrought-iron table on the verandah. "May I put it on your wrist?" he asked.

"Oh yes, please," Caroline said eagerly.

He took her right hand in his left and clasped the rose and ivory lace around her wrist.

"Oh, it's charming. It's truly charming," she looked from the flower up to his eyes and was startled to discover that they were vibrant with excitement. For an instant she thought he was going to kiss her and her heart began to beat wildly.

She watched as he battled to gain control of himself. Finally he said, "I'm glad you like it."

Bewildered by the passion she had seen in his eyes and her own wild response to it, she also struggled for composure. "Thank you so much," she said automatically. She avoided his eyes and willed her heart to slow down. "Every time I look at it, I shall think—"

"Caroline!" she heard Taylor calling from the front verandah. Then he came bolting around the corner. "Caroline!"

He stopped in his tracks when he saw Morgan Randolph holding Caroline's hand. "Oh, good evening, Mr. Randolph. Caroline, darling," he looked straight at Morgan when he pronounced the word darling, "everyone is looking for you. They want to take photographs for the newspapers."

"Oh dear," Caroline started bustling toward the front verandah. "I must go in." She turned back to Morgan. "I'm sorry, but I must get back inside. Thank you again."

She hurried toward the front door with Taylor close behind her. As she entered the light of the entry hall, Taylor demanded, "What's that thing on your arm?"

Caroline raised both of her arms and saw, at the same time, the emerald bracelet on her left wrist and the pink rose on her right wrist.

"What's that pink thing?" Taylor asked again.

His tone sent a surge of irritation shooting through Caroline. "It's a wristlet," she said haughtily, "made from an heirloom rose."

"Why are you wearing that tonight? It doesn't even go with your outfit."

Caroline bit her lip for a moment and then turned and glared up at Taylor. "A wristlet is a 19th century custom. A way for ladies to wear flowers at a ball. It is very appropriate for tonight and quite lovely, I think."

"Well, okay, it's appropriate, it's lovely." Taylor conceded sarcastically. "Where'd you get it?"

"Mr. Randolph brought it."

"Oh, well, I guess you have to wear it then."

"Yes, I suppose I have to wear it," Caroline agreed, disgusted with the discussion. "Where are the photographers, Taylor?"

"Oh, they're in there in the front parlor by the main Christmas tree."

"Will you excuse me?" Caroline asked icily and swept into the front parlor.

After the photographers had taken the newspaper pictures, it was time for the formal welcoming to Randolph House that Caroline had planned. She took a crystal bell from a table in the hall, stood on the third step of the elegantly curved staircase, and rang the bell until people began to gather in the hall and at the double doors of the parlors and dining room. The harpist who was seated next to the staircase began to play old English Christmas carols as Caroline waited. After several carols, the harpist paused, and Caroline spoke in a gracious, but formal tone to the guests.

"Welcome to Randolph House. I would like to take this opportunity to thank you, each and every one, for your contributions that have made this moment possible. Because of you a historic, beautiful home is being restored and opened to the public. Texans, and indeed visitors from around the world, will be able to see a piece of Texas history because of your generosity. It is impossible to enumerate what each person has done or even to mention the special gifts that have often come at very critical moments.

However, I thank each and every one of you for your contributions of money, time, encouragement, creativity, and hard work.

"It is now my happy opportunity to continue a tradition that the Randolph family cherished in this beautiful house for over 130 years. The Randolphs began the Christmas season in this community by opening the doors of this mansion to their neighbors and visiting relatives. Randolph House was always the place where the Christmas season began. And this year we would like to re-establish that tradition.

"The Randolph receptions always included delicious food, excellent conversation, and beautiful music. Tonight we would like to continue a very special tradition of the Randolph Christmas receptions by having our guests join together in singing some of the old carols that have been sung in this house for over 130 years. Traditionally the carol singing was accompanied by a harp, which was placed here at the foot of the staircase, and a member of the family played that harp. We no longer have a member of the family who plays the harp, but we do have a very special surprise for you."

At that moment, the harpist stood up and moved away from the harp.

"Ladies and gentlemen," Caroline announced, "it is my pleasure to tell you that the magnificent harp that stands before you is the actual Randolph harp."

Murmurs of appreciation flowed through the crowd.

Caroline continued. "After extensive research, we discovered that the Randolph harp had been sold out of the family, but it was still in relatively good condition. It has been made available to us through a very generous gift from one of our patrons. It is a grand old instrument, and our research indicates that this harp was brought to the Randolph mansion by the first Mrs. Randolph over 130 years ago. The house was new then, constructed by Mr. Morgan Randolph for his bride to be. After their wedding Mrs. Randolph brought her beloved harp and her musical genius to grace her new home. Tonight we are thrilled to welcome home the Randolph harp." Caroline paused as the guests applauded.

"Please join us now in song to celebrate this Christmas season and the Randolph family who have been the supporting pillars of our community for so many decades. We have chosen a list of songs that were particularly beloved by the Randolphs and were sung by the family every Christmas. I think you will recognize the tunes, but you may not know the words, and so we have printed them for you. Some of our docents are now passing out copies of the lyrics. If you can get into a position where you can see a copy—"

There was a great deal of shuffling in the crowd as various people took the parchment-colored sheets of paper that were being passed out and moved together into groups.

"Thank you. We are proud to have with us tonight the music director of St. Alban's Church, George Howard. He will lead us in our carol fest, but before we begin, please allow me to mention another historical note. We want to begin the way the Randolphs began. They were a family dedicated to the Christian tradition, and it was their choice to begin with a special hymn, 'Silent Night,' to emphasize the spiritual element of their celebration. Then, as you will see from the paper in front of you, they sang a variety of hymns plus some songs just for fun, but they always ended with the first verse of 'Silent Night.' By so doing, they encapsulated their musical celebration of Christmas with 'Silent Night' to symbolize the holiness of the holiday. Even though they had decorated their house and thought a great deal about gifts, parties and ball dresses, they were very aware that they were celebrating the birth of Jesus. Let us follow their tradition this evening. Please welcome the music director of St. Alban's Church and the Randolph harp."

Caroline stepped down two steps and over to the right as a white-haired, distinguished-looking man stepped up a few steps higher than she and began directing the group in the singing of "Silent Night."

The formal welcoming of the patrons had been an exhilarating time, and Caroline's pulse was racing. She was grateful to sing quietly the first verse to "Silent Night" to calm herself. As the group began the second verse, she looked across the hall, seeking the face of Morgan Randolph. When their eyes met, she forgot her pounding pulse, and the sound of the singing faded away. Caroline was overwhelmed by a mysterious feeling, totally new to her. Her mind struggled to understand. She could only describe her feeling as a combination of pain and elation at the same time. It was as if pain and elation were stacked on top of each other and were being folded together. Confused, Caroline wondered, is this love? Is this the way it feels when it's the true thing, a bond for eternity? Why is my heart both hurting and soaring?

It was obvious that something profound was also being felt by Morgan Randolph. He was staring at her as if he had never seen her. His eyes were intensely bright. Instinctively Caroline raised her right wrist to her face and placed the pink rose against her cheek. The coolness and softness of the blossom calmed her, and she slowly became aware again of the singing people around her. The group had finished "Silent Night" and had embarked on a rousing chorus of another Christmas carol.

Caroline shyly walked down the steps as the people continued singing; she felt a great need to be less visible for a few moments to regain her composure. However, she was quickly embraced by an excited guest who thrust a paper in front of her, and she found it necessary to sing along, as the group continued the carols. When the carol fest moved toward its end, and they began to sing the first verse of "Silent Night" again, she finally allowed her eyes to rise from the paper and to gaze in the direction of Morgan Randolph. She could not see him; she was both sorry and relieved.

For the remainder of the evening she felt almost dizzy from the swirl of compliments and well-wishes that were thrust upon her. She was hugged and congratulated, and the chatter of the room filled up her senses as she moved from group to group, seeing to everyone's needs and graciously accepting their compliments. From time to time she would feel Morgan's presence, and she would turn her head, and her eyes would meet his. No matter where he stood in the room, when she felt his presence and looked up, her eyes automatically found his. She was afraid of the power that drew her to this man; nevertheless, she allowed it to work on her. For the remainder of the evening she avoided his actual presence as a struggle took place deep inside of her. She knew without a doubt that her life had begun to change somehow, the moment her eyes met Morgan's while they sang "Silent Night." She had not chosen to stop that change; indeed, she had welcomed it. Something inside of her was moving her, re-making her. It was not passion. She knew about passion, and passion's power was infantile compared to this feeling. This power dug deep into her soul to the place where she kept the ultimate essence of herself. Morgan had not halted the change that was obviously occurring in him either. Whatever was affecting her so painfully and so joyously was in his eyes too. The same force was remaking him, and she knew it.

It was two o'clock in the morning before the merry-makers had all left. She was exhausted, but happy with her success. Taylor was impatient to take her home and wanted to race through the house, extinguishing candles and turning off the lights, but she wanted to be with this house—simply to be with it. She had given a year of herself to bring this house back to life. So when Taylor pressed her to go home, she said quietly, "You go on, I want to be by myself."

"You've got to be kidding," he said irritably. "It's two o'clock in the morning. I'm wiped out. You must really be wiped out. I'm just going to blow out all of these candles, turn off the lights, and see that you get home safely."

"No, Taylor, I don't want you to extinguish a single candle or turn out a single light. I just want you to go. Let me be here a while by myself."

"But why?" he demanded.

"I don't know if I can explain it. I've spent a year reaching this point, and this night will never come again. These candles, these lights, these decorations. It will never be this way, not exactly this way, again. And there's been so much hustle and bustle tonight. I just want to experience this fleeting time in quietness."

"You're nuts," Taylor announced. "But then you always were. That's one of the things I love about you. Okay, darling," he kissed her on the lips. "I guess that's one of those weird things about you artist types that we lawyers will never understand. I'm bushed. Are you sure you'll be okay?"

"Of course. When has it ever been anything but safe out here?"

"Okay. Well, I don't get it, but that's all right. I'll talk to you tomorrow. Sometime in the afternoon."

"Right. Taylor, thank you for all the support you've given me. I can't tell you how much your friendship has meant to—"

"I should hope I'm more than a friend!" he exclaimed. "Don't start giving me one of your formal, curator-type speeches. I'm in love with you. You know that. You've known it for several years."

"Yes, I have," Caroline conceded. "Good night, Taylor."

He bent over and kissed her firmly on the lips. "Good night, darling, I'm proud of you." He turned and walked out.

She heard his car when he started it, and she heard it as he drove down the drive and out of the gate. Then she knew she was finally alone with the house. She looked around at all the lights and candles.

"I guess this is silly," she said to herself, "but oh, why not? Just this once."

She walked from room to room, touching things, looking at them carefully. Her journey ended in the hall where she stood and stared at the Randolph harp. Candlelight flickered around her, sending its quick rays of light to illuminate the rich mahogany of the harp and to turn its strings to slivers of gold. She reached out and ran her fingertips across the strings.

"What a magnificent, magical sound," she murmured. "I wish I could play it. If I could, I would have the power to make this fantasy evening go on and on." She ran her fingertips across the strings once more, then sighed. "I guess the evening's over, and I just have to accept that fact, but it feels like I'm letting go of something I'll never know again." Then she remembered what Morgan Randolph had said about seeing the house in the moonlight, and suddenly she hungered to see the house from the gate. A surge of adrenaline pushed away her exhaustion, and she laughed at the thought of this perfectly silly, perfectly romantic indulgence she would give herself. "I will walk out to the end of the drive and walk back toward the house as if it were mine." She joyously clapped her hands together, then hurried to the front door and started across the threshold. Out on the verandah a man was silhouetted against the moonlight. She felt no fear. In her heart she knew who it was, and she found that she was not surprised he was there.

"Are you ready for your moonlight stroll, ma'am?" Morgan Randolph asked quietly as he approached her.

She imitated his light tone as she answered, "Yes sir, I believe I am."

He held out his arm, she took it, and he formally escorted her down the front steps.

"I believe you must be a mind reader, Mr. Randolph," she said as they quietly walked away from the house.

"No ma'am," he said with a laugh. "I would be a much better businessman if I were."

"Then I must be very transparent."

"You're anything but transparent," he disagreed.

"Then how did you know I would decide to do this—especially at this hour?"

"I wish I could answer that," he said quietly. "There are a lot of questions that have come up tonight that I wish I could answer."

A sharp thrill ran through her at the thought that his mysterious questions might relate to his feelings for her, but she said nothing. She felt both frightened and excited.

They reached the end of the long driveway and turned to view Randolph House. When she saw it in the moonlight, she was astonished. "It's truly incredible. I thought after seeing the inside, that nothing could be more beautiful, but out here in the moonlight its beauty becomes so ethereal, like something that's too precious for this earth. Do you think it might just disappear like a vision?"

"It's home," Randolph said simply. "Home is a vision; that's for sure. As for it disappearing, I guess that's up to the people who share the vision."

"Did you spend lots of time here, Mr. Randolph?" Caroline asked, as she suddenly realized it was, in fact, his home.

"Yes, many happy years. I grew up here. Of course, I haven't lived here for about twenty-five years, since I left for college as a young man, but I always came back every chance I got. You did a good job this evening of characterizing my family and our life here. We were very contented; my mother knew how to make a family close."

"Weren't you surprised," Caroline chose her words carefully, "when your mother left the house to the historic trust?"

"No," Randolph answered. "We talked that all over, and we were in agreement that the house was of such great importance to the people of the state that it shouldn't be a private residence anymore. I kept a great deal of the land, and if I should ever want to live on the plantation again, I would build a new house. Not that I don't love this old house, but its age and magnificence and the history it has seen have really made it *not* belong to me. It belongs to all the people who have their roots in this county, in this state."

"That is a very magnanimous attitude, Mr. Randolph."

"Thank you, Miss Forrest. But when I said it was home, I didn't only mean that it was my home. I meant that it is so beautiful because it is the embodiment of home, a place we are all trying to get to in various ways. And that's another reason it needs to be available to all people."

"I understand, I think," Caroline said quietly. "This house does have a special spirit, and it has embraced me for over a year now and enriched my life more than I can say. It has made me yearn for things I can't even name, much less define."

Caroline suddenly felt uneasy, as if she had revealed too much of herself, so she began one of her formal curator's speeches. "I have you to thank most of all for this wonderful opportunity, Mr. Randolph—"

"Miss Forrest," he interrupted her. "Could you call me something other than Mr. Randolph? And would it be too presumptuous of me to call you Caroline?"

"Well no, no," she stammered. "I would be delighted for you to call me Caroline. I certainly want to count you among my friends, and I shall call you Morgan, if you like."

He took her right hand and stroked it gently as he gazed down at the heirloom rose she still wore on her wrist.

"No, not Morgan," he smiled down at her. "Would you call me David?"

"David?" she questioned. "Is that what the 'D' stands for in D. Morgan Randolph?"

"Yes," he said quietly. "David. Only very close people in my life have called me David. I would like for you to be one of those people."

A thrill shot through Caroline that almost made her giddy. She struggled to clamp reason on it and tried to tell herself that she was just exhausted, but she soon gave up the struggle to be reasonable. She could not deny her feelings.

"I'd love to call you David," she confessed honestly.

He lifted his head and looked longingly at the house, and she stood there beside him, her hand resting in his, and looked at the house with him, wishing desperately she could be part of his life.

A surge of hope that her wish might be fulfilled rushed through her as he pulled her a little closer.

Chapter 3

The evening after the Randolph House reception Caroline returned the emerald and diamond bracelet to Taylor. In spite of the fact that they had both invested five years of their lives in their relationship, Caroline knew that she could not accept such a gift after David Randolph had captured her heart. She didn't know what to say to Taylor, so she simply handed him the bracelet.

"What's going on?" he asked anxiously.

"Taylor, I can't accept this," she said quietly.

"Why not? Don't you like it?"

"It's beautiful. Any woman would like it, but it's too expensive and personal a gift for the level of our commitment to each other."

"You mean because we're not married or engaged?"

"Yes, that's it," Caroline eagerly agreed, but she felt a twinge of guilt. She was telling Taylor the truth, but not the entire truth; she had made no mention of David Randolph.

"Well, I guess this means that when your birthday rolls around, I just won't have to go shopping," Taylor quipped as he took the bracelet and slipped it into his coat pocket.

Caroline stared at him nervously for a moment before dropping her eyes. Her birthday was in April; it was painfully obvious that Taylor believed they would be engaged by then or even married. Her relationship with Taylor, which she had found so comfortable and taken for granted for so long, was pressing her into making life-changing decisions. She now knew she didn't love Taylor; in fact, she knew she had never felt real love, the kind that makes a lasting marriage possible, until the night before. It amazed her that such love should come into her heart—not in a burst of passion while David pressed her close—but instead during the singing of a Christmas carol, while he stood across a room from her and they were engulfed in a throng of people.

Caroline went back to work on Monday morning confident that she would hear from David before the day was out. Since the debut of the restoration of Randolph House the Saturday before, the house was now open to the public for tours, and the public came in a constant stream. Caroline had trained a group of volunteer docents who could guide visitors through the house. Still, she was very busy herself with all the special arrangements that had to be made to keep the house looking its best.

When David had not called her by the end of the working day, she assumed he preferred to call her in the evening when she was at home, so she rejected a dinner invitation from Taylor, pleading that she was very tired. Actually she chose to stay home for the evening to wait for the phone to ring. Normally she would have tried to pretend, at least to herself, that she was not waiting for a phone call from a man, but her feelings for David Morgan Randolph were so strong she didn't bother to play games with herself.

He did not call, and as the week progressed, she did not hear from him. By Thursday she was quite upset. I wonder if he had to make a business trip, she thought as she sat in her office eating a sandwich, and he didn't even bother to let me know he was forced to leave town. Even if his business was urgent, he could have called. One little call! How long could it take? What if all those feelings in the moonlight Saturday night weren't as important to him as they were to me? I have to know where he is. I can't stand just waiting! There was a quick knock on the door, and suddenly Marcia Wentworth entered in her usual breathless fashion.

"Caroline, darling!" she exclaimed. "Thank goodness I caught you."

Caroline put her sandwich down and started to speak, but Marcia did not give her a chance to say a word.

"Darling, you know we're having our Christmas ball this weekend, and I just had the most fabulous idea this morning. We have an orchestra and all the decorations and everything is going to be absolutely fabulous," Marcia bubbled, "but all of a sudden I thought how super it would be to have that charming little harp of the Randolphs that you found. Now don't say a word! I know that you're going to have all kinds of reservations about moving that fabulous relic over to the country club and all that sort of thing, but I promise you that Larry and I will insure it to the hilt and take care of it as if it were our own grandchild. Now do say that I can use the harp! It will be the hit of my ball, and it will certainly help Randolph House." She stopped her rush of words and peered at Caroline eagerly.

"Well, Marcia," Caroline hesitated. "Won't you sit down?"

"No, darling, I haven't a moment to spare. It's Thursday, and the ball is Saturday, and I have a million things to do. You will let me use the harp, won't you? I can just see it now! We'll set up a second stage and create some kind of fake clouds all around the harp. Something gossamer and floating in the breeze. And we'll have a simply ethereal looking girl with long, long hair trailing down her back to play the harp. Oh! Everybody will think it's simply fabulous. The hostesses for the rest of the Christmas balls will be wild with jealousy. I shall destroy them with that darling harp!"

Caroline stifled a laugh and a keen desire to ask Marcia if she intended to put angel wings on the ethereal harpist. At the same time she thought quickly about the total impossibility of replacing the harp if it should be lost or damaged in any way. She also remembered the large sums of money that the Wentworths had contributed to Randolph House. Looking as unhappy as she could manage, she stood and walked around her desk. "Oh, Marcia, I'm so sorry I couldn't possibly let you use it. You see, the house is booked for a wedding on Saturday night, and I'm afraid the harp is being used for the ceremony."

"But they can get another harp," Marcia insisted. "No one will ever know the difference."

Caroline thought quickly. "Well, normally I would agree with you that no one would know the difference, but you see this is the Berry wedding. You know *the* Berrys, from Houston; they are cousins of the Randolphs. I'm afraid that the Berrys were here Saturday night when we debuted the house, and their harpist has already been in this week to practice on the Randolph harp."

"I don't care!" Marcia flung the words at Caroline. "I've made substantial donations to this house, and I want that harp. I'll be devastated if I don't get it! What's more, I won't give you the money I promised to restore the upstairs."

Caroline no longer felt like laughing at Marcia. Her muscles tightened; she could not afford to lose Marcia's support. To give herself time to think, Caroline rose and walked over to the French doors. "Marcia," she said quietly, "you know I can't disclose the name of an anonymous donor, don't you? Not under any circumstances."

"Of course. So what?" Marcia demanded.

Caroline turned and looked her directly in the eyes. "Surely you can guess why I can't loan you the harp."

"Oh, dear," Marcia threw herself into a chair. She obviously had guessed that the Berrys had donated the harp. "I'm devastated! It was such a fabulous idea." She fluttered her acrylic fingernails in the air and jumped back up. "Well, I'll just have to think of some other novelty item. I must be running along, darling. So many things to do." She hugged Caroline, just as if she hadn't been furious with her a moment before, and hurried toward the door, but Caroline stopped her.

"Marcia?"

"Yes, darling."

"What did you think about Saturday night? How did you think the debut went?"

"Oh it was absolutely fabulous! Totally fabulous, darling," Marcia came running back over. "I should have said so the minute I walked in the door. It was a simply superb evening. I don't know how you could have made it any better. You thought of absolutely everything, and wasn't it absolutely fabulous that Morgan Randolph was here?"

"Yes, it was." Caroline was delighted that Marcia had introduced the subject of David. "It was very special to have a close member of the family here for the opening of the house. And he's such a charming man."

"Oh, he's more than charming, darling," Marcia rolled her eyes and then sighed deeply. "Isn't he just the most handsome thing you ever saw? Not to mention all that fabulous money he has."

"Yes, yes very handsome, very nice looking," Caroline tried to sound nonchalant. "But I assume that he has gone abroad again. I believe he enjoyed the evening, but no doubt he'll be spending the rest of the holidays in Europe."

"Oh no, darling, no. He'll be at the ball Saturday night. He told me so himself; he absolutely promised."

"Oh, really?" Caroline smiled in spite of the fact that she wanted to scream and then burst into tears. "How nice. Well, I'm looking forward to it myself."

"You and Taylor," Marcia grinned at her. "What a marvelous couple you make, darling. We're all waiting for the announcement."

"The announcement?" Caroline did her best to look confused.

"Don't play innocent with me, darling. The announcement. How long is it going to be before you have a hunk of diamond on your left hand? Is Taylor silly enough to wait until Christmas day, when all the major parties are over? That would be just like a man, imitating some old Hollywood sentimentality and waiting till Christmas, when you need that glittering rock now." She sighed her exasperation. "Think what a splendid entry you could make this Saturday night with that hunk of diamond on your finger. I'm sure he's already bought it. Can't you hasten the process just a little bit? No doubt it would do wonders for your new dress."

Caroline blushed. "You seem to know Taylor's mind better than I do."

"Perhaps I do," Marcia grinned again. "Well, if you're not going to hasten the process, I'll just see what I can do."

"I believe," Caroline said quickly, "that you are going to be too busy with your own ball, or at least I hope so, Marcia." She emphasized her last words. "It is best to leave Taylor to his own speed, I think."

"Whatever you say, darling. I get the message. I'm off to the hairdresser. But I expect to see you Saturday night, dressed to kill, with your cute Taylor, and I hope there's a very large rock on your left hand."

She fluttered the acrylic fingernails of her left hand at Caroline, bounced out of the room and slammed the door behind her.

Caroline turned and walked to the French doors and watched as Marcia rushed out to her Porsche, jumped in, raced the engine and tore out of the driveway. *What I need to do is slow Taylor down,* Caroline thought. *Oh dear, so David is in town. Why haven't I heard from him? Of course, what do I know about his business affairs? There may be some emergency deal he has to make or something. I know Randolph Industries is enormous. At any rate, I'll see him Saturday night. Hmm. Saturday night. Marcia's ball is always the event of the season. Still, after the expense of my green velvet gown, I was going to wear my black silk from last year. Maybe I need to rethink this.* She went and sat down at her desk and stared straight ahead for three or four minutes, trying to visualize her entrance into the Wentworth Christmas ball in her black silk. The fantasy in her mind was fine until she pictured David Morgan Randolph looking at her. Then she felt panicky. "I definitely won't look grand enough," she exclaimed. "Half the women there will be wearing black. No, it won't do." She snapped to attention. "It simply won't do," she said to the walls. "But it's Thursday, and the ball is Saturday. What am I going to do?"

Whenever questions of dress came up, one word always popped into Caroline's mind—Grandmother. It would have seemed like such a strange association to anyone else, but Caroline had lived her entire life under her grandmother's social tutelage. Her grandmother was Judith Hamilton, the *grande dame* of Dallas society. Caroline's mother, Marian, was not interested in social affairs, so she had long ago been given up as a hopeless cause by her mother, Judith. Judith had turned all her attention to preparing Caroline to take her place in Dallas society and perhaps to rise to even greater heights than she had.

Caroline picked up the telephone and called her grandmother. The housekeeper answered, but Judith was quickly on the line. Caroline was her favorite grandchild and the jewel of her existence because Judith was now mostly confined to her house by her age and her ill health. Still, she had no intention of being left out of society; she experienced every prominent social affair through her granddaughter.

Quickly Caroline explained about the approaching ball and her need for a new dress. Judith listened without a word. When Caroline had finished her story, from which she had carefully omitted any mention of David Randolph, Judith said in her usual efficient tone, "This is quite a dilemma you've gotten yourself into, young lady. I sense a certain excitement in your voice. What is his name?"

"What's whose name?" Caroline asked.

"Don't play games with me, young lady. I practically raised you. That Taylor what's-his-name couldn't possibly bring that kind of tone into your voice, so what is his name?"

Caroline sighed and resigned herself to the facts of her life. Her grandmother Judith had always been able to read her mind. "His name is David Morgan Randolph," she admitted.

"Morgan Randolph?" Judith's voice sounded so excited that Caroline became worried about her grandmother's health. "When did you meet him?"

"He was at the debut Saturday night, and we had a long talk. He is coming to the Wentworth ball, and—"

"And you were going to wear a dress from last year?" Judith demanded.

"Well, it has all happened so suddenly, Grandmother. I really haven't had a chance to—"

"Never mind, dear, never mind. We have less than forty-eight hours, but believe me, no granddaughter of mine is going to be seen by David Morgan Randolph in anything but the perfect gown. Come over at once."

"Well, there are quite a few things I need to do here at Randolph House, but I could come over sometime in the morning."

"In the morning!" Judith exclaimed. "Certainly not! You are the direct descendant of James Bradford of Charleston, South Carolina—not to mention that you are one of the Dallas Hamiltons. You are a lady, Caroline. Ladies don't work! Whatever has to be done at that old house can be done by someone else, some underling. Put an assistant in charge of everything and get yourself over here right away. This is a crisis, Caroline!"

Caroline stifled her desire to laugh at the word "crisis" because she knew the possibilities of her grandmother's volcanic temper.

"I'll be over in an hour or so," she promised.

As Caroline parked her car in front of her grandmother's mansion in Highland Park, she wondered, has Grandmother ordered some poor designer to the premises and given him or her an hour to appear? She laughed at the idea but thought, I wouldn't doubt it. Whatever Grandmother has done or is about to do, I might as well agree to it. It will save energy; besides, Grandmother will win in the end, and she has never failed to be right on target when it comes to fashion, especially ball gowns.

She hurried up the walk to the front door and wasn't surprised when the door swung open before she could touch the door knocker. It was her grandmother's personal maid who greeted her.

"Miz Judith be waiting' for you upstairs," Monique said quickly. "And I haven't seen her this excited in years." She bustled toward the stairs as fast as her sixty-five years would allow. "Well, come on, Miz Caroline. You know Miz Judith don't like to be kept waiting."

Caroline hurried up the stairs behind Monique, the daughter of the personal maid her grandmother had brought with her from

Charleston, South Carolina, when she had married Franklin Hamilton of Dallas seventy years ago. Judith Kendall Hamilton, at age twenty, had taken over the city's social life before anyone else could catch her breath and compete with her.

"Where is she?" Caroline asked as they climbed the first flight of stairs but didn't stop there.

"She be in the ballroom."

"The ballroom!" Caroline exclaimed. "She's on the third floor? Grandmother went up two flights of stairs?"

"Like she was sixteen years old," Monique called back over her shoulder as she herself gasped for air.

"Merciful heavens," Caroline said. "What is she up to?"

"You's not gonna believe it." Monique shook her head.

They finally reached the third floor of the mansion, and Caroline entered a huge, airy room that covered the entire floor. Her grandmother was standing in the middle of it, surrounded by a semicircle of ballroom chairs over which were draped ball gowns.

"Grandmother," Caroline rushed up to her and tried to give her a hug.

"None of that now," Judith pushed her away. "We have business to attend to, Caroline. Honestly, I can't believe you waited until Thursday to think of your gown. You should have called me days ago. You should have called me Sunday morning at dawn to tell me you had met Morgan Randolph. How can you keep me in the dark like this? Haven't I spent my entire life making it possible for you to become the great lady of this city? Well, never mind. We haven't got time for that now, but I warn you, I plan to discuss this with you later."

"Yes, ma'am," Caroline said meekly.

"Now," Judith walked around the semicircle of chairs, pausing before each chair as if it were a religious shrine and staring reverently down at the ball gown draped across the chair. She was whispering something to herself as she looked at each dress. Caroline waited patiently, well aware that it was best not to interrupt her grandmother. When Judith had finished her fashion pilgrimage around the semicircle, she looked at Monique and said, "The white silk georgette with the embroidered and beaded bodice, Monique. It should just about fit, Caroline. I believe you will only have to enlarge it at the waist."

"Yes, Miz Judith," Monique said quickly and hurried to the

chair that contained what looked, to Caroline, like only a heap of white, filmy fabric.

"Come on, Miz Caroline, let's get you into it." Monique took Caroline by the hand and pulled her over to the side of the room and started unbuttoning the blazer Caroline was wearing.

"Wait a minute," Caroline interrupted. "Grandmother, I expected a designer. I expected to be ordered to a shop to—what is going on?"

Judith lifted her chin and stood regally straight in spite of her ninety-two years. "What shop do you imagine could possibly equal a custom gown from the best couturier in Paris?"

"None, I'm sure," Caroline agreed.

"Of course not. So I have had to delve into my own collection. Fortunately for you, Monique has kept everything in mint condition just as her mother did before her. You have finally filled out in the bosom, and so now you can do justice to these exquisite dresses. Monique, get the dress on her."

"This is your dress?" Caroline asked her grandmother.

"It is certainly not your mother's!" Judith replied tartly. "She never had a figure worthy of such a dress. Monique, get that blouse off of Caroline."

Monique started unbuttoning Caroline's blouse, and Caroline hastened to take her skirt off. When Monique had helped her into the white, filmy fabric creation and buttoned up the back, she turned Caroline so that Judith could see her, instead of turning her toward the standing mirror that had been hastily brought to the ballroom. Judith walked around Caroline in a circle, staring at her sternly without saying a word. When she had finished the circle, she stood in front of Caroline and suddenly smiled triumphantly.

"Magnificent!" she proclaimed. "Absolutely magnificent. You look almost as grand in that dress as I did when I wore it in 1922."

"1922?" Caroline cried. "This dress is over seventy years old?"

"Caroline," Judith said severely. "If you insist on reminding me of my advanced years, I shall have to remind you that you are twenty-eight years old and unmarried, with nothing but that Taylor what's-his-name as a prospect. Now Morgan Randolph is another matter. This is the man for you. I've been waiting for an eternity for you to meet such a man; we need the perfect dress to catch him, and this is it."

"It is?" Caroline asked. "I wouldn't know. I haven't seen it yet."

"You don't need to see it," Judith retorted, "I've seen it. Believe me, this dress will catch Morgan Randolph. After all, it caught your grandfather, and he was a Hamilton, *the* Hamilton bachelor, but you might as well see how marvelous you look." She turned Caroline toward the standing mirror, and Caroline could not help but exclaim, "Grandmother! It's unbelievable."

The dress was magnificent, something obviously from another era, something that could not be bought in 1996 at any price, and as Judith had said, perfectly preserved. Even though the wind had tossed Caroline's shoulder-length, auburn curls into a mess and her make-up had worn thin as the day had passed, Caroline glowed as she looked at herself in her grandmother's dress. It was the creation of an artist, the kind of dress a woman never sees in actuality but begs her portrait painter to conjure up with his paints. Yards and yards of the finest silk georgette floated down from the empire waistline to the floor. The lace bodice was hand embroidered with white silk thread over the sheer white georgette. The embroidered flowers were strewn with delicate pearls. The whole dress had the patina that comes to the finest silks and laces only with time and careful, loving preservation.

"You must wear your hair up with that tiny pearl and diamond tiara that I have, and of course you must wear the Bradford earrings and necklace."

Caroline was stunned at the thought. She had only seen those jewels a few times in her life. They were kept in the vault at the bank.

"I couldn't," she protested to her grandmother. "What if something happened to them?"

"You can and you will," Judith insisted. "What do we own those jewels for if not to catch the most eligible bachelor in town? Do you realize how much money the Randolphs have, not to mention their social position? You, of all people, ought to know their importance. After all, you are the curator of their mansion. A disagreeable fact indeed, given the legacy you have inherited. No female Bradford heir should ever degrade herself by working, but never mind that now. At least you have met the Randolph heir, and you shall marry him."

"I know, Grandmother. But those jewels are never out of the bank vault, and I just don't know whether I want to risk—"

"It isn't your risk, it's my risk. I own them. They are perfect for this dress. I ought to know. This dress was designed to complement those jewels, and I wore them with this dress in 1922. The jewels are refined, heirloom pieces, another bit of your legacy. Every other jewel in that ballroom will scream *nouveau riche*. Most of the people there won't know the difference, but Morgan Randolph will recognize old money when he sees it. They are delicate, exquisite gems, and you *will* wear them. I shall go call the bank right this minute and have them delivered." She started toward the door but turned back. "Monique, make the dress a half inch looser in the empire waist. No more than a half inch."

"Yes Miz Judith," Monique agreed.

"Thank goodness the dress has an empire waist, Caroline, or you could never have worn it," Judith's comment was an intentional reprimand to her granddaughter. "I had a twenty inch waist—without my corsets on, mind you—but you modern girls—well, never mind. At least your bosom finally filled out," Judith added before turning briskly back to her task of calling the bank.

Caroline turned back to the mirror and stared at herself. Yes, thank goodness, she thought happily.

Caroline entered the country club that Saturday night with total confidence that she would be the most beautiful woman present at the ball. Her grandmother's dress and the Bradford jewels would guarantee her success. Furthermore, she was radiant with expectation of a magical encounter with David Morgan Randolph. Her confidence was quickly confirmed when Marcia Wentworth greeted her in the foyer by exclaiming, "Caroline Forrest, how dare you outdo me at my own ball! Where did you get that fabulous dress?"

Caroline just smiled mysteriously and complimented Marcia's gold lame extravaganza of a gown while Taylor talked enthusiastically to Marcia's husband about something on Wall Street. Marcia took Caroline aside a few steps and whispered, "You didn't buy that dress to catch Taylor. What is going on, darling?"

Caroline blushed but kept her voice steady as she insisted, "I don't know what you're talking about, Marcia. That imagination of yours is running riot again."

"This has nothing to do with my imagination. You look like royalty. There's not another dress like that on the planet. Who are you really after? No wonder you didn't want a ring from Taylor."

"Doesn't Caroline look grand?" Taylor demanded as he walked up.

"Irresistible," Marcia said, then winked at Caroline before turning and walking away to greet more guests.

Halfway down the hall to the ballroom, Taylor stopped Caroline and turned her to face him. "You do look magnificent, Caroline. I've never been so proud of you as I am tonight." Before she could say a word, he put his arms around her shoulders, pulled her to him and kissed her on the mouth, long and hard. Caroline exploded with fury, but she couldn't force Taylor back and free her lips to scold him.

"Excuse me, may I pass?" a male voice asked. Caroline's heart sank at the sound of that voice, for she recognized it. Taylor released her, and when she looked up, there was David, smiling coolly at her. Taylor stepped back and laughed loudly. "Randolph," he exclaimed, slapping him lightly on the shoulder. "Couldn't help myself. Take a look at Caroline here. Isn't she magnificent?"

David looked Caroline in the eyes, paying no attention to the remainder of her figure or her clothing and murmured, "Exquisite."

Then he walked between them as he said, "Excuse me," and disappeared through the doors at the end of the hall.

"Well, let's go show you off," Taylor exclaimed

Caroline felt ill and in no mood to show herself off more than she already had. "You shouldn't have kissed me that way, Taylor," Caroline whispered angrily. "It's not appropriate in this surrounding. It's not appropriate in any public surrounding."

"I'm in love with you; what can I do?" Taylor shrugged his shoulders amiably.

"You're hopeless!" Caroline sputtered. "I'm going to check my lipstick."

"You look wonderful, darling. Let's just go into the ball and have a wonderful time."

"I'm going to check my lipstick, Taylor."

"Well, there's a mirror right behind you," Taylor pointed to it.

Caroline abruptly left his side and walked to the powder room. Slowly she repaired the damage done to her lipstick while she struggled to recompose herself. What on earth does David think of me now? she wondered. I must take control of this situation and enter that ballroom with a regal graciousness. Yes, that's what Grandmother would say. Regal graciousness. She stood up taller and returned to Taylor. Taylor extended his arm, but she refused it. They walked down the hall to the double doors that opened into the ballroom.

When they entered the ballroom, a rush of female guests raced to Caroline's side to compliment her gown. Soon their escorts joined them, and the conversation turned to the wonderful reception at Randolph House the week before. Slowly Caroline and Taylor moved from group to group, carrying on the light conversations typical of such occasions while Caroline searched eagerly but furtively for David. She could find him nowhere. There was an absolute mob of people, and the orchestra was tuning up.

They had made it halfway around the ballroom, when the orchestra began the first tune.

"Let's dance, Caroline." Taylor grabbed her by the waist.

"No," she pulled back from him. "It's too fast-paced a tune. I'd rather wait for something slower. Besides, we've just arrived. We haven't greeted everyone yet."

"But it's a dance, it's a ball," Taylor insisted. "We came to dance."

"Taylor, we have an evening full of dancing ahead of us."

"Well, okay," he agreed and smiled brightly at her. "I'd rather show you off anyway." He put his arm around her, and she felt his clammy hand on her shoulder, but she shrugged it off, so he moved it down to her waist.

The dance floor quickly became crowded with couples. Caroline was finally able to see the lavishly decorated tables and the people remaining seated.

Taylor exclaimed loudly over the music and pointed to a table, "Oh, look, Caroline, there's Stuart. Who's that with him? Is that the French girl he's been dating?"

Caroline looked in the direction he was pointing. "Her name is Camille something or other," she said, "I can't remember."

"Hey, Stuart!" Taylor called as he started dragging Caroline toward them, but as they rounded a corner of the ballroom, Caroline saw David Morgan Randolph. More importantly, she saw the woman standing next to him, the woman who had her body snuggled up next to his and had wrapped her arm inside of his. Caroline stopped in her tracks and stared for an instant.

If ever an opposite of Caroline existed, it was the woman who seemed to possess David Morgan Randolph at that moment. She was tall and statuesque, obviously Mediterranean, with glossy black hair flowing down her back and dark-brown, seductive eyes flashing up at David as she worked to hold his total attention. Every time she spoke, her full red lips opened and exposed gleaming white teeth that contrasted with her deeply tanned face. She wore black satin—and very little of it. Caroline turned away slightly, pretending to listen to Taylor, while she watched the woman from the corner of her eye. She was wondering how anyone could cover her body with so little fabric. The dress was a miniskirt at the bottom, so tight Caroline was sure the woman couldn't walk, and at the top the dress was cut so low that Caroline was positive that if the woman tried to walk, she would expose herself.

"Hey, I thought we were going to go see Stuart and his French girlfriend," Taylor raised his voice to gain Caroline's attention.

"No!" Caroline exclaimed.

"No?" he questioned.

"No," she said in a more controlled fashion. "We need to go to the punch table. We walked right by the Cuthberts without speaking to them. We can talk to Stuart and Camille later, but the Cuthberts are very important donors to Randolph House, and I couldn't possibly risk offending them." She grabbed Taylor's arm and started back toward the punch table.

As the evening progressed, Caroline kept changing her position in the room to avoid a face-to-face meeting with David Randolph and that creature he was escorting. Occasionally she caught glimpses of them, which did not please her, since the woman was always hanging off of David and hanging out of her dress.

The compliments to Caroline continued to flow in, but they did little to soothe the pain inside of her.

After several hours of avoiding David, she and Taylor were dancing to a beautiful waltz that the orchestra had inserted between the faster-paced tunes. Many couples had left the floor, preferring the faster-paced music, but Caroline was especially fond of waltzes. Taylor was not, but he did his best to lead her through the dance.

When a tall man tapped Taylor on the shoulder, he was a little too eager, Caroline thought, to turn her over to someone else's arms. Her new partner put his hand on Caroline's waist and took her right hand in his before she glanced up and saw that it was

David. He danced as smoothly as she would have expected, and she thrilled to his touch in spite of herself.

At first she simply stared over his shoulder with a smile plastered across her face. She tried to control her thoughts, but his closeness had a most confusing effect on her. Once again she was with David Randolph and experiencing a strange sense of being home—something she had never felt before around any man. Reality was a crowded ballroom where she was gliding across the floor in the arms of a handsome man. However, Caroline kept imagining the contentment of watching a sunset over water, the vivid hues of the setting sun blending perfectly with their reflections in the water. In her mind's eye as the sky changed, so did the water. Sky and water were always matched, "in tune," although they were completely different substances. David and I are like that, she thought. But how is it possible? How can we, who are separate entities, blend into one? And why do I want it so much?

"I believe you've been avoiding me," David spoke quietly.

"Why no," she forced herself to look directly into his eyes. "Why should I do that?"

"Why indeed?" he asked.

"Well, that's simply absurd," she insisted. "It's just that there are so many people here, so many friends to see, so many patrons of Randolph House. I've been quite overwhelmed talking to everyone."

"Yes," he responded. "I've been noticing that. You have been quite overwhelmed, especially by admiring men."

"It's been a lovely ball," was all she could say.

"Yes, lovely," he agreed, as he stared down into her eyes. There was a question and something like pain visible in his eyes, but Caroline felt so confused she was afraid to speak. She turned her head to look over his shoulder again until the music finally ended.

"Thank you," he bowed rather formally and took her back to Taylor.

She refused to look back and see him return to that woman. She had discovered in the last two hours that the woman was Italian, someone named Valery Benelli, a resident of Rome, a woman whom David had been seen with frequently at various European social gatherings. She had also, during the course of the last two hours, watched the woman on the dance floor with many different partners,, and she was not pleased with what she had seen. Why would he be with a woman like that, she had asked herself repeatedly during the evening. I haven't seen him dance with her once. Thank goodness for that. But she makes such an exhibition of herself! Why is he with her at all?

After David returned Caroline to Taylor's side, she made a quick excuse and left the ballroom for the powder room. When she arrived in the lady's room, she was relieved to find it empty. She collapsed in one of the vanity chairs in front of the dressing table and stared at herself in the mirror. She still looked beautiful, but there was sadness in her eyes. She felt like crying, and more than anything she just wanted to go home. All evening she had been asking herself, could I possibly have imagined the strong feelings that I felt for David at the debut of Randolph House? But no matter how hard she had tried to dismiss those feelings, she could not do so. She had felt sure she had not imagined those feelings, and just now, when she was in David's arms, extraordinary feelings had risen in her again. As for David's feelings, there was no way to dismiss the fact that at the debut of Randolph House, David had stayed behind to be with her. "Why didn't he call me this week," she demanded of herself in the mirror. "Why didn't he send a note? And why is he here with that awful-looking woman?"

She heard some female voices at the door, so she clamped her mouth shut and opened her evening bag to pull out her lipstick. She stared into the mirror, applying the lipstick and carefully blotting it with a tissue as another woman sat down beside her. Caroline glanced to her left and was startled to see the face of Valery. The dark, almost swarthy skin, the flashing, sensuous eyes, the long, gleaming, black hair. Valery was accompanied by a friend of hers, another Italian woman. She spoke quickly to Valery in Italian, laughing as she spoke. Only one word was intelligible to Caroline, and it was the word "Morgan."

Anger began to boil up in her, anger she had no right to, she realized. She looked back at her own face and saw that the whiteness of her skin was becoming infused with a bright flush. She straightened her spine and lifted her chin as the two women continued to banter back and forth in Italian. It seemed to Caroline that every third word was either "Morgan" or "Randolph." If only she knew what they were saying.

Just as Caroline stood to go, Valery turned to her and said,

"Such a lovely ball, don't you agree?" in her heavily accented English.

"Yes," Caroline agreed stiffly. "Lovely."

"The Wentworths are such lovely people," Valery continued. "And so rich."

Valery turned back to the mirror, and her Italian friend laughed loudly and added, "and such close friends of the rich, rich Morgan Randolph."

Valery pushed forward her thick lips and applied blood-red lipstick to them, then grinned at her friend in the mirror, laughed and said ominously, "Yes, such close friends."

Caroline's blood turned to ice, and she recognized her own personal physiological signal of fury about to erupt. Quickly she took her evening bag and left the powder room. She did not turn left after leaving and go back to the ballroom. Instead she turned to the right. She walked past several small sitting rooms straight to the porter at the door.

"Joseph," she said quietly. "I need to go home, and I don't wish to involve my escort. Do you have any ideas?"

He looked at her sympathetically and said, "The club limousine be in the parking lot, Miz Forrest. I could take you home."

"That would be wonderful, Joseph. I would appreciate it more than I could say."

"You ain't feeling so good, ma'am," he prodded her for an explanation. "You's as white as a ghost."

"No, I'm not feeling well, but there's no need for any kind of confusion, if you would just be so kind as to take me home."

"Yes ma'am." He held out his hand as if she needed him to steady her, but she smiled her thanks at him and walked ahead of him.

The limousine was close to the door, so they arrived at it quickly. Joseph opened the back door, and she was about to settle into the back seat when someone took her arm.

"Caroline, are you ill?" It wasn't Taylor's voice. Without turning around, she knew it was David.

I absolutely refuse to look him in the face, she thought. "I'm quite fine," she said, staring at the back seat. "I simply wish to go home, and Joseph has been kind enough to offer to take me."

"I'll take you home," David insisted, "if you're ill."

"I told you, I am not ill." Caroline tried to avoid any sharp edge in her tone. "I simply want to go home."

"I'll get my car," David said.

"I don't need your car," she continued to stare at the uphol-stery of the back seat. "I have a limousine at my service and a dependable driver as an escort. Thank you very much. I believe your date is waiting for you."

She removed her arm from his hand and climbed into the back seat. Intentionally she turned her face away from the door, and Joseph shut it. He hurried around to the front seat, climbed in and started the car. Caroline refused to look to the right. She had absolutely no plans to ever look into David Randolph's eyes again.

Chapter 4

"That was a difficult night for me, but oh, how I would gladly trade that night for this one," Caroline said as she stood and moved around her candlelit study. She walked to the window to peer out into the dark. A policeman with a German shepherd walked by; the sight of him consoled her slightly. "At least I'm not completely alone in this storm-ravaged neighborhood, but it seems like this night will never end. I wonder if things are getting any worse in the drawing room." She picked up her flashlight, left her study, and went to the doors of the drawing room. Once again she shrank from opening them, but she forced herself to proceed, and when they were open, she stared into the formerly elegant room she had treasured. The tree still lay on top of her smashed furniture. "This room is ruined," she muttered, "what that tree hasn't destroyed, the rain probably will." Her cut hand throbbed, and as she turned the light from the flashlight on it, a chill shivered up her spine. "The room can be repaired, redecorated, but what about my life? Have I ruined it beyond all hope? There seems to be only one way out of this mess I've created, but can I face myself if I do what I'm planning to do?" Caroline shuddered and closed the drawing room doors as if closing out the sight of that damaged room could remove her anxieties about her life. She returned to her study.

"It's gotten cooler, and it's so damp," she said as she entered the shadowy, candlelit room. "Maybe a fire in the fireplace would help; at least it would be cheerful and give me something to do besides wait for this night to end." She crumpled up a few sheets of newspaper, placed them in the fireplace, and topped them with kindling and several small logs. After touching a lighted match to the paper, she stood and watched as the kindling and then the splintered side of the wood quickly caught fire. "If only I could do something besides just wait," she said, "but I can't sleep, and I don't want to think about the present. I can't think about the future, so that just leaves the past." She chose to remember her grandmother's reaction the day after Marcia Wentworth's ball.

"I am appalled, Caroline, utterly appalled," Judith said as she tapped her cane on the hardwood floor with each word she spoke.

"Well, I thought David Randolph's behavior was appalling too, Grandmother."

"I'm not talking about David Morgan Randolph at the moment," Judith's temper rose higher. "I'm talking about you. I am appalled to think that a Bradford would relinquish the battle-field so easily in the face of a minuscule army."

Confused, Caroline stared at her grandmother's angry face for a long moment. Finally she admitted meekly, "I don't think I know what you mean, Grandmother."

"Have no fear, Caroline Bradford Forrest. I plan to tell you!"

"Yes, ma'am," Caroline said as she started toward a chair to sit down while she endured the inevitable scalding remarks of Judith.

"I think you best remain standing, young lady," Judith said.

Caroline turned back and looked at Monique for support, but the faithful maid helplessly shrugged her shoulders. Caroline sighed and waited.

"You must learn, Caroline, that to a woman of substance a little challenge is occasionally refreshing. Morgan Randolph, or David Randolph, as you call him, would not be worth having if you could win him with no effort whatsoever."

"Valery Benelli was no little challenge, Grandmother. You should have seen her. There was nothing little—"

"Oh, I know her type," Judith interrupted. "Voluptuous, totally sensual, and that, my dear, is where your strength should have been put into play. Sensuality does not come in just one form; you'd be amazed at what men find sensual. You are quite mistaken if you think that Morgan Randolph is going to settle for some kind of little sexual creature—or gigantic sexual creature, for that matter—when he could have a lady of beauty and elegance by his side and claim her for his wife. There lies your strength, Caroline. You have been bred for elegance and exquisite tastes. You are beautiful, and you know it. Furthermore, you have the discretion not to flaunt your beauty, to let it work naturally. You are a rare find, and Morgan Randolph is no fool."

"What should I have done?" Caroline demanded. "I could hardly have stayed there any longer under the circumstances."

"Indeed you could have," Judith insisted, "and should have. You were right to ignore Morgan Randolph for the evening, and of course that strategy obviously worked because he sought you out to dance with you. You were right to ignore him after the dance, but you were wrong to be run off by that little Italian hussy, simply because she was talking about Morgan Randolph in the powder room. You should have assumed a position of superior dignity, gone back to the ball, and left with your escort at an appropriate time. You should *never* have allowed Morgan Randolph to see that you were upset about anything. Always remember that, Caroline. A man can only gain control over you if he sees that you are flustered or upset by him. There are, of course, times to use that tactic, to allow him to *think* he has upset you. This was not one of those times."

"I am not as emotionally contained as you are, Grandmother."

"You had best become so, if you intend to be Mrs. Morgan Randolph."

"I'm not at all sure I want to be Mrs. Morgan Randolph," Caroline insisted. "After all, if he is the kind of man who runs after a woman like Valery, I'm not sure that I wish to be married to him."

"Nonsense!" Judith exclaimed as she brought her cane down ferociously on the floor. "Don't be absurd, Caroline, he's the Randolph heir. Who cares what kind of woman he's running around with? You sound just like your mother."

Monique suddenly forced herself into the discussion by protesting, "But he be too old for Miz Caroline."

"What has age got to do with social position and wealth?" Judith demanded.

"She don't love him," Monique added her second point.

"Irrelevant, Monique. Caroline is not French. She is not motivated by the passions. She is a Bradford and must therefore be motivated by cold logic. Bring us a tea tray." Judith dismissed Monique with a wave of her hand.

When Judith turned her attention back to her granddaughter, Caroline seized the moment, "Grandmother, it would seem to me that cold logic would dictate that you should be angry with Morgan Randolph, not with me."

"Why should I be angry with Morgan Randolph?" Judith demanded. "After all, he's only acting like a man."

"Well, I'm sorry I've disappointed you," Caroline finally gave up the fight. "I can see that your way would have been preferable had I been involved in a battle of wits, but I felt that I was simply—"

"Simply following your feelings," Judith finished the sentence for her. "Never mind. The Wentworth ball is history now. The issue is, what do we do next?"

"We?" Caroline asked.

"Of course, *we*. No man on the face of the earth is going to reject my granddaughter without severe consequences. I am now absolutely determined that you shall be Mrs. Morgan Randolph. It's really only a matter of outwitting him, and I think that our battle strategy is quite obvious."

"I suppose that it is decided," Caroline said sarcastically, "that we are going to engage in a battle?"

"Of course it's decided, Caroline. No Bradford ever turned his back and walked off the battlefield, and you are not going to be the first."

"But what if I decide I don't want Morgan Randolph?"

"I shall think you're crazy," Judith answered, "but if you turn him down flat, after he has proposed, at least you will have turned him down from a position of victory. That I can accept. Having him not pursue you and put his heart on the line, not to mention his wealth and prestige, that I cannot accept. So first things first. We must discuss our strategy for you to gain the heart of Morgan Randolph."

"Not to mention his wealth and prestige," Caroline added curtly.

"They all go together," Judith said coldly. "Now it seems to me that what we need is for Morgan Randolph to believe that he does not have a chance in the world of gaining your attention. The social season is just beginning, and there will be ample opportunity for you to ignore his presence."

"I'm not at all sure that I want to participate in the social season this year," Caroline said wearily.

"Nonsense, Caroline. This is the one year when you must participate for the sake of your honor." Judith's eyes gleamed at the thought of the challenge ahead. She walked briskly to her favorite, straight-backed, 18th century chair, and beckoned Caroline to join her. "You may sit, Caroline. We shall make our plans for conquest over the tea table as Bradford women have done for generations."

Caroline did participate in the social season as energetically as a general with his mind set on the conquest of new territory, but to the public she showed only the grace of a queen. Wearing exquisite gowns from Judith's collection, Caroline dazzled Dallas society. She went to every elite function that was held previous to Christmas, and following her grandmother's insistence, she held her head high, ignored Morgan Randolph and flirted discreetly with the eligible young men from the most prestigious families.

The season, however, was tortuous because almost every event that she attended was also attended by David and Valery. She had learned a great deal more about Valery, much more than she wanted to know. It seemed that Valery was the daughter of an old Italian family which traced its roots back to the Renaissance, but which was now in a state of semi-impoverished gentility. She had been dating David Morgan Randolph for two or three years in Europe and had come to the United States to spend the Christmas season with him. It was obvious to everyone that she expected to return to Italy with an engagement ring on her finger. Rumors about her and David Morgan Randolph were numerous, and it was generally assumed that she was his mistress, and had been for several years, but was now pressing him to marry her.

Every time Caroline arrived at a ball and found David there with Valery, she became depressed and wanted to flee. She refused to allow herself that luxury, however. She reminded herself that she was a Bradford, lifted her chin and acted out the part that her grandmother had coached her in, the part of the beautiful, charming, but difficult to attain heiress. Inside, she was miserable. Her feelings for Morgan Randolph had not lessened, but she scolded herself repeatedly about those feelings. After all, she told herself, what reason do I have to think that he has special feelings for me? One night in the moonlight with nothing but a few gentle words hardly means he intends to give up a long-term, intimate relationship with a woman as exciting as Valery. As for my own feelings, they are ludicrous. I can't understand why I should care at all or why I would even be interested in such a man. But she found she did care, no matter how much she scolded herself, and whenever she heard the gossips talking once again about his supposed affair with Valery, she had to clench her teeth to keep from defending him, even though she had no ammunition with which to defend him. For all she knew, he was having an affair with Valery.

In the meantime, Taylor's actions were also making her miserable because it was becoming increasingly obvious that this would be the Christmas that he would insist on a formal engagement and the setting of a wedding date. He seemed to be oblivious to the fact that Caroline was flirting with many eligible bachelors; since he was always her official escort, he obviously assumed that their relationship had not altered in any way. Half the time Caroline found herself wishing that she had encouraged Taylor more in previous years so that she would now be married to him and this whole fiasco with Morgan Randolph would not even exist. The other half of the time she was grateful that she was not married to Taylor because the presence of Morgan Randolph always seemed to remind her that a deeper, more significant relationship with a man was possible. At least it was possible with Morgan Randolph.

Finally Christmas Eve arrived, and Caroline awoke feeling quite anxious and depressed. I'm only tired, she told herself as she dragged herself out of bed and reached for her robe. Randolph House is finally closed for the holidays, and my responsibilities are over until January 15th. I'm on vacation. I just need to slow down, take today off, and pamper myself a bit to get ready for this evening and tomorrow. She tied the sash of her robe as she walked into the kitchen of her condominium and began to make a cup of tea. All my Christmas shopping is done, all my presents are wrapped. There's nothing for me to worry about. I'll just lounge around, shampoo my hair, do my nails and rest up for this evening.

She took her tea and went to sit in her favorite place in her living room, a window seat in front of a large bay window. From there she could stare out into the private, manicured gardens. It was a bleak, wintry day; one of the famous Texas "northers" had blown in during the night.

Caroline found herself thinking of Morgan Randolph, so she snatched up a notepad and busied herself making a list of things she needed to pack for the three-day trip to the country she would make late that afternoon. She wasn't going very far. She was going to spend the next three days with Taylor's family at Idlewild, their estate north of Dallas. Even so, the list was a complicated one because Christmas in her social class was a rather elaborate affair. Her friends and family always lived up to the Texas tradition of bigness and grandness. Her own parents lived only ten miles from Taylor's, so she would also spend some time with them on Christmas Day. Her list grew as she included not only clothing and personal items but also the gifts that she had bought and carefully wrapped for all the members of the two families.

Oh, I hope Taylor won't ask me to marry him, she thought for the hundredth time since she had awakened. It's not that I don't want to marry him some day; it's not that I don't love him at all. I do love him—well, at least I thought I did. The only thing I know for sure is I just don't feel I can make that kind of commitment to him. I suppose it has something to do with Morgan Randolph, but that's so ridiculous that I can't believe I'm even thinking about it. In spite of the fact that I've followed Grandmother's advice to the letter and appeared at every elegant social occasion, he still does no more than dance with me occasionally. And Valery is always with him!

She sighed as she finished the list, then stared out the window without seeing, as her thoughts took another direction. Perhaps all I'm feeling is pre-engagement jitters. Maybe Morgan is only an excuse for postponing something that frightens me, a life-time commitment. I guess what I need to do is just plunge ahead and accept Taylor's proposal. After all, he offers me a great deal that I have wanted for many years. He comes from the right kind of family. His family may not be as rich as the Randolphs, as wealthy as what Grandmother wants for me, but they're quite socially prominent and very well off. Taylor is successful himself. We're very compatible in interests. Well, somewhat compatible in interests. He's my age. I've known him for years and know him well. I know what I'm getting. I know I can live with what I'm getting. I know exactly what my life will be like if I marry Taylor. That in itself is a great plus. In fact, it should be a wonderful comfort to me. The more she talked to herself the less anxious she felt. Yes, it's just a case of pre-engagement jitters, she decided. I'll be a lot happier with Taylor than with David. I mean Morgan. I refuse to think of him as David. It reminds me of that night in the moonlight, and I can't bear to think about it.

Having thought the matter through and reduced her anxiety level, Caroline got up and spent the rest of the morning packing and shampooing her hair. When Taylor came to pick her up at three o'clock, she was ready.

"Good grief," Taylor exclaimed when he saw the luggage and baskets of packages. "Are you going to Idlewild for three days or three weeks?" he laughed.

"I know it looks ridiculous," Caroline admitted. "I didn't realize how much I was taking until I pulled it all together. But there are a great many events in the next three days, and they all require a different outfit, and of course I need to take packages for both families." She turned around in a circle and looked at the mass of gathered items at her feet.

"Well, I guess I should have rented a truck," Taylor said good naturedly. "Somehow, though, we'll get it all in and still find room for the two of us."

He picked up the large suitcase and the hanging bag and started out the door, and Caroline followed him with a large rattan basket of gaily wrapped Christmas packages. After two trips from the condominium to Taylor's Porsche, it became obvious that no amount of juggling and positioning of suitcases and packages would make it possible for them to make the trip to Idlewild in only one car.

"I'll just have to take my car too," Caroline suggested.

"But I wanted us to make the drive together," Taylor said, as he began to look downcast. "Are you sure you have to have all this stuff?"

"Taylor," Caroline answered, as she tried to keep her teeth from chattering from the cold wind. "I've spent the whole morning making lists and pulling all this together. Of course I'm sure I have to have everything. Besides, it's only 30 miles. It's not like we're starting out on an eight-hour trip in separate cars. It'll take us about 30 minutes, and then we'll be back together again, and we'll have both cars out in the country in case we need them for some other reason."

"Well," Taylor gazed around at the items he had not been able to get into his car. "I guess we really don't have a choice."

"The main thing," Caroline said, "is to get packed before we freeze to death and get on out to the country so we can have a vacation."

"Right," Taylor agreed, and they both picked up the remaining items and walked to the garage of Caroline's condominium. In another ten minutes they had everything stowed away, the condominium was locked up, and Caroline and Taylor were on their way to their Christmas holiday in the country.

When they both arrived at Idlewild about four o'clock, Caroline was greeted by Taylor's parents, both of whom had made it quite obvious that they wanted her to be their daughter-in-law. Everyone was in a jovial mood, and with the help of Taylor's mother, Caroline settled quickly into one of the guest rooms. Soon she joined the family in the large living room of the country house. Taylor's brother and sister and their families were there, as well as a collection of aunts, uncles, and cousins. It was a boisterous crowd who had already begun to consume eggnog and were preparing themselves for the light-hearted evening ahead.

The schedule was a bit complicated. Taylor's mother finally got everyone's attention and began to explain. They were all invited to open houses at two neighboring estates before the family sat down for Christmas Eve dinner about nine o'clock. After dinner they would open a few presents and, of course, go to church at midnight. It sounded like fun to Caroline, who had been able to rest that day and convince herself that she did care for Taylor enough to marry him and had only been suffering from last-minute anxiety.

By six o'clock she was dressed for the evening in an outfit that would be appropriate for the receptions, family dinner and a church service. She wore a red-and-green plaid, cotillion-length, taffeta skirt with a beautiful, Victorian style, ivory silk blouse covered in lace. To complete her outfit, she donned a dark green velvet, old-fashioned short jacket that snugly followed her curves and showed off her tiny waist. She had pulled her long auburn curls back and up at the sides with beautiful pearl combs that her grandmother had given her. She turned in front of a full-length mirror and admired herself. "Perfect," she pronounced her appearance. "Old-fashioned, feminine, elegant. I like it."

When Caroline joined the others in the foyer, she found herself surrounded by elegantly dressed people filled with gaiety. She relaxed and blossomed; she was in her element. They all left for the receptions in a parade of cars, and Caroline felt eager for the joys of the evening ahead of her. Going to two receptions and a gala dinner sounded to her like the perfect way to spend a Christmas Eve. The idea of a church service was a little foreign to Caroline, who had omitted church from her life since she had gone off to college. Her mother, a religious woman, had insisted that Caroline attend church while she was growing up, but once Caroline had left for college, she had left her mother's church-going requirements behind. It's Christmas Eve, she silently persuaded herself, and a midnight church service is certainly a traditional part of that occasion, although I have to admit that the solemnness of a church service doesn't seem to fit into the jollity of this social occasion. Oh well, if it makes Taylor's mother happy, what do I care?

The receptions were wonderful. Both homes were brilliantly decorated and full of happy, expensively dressed, talkative people sharing excellent hors d'oeuvres and eggnog. This is what Christmas is all about, Caroline thought. Next year I—no—Taylor and I will entertain all our friends at some elegant affair to celebrate our first Christmas together.

Caroline drove back to Idlewild with a glow on her face and great happiness in her heart. She was positive that Taylor would find a way to propose to her that night or tomorrow on Christmas Day, and she was having fun watching his face and trying to figure out when he would make that special moment happen. Also, she had begun to wonder about the size of the diamond he had chosen for her.

When they arrived back at Idlewild, Taylor opened the car door for her and helped her out of his Porsche. At first she was surprised when she realized that no one else had arrived back at the house for dinner. Then she guessed that Taylor had arranged it just that way. He was obviously going to propose. Putting his arm around her shoulders, Taylor walked with her toward the house, guided her straight into the living room and sat her down on a bench in front of the fireplace, where the coals of a fire were still glowing. He took both of her hands in his, and Caroline looked eagerly into his face.

"Caroline," he began, "I love you."

She smiled encouragingly at him.

"You know how much I love you," he continued without embellishment. "I've loved you for years and years."

Caroline continued to smile eagerly at him, expecting a flood of passionate words, at least as passionate as Taylor was capable of, but no romance came forth from his lips. Instead he said simply, "You know I've wanted to marry you for years. Will you marry me?"

She was stunned by the shortness of his proposal but had already made up her mind to accept him, so she opened her mouth to say "yes," but the word would not come out. She closed her mouth and stared dismally at Taylor as tears began to gather in her eyes and run down her cheeks. What's wrong with you she demanded of herself. This is the moment you have waited for all your life. You're supposed to be overwhelmed with joy—not weeping.

Taylor totally misunderstood the tears, threw his arms around her, and crushed her against his chest. "Oh, Caroline!" he exclaimed. "I was afraid you might say no, but I see that you're so overwhelmed by happiness that you can't even speak."

Caroline's mind was a whirl of confusion. She couldn't speak, but she knew she had to say something. She pushed him away, wiped the tears from her cheeks and opened her mouth once again to force herself to say yes she would marry him, but she could say nothing. She stared down at her hands in her lap. It was only then that Taylor understood that something was wrong.

"What is it, Caroline?" he asked quietly. "You do *want* to marry me, don't you?"

When he asked the question that way— "you do *want* to marry me, don't you"—Caroline finally put away her pride and conceded to herself that in spite of his behavior, the only man she wanted to marry was David Morgan Randolph. The many weeks of gala social events and flirtations which her grandmother had directed her to participate in had neither brought David to her side nor changed her new understanding of what love is. She had known from the evening of the debut of Randolph House that she had never loved Taylor, that she had never even understood what love is. There were many adjectives that she could use to describe Taylor: comfortable, convenient, fun, compatible, predictable, secure, but none of those adjectives had anything to do with love. Love is something that overwhelms one's heart and cannot be reduced to a few words. She had felt it for the first time while the crowd at Randolph House was singing "Silent Night." She felt it when she was alone in the moonlight with David after the debut. In spite of her anger with David at Marcia Wentworth's ball because he was associating with a woman like Valery, she had felt love for him when they had waltzed together. I cannot accept less than love, she told herself as she struggled to understand her inability to accept Taylor's proposal. I prefer never to marry than to marry for convenience, and that is what I will be doing if I marry Taylor. It won't be fair to him, and it will be meaningless to me. Finally she was able to speak.

"I can't marry you, Taylor," she said quietly.

He sat back, stunned. "Why not?"

She lifted her quivering face and looked him in the eyes because she felt he deserved the truth. "I don't love you," she admitted to herself and to him. "I thought I did, I tried to, but I don't love you, Taylor."

"Is there someone else?" he demanded.

She responded quickly to avoid his question. She could not hurt Taylor by revealing her feelings for David, and besides, those feelings were not reciprocated. "You know I've seen no one but you for two years now."

"Listen, Caroline," Taylor leaned forward. "I know you don't love me in a big, romantic, Hollywood kind of way, but we could still have a great life together, and you'll come to love me more and more after we're married. You know I think you're the greatest girl ever, and we have such wonderful times together—"

"Taylor, please don't do this," Caroline begged. "I don't understand love, but I know I don't love you, and I know myself well enough to know that I could never give up my independence for anything less than a truly compelling love. Not just good times and compatibility, Taylor, but truly compelling love. And I just don't love you that way. I thought I could marry you anyway, but I can't. I just can't!"

She felt tears flowing down her face and knew that she was on the verge of sobbing, so she jumped up and ran out of the room and up the stairs to her bedroom. There she sat on the edge of the bed and allowed herself to cry without any restraint.

When she could cry no longer, she went to the dressing table and stared in the mirror at her puffy, red eyelids and the black streams of mascara that had flooded down her face.

"How will I ever get through dinner?" she asked her reflection. "How will I ever get through the next three days?" She felt panicky and then depressed at the thought of the pretense she would have to conjure up. "Somehow I must get through this and avoid any embarrassment for anyone, especially Taylor. I owe him that; besides, I can't bear to give people something to gossip about." She raised her chin a little higher, clamped down on her emotions and surveyed the damage to her makeup. There was nothing to do but start over. Resolutely she walked to the bathroom and washed her face.

When Caroline came down to dinner half an hour later, she was the picture of composure. Taylor looked like a wounded animal, but no one seemed to notice. All eyes were on Caroline. Taylor's mother had planned the traditional, grand Christmas dinner for the extended family, and the table was long and elegantly set with the best linens, china, silver and crystal. It was covered with beautiful dishes of tempting food that surrounded a magnificent floral arrangement and antique candelabra.

Taylor mechanically seated Caroline and then took his own seat at her side. She looked at the maze of faces all around the huge dining room table and was grateful that many of them had had plenty of eggnog before the dinner. They were not likely to be very observant. She kept up her end of the various conversations with charming but false wit and laughter, while Taylor sat at her side in total silence and glumness. Eventually his mother noticed his demeanor and began to glance at Caroline with a concerned, questioning look.

Depression began to creep up on Caroline again. When she saw Taylor's mother nod meaningfully at Taylor's father and realized that Taylor's father was staring at his son's face, Caroline's anxiety rose. Slowly she watched as various members of the family began to catch on to the fact that something was wrong with Taylor. The talk around the table became more subdued and forced, and the light-hearted tone bogged down as people tried to pretend that nothing was wrong. Caroline felt that she would suffocate. Even the beautiful flaming desert that was served at the end of the meal did not seem to distract anyone from the obvious difficulty between Taylor and Caroline. Finally the endless meal was over, and Caroline gracefully extracted herself from the dining room and fled to her bedroom.

She had only been in her room a few moments when there was a quiet tap on the door, and before she could say "come in," Taylor walked in and closed the door behind him. "Caroline," he started and stopped. He looked at the floor, cleared his throat and began again. "Caroline, this isn't over between us. It can't be."

"Taylor, I really think I have finally understood what is in my heart and what is not in my heart. I have at last told myself the truth, and now that I know my true feelings, I must tell you the truth."

"I want to talk about it some more," he insisted, "but we leave for church in fifteen minutes, so we'll have to talk when we get back."

"I don't think there's anything else to say, Taylor," Caroline persisted. "It's going to be hard enough to sit through church as it is. I don't want to sit there thinking that you and I are going to discuss this again."

"Are you planning to just dump me," he demanded angrily, "after all these years? Just suddenly, on some crazy whim of yours, you've decided that I'm out of your life?"

"No, of course not; I'm sure that we can go on being—"

"Friends?" he exploded. "You think we can go on being friends after the kind of relationship we've had? Get real, Caroline!"

"I don't know, Taylor. I just know that I can't be your wife; it wouldn't be fair to either one of us. There must be some civilized way to handle this, but I've never been in this position before, and I don't know what to do."

"Well, I know one thing," he said. "This is my parents' home, and it's Christmas Eve, and my whole family is gathered here, and I have no intention of being embarrassed in front of everybody."

"I'm sorry if you were uncomfortable at dinner, Taylor," Caroline murmured. "I felt awful too. I don't know what to do. I can only pretend so much."

"There's only one thing you can do, Caroline," he walked over to her and put his hands on her shoulders. "You must recognize that you're only feeling frightened of this commitment. We are right for each other. Give yourself a little time and you'll see that. Don't just say 'no.' Don't just cut it off. We can't have invested all of these years in this relationship and have it ended with a single word. You can't just say 'no.' I'll see you downstairs."

He turned and left the room, and Caroline went to the dressing table mirror to straighten her hair before church. When she looked at herself in the mirror, she saw the stricken, panicky look in her eyes, and reality asserted itself over social decorum. "I can't pull it off," she whispered. "I can't pretend anymore. I just can't! Oh, what have I done? What am I going to do now? Poor Taylor, I've hurt him badly, and he deserves better. I can't hurt him any more. Everyone downstairs has figured out the truth and is uncomfortable. Taylor is obviously miserable. I mustn't prolong his misery by giving him false hope." Caroline snatched up her coat and purse, left the house by the back, service steps without being seen, got into her car and left the estate before anyone could stop her. She drove for three or four miles before it occurred to her that she wasn't sure where she was going. About a mile down the highway she saw a lighted building, and as she approached it, she realized that it was a small church. That parking lot, she thought, where people are gathering for a midnight service will be a safe place for me to pull off the road. I must decide what I want to do, what I should do. I can't just drive all night.

After she parked her car in the parking lot, she glanced at her watch. It's a quarter till twelve, she thought, and I'm sitting alone in a strange parking lot of a strange church watching happy families enter the building. Oh, how did I come to this low point? She surveyed the church building. It was a small, white, clapboard church which seemed no bigger than a chapel to her, and the people entering were obviously lower-middle class. Just look at the happiness on their faces! she exclaimed to herself. It's so different somehow. It's not the gaiety I saw at the receptions tonight or at the many balls I've been to. What is the difference? Where does it come from?

She had no plan. She was simply alone in the cold, looking in on the lives of joyful people. The minutes ticked away on the clock in her car until it was five till twelve, and the simple church bell began to toll to call worshipers to this special service. She did not feel a spiritual need, but she felt the need not to be alone in a parking lot that was fast becoming empty. She picked up her purse, opened the car door and hurried to the church door.

Inside she found a very simple, small church with clean white walls that were softened by many votive candles in sconces. The church had been decorated, obviously by amateur hands, with evergreen boughs from the surrounding woods, berries and candles. A large stable scene was depicted in the choir area, but it was empty of the Holy Family. A single, large candle burned in a stand several steps below the manger. Hoping she wouldn't be noticed, Caroline

...d into a pew. The family next to her turned to her and smiled. ...felt wretched when she saw the husband and wife and their three rosy-faced children. They have something I don't have, she thought. What is it? What could they possibly possess that I don't have? They don't even have expensive clothes; the wife looks content though. Maybe they are happy because they keep their lives simple and just accept their place in life. I don't know. Whatever they've got, I wish I had some of it right now. What am I saying? Look at them. They're poor! I don't want poverty. Oh, I'm just in a temporary state of confusion.

The bell stopped its tolling. The congregation rose to its feet and began to sing "Oh Come All Ye Faithful." The wife next to Caroline opened a hymnal and shared it with her. Caroline looked at the woman's simple, polyester dress and compared it to her own silk taffeta skirt, lace-embellished silk blouse and velveteen jacket. She felt terribly out of place, but the woman's happy smile seemed to include her, and her insistence that Caroline share a hymnal helped Caroline feel welcome.

As the service of carols and readings from the Gospel proceeded, Caroline was struck once again by the simplicity of the church building, compared to the usual churches that she had attended. There were no stained glass windows, no expensive pews carved out of mahogany or cherry. The altar was draped in a plain cloth, but there was great beauty that came from the spirit of the people there.

Toward the end of the service the minister announced, "Jesus is born, let us rejoice!" As the congregation stood and began singing, "Hark the herald angels sing, glory to the new born King," a young girl walked solemnly down the aisle. She was dressed as Mary and carried a baby. By her side was a young man depicting Joseph. They took their places in the nativity scene. Soon other youngsters dressed as angels, shepherds and wisemen walked down the aisle and joined them. When they were all in place, the minister took an unlighted candle and placed its wick to the flame of the large candle before the manger. Members of the congregation began to file forward; each one picked up a candle off of a table and lighted it from the nativity candle. They did not return to their pews, but instead they gathered at the front of the church in front of the nativity scene. Caroline was encouraged to go forward by the woman standing next to her, so she joined the worshipers. Soon every man, woman and child held a lighted candle in honor of the Christ child; the lights were turned off, and the congregation began to sing "Silent Night" acapella.

Chills ran down Caroline's back. She did not understand what she felt or what was happening around her, but she knew that what these people were experiencing was a phenomenon she had never experienced. When the hymn was finished, the people bowed their heads as the minister thanked God for sending His Son. At the close of the prayer, the organist played an exuberant "Joy to the World," and the people sang and hugged each other and hugged Caroline. As the last word of the jubilant carol filled the air, they blew out their candles and visited happily with each other as they moved back down the aisle and out to the parking lot. Caroline followed the group's movement, smiling at people and exchanging pleasantries. When she reached her own car, the woman who had shared a hymnal with her joined her.

"I am Joyce Henman," she said. "We would like for you to come home with us. We don't have a big house, but my oldest could sleep on the couch, and you could have her bed. Then you could spend Christmas Day with us. There will be lots of relatives and lots of noise, but if you have no other plans—"

Caroline hugged the woman and wiped away the tears that were streaming down her face. "Thank you," she struggled to speak. "Thank you. My plans fell apart, but now I'm glad they did. They weren't the right plans for me. I see that now. But I do have a place to go, and don't worry, I won't be alone. I'll be with family."

"God bless you," the woman said. She hugged Caroline gently, then drew back and looked her in the eyes. "Why don't you let God make your plans from now on?"

Caroline nodded her agreement, "I'm sure He would do a better job than I have."

The woman smiled again and said, "Have a blessed Christmas," before she turned and left.

Caroline knew that she was not going back to her condominium, nor was she going back to Taylor, nor was she going to her grandmother's house. She knew she was going home to her mother's house.

As Caroline entered the gate of her parents' estate, she

wondered if anyone would be awake. She fervently hoped not; she had no idea what explanations she could give her family since she didn't understand her actions herself.

There were extra cars parked to the side of the house, including her grandmother's limousine. Caroline sighed with relief when she saw no lights in the windows. Her experience of previous Christmases gave her an idea of what had occurred in her childhood home on Christmas Eve. No doubt her grandmother had arrived in the evening with Monique and supervised a Christmas Eve dinner for various family members. One significant person would have been absent—Caroline's mother, Marian. She would have spent the evening serving dinner in the shelter for the homeless where she had volunteered countless hours for years. Caroline was certain Judith had made her usual caustic remarks to Marian, and Marian had smiled that mystical smile of hers, kissed her mother and gone her own way—to the shelter.

Caroline sat in her car and stared at the elegant country house and thought about her mother. She knows who she is, Caroline reflected, although it took her a lot of years to find herself, or maybe it was to assert herself. Grandmother is an incredibly strong personality, but in the end she was no match for Mother's quiet strength. I wonder where she gets that strength. She pondered her knowledge of her mother's youth and her own memories of her mother.

Marian had followed the usual path of a daughter of a wealthy family, people who had generations of money and prestige behind them. She had attended the best girls' schools, made a stunning debut, and married the most eligible bachelor. Then she had fulfilled her duties to her class by producing two sons to carry on the Forrest name and one beautiful little girl, Caroline, to grow up and marry well and thereby form an alliance with another family of old money. Marian had been a typical woman of her class, and Judith had been totally satisfied with her.

Then quite suddenly, when Caroline was in her early teens, her mother had resigned her social position. Caroline could remember no announcements of her mother's decision to change her life; Marian had simply come home from a trip to South Carolina and canceled her social engagements and started spending her days volunteering at various charities. Judith had been horrified and was generous in her condemnation of her daughter. Every argument between Judith and Marian that Caroline had overheard included her grandmother's insistence that Marian was abandoning Caroline, but Caroline had never felt abandoned. She simply became aware of two strong forces in her life—her grandmother's absolute determination that Caroline would become the belle of her generation and her mother's powerful example to Caroline that she would find meaning in life through service to others. Caroline had continued down the path of her first fourteen years of life and continued to embrace her grandmother's values. She loved her mother, but she did not understand her.

Now she was back at her childhood home, and both women with their different attitudes about life were brought together by Christmas. Considering the actions she had taken that evening, Caroline hoped they were both asleep. "But if somebody is awake," she whispered, "please let it be Mother."

It was 2:15 in the morning, so Caroline closed the car door quietly and walked to the front door. She started to use her own key to open the door, but it was opened from inside by Marian.

Caroline simply looked at her. She shed no tears and spoke no words. Her mother waited a moment, then asked, "Do you want to talk about it?"

Caroline was amazed at her serenity, her acceptance of what should have been a startling arrival in the wee hours of the morning.

"There's nothing to say really, Mother. I refused Taylor's proposal, and I just couldn't stay at his parents' house. I refused his proposal," she repeated.

"Good," her mother said calmly.

"I can't make that kind of commitment to him," Caroline's voice rose.

"No, you can't, dear," her mother assured her.

"But I thought I loved him."

"But you didn't, did you?"

"No," Caroline answered. "But I didn't know that until it had gone too far, and now he's hurt. But it seemed better to break it off suddenly and just leave and not pretend. I couldn't pretend now that I know."

"You've done the right thing, Caroline. There's no doubt this will be painful for Taylor, and it won't be easy for you."

"But I don't love him," Caroline felt that she was repeating herself obsessively. "I don't love him."

"No, dear. You don't."

There was a long silence, and Caroline's mother came forward and put her arms around her daughter's shoulders. Caroline did not cry; she said nothing more, as her mother stood there and held her close, a gesture Caroline found as comforting as if she were six years old.

"Your room is ready, dear," her mother said finally. "Perhaps you need to get some sleep."

"Yes," Caroline agreed wearily and turned toward the stairs. When she reached the bottom of the stairs, she turned back toward her mother and said, much to her own amazement, "Mother, I—I stopped at a little church on the way here. It was the most remarkable experience."

Her mother smiled at her in a way that Caroline had seen since she was fourteen years old but had never understood. "A special Christmas gift for you, perhaps?" she asked.

"Yes, I guess that's the perfect description of it. I saw something—something beautiful—a kind of love I've never seen. And the joy! Yet those people had so little—just each other and—and—"

"God come to earth," her mother finished Caroline's sentence and smiled serenely. There was a moment of quiet between them.

"Don't we have the same thing happen in our church at Christmas Eve services? Doesn't God come to earth there?" Caroline asked.

"Of course. The question is: do we notice?"

"I haven't—not until tonight," Caroline admitted.

"But He did come, Caroline, and for a specific purpose. Sooner or later each one of us has to confront that purpose and decide where we stand in relation to it."

"You have decided, haven't you, Mother?"

"Yes, Caroline. I have decided."

"And it's changed your life." Caroline spoke the words as a statement of fact and a summary of what she had observed in her mother's choices and actions.

"Yes, Caroline. My decision caused a glorious revolution in my life."

Caroline fingered the silk taffeta of her skirt, then caressed the velvet of her jacket as she observed her mother's Christmas Eve outfit of a denim dress and solid shoes. When she returned her gaze to her mother, she saw on her face a glow of joy she would have given anything for.

"Merry Christmas, Caroline," Marian said softly.

"Merry Christmas, Mother." Caroline ran back and gave her a hug and then went upstairs to rest.

There was a strange combination of heaviness and peace in her heart.

Chapter 5

"What a long winter that turned out to be," Caroline said to herself as she rose from the sofa and went to tend the fire. "I never found my way to that joy Mother has. I wish I had. Instead I accomplished what Grandmother wanted; I continued the Bradford legacy and married for wealth and prestige. Fortunately for me I was madly in love with D. Morgan Randolph, my wonderful David. But I wouldn't have bet a dime that long winter six years ago that I would ever become Mrs. Randolph." Caroline added another log to the coals and stood there watching. The log just sat on top of the shimmering, red-rose coals and refused to ignite. "What a perfect metaphor for that awful winter. My heart was as full of fire for David as those coals are full of fire, but he had gone back to London, so my life was like that un-ignited log. It just lay on top of my feelings, a great burden to me, a life of dead weight with no warmth and light in it. Oh dear! Life could be that way again if he finds out what I've done."

"Oh Caroline! You're getting morbid." She scolded herself as she glanced at the clock. "No wonder. Three o'clock in the morning. Will this night never end?" She walked to the window and stared out at the fallen tree lying across the front yard. "Things did work out with David, you know. At least they did until now. No! I won't think of that. I'll put some paper under that log and *make* it burn. At 3:00 in the morning I simply refuse to think about anything except victories."

The azaleas were blooming when Caroline next saw David Morgan Randolph. He came striding up the brick walk of Randolph House, just as if he were coming home for dinner. She saw him through the French doors of her office, and her heart began a staccato beat as she prayed fervently that someone would detain him in the foyer until she had regained her composure. Then she remembered that the sun was setting outside; the staff had all gone home.

What can I say to him, she wondered frantically. How much does he know? Does he know I rejected Taylor's proposal? Does he know that I haven't accepted a single date since Christmas Eve? Panic rose in her, and she decided that she could not possibly confront David Randolph at that moment. She bolted out of the French doors onto the western verandah of Randolph House. She paused at the edge of the verandah and stared out over the gardens trying to decide whether to take the foolish step of running away, assessing whether or not she had the courage to smile and pretend that thoughts of him had not been disturbing her all these months.

Don't be an idiot, she scolded herself. Of course he's heard you aren't dating Taylor. He has no special feelings for you, and you are not going to make a fool of yourself by revealing your feelings for him in any way. He's made no effort to contact you at all, and what about Valery? Obviously he still has a relationship with her, and it isn't hard to guess what kind of relationship it is. No doubt he's been in London all these months with Valery. Your one night in the moonlight with him here at Randolph House meant nothing to him. He just wants a woman available on both sides of the Atlantic. This is just like him; her anger rose as she determined to stand her ground and speak her mind. He always appears so suddenly. I never have a chance to prepare myself, or if I do, it turns out like Marcia Wentworth's ball. That memory flashed an infuriating image through Caroline's mind, the picture of Valery wearing one yard of black satin, which strained to cover her body as she gyrated on the dance floor.

"Caroline?" she heard David's voice behind her. She lifted her chin and slowly turned around to greet him. Determined to maintain a detached composure, she looked directly into his eyes. The eagerness of his expression changed to a startled look which melted into admiration. The rapid change of expression on his face confused her until she looked past him and saw herself in the reflection of the French doors. The final performance of the disappearing sun had bejeweled the sky with magic sweeps of crimson, rose and gold. It was the perfect backdrop for her vibrant auburn hair and her creamy complexion. Her normally blue-gray eyes had turned sapphire, as they always did when she was angry or excited. She realized that no amount of makeup or other artifice had ever made her more beautiful than she was at that moment.

"How beautiful you are!" David blurted out.

She glared into his eyes. "You have no right to say such a thing to me."

"No, of course not," he agreed hurriedly. "But that doesn't make it possible—I mean—at such a time, a man doesn't think of his rights. Honestly, Caroline, at this moment you are the most beautiful woman I have ever seen."

"I'm surprised to hear you say it," she retorted. "I should think I'm wearing far too many clothes to appeal to your taste."

A dark flush spread across his face, and a chilling silence created a chasm between them.

"Is that a reference to Valery?" he finally asked quietly.

"Should I make a reference to Valery?" Caroline intentionally made her tone light and flippant.

"Are you asking me for an explanation?" David asked.

"I'm sure you owe me no explanations," Caroline answered. "And I'm equally sure that I wouldn't be interested in any you had to give."

"Nevertheless," he said, "won't you give me an opportunity to speak? If you hear nothing of interest to you, then you'll have wasted nothing on me but your time."

He stepped closer to her, and she felt her pulse quicken as he looked longingly down at her. She turned her back, rather than allow him to see that she could not maintain a composed look on her face.

"Won't you even listen to me?" he asked gently.

How easy it must be for him to break women's hearts, she thought. "I'm still here," was all she said.

"I'm sure you're aware that I've had a long-term relationship with Valery. A relationship that one might call intimate."

Caroline continued staring out at the sunset but replied caustically, "How very non-specific a word—'intimate.'"

"You must understand," David said calmly, "that I've known Valery many years, perhaps as long as ten or twelve years. I don't really recall when I met her—"

"I don't think it's necessary for me to understand anything about your relationship with Valery," Caroline cut him off coolly.

"It may not be necessary to you, Caroline, but it's important to me. I can well imagine what you must think of me."

"Can you?" she demanded as she whirled around and stared up at his earnest face.

David was silent for only a few seconds before he plunged in with renewed resolve. "I have known Valery for ten or twelve years, and over that time a relationship has developed slowly but surely, and for about the last two years it has been a very serious, intimate relationship. At that time I did not know you, of course. When I first met you, the day of the reception here at Randolph House, I was overwhelmed by feelings I have not felt since I was a young man. Feelings I most definitely did not have for Valery. I'm afraid I did not handle those feelings very well, particularly in light of the fact that you were quite involved with Taylor. I can't excuse myself. I knew of your close relationship to Taylor. The night of the reception I stayed behind after everyone left with the hopes of being alone with you, enjoying a quiet time with you. It was my only opportunity to double-check the feelings I had."

"Apparently the feelings did not turn out to be accurate or true," Caroline replied.

"You're quite wrong there," David reached forward and put his hand on her arm. When Caroline looked scornfully down at his hand, he removed it.

"You see," he began to walk up and down on the verandah in front of her, "I had already arranged for Valery to come to Dallas to spend the Christmas season. In fact I met her plane the morning after the reception here. I wanted to spend time with you. I wanted to get to know you, but there were two things in the way. First, there was Valery; it would have been cruel of me to back out on the invitation I had issued to her. And then there was Taylor; I was very aware of your close relationship to him. Marcia Wentworth told me that it was only a matter of days before your engagement was to be announced. What was I to do? I struggled with myself. Every time I saw you at one of the Christmas parties I came close to breaking what I consider to be my code of ethics and speaking directly to you about my feelings."

"And did Valery stay through New Years?" Caroline asked. She already knew the answer; she knew that Valery had left the day after Christmas.

"No, she left the day after Christmas."

"Were you suddenly struck mute?" Caroline demanded.

He stopped in front of her. "In a way, yes, of course I was. I could hardly approach an engaged woman and express my feelings for her."

In an instant Caroline felt confused and apprehensive; her anger dissolved.

"What engaged woman?" she asked quietly.

"Why you, of course," David replied. "Taylor asked you to marry him on Christmas Eve, and you accepted. The day after Christmas, Valery went back to Italy. I was finally free of half of the reason I hadn't spoken to you about my feelings. But it was too late; you were an engaged woman with a wedding date set."

"Oh really!" Caroline exclaimed, "and just how did you come to that preposterous conclusion?"

"Marcia Wentworth told me."

Caroline was so stunned by his words that she couldn't think clearly for a moment. "Marcia Wentworth told you I accepted Taylor's offer of marriage?" she finally managed to ask.

"Yes, she called me the day after Christmas to tell me all the wonderful news about you and Taylor, that you were engaged and that there was to be a wedding in March. I knew that if I stayed in Dallas, I couldn't keep quiet. So I returned to London and went on with my life as I had led it before."

"Why would Marcia do such a thing?" Caroline demanded. "She knew very well that I rejected Taylor's offer. Everyone in our circle of friends knew that Taylor and I were not even speaking to each other. It was a horrible scandal; people had a wonderful time trying to guess what had gone wrong between Taylor and me. There was never a wedding date set. There was never even talk of a wedding date, certainly not a March wedding date."

"I know that now," David said quietly. "And that's why I'm here."

"How did you finally learn the truth?"

"March has come and passed, and there was no announcement of a wedding between you and Taylor. I knew your marriage would be a great society affair, and when there was no announcement of it, I flew back to Dallas and confronted Marcia."

"I don't believe you," Caroline said, although she was hoping desperately that he could persuade her. "Why would Marcia Wentworth do such a thing to me?"

"Because she is Valery's first cousin."

"Valery's first cousin?" Caroline was incredulous. "Marcia

Wentworth is Valery's first cousin?"

"Yes, Marcia's maiden name is Benelli."

Caroline just stared at him in amazement. "Did you know they were cousins?"

"I knew," he admitted, "and it would be dishonest of me to pretend that they totally tricked me—that I was a completely innocent victim of their scheming. You see, there was a part of me that wanted to be prevented from relating to you. I didn't understand what I was doing to myself then, but I see it now."

"I don't understand," Caroline shook her head slowly.

"Well, it's one of those things that are both simple and complicated. The simple version is, I was married in my twenties—very happily married. My wife died trying to give birth to our first child. She was only twenty-six years old. They took the baby by caesarean after she died. Our son struggled to live, but he died two months later. All the hopes of my youth were ashes, and I felt I had lighted the match myself."

"How horrible for you." Caroline wanted to touch him, to place her hand on his arm, but his grief seemed so private that it made him quite remote.

"The complicated part is the way that that experience scarred me. I never wanted to love anyone again."

"But why not, David? I know it was devastating at the time, that your grief must have been immobilizing for a while, but it was a long time ago. People can deal with their grief and go on."

"You don't understand, Caroline. I blame myself for her death. She would be alive today except for me."

"You don't know that, David. She might never have met you and still have died. She might have died in a car accident or—"

"I've reasoned with myself over and over, Caroline, but my feelings don't change. She died because I loved her, because I loved her so deeply that I wanted to create a family with her. It wasn't lust; it was lifelong love, and it killed her."

"Your feelings of love were perfectly natural," Caroline insisted. "They were beautiful feelings, obviously a desire for the best kind of commitment between a man and a woman."

"I understand what you're saying; I even understood such logic back then, after I recovered from my initial grief, but the fact is I never allowed myself to love that way again. That's why I've associated with women like Valery and avoided women like you. But something has happened to me lately. Maybe it's just age or something. I don't know. I want a wife, Caroline—not a mistress. There's all this emotion—I guess it's that same kind of love I felt in my twenties—bottled up inside of me. But I never want to cause death again."

"Death doesn't automatically follow that kind of love, David."

"It's getting chilly out here," he suddenly changed the subject. "Let me take you back inside."

"No," Caroline refused. "This is all so surprising to me and so confusing. I don't think I want to be contained by four walls right now. I need to be out here in the quiet dusk."

He nodded, and she turned away from him to stare at the sunset again. Only a vivid crimson ribbon lying on the horizon remained of the earlier fiery glow. Because the sun was so diminished, Caroline was able to see a full moon rising. Through all the fiery passion of the sunset, the moon had been there all the time, a white disk radiating its serene light, waiting for its moment of gentle glory.

Caroline felt motion behind her, and then she felt David's suit coat as he draped it over her shoulders. After he had covered her shoulders with his coat, he let his hands rest on her arms.

"Caroline," he spoke softly, close to her ear, "I have very strong feelings for you. I believe you have some feelings for me. The past still frightens me, but I would like to investigate the feelings we have for each other, to determine if there's any future for us. I realize I have great disadvantages. I am older than you are, and I have had some relationships you would be uncomfortable with, to say the least. Knowing what I know of you and your standards, I realize you cannot think highly of my relationship with Valery. But if you will only consider what I've told you, perhaps it will be easier for you to understand the kind of relationships I have chosen."

Caroline nodded, and he placed his cheek against the softness of her hair as he continued. "I don't want to live out my life denying my deepest feelings. I want a woman I can love for the rest of my life, a woman I will be proud to call my wife. You are such a woman, Caroline. If you will allow me to spend time with you, I believe I can show you that you can love me."

Caroline stared at the full moon as it ascended, casting its pure light on the countryside. It seemed to fill her with the quiet courage she needed. "I hurt Taylor, David, really hurt him because I never stopped and took a serious look at myself. I didn't take the future seriously. Time seemed to spread out endlessly before me, so I avoided the hard decisions. I was not in touch with my true feelings for Taylor, and because of that fact I hurt him badly. I shall always regret the pain I caused him and the years that we both lost in which we could have been dating others and perhaps finding that special someone we both wanted. I just don't want to harm anyone else in that way, and, David, I cannot guarantee you anything." She paused to give herself time to choose her words carefully. Then she turned and looked into his eyes, "I do not want to live out the rest of my life without risking a relationship with you, without knowing whether I care for you in the way that would make a marriage possible, but I don't want to hurt anyone else."

"I'm a grown man, Caroline," David spoke firmly. "And if there's the slightest chance that you could love me, I will take the risk gladly. You are worth it."

Caroline's eyes filled with tears; embarrassed by them, she dropped her gaze from his. He enclosed her in his arms, held her tight against his chest, and buried his face in her hair. "Once again we are alone at Randolph House in the moonlight," he murmured. "Can't we just begin again, wipe the slate clean and start over?"

"Yes," she whispered. "I would like that."

What an enchanted spring that was, Caroline thought, as she lay on the couch in her sitting room in her storm-damaged house and watched the strange shadows that the flickering candles made on the walls. Those were the happiest months of my life, and if there was anyone happier than I, it was definitely Grandmother. It was obvious that the greatest ambition of her life would be accomplished when I married David Randolph. From the moment I raced into her parlor to tell her that David was back, she seemed to be immediately rejuvenated. I don't think a day of our courtship passed that Grandmother didn't call and demand a minute-by-minute description. I suppose it's easy to understand her excitement. She was eighty-six years old, and she viewed this vicarious romance, which was a greater match than even she had made, as the final triumph of her life, as the continuation of the Bradford legacy.

Mother did not see it the same way. When I went to tell her that I was head over heels in love with David Randolph, she was happy for me, but she had some probing questions, questions I didn't want to deal with, questions I had never wanted to deal with in any area of my life. Grandmother was ecstatic about David's wealth and social position, but Mother was concerned about something she called his spirituality. She wasn't concerned about his churchgoing. It was something deeper than that, something obviously more important to her, something I don't understand even now. Of course, I paid no attention to her cautious optimism or to her pleading that I go slowly. I much preferred Grandmother's enthusiasm, so I limited my visits to Mother rather than hear the reserve in her voice. On at least one issue, I now painfully see that she was right to be concerned. When David proposed to me in June, I was so in love with him and so in love with the picture of our future life that I had conjured up, I would have agreed to anything he required of me. Of course, I wasn't really very surprised that the only requirement he had was that I agree that we would not have children. After all, he was past forty and had been through so much pain from the deaths of his first wife and his child. I was twenty-eight and madly in love and—yes, I admit it—confident that I could talk him into children later if I wanted a child.

Mother knew more about me than I did, obviously. I made my promises to David about not having children without giving it much thought. We had a grand wedding in the fall, a wedding that included every detail of elegance and happiness that Grandmother could dream up, and there wasn't anything she couldn't dream up. It was certainly the happiest day of my life and perhaps the happiest of hers. Mother was happy too, but her eyes indicated clearly that she was saying some kind of special prayers. Apparently those prayers didn't work. If they had, how could I have ended up in the mess I'm in, and what on earth am I going to do to save myself from my own foolishness?

Chapter 6

"Will morning never come?" Caroline jumped up from the loveseat, walked to the window, and stared out into the darkness at the rain. "This has got to be the longest night in history." She let the curtain fall from her hand and wandered listlessly around the room, feeling trapped by the circumstances created by the storm, as well as by her predicament with David.

How could I ever have broken my promise to David? she silently demanded of herself. How could I have tricked him into fathering a child, and what am I going to do to keep from losing him? Our marriage was so happy; all I needed in my life was him. Then things changed, things inside of me. I don't know how to explain it, but I just began to feel that our happiness was incomplete somehow, that I was incomplete. So I tried to talk him into having a baby. Is that so bad? Am I a horrible woman because I want a child? Don't I have any rights? Of course I do! So I took matters into my own hands just like women have always done. I intentionally stopped taking the pill, and now I'm pregnant. That's a reality that's as unavoidable as the fact that there is a tree lying in the drawing room at this very moment. What a fool I am! I convinced myself that a man who had suffered such grief from fatherhood, who had made me promise that I would never put him through such a thing again, and who is nearly fifty years old now—I convinced myself that such a man would change his feelings in some Hollywood fashion the minute he knew he was going to be a father. Grandmother is right. I haven't got a realistic bone in my body, and perhaps Mother is right too when she says that I need to think in more spiritual terms. Breaking my word to David definitely falls into the arena of spiritual problems. But I was absolutely convinced that when I told him that I was pregnant, he would be happy. Of course I knew he would be worried for the entire pregnancy, but I'm so healthy, and there's no problem like there was with his first wife. She had a heart condition. I'm in perfect shape to have a child; the doctor said so.

Oh, if David had only left for London one day earlier! He would have missed Scott's tirade yesterday at the office. He wouldn't even have known that Suzanne tricked Scott into having another baby. Then I would have joined him in London this weekend, and we would have gone on to our holiday in sunny, carefree Greece. I just know I could have found the perfect time to tell him about our baby. Sometime when he was relaxed, maybe on a clear, bright-blue morning when all the world seems new and nothing bad could ever happen. In the right place I could have convinced him to deny his fears and be happy about our baby.

But there was no mistaking the anger in his voice when he told me what Suzanne did to Scott. What could I do? I couldn't just sit there and say, "Yes, I know, David, what Suzanne has done to Scott because I knew about her plans from the beginning, and I decided to do the same thing." How he ranted around this house last night! He was furious with Suzanne. Then he said emphatically, "If I had a wife do that to me, I would divorce her!" I thought I would be sick right there. I thought it was the worst moment of my life, that I could never feel worse, but I was wrong. When his face softened and his tone changed entirely and he turned to me with the most loving look, took me in his arms and praised me for my honesty—that was the worst moment of my life.

"Thank God," he said, "I don't have to worry that you will ever lie to me the way Suzanne has lied to Scott. I can't tell you how wonderful my life is because I can trust you, Caroline. Not just with the pregnancy thing and my overwhelming fear of losing you, but also the countless trips I have to make abroad, the many nights we're away from each other because of my work. I know I have a wife I can trust without reservations. I know you, Caroline. You are pure through and through."

I started crying. Of course, he thought my tears were the result of his praise, not because of the wrenching guilt and shame I was feeling. How I wrestled with all that he said! How grateful I was when he left this morning for London, grateful to have this time alone to work through this problem. But why does it have to be such a problem? Surely I can make him see that I will be fine and our child will be born healthy.

Oh, what a fool I am! Even if I have a healthy baby and breeze through the pregnancy and the delivery, it won't change the fact that I've lied to David. I've broken my word. Nothing will ever be the same between David and me again. But what can I do? I'm pregnant, and there's only one way out—an abortion. But I want a baby! Caroline paced around the room like a prisoner in a cell. Finally she stopped before the fireplace, picked up the poker and jabbed at the log. When she put the poker down, she stared hard at the flames. She was finally ready to be honest with herself. I want David more than I want this baby, she confessed. I love him. I love our life together. And yes, it's true, I love the wealth and social prominence. What if he did divorce me? What would I have then? Think what I would lose! Maybe I just need more time with him, another year or so, to talk him into a child. Maybe I can have both this wonderful life with him and a child, if I just wait another year. So maybe an abortion is the best thing for now. Thank goodness he's in London, and this storm and the damage to the house give me the perfect excuse to cancel our vacation. I need more time to think and to get an abortion if—oh, I'll go crazy if I keep thinking about this now! It's 5:00. Surely it will be light in a couple of hours. I must get my mind on something else. Caroline wandered over to her desk and saw the vest she had rescued from the drawing room earlier.

"Think about James Bradford's vest," she ordered herself aloud. She sat down on a chair and began to study the vest again, but she had a hard time controlling her mind. She sighed with frustration when she couldn't concentrate on the vest, so she turned her attention to the note. She opened the small piece of paper and read the cryptic words again. "He knows nothing. Meet me at midnight." Determined to divert herself from her own problems, she leaned back in the chair and thought, I'll try to imagine why this note was put into James Bradford's pocket.

Caroline stared down at the note for a few minutes with its faded brown ink. This is obviously a woman's handwriting, she concluded, and the very fact that it's not addressed to anyone or signed by anyone suggests something very secretive was going on. Hmm, what secretive thing could possibly have been going on at midnight between a man and a woman? I guess the answer to that is pretty obvious. And who is the "he," the guy who doesn't know? Her husband, perhaps? Sounds pretty deceitful. Well, maybe people haven't changed very much after all in the last 125 years. Maybe my great-great grandfather, the prominent James Bradford of Charleston, South Carolina, was having some sort of secret liaison with a woman. It's almost comforting to think he did. It makes me feel better about myself, about what I've done to David. No, I don't want to think about that!

I'm going to sit here, and I'm going to imagine myself in Charleston, South Carolina around 1865. The War would have ended, but I think Charleston was occupied by federal troops for a long time after the War. It probably took a while for James Bradford to get home, but he eventually came back and started picking up the pieces of his life. One of those pieces would have been his social life. He probably went to some public gathering where a lady who was quite well-known greeted him. Perhaps she allowed him to kiss her hand, and when he did so, she slipped a note into his hand, which he quickly put into the pocket of this vest. Both of them continued to act perfectly normal and made conversation about the weather or perhaps the horrid federal troops that were still in Charleston, or perhaps the shortages of food. Of course, as soon as he possibly could, great-great grandfather James Bradford found a private moment in a private place to read the contents of this note. And when he did, how did he feel? Did he meet her at midnight? Of course he did. And I think it's just about at that point in my story that I should stop speculating about my ancestors, before I start thinking about things I have no business thinking about.

Caroline laughed for the first time in quite a few days. I guess it's horrible of me, but I'm dying of curiosity. Wait a minute. Maybe I don't have to imagine what happened. After all, this was Grandmother's grandfather; she was very close to him when she was growing up. She owned this vest and thought it was so important for me to have it that she gave it to me as a wedding present. It's a beautiful thing. I always assumed that she gave it to me because of her constant references to our wonderful legacy from James Bradford. I just hung it on the wall and gave it little thought, but there *could* be some mystery about James Bradford. Perhaps she knows the story that I'm trying to make up to pass this awful night. As soon as I can get the mess cleared up here, I'll go visit her. It'll be fun. If she doesn't know what happened, we can have a good laugh speculating about what her wicked grandfather might have been up to. Caroline stood up and moved the candelabrum away from the loveseat. Then she carefully placed the vest on the table next to the loveseat.

Dawn finally came. At the first sign of light Caroline peered out the window and discovered that the city crews were arriving to clean the debris from the street. Part of that debris was the enormous live oak that had been uprooted in the yard across the street, had stretched its thick, long arms across the pavement and had ended its journey by crashing into her drawing room. Men carrying chain saws began the grinding noise of removing the major trunk of the tree from the street. She knew that they would soon need to come into the house to remove the top of the tree from the drawing room, so she hurried upstairs, changed clothes and left the house, hoping to find the closest working telephone. She barely made it off the front porch before she was stopped by a city disaster worker who ordered her to stay in her house. After much pleading on her part, she convinced him to have someone call her housekeeper, Hannah Tulaney, and tell her to send a carpenter. Caroline hated the idea of more waiting, but she was still stuck. *It's just a matter of time before they have that tree out of the yard,* she encouraged herself. *I just hope Hannah can find a carpenter.*

Caroline remembered that she had not eaten any supper or breakfast, but there was no way to cook until the utilities were restored. She wandered back into the kitchen and found some French bread to munch on. She immediately felt queasy but dismissed the fleeting idea that it was because of her pregnancy. She made up her mind not to think about that problem today.

By three o'clock that afternoon Caroline had endured the sound of chain saws for hours as they cut apart the tree and removed it from her yard and drawing room. Hannah had sent a carpenter who had come with massive sheets of plywood and boarded up the gaping hole in the wall. The police flatly refused to allow Hannah into the neighborhood, so Caroline had busied herself cleaning up the wet, muddy mess left by the tree, as well as the broken glass, broken bricks and bits of mortar in the drawing room. She was exhausted by the vigil of her long night alone in the house, as well as the general stress she was feeling from the problem she now faced with David. However, with the aid of the carpenter she cleaned up as best as she could. Both of them marveled at the precise and restricted damage the tree had done. "It's as if that tree was just aiming for that one spot on the wall," the carpenter said. "There's furniture smashed, but that vest you showed me is the only thing raked off the wall. Why, those little lights on both sides of it haven't even been touched."

"It is odd, isn't it?" Caroline stared at the wall which was only damaged in a three foot wide strip where the vest had hung.

"It's spooky, is what it is," the carpenter declared. "That tree just reached as far as it could and snatched that old vest off the wall."

Caroline didn't mention the note she had found, but occasionally she stared at the wall for a moment, and every time she did, a little shiver went up her spine. She told herself it was the result of her excitement about the note, but she couldn't deny that that shiver had an edge of fear to it.

She was eager to talk to her grandmother about the vest. Finally the house was secured, and it was almost tea time. There was still no electricity, but the police were allowing a few residents to leave. Caroline changed into fresh clothes and left to visit her grandmother.

When Caroline arrived at her grandmother's around four o'clock in the afternoon, Monique met her at the door with a warning. "Miz Judith is all riled up," she said grimly. "You best watch your step."

Caroline sighed and walked on into the entry of her grandmother's mansion. "What's she angry about, Monique? Because I didn't come over and spend the night here? I couldn't possibly leave my house unwatched."

"No, Miz Caroline, she done gotten over that one, but she got a phone call from Mr. David about five minutes ago, and he was good and worried cause he found out the phone lines to your house was damaged by a storm."

"Oh," Caroline said. Even though she had thought of David all night, she had been grateful she couldn't call him; she simply wasn't ready to talk to him yet. "Well, perhaps I should call David before I see Grandmother then."

"I think you better get on up them stairs to that drawing room and let her get over her hissy fit and then you can call Mr. David." Monique ushered Caroline along as she talked. The muscles in Caroline's neck began to tense at the thought of her grandmother's anger, although she knew Judith's temper was usually a sharp flash of indignation that never lasted very long with Caroline, even though Judith could hold a grudge against others for a lifetime.

Caroline paused outside the double doors of the drawing room and put on her best smile before opening the doors and walking in. "Well, here I am, Grandmother, all in one piece in spite of everything," she said as cheerfully as she could manage.

"No thanks to you," her grandmother replied curtly. She was sitting in her favorite mahogany, Queen Anne chair, which was upholstered in silk brocade. In front of her a tea table covered with a linen battenburg lace cloth held an elegant Limoges tea service. The precious, translucent china waited to serve the dignified woman who had owned it for over seventy years.

"I declare, Caroline, it makes no sense for you to stay in an empty house, totally unguarded through a long, dreadful night like last night. I didn't sleep a wink for worrying about you."

"I'm very sorry, Grandmother, that you worried." Caroline walked over and gave her grandmother a kiss on the cheek.

"I told that man who called me, to tell me that you were alive, that I did not want you staying there. Did he give you my message?"

"No, he didn't."

"It's just as well he didn't bother. You wouldn't have come and stayed here anyway."

"But I was fine, really. There were officials patrolling the street all night long. There was absolutely no danger of any looting or other problems."

"Well, in that case you certainly could have left your house, couldn't you?" Judith asked, proving that her wits were as sharp as ever in spite of her ninety-two years.

"In retrospect, Grandmother, I suppose I could have, but it seemed better to stay at the time."

"Well, don't bother to sit down," Judith said sternly. "David has just phoned from London. He is beside himself with worry. I can't believe that you didn't call him the very instant you were able to get to a telephone."

"I didn't want to worry him," Caroline partially lied. "He only left yesterday morning for London and was not certain whether he would spend last night in our townhouse."

"Well, he's certain where he is now. He's waiting in your London townhouse, and I want you to go and call him this very instant. He is quite perturbed with you."

Caroline looked hesitant and did not move quickly enough for her grandmother.

"Don't stand there, child! Go call your husband," she ordered. Then a conniving look appeared on her grandmother's face and her eyes twinkled a bit. "On the other hand, it doesn't hurt a husband one bit to be worried about his wife, you know. It's a very good thing for a marriage, in fact. Always keep him on the edge of his chair. How many times have I told you that? I declare, I don't know what you're going to do when I'm no longer around."

Caroline realized that when her grandmother took that tone, the tone of conspiracy against the men of the world, that she herself was off the hook. So she grinned at her grandmother, excused herself, and turned to leave the drawing room. Monique was waiting out in the hall, ready to serve tea when Judith called for it.

"I'll go across the hall into the library and call David."

"Don't be too long," Monique warned. "You know Miz Judith. She isn't gonna be patient about tea time."

"I'll hurry," Caroline said as she entered the library and closed the door behind her. She leaned against the door for a few minutes. The fact of the matter was that she still did not want to talk to her husband. *I guess it's guilt,* she thought. *Or maybe fear that he will suspect something. But I must call him.* She went over to the desk, sat down, and stared at the phone. *What a joy it would be,* she thought bitterly, *if I could still look forward to sharing my good news with him. But I can never tell him. Oh, it's not supposed to turn out like this! A baby is supposed to be good news.*

Caroline felt a wave of nausea, so she put her head down on the desk until it passed. She wanted so much to feel the excitement and joy she had felt at the doctor's office. She rested her head and tried to summon up those positive feelings so she would sound cheerful on the phone and not alarm David into flying back home. But the joy wouldn't return. From the entire hour she had spent in the doctor's office, only one image came back to her. She could plainly see a large, cross-stitched sampler that proclaimed in bold letters, "Children are a gift from God." A deep sense of satisfaction had permeated her whole being when she had seen it. Now she felt robbed.

"I have some rights here, too," she whispered belligerently. "David's fears are perfectly natural, but he could get over them if he would only try. Don't I have a right to be a mother? Isn't that a part of what being a woman is, at least having the opportunity to be a mother?"

"Yes, you have a right, Caroline," she answered herself, "a right to this baby, if you're willing to take the consequences. Are you?"

Caroline raised her head, placed her phone call and managed to convey to David that she was safe, but a bit shaken up by the storm. Fortunately for her, because of business in London he really needed to cancel their short vacation to Greece. Also he had caught a cold and was in no mood for a vacation, so when she emphasized the need to repair the house, he agreed that they should postpone their trip. After her brief call she reluctantly returned across the hall to have tea with her grandmother.

"How's David?" Judith demanded as Caroline entered the drawing room again.

"Actually, he sounds horrible," Caroline sighed as she sat down in a chair opposite her grandmother with the elegant tea table between them. Her eyes were full of worry. "He could hardly talk to me, he was coughing so much. At least I managed to make him understand that I'm okay and that the house is damaged but not so badly damaged that he needs to turn around and fly home. I just hope that Mrs. Watson will force him to take care of himself."

"If he's as sick as you think," Judith insisted, "he needs more than Mrs. Watson. She's only your London housekeeper. I think you should go, Caroline."

"Yes, I suppose I should," Caroline agreed aloud as she silently thought, but I don't want to. I'm not ready to see David yet. I'm sure he'd have no problem noticing that I'm very disturbed about something. I don't know yet whether I just want to handle the situation myself or whether I want to discuss it with him.

"Weren't you two planning a vacation in the next few days?" Judith asked.

"Yes, we were. I was supposed to join David on Friday, and we were going to go to Greece for a week's holiday."

"Well now, that's perfect," Judith insisted. "You'll just go a few days early. Hopefully with the proper medication and some good rest you can get him back on his feet, and you can still have a week together in Greece."

"There are several things you're not considering, Grandmother. First of all, David has canceled the holiday himself."

"But why?" Judith asked. "For the last month he's been

talking about wanting to steal you away to Greece. The man wants a second honeymoon, Caroline. Give him what he wants. It's the surest investment for your future."

"There's a business deal of some kind going on, Grandmother. You know how men are about business. When he left here yesterday morning, he was eager to get away to Greece with me, but one day in London has changed all that. Some kind of wonderful opportunity has arisen in the business world that he simply has to be a part of, so he's perfectly happy to postpone the holiday. In fact, after he found out I was unharmed by the storm, he almost sounded grateful that the storm had happened and that I needed to stay here to see that the house was repaired."

"Caroline, I have to tell you that when I spoke with David, he sounded very ill to me. You mustn't forget, dear, that he had pneumonia just last year, and once you've had that dreadful stuff, it's very easy to get it again. Do you really need to stay in Dallas to take care of the house?"

"No, of course not, Grandmother. A carpenter came this morning and boarded up the gaping hole in the front of it. The roof is sound. My housekeeper will look after things until I can return. I just don't think it will do any good to go to London. David may be sick, but he can be a very stubborn man."

"I've never known a man who wasn't stubborn," Judith said, "or at least I've never known a man worth anything who wasn't stubborn. I've also never known of an occasion when a woman couldn't get a man to do exactly what she wanted him to do, if she tried. I don't think you want to go to London, Caroline."

"Nonsense, Grandmother. If David is really ill, of course I want to go. It's just that I don't want to go over there and have a big fight with him over his health and have him end up going off to his business meetings in spite of everything I do."

"I still think you need to do something, dear. Why don't you call that London housekeeper of yours and see what she thinks about the state of his health?"

"That's a good idea," Caroline agreed hurriedly, wanting to change the subject, "and I'll talk to David later this evening or early in the morning. After all, it's almost midnight there now, and these colds and respiratory problems always sound worse at night."

"Just remember that David is your very best investment, Caroline."

"I prefer to think of him as a husband, Grandmother," Caroline laughed to cover her annoyance.

"Think of him as a husband if you like, dear," Judith said airily, "but remember he is still your best investment."

"Yes, Grandmother, I won't forget. Now how about that tea you promised me?"

Judith picked up a silver bell on the tea table and rang it. "Exactly what is the degree of damage to your house?" she asked.

"Well, most of the damage was caused by a large oak that fell across the street. You know that magnificent, old oak in the Windfield's yard, the one that spread so gracefully across the width of the street? I'm afraid the storm must have caught it just right and uprooted it. It fell across the street, across my front garden and straight through the bay window in the drawing room."

"Mercy!" Judith exclaimed. "I hope nothing of value was destroyed."

"The window is certainly gone and a part of the wall. Fortunately, only the very topmost part of the tree actually came into the room. I'm afraid it did smash some very beautiful furniture, Grandmother."

"Nothing from the family, I hope," Judith began to sound more alarmed. "I don't think I could bear it if you tell me that the Sheridan sofa is gone."

"No, Grandmother, nothing from the family was destroyed. The Sheridan sofa was over to the side of the room. That's what is so peculiar about the results of the storm. A few reproduction pieces were smashed, and some lamps and porcelains were broken. The most fascinating part of the whole story is that the topmost part of that old oak tree just scratched its way down the interior wall and ripped James Bradford's vest off the wall."

"James Bradford's vest?" Judith sprang up from her chair and leaned weakly on her cane. "Merciful heavens, Caroline! You're not sitting there calmly while you tell me that my grandfather's vest has been destroyed?"

Caroline rushed over to settle her grandmother back into her chair as she soothed her. "No, Grandmother, the vest is fine. I went in immediately after the tree had crashed and found the shadow box the vest was in. The box was in a hundred pieces, but the vest itself was fine. I took it out of the room and away from the rain. It's not damaged in the least, I assure you."

"Caroline, I certainly hope you are telling me the absolute truth. You know how important that vest is to me. I couldn't bear to think that we had lost James Bradford's vest. It is the most tangible proof of our Bradford legacy."

"Grandmother, I promise you. Please don't excite yourself. The vest is in very good condition. I took great care with it; it is perfectly safe."

At that moment, Monique entered the drawing room with the tea tray. She calmly set it on the tea table, but when she looked straight into Judith's face, she stood up straight and demanded of Caroline, "What's wrong with Miz Judith?"

"She's fine," Caroline said quietly.

"I am not fine!" Judith contradicted her. "Monique, James Bradford's vest was almost destroyed by that storm."

Monique said nothing, which seemed to increase Judith's sharpness. "Don't you understand? The vest of my grandfather, James Bradford, was almost destroyed by that storm. Caroline had to rescue it from a pile of broken tree limbs and smashed furniture."

"But it's okay, Grandmother," Caroline insisted. "The vest is fine."

"I want to see it," Judith demanded. "Where is it?"

"It's at home, safe in my study."

"I shall not rest until I see with my own eyes that it is not damaged."

"Then I shall bring it over and show it to you," Caroline said patiently. "Now please, let's have some tea, and you calm down. I have something interesting about the vest I want to tell you."

"Something interesting?" Judith looked at her sharply. "You said it was not damaged, Caroline."

"It is not damaged, Grandmother, but I spent quite a bit of time looking at it last night, and I discovered something quite fascinating about it. It's just a fun thing. Something for us to speculate about, have a little fun pretending. Would you like me to pour the tea?"

"Yes, dear, I think you best." Judith settled back in her chair as Monique hurried around to put a cushion behind her.

Caroline quickly poured her grandmother a cup of tea and added the milk and sugar that she knew Judith preferred. Then she handed the cup to Monique, who handed the cup to Judith. "Take a few sips, Grandmother," Caroline insisted. "You'll feel better in just a moment, I'm sure."

"Of course I will," Judith began to regain some of her tartness. "Pour yourself a cup too, Caroline. If the vest is safe, there's nothing else for me to be concerned about. We can always replace a wall or a window, and as far as reproduction furniture is concerned, well, I wouldn't even bother to replace it. I'm sure I have plenty of things in this gigantic house that would be much more appropriate for your drawing room."

"I'm sure you do," Caroline smiled patiently. "Now please drink your tea, Grandmother."

Judith put the cup to her lips and began to sip the warm liquid. Caroline exchanged a look of relief with Monique as she turned to pour herself a cup of tea. Monique backed away several paces and watched her mistress, a look of worry still lingering in her eyes. But after Judith had drunk half of the cup of tea, she seemed perfectly calmed. She put the cup back in the saucer and turned to Caroline. "Now tell me this interesting thing about the vest, Caroline."

Caroline put her own cup down, and a new eagerness entered her voice. "Sometime during the night, Grandmother, I was trying to stay awake, and of course there was no electricity, so I couldn't entertain myself in the usual ways. I took a very close look at the vest. It is a magnificent piece of work. I've never held it in my own hands and been able to examine the incredible stitchery on it, so I was almost glad that the shadow box had broken and allowed me a chance to handle such a precious item."

"It is a beautiful thing," Judith sighed, as she took another sip of tea. "I didn't want to put it in that shadow box, I must confess, but of course the museum recommended that it be completely protected from air and light. So I put it behind that glass, knowing that I would never be able to touch it again."

"It must have been difficult for you," Caroline agreed. "I don't think I understood that until last night, but once I held it in my own hands, it seemed to come alive. I felt like it wanted to talk to me. That's silly, of course, but I did think a lot about my great-great-grandfather and remembered some stories you have told me about him. Anyway, Grandmother, I was examining the vest very carefully when I suddenly felt something odd."

"What do you mean, 'something odd'?" Judith sat up a little straighter and put her teacup on the table.

"It felt like something stiff and a little crisp. It was up close to the shoulder seam of the vest, and when I moved the fabric, I heard a little crinkling kind of noise."

"Oh really?" Judith looked puzzled. "What was it?"

"It was a piece of paper, a very old piece of paper. It took some time and some careful work, but I managed to move it down to the pocket area, and I saw that the pocket had been repaired. I guess the seamstress who sewed the bottom of the pocket closed didn't know that that piece of paper had gotten loose inside the vest."

"Did you try to get it out?" Grandmother demanded.

"Yes, I did. Now don't get upset, Grandmother. I just took my needlepoint scissors and cut a few stitches—"

"Caroline, you didn't!" Judith gasped.

"Grandmother, these were stitches that were repair work, not the original stitches. Someone had repaired the inside of the pocket and done a very clumsy job of it. I only had to clip a few stitches to get the paper out. No historical damage was done. You know I wouldn't have done that."

"So you got the paper out," Judith waved her hand impatiently. "What did it say? What was it?"

"Well, that's the exciting thing. It's a great mystery. On the paper there was some spidery handwriting in a faded brown ink, and all it said was two short sentences: 'He knows nothing. Meet me at midnight.'" Caroline sat back with great satisfaction and looked at her grandmother's face, expecting to find some sort of excitement there.

Judith turned white and gasped.

"Are you okay, Miz Judith?" Monique sprang to Judith's side.

"Grandmother!" Caroline stood and hurried to the other side of the table. "What's wrong?"

"Caroline," Judith struggled to speak. "Give me that note this instant."

"But I don't have it," Caroline said quickly.

"I want that note," Judith insisted. "Is it in your purse, is it in your car?"

"No, I don't have the note with me. Grandmother, please, calm yourself."

"Miz Judith, you gotta go lie down," Monique said.

"Caroline," Judith pushed Monique back, stared into her granddaughter's face and commanded. "I want the note and the vest; I want them now."

"I will bring them to you, Grandmother. I promise. Just, please calm down."

"You don't understand!" Judith's voice rose.

"Miz Judith," Monique interrupted her. "I think you're making too much of this note."

Judith looked at Monique, and when their eyes met, Caroline could see that some kind of secret communication passed between them. Quite suddenly Judith regained her composure, sat back quietly against the pillow behind her and relaxed her hands on the arms of her chair. "Of course, Monique. You're quite right. This is perfectly silly. We needn't discuss it any more. Caroline, please bring me the vest and the note as soon as it's convenient, dear."

"Well, of course," Caroline said. She was totally baffled by her grandmother's sudden change in demeanor and tone.

"Goodness, Monique," Judith suddenly changed the subject, "this tea has grown quite cold. Bring some more hot water, and offer Caroline some of those delicious tea sandwiches that you made and some little cakes, perhaps."

Monique stood and looked at Judith for one more moment before she bustled out of the room as quickly as her sixty-five years allowed.

"Now, Caroline," Judith said. "Goodness gracious. Sit down, child. Tell me all about your plans for restoring the front of your house. You say they have removed the tree. Such a shame to lose that beautiful old oak. I remember it well, the most striking tree on the block."

"Yes, yes," Caroline stammered as she returned to her chair. "The city crew came early this morning about dawn and started work on the tree. Of course they removed it from the street first and then came and took it from the house. As I said, I had a carpenter come and board up the window."

"Well, I hope you didn't endeavor to clean up that mess yourself, dear."

"Well," Caroline paused. "The carpenter helped me."

"Mercy, Caroline! Your hands could have been ruined. You did wear gloves, didn't you? How many times have I told you?

otects her hands."

gloves, Grandmother."

e so. Now about your drawing room. This will
⸺ wonderful opportunity to redecorate it, Caroline. We must set our minds to it and come up with something really spectacular."

"But appropriate to its 18th century style," Caroline insisted.

"Oh, of course," Judith agreed. "Appropriate to the 18th century style. As I said, don't bother to buy any furniture. This mansion is stuffed with beautiful pieces from the Hamilton family and some marvelous Bradford pieces. It would be ridiculous for you to go out and buy reproductions. I should be passing more of these things on to you anyway. They would certainly be wasted on that mother of yours."

"That would be wonderful, Grandmother," Caroline hastily agreed to avoid a discussion of her mother, "assuming no more trees are going to be crashing into the drawing room."

"Indeed," her grandmother tried to chuckle a little bit. "If that old oak is gone, I suspect the drawing room will be quite secure for some years to come. Do you have a new color scheme in mind, dear?"

"Well, no, I really haven't had time to think about it."

"Ah, here's Monique back with some more hot water. Let me pour you a cup, Caroline."

"I'll pour Miz Caroline's tea," Monique looked concerned as she examined Judith's face.

"Nonsense," Judith exclaimed. "I'm perfectly capable of pouring a cup of tea. You must expect these little sinking spells of mine occasionally, Monique. After all, I am advancing in years."

"You's ninety-two years old and you oughta be taking better care of yourself," Monique insisted.

"I don't need you to remind me of my age, Monique." She leaned forward and poured some hot tea into a fresh cup that Monique had provided for Caroline.

"Don't just stand there, Monique. Offer Caroline some of those marvelous tea sandwiches you made. Oh, Caroline, Monique has come up with the most delicious mixture for tea sandwiches. It's a very delicate blend of salmon with a few herbs and just the slightest, slightest touch of a French mustard sauce. What do you call that sauce, Monique?"

"I don't call it nothing yet."

"Well, it's one of Monique's new creations, Caroline. You must try it. Monique, give her a sandwich."

Monique picked up a beautifully arranged plate of tiny tea sandwiches and held it in front of Caroline so she could help herself. The aromas of salmon and sharp mustard rose to Caroline's nose, and suddenly Caroline felt horribly nauseated.

She put her teacup down so forcibly it clattered in its saucer. Monique stared at her, and Judith put down the teapot without pouring her own cup of tea.

"What on earth is wrong with you, dear?" she demanded.

Caroline felt that she was about to faint.

"I'm not feeling very well, Grandmother," she said weakly as she struggled to make her brain produce a plausible reason. "No doubt it's the strain from the storm. I didn't get any sleep last night." She began to feel positively dizzy. "I think I'd better lie down," she murmured.

"Monique!" Judith exclaimed. "Help Caroline over to the sofa, and go get a cold cloth immediately."

"No, I had better get to the bathroom," Caroline said as she stood up. "I'm very afraid I'm going to be ill."

"No, you will lie down," Judith ordered, and Monique took a firm hold of Caroline's arm and helped her over to the sofa.

"A cold cloth, instantly," Judith ordered Monique as she rose from her chair and hurried to Caroline's side as quickly as she could.

Caroline felt better the minute she lay down because the dizziness began to pass. Monique was back in just a few moments with two cold cloths, one of which she laid across Caroline's forehead and the other across her neck.

"Lavender water, Monique," Judith said imperiously. "Have you no sense? We need lavender water, of course."

Monique hurried off again. Judith leaned over Caroline and stared at her.

"Perhaps I should call Dr. Phillips," she said.

"No," Caroline answered far too promptly. "Really, Grandmother, I'm quite all right. I just had a very strenuous night."

"I knew you should have come and stayed here," her grandmother tapped her cane firmly on the wooden floor. "But would you listen to me?" she tapped it again. "No!"

she tapped it twice. "You are a stubborn child."

"I'm sure I should have listened to you," Caroline murmured as she closed her eyes. The nausea was almost gone, and she had hopes that she could keep her grandmother from suspecting the truth. "The night was more difficult than I expected it to be." Monique entered carrying a cut crystal decanter of lavender-colored liquid. She poured the liquid onto a lace-trimmed hand-kerchief and began to bathe Caroline's temples and wrists with the lavender water which Judith believed to be the remedy for most of a lady's ailments.

"Thank you, Monique. Grandmother's lavender water has done the trick. I'm sure I'll be quite fine now," Caroline insisted. "I'm going to get up."

She sat up slowly and swung her feet to the floor. "There, see, I'm quite fine. It's just exhaustion from last night, perhaps a little bit of nervousness from the storm. It was a very frightening storm, after all."

"I should think so, my dear," Judith agreed. "But don't try to stand just yet. A cup of tea and some of Monique's cakes will certainly make you feel better. Monique, bring Caroline a fresh cup of tea."

Caroline started to rise.

"No, dear, just sit there on the sofa, and I shall sit here in this chair, and we shall have our tea over here. Bring some sandwiches too, Monique. No doubt Caroline hasn't eaten at all today."

"Really, just some tea would be fine," Caroline was a little afraid to confront the sandwiches again, but Monique appeared with tea and sandwiches. Caroline took her tea and began to sip it.

"You must have a sandwich," her grandmother insisted as she picked up a spicy smelling sandwich and handed it to Caroline. "Eat this. It will make you feel better."

The minute Caroline smelled the spicy salmon, she felt nause-ated again. She thrust the sandwich and the tea into Monique's hands and lay back down on the couch.

Monique stood there and stared at her, as silence reigned in the room. Then Monique turned, in what seemed to Caroline like slow motion, to Judith and a knowing glance passed from Monique's eyes to Judith's.

Judith suddenly announced, "That will be all, Monique."

With no argument whatsoever, Monique took the teacup and

the sandwich, left the room and closed the doors behind her.

"You are pregnant, Caroline," Judith accused. "Don't deny it. Both Monique and I know."

Caroline sighed. "Yes, I am pregnant, Grandmother, and I would appreciate something other than an angry tone from you."

"What does David say about this state of affairs?"

"I haven't told him yet," Caroline confessed.

"I wonder why not," Judith said caustically. "Really Caroline, have you lost your mind? Well, when are you going to tell him?"

"I don't know. I may not tell him at all. I don't know what I'm going to do."

"What do you mean you're not going to tell him at all? Don't you think he'll notice? You can't keep a thing like that a secret. Really, Caroline, you're not telling me that David did not agree to this, are you?" Caroline said nothing. "Merciful heavens, Caroline! What were you thinking?"

"I was thinking that I would like to have a child. Is that so very strange?"

"There are good reasons for having children, and there are good times for having children, Caroline. The best time is when your husband is in agreement."

Caroline said nothing because she felt so tense that she had become sick again.

Judith stared at her suspiciously. "There's something you're not telling me. Don't try to pretend with me, Caroline. I've known you since the day you were born. I've spent twice as much time with you as your mother has. I know when I'm not being told everything. What are you holding back?"

Tears began to slip from Caroline's eyes and flow down her cheeks.

"I knew it," Judith said. "You're not the type to cry. Even when you were a little girl, you didn't cry unless something perfectly horrible had happened. It's got something to do with David, hasn't it? He's going to be more than a little angry with you about this pregnancy thing, isn't he?"

Caroline nodded her head as she continued to cry quietly.

"Well, you might as well tell me," Judith insisted. "You certainly ought to know by now you can trust me, dear, and I shall help you deal with whatever it is. There's always a way to get around a man, Caroline." Judith got up from her chair and pulled it close to Caroline's side and sat back down. She took Caroline's hand, and with as compassionate a voice as she was capable of using, she said quietly, "Just tell me the situation, child. I can't help you if you leave me in the dark."

"It's very simple, Grandmother," Caroline's voice quaked as she tried to talk through her tears. "I promised David before we were married that I would see to it that we would have no children."

"Why on earth did you do that?" Judith's supportive tone suddenly disappeared.

"I had to," Caroline insisted. "It was his idea. He didn't want to have children because he never got over losing his first wife and their child."

"Oh that," Judith said impatiently. "That happened years ago."

"Well, it didn't happen years ago as far as David was concerned; he remained quite upset about it, so much so he simply avoided marriage or the kind of woman that he might be tempted to marry for fifteen years because of it."

"Until he met you," Judith pointed out, "but you agreed not to have children."

"Yes, I had to."

"But now you're pregnant. How did that happen?" Judith demanded.

Caroline said nothing. She just stared at the ceiling and avoided her grandmother's eyes.

"Oh really, Caroline! I never thought you could be so stupid." Judith leaned back in her chair. "Why did you do it?"

"I want to have a baby. There's nothing strange about that, Grandmother."

"Well, I have to admit that I can't understand why any woman would want to have a baby unless there was some gain in it, and as far as I can tell, in your situation you knew that there was nothing but trouble ahead if you conceived a child, and yet you proceeded to allow yourself to become pregnant."

"Yes, it's entirely my doing. I thought David would get over his feelings, and I thought we could have a happy family life, which is something that I want, even if you don't think it's valuable."

"Well, it's not that I don't think that family life is valuable, dear. You know how much I enjoy you, and I certainly couldn't have had you if I hadn't had your mother, Marian, even though she has certainly turned out to be a disappointment. And, of course, I want you to have children. I want there to be more Bradford heirs. But it's just that, as I said, there is a time for these things, and apparently this is not the time. So what are you going to do?"

"I don't know," Caroline said.

"How angry do you think he will be?"

"Furious." Caroline told Judith about David's reaction when Suzanne tricked Scott.

"Oh dear, oh dear," Judith shook her head. "Well, the answer's obvious."

"It is?" Caroline asked.

"Of course it is. You can't have this child."

"But I'm already pregnant, Grandmother."

"I know that. I haven't forgotten. You may be able to pull this little scheme of yours off later, but not now. Fortunately this is 1996, and there are ways to become unpregnant which are legal."

"An abortion. Why don't you just use the word?" Caroline accused. "Why don't you just say that you're recommending that I go abort your great-grandchild?"

"'Abortion' is an unpleasant word, Caroline. Surely we needn't descend to such language. Don't think of this baby as a child. It only makes things more complicated. Just think of it as a difficult situation which you can solve. After all, this is an age-old problem. Women have been dealing with this problem from the beginning of time. Why, in my day, if we hadn't dealt with it, we would have had a child a year and not lived past the age of forty."

"I don't want to talk about it right now," Caroline said. "I just feel angry and disappointed and very upset, and I don't want to talk about it."

"You can refuse to talk about it as much as you wish, but reality is reality, and as I have told you many times, Caroline, you're not very good about facing reality. You are going to have to make some arrangements. You cannot allow this slip-up of yours to ruin your marriage."

"This 'slip-up' is my baby, Grandmother!"

"Stop thinking of it as a baby, Caroline. Sometimes we have to play little word games with ourselves for comfort's sake. Do you want to lose David and all that he has given you?"

"No, of course not, but I want to have this baby."

"It isn't a baby!" Judith raised her voice and struck the floor with her cane "And you can't always have what you want, Caroline. Life is like that. We want a lot of things we can't have, and no one is saying you can never have a baby. But you must be smart about it. You must coax David into wanting a baby, and you haven't time to do that this time. As soon as you get yourself out of this little mess you're in, we'll start working on him. After all, the Bradford legacy must be continued by your heirs. Why, by this time next year, I'm sure we'll have David persuaded."

Caroline stood up abruptly. "I'm going home. I haven't had any sleep. I'm exhausted, I'm upset, I feel horrible, I'm going home and rest. I won't think about this now; I'll think about it tomorrow."

"You and Scarlett O'Hara," Judith said caustically as she rang the bell for Monique. "Sometimes, Caroline, you sound just like your mother."

"Perhaps I do. I am my mother's daughter after all."

"Yes," Judith sighed dramatically. "There was no way to avoid that. We'll talk about this later, my dear. How pregnant are you?"

"Just a few weeks."

"Well then, we have plenty of time to deal with it."

"Deal with it! I don't want to 'deal with it.' I want to rejoice."

"You don't want to deal with it now, dear, because you're not thinking. Go home. Get some rest. Then you'll be able to think more clearly, and we'll talk about it again. Oh, there you are, Monique. See Caroline out."

Caroline started toward the door but turned back to say quickly, "They expect to have the phones working by tomorrow. I'll call you then or the next day."

"You won't need to call me tomorrow," Judith said. "You will return with the vest and the note tomorrow—no later."

"I can't promise—" Caroline began.

"Tomorrow," Judith interrupted her.

"By the way," Caroline intentionally changed the subject. "You did call Mother, didn't you, and tell her that everything is okay?"

"Yes, yes," Judith waved her hand impatiently. "I called that mother of yours. She said one of those absurd things she always says."

"What absurd thing?" Caroline asked.

"Oh, you know, one of those things about you were in God's hands or something like that," Judith said bitterly.

Caroline sighed and wished for just an instant that it was her mother sitting there and not her grandmother. "I'll call her as soon as the phone is working. Tell her I'll call her, if you talk to her."

"Oh, I don't think she'll be calling to check on you. After all, she's left you in God's hands."

"Grandmother, please, let's not get into that now."

"No, dear, let's not ever get into it." Judith rose from her chair and walked toward Caroline. She put her arm around Caroline's shoulder. "You go home and rest. I'll see you tomorrow when you bring over the vest and note. You'll be much clearer-headed then, and we'll deal with this problem of yours."

Every inch of Caroline ached to scream, "It isn't a problem!" Instead she kissed her grandmother on the cheek and started to turn away, but Judith clutched her arm with surprising strength.

"I'll expect to see you by noon at the latest with the vest and the note. By noon!"

Chapter 7

Caroline arrived back at her own neighborhood, sick at heart and sick in body. She felt depressed, anxious and physically weak. The destruction of her neighborhood was painfully obvious; the work crews were still there toiling to clean up the mess from the storm. She had left so hurriedly that afternoon to go to her grandmother's she had paid little attention to the destruction in the area around her block. However, as she now drove back through her neighborhood, she realized how violent the storm had been and how lucky she had been to have suffered so little damage to her house. She was three blocks from her house when the rain started pouring again from the low, dark clouds. A policeman signaled for her to pull over to the curb. He moved quickly to the car window, and she opened it to hear what he had to say.

"I'm sorry, ma'am, but nobody can drive into this area right now."

Caroline's spirits sank even further, and she felt totally exhausted. "But I live here," she insisted. "My house is only three blocks away. All I need to do is drive three blocks further and get my car into the garage before this weather gets any worse."

"I'm sorry, ma'am, but the electric company has had a really tough time here today, and they've got wires down everywhere. I just can't allow you or anyone else to drive a vehicle into this area."

"Could I walk in?" Caroline asked desperately. "Officer, I was up all night in my house, and I'm exhausted. I just need to get home. Is it possible for me to walk in?"

He looked around the street for a few seconds before returning his gaze to her face. "You could walk in if someone escorts you who knows how to watch for the wires that are down, but you'll have to leave your car here, and I'll have to see some identification."

"Whatever you say," Caroline sighed as she reached for her purse and her driver's license.

The officer took a close look at her license, handed it back to her and said, "Why don't you pull around the block there." He pointed to a side street. "They've got the wires up over there. There's no danger to your car. They'll be patrolling all night for vandals, so I think it's perfectly safe to leave it on the street. Then if you really want to do this, I'll walk you to your house. Are you sure you need to get to the house?"

"Positive," Caroline insisted.

"Well, I'll be here. You stash your car and come back."

Caroline parked her car about a block and a half away and walked back as quickly as she could, hoping the same policeman would still be there. He was waiting for her, and he escorted her the three blocks to her house. When they began their walk, it seemed absurd to her that she needed an escort, but she was soon glad the policeman was with her. The street was literally filled with trucks and men; all the wires were laid carefully on the sidewalks. The policeman escorted her across the grassy gardens in front of the houses until he finally got her to her own front door.

"Maybe I better go in and check the house," he suggested.

"I don't think that will be necessary," Caroline insisted as she turned her back on the front door to face the policeman. "It's been boarded up since this afternoon when I left. And as you say, the area has been full of workmen."

"Just the same, this is an awfully big house, and I don't like the idea of you going in there alone."

Quite suddenly the front door opened, and Caroline whirled around in surprise. There stood Marian, Caroline's mother.

"Mother, what are you doing here?" Caroline asked.

"Waiting for you, of course," Marian answered, then turned her attention to the officer. "I'm Mrs. Randolph's mother. I've been here for about an hour. Another policeman walked in with me and made sure the house was safe."

"Okay, ma'am, but remember, don't try to leave the house without some sort of an escort until these wires are all up." Caroline nodded and followed her mother into the hall.

"What are you doing here?" she asked her mother again as they stood in the dimly lit main hall.

"I just came by to check on you, dear," her mother put her arm around Caroline's shoulders, "and from the looks of you, I would say somebody needs to tuck you into bed with some hot chicken soup or something."

Caroline picked up the long, wet strands of her hair that were hanging limply on her shoulders and pushed them back away from her face. "I may be thirty-two years old, Mother, but right now I feel about five."

Her mother patted her on the shoulder. "I'm not surprised, dear. It's quite a mess around here. I didn't realize it was as bad as it is from what your grandmother said."

"She did call you?"

"Oh yes, she called, said you were fine, that you could handle your own life, and—well, you know your grandmother." Marian shook her head a little, a clear indication that Judith, her own mother, baffled her.

"Yes, I just left her house. She's her usual perky self."

Marian laughed a quiet, understanding laugh that suggested that once again she was choosing to accept a personality very unlike her own. "Come back into the kitchen, dear, and let me get you some hot tea or something. You do have a gas stove, don't you? Why don't you go get a towel and dry off."

"I think I'll just run upstairs and get out of these wet clothes and put on a robe or something," Caroline started toward the staircase.

"I'll put the kettle on," her mother said as she walked toward the kitchen.

When Caroline joined her a few minutes later, she already felt better because she was dry and in her own house, but also she had taken three or four minutes to talk to herself while she stared at her face in the mirror. During that time she had convinced herself that her grandmother was right, that she could take control of herself and handle whatever situation she had to handle.

"Still feeling five years old?" her mother asked cheerfully when Caroline walked into the kitchen.

"No, actually, I think I may have made it all the way to fifteen," Caroline tried to match her mother's easy tone.

"I made you some peppermint tea. Hope that's okay." Marian was poking around in the refrigerator and spoke without looking at Caroline. "I found some sandwich makings in here. I don't know about you, but I'm starving." She pulled out several handfuls of sandwich meats and cheeses and turned around and threw them on the counter. "This stuff isn't really cold; the refrigerator's been off too long, but the cheese should be safe." She went to the pantry and brought out bread and chips. Caroline stared at the meat. Even though it was wrapped in plastic, she could smell the strong scents of salami and ham. Worse still, amid the packages of cheese there was definitely some kind of blue cheese. Her stomach immediately churned, and she felt faint as nausea washed over her.

"Well, it won't be a feast," her mother said as she turned around again. "But I've never been so hungry—" She stopped and stared at Caroline, who was gripping the counter so tightly that her knuckles were white.

"Caroline, what on earth? Are you all right?"

Caroline shook her head, turned and dashed from the kitchen to the closest bathroom. When she came out of the bathroom, her mother was standing outside the door.

"I wasn't sure how old you were when you went running out of the kitchen," her mother said, trying to sound lighthearted but failing miserably. "Right now you look thirty-two, but I sense that you're not quite fifteen yet for some reason."

"I'm all right, Mother," Caroline assured her with as much composure as possible.

"You're as white as a ghost, if you don't mind a trite cliché," Marian took hold of her daughter's arm. "Come in here and sit down." She began to guide her back toward the kitchen.

"No," Caroline stopped. "Not the kitchen."

Her mother peered down at her for a few moments and then a smile splashed across her face. "Caroline, you're pregnant!" She beamed at her daughter.

Caroline said nothing.

"Caroline Randolph, don't you try to pretend with me." There was undeniable delight in her mother's voice as she spoke. "I've had three children. You're pregnant, aren't you?"

Caroline finally nodded her head grimly.

"I know you feel perfectly rotten, dear, and you wish that you'd never gotten yourself into this condition, but believe me, it's going to pass, and there really is abundant reason to be happy. Even so, I guess it would be absurd to try to coax a smile from you. Right? Come on, let's just go sit down in the den. Let me get that peppermint tea for you and some soda crackers. You'll feel better in just a few moments, and we'll be able to share the happy side of this wonderful news."

She ushered Caroline into the den, seated her on the sofa and went to get the peppermint tea. Caroline sat there and argued with herself. Should I tell her what I've done, she wondered. Maybe she could advise me. No, I can't tell her. She opposes abortion. Oh, why did anyone have to find out? I don't want Grandmother pushing me into an abortion. On the other hand, I certainly don't want to face Mother's disapproval if she finds out I'm considering abortion. This doesn't concern anyone but me!

Marian bustled back in with the peppermint tea and some plain soda crackers. "Now, every time you feel the slightest bit of nausea, dear, if you'll just use this old remedy. Keep soda crackers with you at all times so you can get something very bland in your stomach when you feel sick. There's nothing better. Remember, this nausea is only temporary; you'll get through it. It's an old wives tale that it can only happen in the morning. It can happen at any time, so keep your purse full of crackers, keep your pockets full of crackers, and you'll be fine. Just try to concentrate on the incredible joy that is ahead of you, once you get through the pregnancy and you have that beautiful baby in your arms. Oh, I'm ecstatic about this! I really am trying to temper my emotions because you're sick at the moment, but I'm going to be a grandmother."

"You're already a grandmother," Caroline said dryly.

"Well, that's true. The boys and their wives have already produced grandchildren for me, but this is different. You're my daughter, my only daughter, and you're going to have a baby. This is such a precious thing to me, Caroline." Her mother pulled up a footstool and plopped down on it, close to Caroline's knees. Caroline drank her peppermint tea and nibbled at crackers but said nothing, either joyful or troubled.

Her mother watched her face for a minute or two as Caroline carefully averted her eyes. After studying Caroline, Marian's face darkened with anxiety. When she spoke, there was uneasiness in her voice. "Something is wrong, Caroline. There's something you're not telling me. Is something wrong with the baby? What did the doctor tell you? You have been to a doctor, haven't you?"

Caroline could not help herself. Her control broke; she started crying. Her mother stood up, leaned over her and pulled Caroline close to her. As she stroked Caroline's head, Caroline began to sob uncontrollably. Her mother held her close until she was quiet again, and then Marian sat down on the sofa next to her daughter. She reached out her hand, turned Caroline's face toward her and said firmly, "These are not the tears of the typical pregnant woman suffering from nausea. These are certainly not the tears of a woman who is happily married, financially secure, and has every reason to welcome a child into her life. What is going on, Caroline?"

"Oh, Mother, it's David."

For a moment her mother stared at her with a puzzled look on her face. Then her eyes brightened with understanding. "David does not want the child," she concluded wisely.

Caroline nodded her head and tried to choke back another round of tears.

"Oh dear," Marian said. "This does make it difficult, I know, but believe me, honey, many men are upset when they're told they're going to be fathers. Your own father was no exception. It's a very common reaction in men, and considering David's past experience of losing his wife in childbirth, you can expect his reaction to be a little bit more dramatic than normal, but he'll get over it. Just give him a little time."

Caroline hated being so out of control, but she could not keep more tears from washing down her face. She desperately needed to blurt the situation out before it blew up inside of her. "He doesn't know, Mother," she wailed. "He doesn't know, and I can never tell him."

"But you must tell him. What do you mean you can never tell him? Caroline, you're not making much sense. I know you're upset, and you've been through a traumatic situation with this storm and everything, but—" Marian, seeing the hopelessness of trying to reason with Caroline, reached for a box of tissues on the end table and handed them to Caroline. As Caroline dried her face and blew her nose, Marian waited patiently. Then she quietly asked, "How long is David going to be in London?"

"At least two weeks, maybe three," Caroline shredded the soggy tissues that lay in her lap.

"Well, maybe that's for the best," Marian said thoughtfully. "You certainly want to talk to him face-to-face, and if he's going to be gone for several weeks, you'll have time to get some rest and regain some kind of composure. Honey, I assure you, David is going to want this child. He may say he doesn't at first; he may be upset. He may very well worry through this whole pregnancy, but this child is his flesh and blood, and he is going to want it. He's a very responsible man, and after he's had just a day or two to adjust, he's going to recognize his responsibility here."

"Oh, Mother! You don't understand."

"What is there to understand? He is a partner in producing this child. You didn't do it without him. He made choices that led to this child, just as you have. So after he gets over the initial shock and deals with the anxiety he feels, he's a responsible man and a strong man, and he will support you—"

"He didn't make any choices in this," Caroline blurted out. "I tricked him!"

First Marian looked surprised and then amazed as Caroline quickly confessed her deception of David and his reaction when he heard that Scott had been tricked into a pregnancy.

"So you just let him go off to London without telling him," her mother concluded quietly.

"He had to make the trip, Mother. He'll be back in two or three weeks. He was so angry about Scott's situation. It just didn't seem like the time to get into it, and frankly I felt so rattled by his extreme reaction to Scott's situation. I just needed some time to think things out."

"But you are going to tell him when he returns." There was a definiteness in Marian's voice that Caroline wanted to avoid.

"I suppose so," Caroline said evasively.

"You suppose so?" Marian asked. "How can you not tell him?"

"Well," Caroline looked at her lap and stammered, "there are other options I could take, Mother."

There was a prolonged silence between the two women. Caroline was very aware of her mother's attitude about children, and she expected a very strong condemnation of the whole thought of abortion, but her mother did not broach the subject at all. Instead she asked, "Do you think you could eat something like oatmeal?"

Startled by Marian's sudden change of subject, Caroline lifted her head and looked at her mother.

"A bowl of oatmeal, Caroline, would be just the thing you need. Then I want you to pack a few things and come home with me."

"No, Mother, I'd rather stay here tonight."

"Caroline, I don't know if I have any rank to pull here, but I'm going to try to pull some anyway. This street is going to be a mass of confusion all night. The police told me so. There is still no power in this house, and there's no telephone service. You've been here one night by yourself, and you're a wreck. If you were totally yourself, I'm sure you could go through another night here without much rest, but I think, considering your condition, you need a quiet place. I want you to come home with me, just until the power and telephone services are restored. It won't be for more than one night, maybe two. I want you to come home."

"Mother, I'm sure that I—"

Marian interrupted her with a firm voice. "I want you to do this for me, Caroline, so I won't worry about you."

Caroline could not argue with that. "Okay," she muttered, "but, Mother, remember I am thirty-two years old. *I* will decide—"

"I know, I was there when you were born," Marian said lightly in an obvious attempt to deflect any argument. "Now, do you want me to fix you some oatmeal?"

"No, I think I'll just keep munching on these crackers." Caroline picked up a cracker and stared at the coffee table as she ate. She could not comfortably meet her mother's eyes.

"Do you feel like going upstairs and packing a bag?" Marian asked. "I could do it for you."

"No, I can handle it," Caroline got up from the sofa and picked up the package of crackers to take with her. "It won't take me long to put together a few things." She started toward the door. This is too simple, she thought, too casual. Mother would never drop the abortion issue without a fight.

"You're going to be amazed at how much better you feel tomorrow, Caroline," Marian called after her, "after you've had a truly restful night. You must have been upset night before last, too, before David left."

"Yes, I've lost several nights of sleep," Caroline agreed quietly. "I'll get my things." Mother is just biding her time for the right moment, Caroline decided. I should stay here, but I'm so tired. Besides, sooner or later she'll have her say.

Caroline awoke the next morning at her mother's country estate in the bedroom that had been hers through all the years of her childhood and adolescence. It still had sheer Priscilla curtains criss-crossing the tall, old-fashioned windows; it faced east, so the sun was dancing across the highly polished, wooden floor all the way to the bed, where it bathed Caroline in its cheerful, soothing warmth.

Mother was right, she thought. I do feel like a different person. She turned her head and looked at the clock. Merciful heavens, it's ten o'clock! I've been asleep at least twelve hours. The house is so quiet. Of course, it is ten o'clock, so Dad has gone to his office, and I'm sure Mother left early to go down to the shelter to serve breakfast. At least, I think that's what she does down there. Or maybe she just acts as some sort of administrator. Surely she doesn't actually dish out food. Come to think of it, I don't know what she does down there. I've never asked. Oh well, to each her own.

Caroline would have lain in bed the rest of the morning enjoying the tranquillity if she hadn't been starving. "This so-called 'morning sickness' is not very well named," she muttered as she sat up, turned back the bed covers and swung her feet onto the floor. "It's morning, and I feel wonderful. At night I feel horrible. Well, I better eat while I feel good, I guess."

She walked across the room and looked out a window at the acres of Texas land her family owned. "This was a wonderful place to grow up," she murmured, "so fun and free, so safe. And it's also a wonderful place to retreat to. All that land and only the sounds of the birds and the wind." She slipped a robe on and wandered down to the kitchen with the idea of fixing herself a good breakfast. She was startled to find her mother there, sitting on a window seat, working on some kind of paperwork.

"Well, there you are," Marian said happily. She put the papers aside, stood up, and came to Caroline to give her a hug. "You look like a different woman. It's obvious you feel better."

"I feel perfectly normal," Caroline shrugged her shoulders as she spoke. "This morning sickness stuff is really bizarre."

"That's a good word for it," her mother agreed. "I bet you're hungry."

"Very," Caroline said. "I could eat a lumberjack's breakfast."

"Well, let's seize the moment and fill you up while your stomach wants food. What would you like?"

"Oh, anything, just so there's lots of it."

"I ought to be able to handle that," Marian laughed as she went to the refrigerator.

Caroline settled herself on the sun-drenched window seat.

So Mother has stayed home from the shelter this morning, she thought. I bet we're about to have our little talk about my pregnancy, and I'd just as soon skip it. I'm thirty-two years old. I could just say I don't want to talk about it. That's what I should have said to Grandmother yesterday. This is totally my mess, and I'm the one who has to live with my choice. I have a perfect right to be left alone to make my own decisions. That's exactly what I'm going to tell Mother when she brings the subject up any minute now. That's also what I'm going to tell Grandmother. Oh no! Grandmother! I promised to bring that note and the Bradford vest to her. I'll have to call her. For once in her life, she's just going to have to wait .

Marian was humming a tune as she quickly fixed a large country breakfast. In no time she set a plate of steaming food on the table, and Caroline eagerly took a chair and started eating. Marian poured herself a cup of coffee and pulled out a chair opposite her daughter.

Well, here it comes, Caroline thought, the inevitable pressure.

"Here are some strawberry preserves," her mother pushed a jar toward Caroline, "that one of the neighbors sent over. They're absolutely delicious. Be sure to try some." She paused, then abruptly changed the subject. "It's nice to see the sun again. I'm definitely ready for spring this year. It seems like the older I get, the more impatient I am with winter."

"Mother, why don't you just say what's on your mind?" Caroline blurted out.

"I have a lot of things on my mind," Marian replied calmly. "If you're referring to your baby, you're thirty-two years old. You know what I think about abortion. You've just been through several very difficult days. You're far too intelligent to make any hasty decisions or do anything irrational. So we can discuss your child later. In the meantime, I'd like for you to go somewhere with me."

"Go somewhere with you?" Caroline was surprised. "The only place I can go this morning, Mother, is back to the house to check on things."

"There's no need for that, dear. I called Hannah and told her to go over there, spend the day and watch over things. She called back about half an hour ago from some store and said that there is still no power and no telephone. So I'd like for you to go someplace with me. We haven't been anywhere together in a long time."

"Mother, we're not going shopping for baby clothes or anything like that, are we?" Caroline demanded suspiciously.

"No, Caroline. If I'm not going to discuss your baby with you today, I'm certainly not going to take you shopping for baby clothes."

"Good," Caroline took another bite of her breakfast.

"Actually I'd hoped that you would come down and look at the site for a second shelter that I'm planning. I really need your advice."

"My advice?" Caroline questioned. "Mother, I don't know anything about shelters for the homeless."

"Well, this is a very special situation. You see, I have to start with an old house in the inner city. It was donated to us. It's quite a wreck, but it's very large and perfectly located. We only have the house and a little money to fix it up—very little money. But we have to try to make it function as a shelter as quickly as possible, and my strength has never been in converting old structures into useful space. I thought, because of your experience as a preservationist, you could give me a quick appraisal of the condition of the house and perhaps make some suggestions about how to use the space to the best advantage. And maybe you could give me some names of contractors that I can go beg services from. You wouldn't mind doing that, would you, dear?"

"Well, no. If you think I could help in some way, I'll take a look. And of course I do know a lot of people who are willing to donate services to old houses. But remember, Mother, the people I know support elegant, historic properties—not shelters for the homeless."

"A tax break is a tax break—at least I hope that's how donors will see it. Anyway, I'd really appreciate your advice. I feel totally over my head in this part of the project."

"It's a deal," Caroline said as she finished her breakfast. "You're just as good a cook as ever, Mother."

"I never could cook and you know it, but I can throw breakfast together," Marian laughed.

"When do you want to go?" Caroline asked.

"The sooner the better, I think. It's warming up outside; it's really a beautiful day to be out. So whenever you're ready, we'll go."

"It shouldn't take me long to get ready," Caroline said as she pushed her chair back. "If all I'm going to do is visit a ghetto, I suppose I don't have to look like a model."

"Hardly," Marian smiled as she picked up Caroline's plate and took it to the sink.

"I'll be down in just a few minutes, then."

When Marian drove into the slum area of Dallas where the donated house was situated, Caroline felt quite anxious, even though her mother was perfectly at ease. "You look tense, dear," Marian said. "There's really no danger. You may see some people who are not quite like you are in their outward appearance, but they know why we're here, and they're very grateful we're here. Oh, a few people can be resentful and hateful, of course, but that's true in any human situation, isn't it?"

Caroline nodded and tried to relax the muscles in her neck.

"Just keep your mind on our purpose, and you'll be fine. We have an old building that we have to restore, but keep in mind, dear, that we have very little money. No frills here. We need to have as much usable space for classrooms and dormitories as we can possibly manage, and, of course, we'll have to have a sizable dining area and a very efficient kitchen."

"Classrooms?" Caroline was surprised.

"Yes," her mother reached for the door handle of the car but turned back for a minute. "Didn't I mention to you that we're going to do some preschool sheltering here for single working mothers? Also, some after-school tutoring for kids who need extra help to stay in school. So we need some classrooms, some recreation rooms, and we'll want to maximize those spaces by also having the possibility of bedding people down in them at night whenever it's necessary."

"Sounds like a tall order," Caroline said.

"It is a tall order, but I'm sure you're up to it." Marian jumped out of the car eagerly.

Caroline opened the door on her side and followed less eagerly. "I'm used to restoring things, Mother, which means returning them to elegance and grandeur, not turning them into classrooms, dormitories and kitchens."

"Surely there are some similarities, in the beginning at least," Marian insisted. "Even when you restore an elegant mansion, you have to deal with plumbing, wiring, structural problems and all that kind of thing first, don't you?"

"That's true," Caroline agreed.

"That's exactly where I need your help. This is Day One of this project."

"Well, you've got it." Caroline felt a wave of happiness come over her at the thought of using her skills again. "Actually it ought to be kind of fun. I've missed working as a preservationist. Even though this is not restoring elegance, maybe at least I'll feel a little useful."

The minute they walked into the hall a young woman came racing forward. "Marian!" she exclaimed. "Thank goodness you're here. We've got a real crisis on our hands. Mr. Hollins called."

"Oh no!" Marian shook her head quickly, her face suddenly furrowed by her frustration. "Not again."

"Yes, again," the young woman emphasized the word 'again' so vigorously that Caroline's happy feelings faded to frustration, even though she didn't know the problem.

"What is it this time, Gail?" Marian asked, then remembered her manners, "Oh, Gail, I'm sorry, this is my daughter, Caroline Randolph. Caroline, this is Gail Patterson."

Caroline started to greet the plain-dressed, efficient woman, but the woman nodded at her before saying, "It's the same thing. He doesn't want to continue donating his bread to the shelter, and he isn't planning to make a delivery today, and if he doesn't, we'll have no bread at the shelter tonight for supper."

"Great," Marian said dryly.

"You've got to call him," Gail said. "He's at least got to give us time to make other arrangements. This is really outrageous, just pulling out on us at the last minute like this. It's just—what will we do?"

"I don't know," Marian confessed. "I'll call him. Maybe I can talk him into giving us a little bit of time to work out another arrangement with someone else. I'll try. That's the best I can do."

"What's wrong with this guy, Mother?" Caroline demanded.

"Mr. Hollins has been giving us the old bread from his bakery, the bread they pull off the grocery store shelves because it's not fresh enough to sell there. They've just been trucking it over to the other shelter and dumping it. That's been our bread source for the people we feed over there, about two hundred women and children. But Mr. Hollins doesn't think it's worth the effort or the gasoline to bring the bread to us. He'd rather throw the bread into a dumpster and let it rot in the landfill."

"You're kidding!" Caroline exclaimed. "What kind of thinking is that? Why, Hollins Bakery is the largest bakery in town."

"I'm afraid the sad fact is, Caroline, that feeding homeless women and children is just not profitable. This is the second time he's pulled this. I should have found another supplier last time. Well, I'll go call him, Gail. Caroline, why don't you just look around and get acquainted with the building?"

"We had to put a few women up here last night, Marian," Gail said, "I didn't want to, considering the state of the building, but we had such an overflow at the Seton Shelter. I really didn't have any choice."

Marian nodded and turned back to her daughter. "Caroline, just make yourself at home and make some mental notes on what needs to be done. I'll be back as soon as I can."

"Do you run the shelter with Mother?" Caroline asked Gail.

"Technically I'm the director of the Seton Shelter. However, your mother does more work than anybody can describe—everything from begging large corporations to give us hand-outs to serving soup. She ought to be given the title of Director Emeritus or something, but she has no use for titles. So, you're going to help us?" Gail asked eagerly.

"Well," Caroline hesitated. "Mother just asked me to come down and look over the building because I have a degree and some experience in restoration work."

"That's fantastic! So you've restored old buildings like this into shelters?"

"Well, actually no," Caroline began to feel something like guilt. "When I say 'restoration work,' I mean restoration of historical properties."

"Oh," Gail said a little flatly, but then her face brightened again. "We need any kind of help you can offer—as you can see." She waved her hand at the walls of the dilapidated building. "Let me get you some paper so you can make some notes." She turned and walked briskly away. When she returned, she held a half-used legal pad and a ball-point pen.

"I've got to get back down to Seton Shelter to see that lunch is served. Almost everybody there is a volunteer, you know. Tell your mother I'll talk to her later this afternoon, and that I'm praying she can find us some bread for tonight."

Caroline nodded and watched as the young woman hurried out the front door. Suddenly feeling quite useless, she began to wander from room to room to avoid thinking about people who had no food to eat. She tried to picture the run-down, dilapidated old mansion turned into some kind of clean, useful shelter for the needs her mother had listed. After she'd examined the whole house, she walked out into what had formerly been the back garden of the mansion. Only the dimmest outlines of the formal flower beds were still visible. It was now a wreck of abandoned appliances, bits and pieces of cars, rank weeds, molding newspapers, rotting cardboard, and stinking cans and bottles.

"What a mess!" she exclaimed. "This will never be a playground. Mother must be crazy. Why does she even get involved in this kind of stuff? Why does she leave the comforts of her country estate and come down here? Why would she choose to even look at something like this?" Caroline looked down at the ground close to her feet and saw some rusty tin cans. Then her eyes lighted on a broken hypodermic needle. She inhaled suddenly and involuntarily, then moved quickly away. She wandered further into the garden area and noticed spots on the ground that were blackened, that were obviously places where campfires had been built during the winter. There were large, broken-down cardboard boxes, now abandoned, that she began to realize had been the homes of people. A great sadness descended over her, and she felt helpless.

I just want to leave, she thought. I don't even want to know about what goes on down here. It's totally depressing thinking about people living like this. She looked back at the house and remembered the problem with the bread. I can't insist we leave now; Mother is in there trying to find bread for people. Grandmother is right; Mother is crazy to do this. But I'm stuck for the moment, and I promised to help. I just won't think about the people. I'll think about this as just some land that needs to be cleaned up and turned into a playground—somehow.

Idly she started kicking at a large cardboard box. Suddenly she felt movement in the box she was absent-mindedly kicking, and she jumped back and stared at it. There's somebody inside, she thought, as fear swept over her. Or maybe it's a dog or something. She started to run back to the house, but the box became perfectly still, and her curiosity overcame her fear. She stepped back five paces and walked around the box until she could see inside. "Good heavens!" she exclaimed. Three little grimy faces were staring back at her, and they were far more frightened than she was. She crouched down to look at them more closely as she tried to think of something to say. All she could manage was a sharp question, "What are you doing in there?"

The children froze and stared back at her without a sound. Caroline realized that her tone had been far too threatening. She tried to smile warmly and changed the tone of her voice.

"I'm sorry," she said. "I didn't mean to sound angry. It's just that you scared me. I didn't know anybody was in there, and then all of a sudden I thought somebody scary was in there. But you kids look like you're someone I could be friends with. Why don't you come out in the sunshine and talk to me?"

The children said nothing. Caroline looked them over quickly. There was a little boy, who might have been three, and a little girl of about five—it was hard to tell—and she was holding a baby. Caroline forgot about the filth all over the yard and sat down in the midst of the dirty paper and tin cans. She folded her legs, so luxuriously encased in their cashmere slacks, and tried harder to relate to the children.

"Please come out and talk to me," she smiled at the girl. "You must be hungry. It's almost lunch time. I could get you some food. Aren't you hungry?"

The three-year-old boy nodded his head and started to crawl out of the box, but his older sister of five jerked him back and said to Caroline, "We ain't hungry."

"I won't hurt you," Caroline said softly. "I came down here to help you. I know you must be hungry. It's time to eat."

"We ain't hungry," the little girl insisted, while her little brother stared up at her with starved eyes.

"Well then, will you tell me why you're in this box?" Caroline tried to keep the tears that were stinging her eyes from affecting the sound of her voice.

"We're waiting for Mama," the little girl announced with great finality. "She's gonna come back and get us, and we gotta be here so she can find us."

"Where has your mother gone?" Caroline asked.

"Work," the little boy spoke up.

"And she left you here?" Caroline was stunned at the thought, and her amazement sounded in her voice.

"We stay here everyday," the little girl said defiantly. "It's a good place to stay. Mother found it for us, and it's a good place to stay."

"I'm hungry," the boy complained.

"No, you're not," his sister said.

"Yes, I am," he insisted.

"What kind of work does your mother do?" Caroline asked the little girl.

The little girl shrugged her shoulders. "Whatever she can get to do. She just goes out and works, and if she gets some work, she comes home with some food."

"Home?" Caroline asked. "So you do have a home? You only stay here during the day?"

"We sleep here," the little boy said.

"Shhh," his sister slapped him. "You're not supposed to tell that."

Caroline's heart sank, and she felt a kind of grief she had never known. How many times have I seen this on television, she thought, and it didn't hurt at all. How different this feels!

"Mama loves us," the little girl announced suddenly. "She takes care of us. We don't need you to take care of us. We'll wait till she comes home."

Caroline nodded, got up off the ground, and turned back toward the building to keep the children from seeing the tears on her cheeks. When she walked back into the building, through what were formerly elegant French doors, her mother met her.

"Caroline, what's wrong?"

"There are three little children out there in a box—" Caroline choked up and could say no more.

"There are little children in boxes all over this part of the city, Caroline. Did you learn anything about them? How old are they? How long have they been there?"

"They live there," Caroline wiped the tears off of her cheeks and tried to take the quiver out of her voice, "or at least that's what the girl said. She looks like she's about five years old, and there's a little boy who looks about three and there's an infant. The little girl said they live there. The mother is out working, and they're waiting for her to come home with some food." Caroline broke down and started crying openly.

"I know you've never seen things like this up close, honey, and it's very hard to accept that in this country we allow such things to happen. Your tears are justified, I don't deny that, but wouldn't it be better to turn that energy into trying to help?"

"I don't think I can face this kind of thing, Mother."

"Not everybody can face the miseries of suffering people directly, Caroline, but everybody can contribute in some way." Marian ran her hands through her graying hair, as if by doing so, she could clear her mind to think. "Maybe God did not make you to work with people like this in a hands-on situation, but He has given you skills, influence and friends. You could use all of those to turn this into a working shelter so those children and other children like them don't have to wait in a box while their mothers try to find work."

"Is she really out there working?" Caroline demanded as her tears continued to flow. "Does she really get up every morning, leave her children, go out to work, and come back at night? What does she come back with?"

"Very little, if she's typical, and apparently she is. Usually such a woman can only make enough to feed her children one meal."

"How does she go on?" Caroline asked. "How do the children survive such a life?"

"Actually they have the easy part, Caroline. They trust their mother. They believe she's big and strong enough to take care of them. It's the mother who has the hard time. She has to go out and do anything she can to get money to buy a little food for her children."

"Doesn't the government help? I thought the government was supposed to take care of people like this. They're only children!"

"That's what we would all like to think is happening, but many people are simply left on the streets. Obviously this woman is one of them."

"I just can't see how this woman gets up every morning and goes out—where does she find the strength to do it?"

"She loves her children, Caroline. She thinks no sacrifice is too big to keep them alive and with her."

"Where is the father of these children?"

"No doubt he's gone. I don't know the circumstances of

this particular woman. Obviously there's no father present to help her. For one reason or another he's gone; probably he's deserted her. She fits a very typical stereotype. The fact that she has an infant out there probably would answer your question if you could ask her."

"What do you mean?" Caroline asked. "What has the baby got to do with the problem?"

"Most of the homeless women we deal with who have children, Caroline, have been abandoned by the men in their lives because they will not give up their children."

"Well, of course they're not going to give up their children," Caroline retorted. "How could anyone give up a five-year-old girl, or a three-year-old boy, or a baby?"

"She could have given up any one of them before they were born. At least that's the way many people see it. Abortion is legal. I don't know this woman's situation, but I suspect strongly that if we talk to her, we'll discover that when she chose to give life to her baby, her husband, or whatever he was, walked out on her."

"Then why did she have the baby?" Caroline demanded. "You're right. Abortion is legal. It's even free for women like that."

"I would assume she had the baby because she loved the baby, Caroline. She decided that the child's life was worth whatever risk she had to take to give it life and whatever work she might have to do to support it."

Caroline said nothing for a few minutes and turned away from her mother to stare out the doors at the cardboard box where she knew the children remained and would remain until their mother came back.

"Sometimes, Mother," she said quietly, "I think I don't know anything about love."

"I'm sure I knew very little about love, Caroline, until twenty years ago, certainly nothing about sacrificial love. It's hard to know about love when life is easy, because to feel real love, you have to sacrifice some of yourself. As you know, I grew up with a very easy life, never needing anything, always plenty of security, plenty of social prestige, every material item that I ever wanted and more. I never had to make any sacrifices. It's hard to learn about love when you grow up like that."

"You know I'm considering aborting this child, don't you, Mother?" Caroline asked quietly

"Yes, of course I do."

"Grandmother sees nothing wrong with an abortion."

"I can only say, Caroline, that your grandmother, who is my mother, has a very different opinion from mine. I might very well have shared her opinion twenty years ago. Indeed I'm sure I did share her opinion twenty years ago. I shared all of her opinions until I began to think for myself, and then I discovered that I shared very few of her values. I still love her, but she is wrong about so many things, and she is wrong about your child."

"I didn't plan to discuss it with her, you know, but got sick when I was over there yesterday, and she guessed instantly and—"

"And she demanded that you protect your relationship with David at all costs, even at the cost of destroying your child," Marian finished Caroline's sentence.

"That's about it," Caroline wiped the tears from her face again. "She sees my marriage to David as the most important thing. She knows how he feels about children, and she doesn't think I should risk losing him over a child."

"Is it David she doesn't want you to lose or is it his money and social position?"

"You know the answer to that," Caroline said sadly.

"Yes, I do. She hasn't changed in all the years I've known her. I don't think she ever will. But you're *not* your grandmother."

"I'm not you either," Caroline snapped at her mother.

"No, you're not, nor should you be, either your grandmother or me. You must find out who you are. We all have to find out who we are. Many of us, especially those of us who have money and privilege, manage to ignore that question all of our lives. And those at the other end of the spectrum, those who have nothing, don't have time to think about it. They're working too hard to put food into the mouths of their children. But you have now put yourself into a situation, by your own choice, where you're going to have to decide, Caroline, who you are and what counts most with you."

"You're talking about the fact that I'm pregnant, aren't you?" Caroline's temper flared. "I knew you'd get around to pushing your values on me eventually."

"Of course I'm talking about your baby. I'm talking

about life, and your baby is alive."

"You brought me down here to play on my emotions, to persuade me—"

"I brought you here to show you life is bigger than you and your search for your own pleasure, Caroline. You broke faith with your husband because you thought you would enjoy a baby. That was a mistake, but now, by your own actions, you have moved yourself into a bigger arena. You are pregnant. Your dilemma is not, should you have a baby. You already have a baby. Your dilemma is, should you kill your baby. You can no longer make your decisions based only on your own happiness. There is another life involved—not a bit of tissue—a life."

"That's your opinion!" Caroline retorted.

"It must be yours too, or you wouldn't be agonizing over an abortion."

"I don't know what I think," Caroline admitted. "I certainly don't know what to do."

"Don't make any hasty decisions," Marian pleaded. "Don't embrace your grandmother's view of life just because it's available to you. You are one of the lucky ones. You are at the top of the social strata. You can abort your baby and protect your luxurious lifestyle, go on with your head buried in the sand and just enjoy life. But ask yourself, what will you have when you're my age, if you do that? What will you have when you're your grandmother's age, if you do that? Think long and hard, Caroline. I don't have the power to tell you what to do. You know I oppose abortion. I beg you to think, to look beyond your present difficulties, to dare to move out of your cocoon of safety and self-concern. There is more at stake here than your happiness or David's anger with you or even his anxiety about losing you in childbirth. Life is at stake."

Her mother fell silent and when that silence continued, Caroline looked up at Marian's face. Her mother was staring out the window in the direction of the cardboard box. Caroline also looked at the box.

"I couldn't get the children to come out," Caroline said sadly. "I tried, but they wouldn't trust me."

"They'll wait for their mother, dear, and so will we. Don't worry, we'll take some sandwiches out to the children and a bottle for the baby. I'll see to it that someone is here until their mother returns, and we'll talk to her, and we'll applaud and support what she is trying to do and help her in every way we can. If she's willing, her children won't sleep in that box tonight."

"She's so courageous," Caroline murmured, "truly courageous. Mother, how can I help her?"

Marian looked at Caroline's face intently. She raised her hand and stroked her daughter's cheek. "I think you have it backwards, dear," she said gently. "Right now you need her more than she needs you. She is a star sent to guide you."

Caroline simply nodded.

"I'm going to get some sandwiches for those children," Marian started to walk away briskly.

"What about the bread man?" Caroline called after her mother.

"Oh, he's decided to give us another week," Marian replied with a smile.

"Just a week?" Caroline exclaimed.

"A lot can happen in a week, Caroline."

Caroline nodded her head as she acknowledged to herself that she had entered into a world she didn't understand, a world that had changed her forever.

Chapter 8

Caroline was delighted to see light shining from the windows of her house as she pulled into the driveway in the early evening hours. The electric company must have made faster progress than they expected, she thought. I should be able to spend the night at home. Thank goodness! I need some time to myself. She walked to the front door of the house which she had so lovingly restored for herself and her beloved David. She paused to admire the beautiful, leaded-glass panels on each side of the door. Each panel was a mosaic composed of many pieces of curving, beveled glass that some gifted craftsman had assembled over one hundred years before. The beveled glass caught the golden light from inside the house and caused it to dance across Caroline's face. She felt like a little girl again watching a Christmas tree being lighted for the first time. An involuntary laugh escaped her lips as she reached her hand toward the glistening glass and watched the sparkling light play across the creamy skin of her finger. "Home," she sighed.

As she unlocked the door, she heard the telephone ringing. Fantastic, she thought, the phone's on too. Things are really returning to normal. She raced to the phone, and when she jerked the receiver up to her ear, she heard Marian's voice, "Caroline? Is that you?"

"Yes, Mother," Caroline struggled to catch her breath, "just a second. I've got to check the security system." She put the receiver down and hurried to the control box and punched in the code that would keep the alarm from ringing.

"You sound funny, dear," her mother commented when Caroline returned to the phone. "Are you okay?"

"I'm fine. I was just running to catch the phone, and then I remembered that Hannah always leaves the alarm on. The electricity is on, and the street is totally clear of workmen. I'll be able to stay here tonight."

"You sound so excited."

"I am. I don't know why, Mother, but suddenly I feel like I can handle things. I really am lucky to have so much."

"We all are. Well, I'll miss you," Marian replied, "but I can certainly understand why you want to sleep in your own bed."

"Thanks for dinner; and, Mother, thanks—thanks for everything, for caring."

"That's easy, dear," Marian laughed, "comes with the territory. You'll find that out soon enough."

"Yes," Caroline responded vaguely. A little shadow had passed over her spirit as she thought of her pregnancy. "I'll talk to you tomorrow, Mother." Caroline put the phone down and stood perfectly still. She looked inside her mind at the shadow that threatened her happy mood. "I don't want you," she whispered to the shadow. "I want my baby."

She walked through the house to the kitchen. There on the drain board was a note from her housekeeper with 6:00 written at the top. She's only been gone a half an hour, Caroline calculated as she glanced at her watch. She continued reading the note which explained that Hannah had cleaned out the refrigerator and restocked it, and that she would be back in the morning at her usual time. Well, it looks like I'm going to have a quiet evening alone at home, Caroline thought, but it will certainly be an improvement over the last evening I spent here by myself. Was that really only 48 hours ago? A cup of tea sounds good. I think I'll make one and drink it, go upstairs and take a long bubblebath. Then I'll crawl into bed with a good book.

Caroline walked into the laundry room and activated the security system of the house. She yawned as she returned to the kitchen and put the tea kettle on. It seems like no matter how much rest I get, I'm still tired, she thought. I guess that's the way it is when you're going to have a baby. Oh dear, I'm a fool to allow myself to think things can work out with David, but I don't care! I refuse to think about any problems tonight. I deserve a worry-free rest.

Caroline drank her tea, then went upstairs and was soon lying dreamily in her bubblebath. She had finished her bath and had just slipped her weary, but relaxed, body between the crisp, monogrammed sheets and rested her head against plumped-up pillows edged in battenburg lace, when the phone rang again. "Now who could that be?" She picked up the receiver and was just beginning to say "hello" when a frantic voice shouted at her, "Miz Caroline! Miz Caroline! You got to come now. You got to come quick. Something terrible be wrong with Miz Judith!"

"Monique? Is that you?" Caroline demanded as her heart lurched. "What's wrong with Grandmother?"

"I don't know what's wrong with her. She been acting crazy. She gone clean out of her head. She be sick, Miz Caroline, real sick. You gots to come now!"

"Call an ambulance, Monique. Just dial 911 and give them the address and—"

"No ambulance!" Monique broke in. "She won't let me call no ambulance."

"I'll be there in five minutes!" Caroline slammed the phone down and jumped out of bed. She pulled her nightgown over her head as she dashed across the room and started jerking clothes out of drawers and the closet. In less than a minute she was dressed and racing down the stairs. Just before she bolted out of the house, she snatched up the phone in the main hall and dialed 911. After ordering an ambulance, she dashed out the door, jumped into her car and sped out of the driveway.

Monique threw open the front door seconds before Caroline reached it. The old servant was crying and hysterically repeating, "She make me build a fire, a big fire, a bonfire she call it. Oh, Miz Caroline, she make me build a fire. She got all them old papers out. They's scattered out all over the place—"

"Where is Grandmother?" Caroline demanded, cutting through the woman's hysterics.

"It be too warm for a fire," Monique continued. "I told her that. I say, it be too warm for a fire, Miz Judith. But she make me build a fire. She say she gonna burn up—"

"Monique, stop it! Where is Grandmother?" Caroline demanded again as she took Monique firmly by the shoulders and shook her.

"In her bedroom," Monique blurted out. Caroline ran through the hall and dashed up the first flight of the elegant staircase, as Monique followed her more slowly. She flung open the door to her Grandmother's room and stopped suddenly when the bizarre scene she saw registered in her brain. Her elegant, ninety-two-year-old grandmother was sitting on the floor in front of a blazing fire in the fireplace. Her white hair was disheveled, and her eyes were wild as she stared at the papers on the floor around her. In the seconds while Caroline watched, Judith snatched up a handful of papers, looked at them, and muttered something incoherent before she threw them into the fire.

"Burn! Burn, burn, burn!" Judith babbled as she scrambled closer to the fire and snatched up papers that had escaped the flames and thrust them directly into the fire.

"Grandmother!" Caroline cried as she ran across the room and knelt next to her grandmother. "You'll be burned." She pulled Judith's hand out of the flames and dragged her back a few feet. Judith stared at her with angry, unrecognizing eyes. Then suddenly she knew Caroline. She dropped the papers, grabbed Caroline's blouse with both hands, and demanded, "Caroline, did you bring the vest? Did you bring the note?"

"Grandmother," Caroline spoke as steadily as she could. "Grandmother, please calm down." She put her own hands over Judith's hands which were still clinching Caroline's blouse. "Please come get into bed. You must rest."

"There's no time!" Judith screamed. "Don't you understand? There's no time. Go get the vest, and don't forget the note. I want that note. All the old papers. Burn them, burn them!"

"Grandmother!" Caroline quickly took the old lady by the shoulders and gave her a gentle shake. "Grandmother, stop it! There's plenty of time. No matter what's wrong we can fix it."

"No!" Judith exclaimed. "No, it's too late." She wrenched herself free of Caroline and grabbed another handful of papers and threw them at the roaring fireplace. "It must be finished!" she screamed. "It must be finished now. No one must ever know!"

Caroline was totally confused about the meaning of Judith's hysterical rambling, but she was certain that Judith needed to be calmed down at any cost. She scrambled around in front of her grandmother to block her from the fireplace and once again took her by the shoulders. "Grandmother, I insist that you get into bed. Whatever needs to be done, I will do it. But I insist that you get up off this floor and get into bed and calm your-self down."

"Please, Miz Judith," Monique begged. "Listen to Miz Caroline."

Judith looked at Caroline for one quiet instant, and then she demanded in an imperious tone that Caroline recognized as typical of her usual commanding demeanor, "Don't you understand, child? Everything depends on these papers being destroyed.

Everything can come tumbling down, tumbling, tumbling down, Caroline. Smashed. Everything I've worked for."

Caroline had absolutely no interest in the content of what her grandmother had said, although it struck her as bizarre. She wanted only to save her grandmother's life, and she recognized that the old woman was on the edge of exerting herself to death.

"They must be burned!" Judith suddenly screamed as she returned to the irrational, old woman Caroline had never seen before that night. She wrenched away from Caroline and grabbed a needlepoint-covered box. She struggled to open its brass clasp, but it was locked. "The key, Caroline, the key!" Judith shrieked. "I must burn them. The key, Caroline."

Unable to stop her grandmother, Caroline decided it was best to aid her. "Where is it? Where is the key?"

Judith fell forward and seemed to faint. Monique cried, "Miz Judith!" and burst into sobs.

"Stop that," Caroline commanded. "Bring pillows from the bed. I want her to lie here on the floor. An ambulance is on its way."

"Miz Judith, Miz Judith!" Monique ignored Caroline and raced to Judith's side. "Oh, Miz Caroline, she be dying!"

"She's not dying," Caroline insisted. "Get the pillows, Monique." Caroline was holding her unconscious grandmother in her arms as she spoke. "Do as I say—now!"

Monique rose laboriously from the floor as Judith regained consciousness. Weakly she fumbled with the needlepoint-covered box.

"Leave that alone, Grandmother," Caroline said. "Please, leave it alone."

"The key," Judith called feebly.

Caroline was torn between forcing her grandmother to lie down and doing what her grandmother wanted in order to bring her some kind of peace so that she would rest. She knew her grandmother's disposition well and chose to give her what she wanted as the best hope of encouraging her to relax. "Where is the key?" Caroline demanded again.

"It be in her desk," Monique said.

"Yes," Judith mumbled. "My desk, my desk. The secret compartment."

"Secret compartment?" Caroline demanded in dismay,

wondering how on earth she'd ever find a secret compartment in Judith's ornate old secretary.

"I knows where it is," Monique said.

"Then get it," Caroline commanded.

Monique hastened to the secretary. Caroline turned her eyes back to her grandmother, who was still conscious but limp against Caroline's arms.

"Caroline," Judith said quite calmly, "promise me you will burn the papers."

"I will, Grandmother," Caroline promised immediately, "just relax. I will burn the papers. Help is on the way for you, and I promise that I will burn the papers."

"Now!" Judith demanded.

"Monique, bring the key," Caroline called back over her shoulder. Monique hurried toward her with a small gold key in her hand.

Caroline snatched it from her and inserted it into the lock of the needlepoint box that her grandmother was still clasping. When she turned the key, the clasp loosened and her grandmother jerked open the top of the box. "Burn them, Caroline!" she cried, and then she collapsed in Caroline's arms.

There was a loud pounding on the front door downstairs.

"It's the ambulance," Caroline said. "Quick, Monique. Go to the top of the stairs and shout at them to come in." Monique started toward the door as Caroline held her grandmother in her arms. Her grandmother had regained consciousness but could not speak. Her eyes were full of a plea that Caroline understood. "I will burn the papers, Grandmother," Caroline promised. "Please just be still." She stroked her grandmother's face as the paramedics burst into the room. "I think she's had a stroke," Caroline said quickly.

"Did she fall?" the paramedic asked briskly.

"No, she hasn't fallen."

"Then let's get her on the bed," the paramedic said. Gently he and his assistant picked up Judith and carried her to her bed. When they placed her on it, her body sank into the pillows propped up against the headboard. Caroline stood at the end of the bed, staring at her grandmother, who looked like she desperately wanted to speak. The emergency crew members were bringing in oxygen and various equipment, and the paramedic was asking a stream of questions.

"How old is your grandmother? Does she have a history of heart problems? When did she become ill? Exactly what has happened since you've been here?"

Caroline answered automatically, unable to take her eyes from Judith's face. Judith's eyes were piercing into her own as she lay in a paralyzed state. Caroline knew that Judith was helpless in body but that her mind was still determined on one point. Caroline looked her in the face and said, "Yes, Grandmother, I will burn them."

She walked to the needlepoint box, picked it up and turned so that her grandmother could her actions. She removed the papers from the box, walked to the opening of the fireplace, held up the papers so that her grandmother could see then, and threw them into the fire. Her grandmother watched the fire consume the papers that had tormented her into her present condition. Caroline walked back to the bed, but was prevented from reaching her grandmother's side by the emergency workers. She stood at the foot of the bed and said, "It is done; they are gone."

Judith looked at Caroline and her eyes registered satisfaction and then blankness.

"We've lost her," the paramedic said. "Get a respirator," he ordered one of his crew, then quickly turned to Caroline. "I'm sorry, ma'am. She's dead. She had a massive stroke, I think. She's ninety-two, you say? We can put her on a respirator, but I doubt it will do any good. It's your call."

"Leave her alone," Caroline said quietly.

"Oh, Miz Judith!" Monique wailed as she clutched the bedpost at the end of the bed.

"Are you sure, ma'am?" the man asked as his crew member ran in with some more equipment.

"Yes," Caroline insisted, "My grandmother lived with dignity, in total control of her life. She would not wish to live any other way."

Monique sobbed as the man directed his crew to move away from the bed. Caroline walked around, sat down on the edge of the bed and looked at her grandmother's face.

"I'm sorry, ma'am," the man said. "Would you like me to close her eyes?"

Caroline hesitated, but Monique cried, "No, I take care of Miz Judith." She went to the other side of the bed, opposite Caroline and looked at Caroline for permission. Caroline nodded her head, and Monique reached over and closed the eyelids of her mistress. Then Monique fell to her knees beside the bed and began to pray and weep.

"I'll have to call for a coroner," the paramedic said gently as he waved his men out of the room.

Caroline said, "Yes, do what you have to do. Just give us a few minutes."

He quietly left the room. After she heard his steps on the staircase and heard him close the front door, she sighed with relief. Denial of what she had just experienced flooded her mind. She leaned over and kissed her grandmother on the cheek. She didn't feel that she was saying good-bye. Her grandmother had been such a vital creature that it was impossible for Caroline to accept the fact that she could cease being. Caroline felt that she was just watching Judith sleep, that after her nap Judith would sit up and order a tea tray. Caroline listened briefly to Monique's prayers, but she felt no inclination to pray herself.

She was unaware of the passing of time until Monique came to her side and gently shook her. "Miz Caroline, Miz Caroline," Monique said. "Miz Judith wanted these papers burned."

Caroline did not look at her, but whispered in a faraway tone, "I know, Monique, that's why I threw them into the fireplace."

"But you didn't burn all of them."

Startled by that revelation, Caroline took her eyes from her grandmother's face and looked at Monique, who was holding the needlepoint-covered box. The sight of that box jolted her back to reality; immediately she turned her eyes back to Judith as the memory of her struggle with Judith in front of the fireplace and Judith's collapse raced through her mind. Then once again she saw the blank look in Judith's eyes when she died.

"Is she really dead, Monique?" Caroline's eyes filled with tears and her voice shook.

"Yes, Miz Caroline," Monique answered, "and you got to do what she wanted. See here in the bottom," Monique pointed. "There's still papers left in this box."

"Monique," Caroline asked wearily as she looked at the aging servant. "What are these papers? Why are they so important?"

Monique looked away from Caroline's face and would not answer her.

"What are they, Monique?" Caroline asked again. "These papers that are so important that grandmother died trying to destroy them? What are—" Caroline's voice broke and she could not speak as grief grasped her.

"I promised—promised Miz Judith," Monique insisted.

"Promised her what?" Caroline struggled to control her voice.

"That I'd never talk about it." Monique turned back to Caroline. "We gots to burn them, Miz Caroline."

Caroline took the box from Monique and stood up. "I can't deal with this now. Don't you understand? Grandmother is gone, Monique. I must call Mother." Caroline went to the telephone and tried to dial her mother's telephone number. Twice she stopped in the middle of the number and put the receiver down and cried, "I can't bear to tell her."

"You got to burn the papers first," Monique said.

"I've got to call my mother," Caroline insisted as she savagely punched the numbers out on the telephone. When Marian answered, Caroline tried to remain composed, but she barely managed to sob out the fact that Judith was gone. Her mother promised to come immediately, and Caroline put the phone back down.

"Please, Miz Caroline," Monique was more determined than ever. "You got to burn these papers."

"I can't think about a bunch of old papers now, Monique," Caroline snapped at her as the tears flowed down her cheeks. "What do I care about a bunch of old papers? Grandmother's lying over there dead."

"But Miz Marian can't see them," Monique insisted. "Miz Marian gonna come and see these papers, and Miz Judith have a fit."

Impatiently Caroline took the needle-point covered box and stuck it into a built-in cupboard by the side of the fireplace. "I can't think about them now," she told Monique. "They mean nothing to me." She returned to sit by Judith's side. In spite of all logic she kept looking for a tiny sign of life.

When Marian arrived, she gave Caroline a firm hug, went to the bed where Judith lay, then turned to Caroline and Monique and said, "I'd like to be alone with her."

Monique slowly left the room. Caroline said to her mother, "I guess I'll go downstairs and call David. Is there anyone else I should call?"

"No, dear," Marian said tearfully. "Your father is making the arrangements."

Caroline left the room and closed the door behind her quickly before her own tears upset her mother. Outside Judith's bedroom she leaned her forehead against a wall and wept. Finally she dragged herself downstairs to the drawing room and across the room to the phone.

Caroline stared down at the rose-colored, damask fabric covering the 18th century chair that awaited her in front of her grandmother's mahogany writing table. The elegance of the chair struck Caroline as the epitome of what Judith stood for. It was not a reproduction. It was an 18th century piece, meticulously crafted from mahogany with an intricate shell pattern carved on the top of the cabriole legs. The arms of the chair curved so gracefully, it was difficult to believe they were made of wood. Almost two centuries had passed since some loving artisan had crafted the chair, and those years had produced a rich patina on the wood which reflected all the colors that were near the chair in the room. Caroline sank into the chair and faced the writing desk. It too was an 18th century piece, a beautifully carved work of art from some very talented woodworker of two hundred years past. Its hand-rubbed finish reflected light and color like a mirror. She studied the top of the writing table where she found a hand-cut crystal lamp and a gilded, porcelain ink stand that she judged to be a French antique. On the right side of the desk there was a Wedgewood vase containing the lilies her grandmother favored above all flowers. Even the writing pad was exceptional. Meant to be a purely utilitarian object to protect the surface of the desk, Judith Hamilton's writing pad was covered in silk moire of a pale sea-foam green color. On it lay sheets of Judith's monogrammed note paper, the parchment color with the deckled edge and the elaborate engraved monogram that Caroline knew so well. Her grandmother's favorite pen lay across several sheets of note paper, as if she had only left for a moment and would soon return to finish her daily social correspondence.

Caroline raised her eyes to the painting above the desk and studied the beautiful garden scene depicted there. It was an original canvas from one of the lesser known Impressionists of the late

19th century, a picture depicting elegance and ease. The colors of the garden were soft, bathed in the gentlest sunlight from a clear, blue sky. In the picture there was a rather prim-looking woman dressed in white walking on a garden path. She appeared to be walking straight toward Caroline. Caroline's mind was confused and numbed, and she had the impression that the woman was her grandmother walking toward her and into her own drawing room. Caroline turned slowly in the chair and gazed across the drawing room. The room was large, exquisite, decorated to perfection in shades of rose and the sea-foam green that Judith so loved. Every object was perfectly placed in the room, every pillow plumped to its fullest, not a speck of dust or imperfection was visible anywhere. Caroline looked back at the picture and realized that the woman had not advanced even one step toward her. "You will never come again, Grandmother," she said to the woman in the picture. "So why were you ever here?"

A picture of the cardboard box behind the dilapidated mansion in the slums flashed into Caroline's mind. She saw the dirty, hungry children, three sets of anxiety-filled eyes in a discarded cardboard box. An ocean of confusion crashed through her mind as she struggled to reconcile her experiences of that day. At that moment, she sat surrounded by incredible elegance and wonderful ease of life, while only a few miles away there was such devastating poverty that even a morsel of food was hard to come by, and home was a cardboard box that could not keep out the cold or rain. Her grandmother lay dead in the room above her. Dead from the exertion of trying to destroy a record of the past which she had spent her life verbally adoring. Inside Caroline there was new life waiting to be born. "What is real?" Caroline cringed as she whispered the words. Suddenly she felt great panic, and she clasped the edges of the heavy mahogany desk as she felt her body reeling. She flung her arms on the desk, buried her head and sobbed. After she had cried for several minutes, gentle hands began to stroke her hair, and she heard Marian's voice, "You must not allow yourself to become overwrought."

"Grandmother is gone," Caroline cried.

"Yes," Marian said quietly. "She is gone."

Caroline raised her head and turned to look her mother in the face. "If Grandmother is gone, then her world is gone too."

"Her world is gone, Caroline," Marian nodded, as tears filled her own eyes. "But your world remains. My world remains, and in both of those worlds there is someone very precious we must protect."

"I don't know what you're talking about," Caroline mumbled.

"I'm talking about your child, Caroline, my grandchild. You must go home now and rest. There is nothing you can do. The next few days will be difficult enough, but your father is making all the arrangements, so you need not concern yourself with that. We will all be grieved for a long time, but we must go on. And it is imperative that you moderate your grief to protect your child's life."

"How can you be so calm?" Caroline demanded angrily.

"If I seem calm to you, Caroline, it's because I'm dazed. But I'm not so dazed that I can't grasp the reality that your grandmother is beyond our help, but your child is within the reach of our tender care. I don't know how I'm going to get through the next week, frankly, but I do know that if anything happens to you or your baby, I can't make it. Please, Caroline, do your best to stay as calm as you can. I want you to go home. I want you to go to bed and rest. This has been a dreadful shock to you. Your father has come to help me. Your brother will be here soon. We are all in better condition than you are to handle the pain of the details. I want the comfort of knowing that you are at home resting. Please do this for me."

"Okay, Mother, I'll do it, if that's what's best for you."

"I want you to take Monique with you to take care of you, and I want you to call David. He needs to be with you at this time, and he will want to be here."

"I know that." Caroline hesitated and looked down at her lap where she was wringing her hands.

"What is it, Caroline?" Marian asked softly.

"I'm just not sure I'm ready to see David," Caroline whispered.

"You need your husband, dear. It is not necessary to talk about your child immediately. You just need him with you in this difficult time."

"Yes, I suppose so," Caroline agreed. "I'll call him when I get home." She stood and put her arms around her mother and tried to be unselfish and think about the pain her mother must be feeling.

Her father came into the room and said quietly, "The funeral director is here, Marian. They are ready to remove Judith's body."

"Of course," Marian said. "I'll go up to Mother's room."

"There's no need for you to do that, honey," Caroline's father replied.

"No, I want to be there," Marian said more firmly.

"I'll go with you, Mother." Caroline put her arm around her mother's shoulder, and they left the room.

An overwhelming sadness rose up in Caroline as she watched the men gently remove her grandmother's body from her bed. They put her on a rolling stretcher, and Caroline began to sob as she realized that she would never see Judith again in this room. Marian held Caroline close, took Caroline's face in her hand, and said, "You promised to go rest."

Caroline nodded her head in agreement. Marian turned to Monique, "I want you to go home with Caroline, Monique, and take care of her."

"Yes, ma'am," Monique said through her own tears.

Marian looked around the room, then followed her mother's body out the door.

Caroline and Monique were left alone in Judith's bedroom. Monique looked at the empty bed, and Caroline's eyes followed hers. Then Monique came toward Caroline and put her arm around Caroline's shoulder. Caroline buried her face in Monique's neck and sobbed. After a moment, Monique said brusquely, "That's enough, Miz Caroline. Miz Judith wouldn't want you crying or hurting yourself. We gots to take care of you, just like we would Miz Judith."

Caroline nodded and started to walk toward the door, but she stopped when Monique went to the cabinet where Caroline had hidden the papers, took out the needlepoint-covered box, walked to Caroline, and gave the box to her. "This be the last thing we can do for her," Monique said.

"Yes," Caroline agreed. She put her arm through Monique's and they left the room with Caroline carrying the box.

When Caroline and Monique arrived at Caroline's house, she forced herself to go to her study and close the door. For a moment she leaned against the door, thinking of David, torn between her great need for his reassuring presence and her fear that if he came, she could not hide her pregnancy. *I need more time,* she thought desperately. *Nothing has gone as I planned.*

How can things move so fast sometimes in your life and so slowly in other times? No wonder I feel confused. In two days' time I've experienced David's explosion about Suzanne's becoming pregnant by tricking Scott, a horrible damaging storm, Grandmother's insistence that I abort my child to save my marriage, Mother's insistence that I not abort it, and now Grandmother's death. It's all so confusing! I can't sort it out. And no matter what part of it I think about, I keep seeing the eyes of those little children living in that cardboard box. I keep thinking of their mother working to keep them alive, risking everything, losing her relationship with the man in her life. I feel like such a coward. Mother's probably right, David would understand eventually. It could all be worked out. Oh dear, Grandmother has died! I just have to put all of this away for the time being. Grandmother has died trying to burn papers from the past. It's all so absurd I—Mother's right. I must have David's steady hand. I don't need to talk about my pregnancy with him; I just need to focus on the funeral and get through the next few days.

With that resolution clearly in mind, Caroline walked quickly to her desk and put the needlepoint covered box down. She reached for the telephone, considered the time difference, and phoned the townhouse they owned in London, hoping she could catch David before he went to the office. Their housekeeper, Mrs. Watson, answered the phone in her typically prim manner. "Randolph residence."

"Mrs. Watson, this is Mrs. Randolph. Has Mr. Randolph left for the office yet? I must speak to him."

"No, ma'am, he hasn't left," Mrs. Watson hesitated for a moment. "And he isn't going to leave, not if I have anything to say about it."

Caroline was stunned by her words. "What do you mean?" she demanded. "Is something wrong with Mr. Randolph?"

"Mr. Randolph has one of those terrible bronchial colds he gets," Mrs. Watson reported. "He insists on going to work even though the doctor told him not to, but I am not going to let him out of this house, even if he should fire me. I am worried about him, Mrs. Randolph. He could very well have pneumonia, just as he did last year."

"Where is he?" Caroline asked.

"He's upstairs trying to get dressed, insisting I put breakfast on the table in the dining room. But, Mrs. Randolph, you must speak to him. He cannot quit coughing; he has a temperature. The doctor insists that he take antibiotics and stay home and rest, but he won't cooperate. I tell you, he's going to have pneumonia again."

"Put him on the phone immediately," Caroline commanded. "He is not going to go to work."

"Just as you say, Mrs. Randolph." Mrs. Watson was obviously relieved.

Caroline's heart thumped wildly in her chest as she waited to hear David's voice across the trans-Atlantic lines. He had a horrible case of pneumonia last year, she thought. What can he possibly be thinking to risk such a thing again? And, of course, he can't possibly travel now. A little sigh of relief filtered through her mind at the thought that she would not have to be confronted by David now. She immediately felt guilty, and at the same time she felt regret that she would not have his help.

Finally David picked up the line, "Caroline?" he said and then broke into a deep, harsh cough.

"David," Caroline spoke firmly as soon as he had quit coughing. "David, you sound perfectly horrible. Mrs. Watson says that you have another bronchial cold and the doctor told you to stay home."

"I'm fine," David insisted in as strong a voice as he could muster.

"It sounds to me like you're very ill," Caroline insisted. "And if the doctor has put you on antibiotics and is warning you to stay home in bed, you'd better do what he tells you to do."

"I've got to close a very large business deal today, Caroline. It won't take but a half a day, and then I can come home and rest."

"No, David, I know how these half-a-day business deals turn out. You end up having lunch, and then there are more negotiations in the afternoon, and you end up having dinner, and you come dragging home at midnight. If you do such a stupid thing, you'll be in the hospital in the morning."

"I'll be fine," he insisted, but his voice cracked as he began to cough again. Caroline waited patiently, suddenly worried about how she could tell him of Judith's death without encouraging him to risk his health to come back to Dallas. For a fleeting moment, she thought of not telling him at all, but she knew he would be furious with her once he found out. David finally quit coughing, and after a moment of silence during which he was clearly trying to catch his breath, he suddenly asked, "Why are you calling at this hour?"

"I have some news to tell you," Caroline's own voice choked as her mind turned to the purpose of her call. "But before I tell you, David, promise me that you will give up this insane idea of conducting business today. Promise me that you will go back to bed, at least until your temperature breaks, no matter what."

"I don't like the sound of this," David said hoarsely. "Something's wrong. Has there been another storm? Where are you?"

"I'm at home, David. I'm fine, but something has happened. Oh, I wish I didn't have to tell you."

"Tell me, Caroline," he demanded impatiently.

But before she could speak, he began to cough again. Suddenly Caroline wanted above all other things to keep David safe. The thought of another bout of pneumonia and even the slightest chance that she might lose him to death terrified her. She began to cry, and by the time David had finished coughing, she was sobbing. "David, David, please, promise me you'll go back to bed. I can't face the thought of losing you."

"Losing me? I'm not going to die, Caroline," he insisted. Then his voice turned suspicious. "Something has happened over there. It's not like you to be hysterical. What's going on?"

"Promise me you'll go back to bed," Caroline continued to cry, but she made her voice as commanding as she could. "Promise me! I couldn't bear to lose you too."

"What do you mean, 'lose me too'?" David demanded. "Caroline, what is going on?"

"Promise me, David," she pleaded through her sobs.

"Okay, okay, honey," he tried to placate her. "I'll cancel my meeting. I'll postpone it. I'll do whatever will make you calm down. I'll go back to bed. Now what has happened? There's been another storm, hasn't there?"

"No," Caroline tried to regain control of her voice. "No, David, it isn't another storm." There was a long pause as Caroline swallowed hard and wiped the tears off of her cheeks. She couldn't speak the words that would make her grandmother's death even more of a reality to her.

"What is it, Caroline?" David asked quietly. "Tell me, tell me, honey, please. Just say it. Once you've said it, it will be easier. Just say it." He waited quietly.

Caroline listened to the static of the trans-Atlantic line and finally spoke barely above a whisper. "Oh, David, Grandmother is dead." She didn't need to say any more. She knew that he was well aware of her devotion to Judith.

"I'm so sorry, honey," he said quietly. "I'll come home."

"No!" Caroline cried suddenly. "I don't want you to come home."

"But of course you do," David answered. "You're not thinking straight, Caroline. You're horribly upset. Of course I'm coming home. Surely you don't think I would let you go through this alone."

"But David, if you're too sick to go to a meeting, you couldn't possibly get on an airplane and fly across the Atlantic Ocean."

"Nonsense," David insisted. "I'll just get on the first flight available. I'll sleep on the flight and take my medication. I'll be home in a matter of hours."

"No, David!" Caroline started sobbing uncontrollably and gasping out phrases as she cried. "I can't bear to lose you too. You must keep yourself safe. Grandmother's dead. I can't let you die too."

David tried to break into Caroline's hysterical wanderings, but he finally gave up and waited for her to cry it out.

Monique heard her sobbing and came into the study. When she saw that Caroline had totally lost control, she took the telephone from her hand and spoke into the receiver. "Mr. David, this be Monique. Yes sir. Miz Judith be dead, and Miz Caroline be very upset."

"He mustn't come home," Caroline insisted. "He's very sick, Monique. He'll have pneumonia again. He'll die too."

"Monique," David started coughing and couldn't go on. When he regained his voice, he said, "Monique, calm Caroline down, get her into bed, and when she is calm, tell her that I'll be home as soon as I can get there."

"No, Mr. David," Monique disagreed. "If you's sick, you don't need to be here. Miz Caroline has her mother and father and all the family to take care of her. She gonna lose her mind if she thinks you's risking your life to come here. There's nothing ahead but a funeral, Mr. David. Miz Caroline will be fine. We all gonna help her. But if she got to worry that you's gonna die too, she ain't gonna make it. You gots to stay there till the doctor say you can travel. Miz Caroline gotta know you's safe."

Caroline was nodding her head vigorously as Monique spoke, then she grabbed the phone from Monique and begged, "David, please, please. Monique is right. Mother and Daddy are here. Everyone is here. Nothing will bring Grandmother back. You know how funerals are. There are so many people around, you can't feel anything. I'll be fine. It's just been such a shock because it just happened about an hour ago. But please, David. If I have to worry about you, if I have to worry that you could have pneumonia again and even die—"

"Caroline," David interrupted, "I won't come now. Go to bed. Get some sleep. I'll cancel my business meeting and go back to bed myself, and we'll talk when you wake in the morning." He began coughing, and Caroline waited anxiously. "I'll call you," he was finally able to go on, "and we'll talk after you've had a good night's rest."

"Promise me you won't try to come home, David," Caroline pleaded.

"I promise, Caroline. I'll go back to bed. I'll take my medication. Maybe I'll be stronger by this evening. You sleep through the night, and I'll rest through the day. I'll call you tonight, which means I'll call you first thing in the morning, your time."

"Okay, David," Caroline agreed.

"I love you, Caroline."

"I love you too, David. Please believe me. This is best. I can only worry about so much at one time."

"I see that, honey. We'll talk in eight or ten hours, after you've slept and I've rested. Now go to bed."

"I will, David, I promise, if you promise that you'll stay in bed."

"I promise, Caroline. Now good night. Please rest."

"I will, David. Good night," Caroline said sadly and replaced the receiver. "He's not coming," she looked up at Monique, "at least not right away. Oh, Monique, I'd die if anything happened to him."

"I know, Miz Caroline. And he'll die if anything happens to you, so let's get you up into that bed and get you settled for a good rest."

"I don't know why everybody keeps talking about my resting," Caroline said bitterly. "It's not as if I can wipe my mind free of all that's happened. Surely people don't think I can just lie down and go to sleep and forget everything."

"Of course not, Miz Caroline, but you can still rest your body."

"Maybe I can take some kind of sedative," she began, but then she stopped short. "No, I guess that wouldn't be safe for the— that wouldn't work, would it?"

Monique shook her head and ushered Caroline out of the study.

"We'd better find a place for you to sleep," Caroline said.

"I's gonna sleep upstairs, in case you needs me," Monique insisted.

"That's fine, Monique. Let's just pick one of the guest rooms that you like, and we'll settle you in there."

"I's gonna settle myself, after I settles you," Monique had her arm around Caroline's waist and was partially supporting her as they walked up the stairs.

"Monique, I'm not an invalid. I'll be fine. Let's just get you settled."

"I's gonna take care of you," Monique suddenly stopped in her tracks and turned and looked Caroline in the eyes. "Miz Judith would want me to."

"Yes, I'm sure she would," Caroline patted the old servant on the shoulder. "Thank you, Monique. I'm glad you're here tonight."

"I's gonna get you in bed where you can rest, Miz Caroline," Monique started back up the stairs, gently pushing Caroline along with her.

Caroline made no more protests as Monique settled her into the bed she had jumped out of several hours before to rush to Judith's side. Monique pulled the covers up to Caroline's chin as if she were a little child, then asked, "Does you need anything else, Miz Caroline?"

"No, Monique. You go rest too. Just pick any room you want."

"I'll be fine," Monique insisted. "Now you sleep." She turned off the lamp, reached over and patted Caroline's arm, and left the room.

Caroline lay there trying to absorb the incredible events of the evening. Every time she thought of her grandmother, tears began to flow down her cheeks. She listened as she heard Monique settle for the night in a bedroom down the hall from her own. Monique had left the door to Caroline's bedroom open, and Caroline watched as the last light, Monique's light, was turned off.

Still she could not sleep. Everything in the world seemed wrong. Wherever she placed her mind, she found trouble. She couldn't bear to think of her grandmother, and when she thought of David, she felt frantic with worry. The minutes ticked away on the clock over the mantel as Caroline stared at the ceiling.

After Monique had been in bed for over an hour, Caroline finally gave up her efforts to sleep. As noiselessly as possible, she rose from her bed, donned her robe, and walked barefoot out of her room and down the hall. She descended the staircase and went to her study where she picked up the needlepoint covered box and opened it. She took the papers that were left in the bottom of the box and spread them on her desk. She wondered, what was so important about these? Why did Grandmother want everything burned? It makes no sense. She always wanted to preserve her past; she was so proud of her family. Caroline picked up one old paper and then another, but they were meaningless to her, just old writing where the ink had weathered to a brown shade. She had no heart for them, no interest whatsoever in events that were so long dead. She asked herself, what difference does it make now? Grandmother is dead. Caroline's tears began to flow again. She tried to give her attention to the papers, but about five minutes later she confessed to herself that even these papers could not divert her mind from the painful emotions that were overwhelming it. Finally she thrust the papers back into the box, closed the lid, turned out the light and left the room. As she climbed the stairs, her physical exhaustion began to overwhelm her emotional distress; by the time she had climbed back into her bed, her mind had clicked off, and she fell asleep.

Chapter 9

Caroline awoke the next morning when Monique shook her and said, "That housekeeper in London be on the phone."

Caroline's mind instantly became alert as she reached for the phone next to her bed. "Mrs. Watson?" she answered in alarm. "Is Mr. Randolph okay?"

"No, ma'am," Mrs. Watson said briskly. "He's lost his mind as far as I'm concerned. He's much sicker. The doctor's been here and given him a shot, but Mr. Randolph is still preparing to leave and come to Texas. I decided to call you, even if he fires me."

"Put him on the phone, Mrs. Watson." Caroline swung her legs over the side of the bed and sat up straight. "I want to talk to him."

"He can't talk to you, Mrs. Randolph. His voice is completely gone. Every time he tries to talk he has the most horrible coughing fit." She stopped and changed the tone of her voice to one of pleading concern. "Mrs. Randolph, you must stop him. The doctor says he has pneumonia now and should be in the hospital."

"Get him to the phone," Caroline commanded. "Don't worry, I'll stop him." She waited impatiently as Monique stood there downcast with worry. Caroline covered the phone and stared pleadingly up at Monique. "I've go to stop him, Monique. He should be in the hospital right now. But what am I going to do? You know how stubborn he can be."

Monique thought a few seconds, her eyes lighted up, "It won't do him no good to come here if you's gone there."

"You're right, Monique, I'll go to London. Oh, this is horrible! I have to choose between being with my husband who's ill and being with my mother while she buries Grandmother. What am I going to do?"

"That Miz Watson take good care of Mr. Randolph, don't she?" Monique asked.

"Of course she does," Caroline said. "She has worked for him for years, and he has always helped her financially when she needed it."

"Then he don't need you in London."

"But you said I should go," Caroline insisted.

"I didn't say you should *go*," Monique said sharply, emphasizing the word "go."

Caroline smiled sheepishly. "I understand, Monique. You didn't live with Grandmother all those years and learn nothing, did you?"

Monique shook her head sadly.

Caroline heard David pick up the telephone. In a raspy whisper, he said, "Caroline, I'm coming." But those were the only words he could speak before he was stopped by a devastating coughing fit. Caroline waited until she could get his attention. The moment he quit coughing she said calmly but with fierce determination, "David, you are *not* coming to Dallas. It will do you no good, because I will not be here. I am coming to London to take care of you. It's obvious that you don't have the good sense to let Mrs. Watson take care of you, so you leave me no choice but to abandon my family and come to London to nurse you."

David whispered, "But Caroline, you need me now."

"I need you alive!" Caroline shouted at David for the first time in their six year marriage. "What good are you to me dead? I need you alive. Apparently I must come to London to make you stay alive."

"No, Caroline," David struggled to whisper. "You're not up to it."

"That's true, David. I'm not up to it. I feel like I'm being barraged with cannons from all sides. Most of what's happening I have no control over, but I can see to it that you don't kill yourself, so I'm coming to London to keep you from coming to Dallas. I wish I didn't have to, but you're forcing me to do it. I need to be here. I'm too tired to come to London. My mother needs me, but the most important thing in the world to me is for you to get well and for us to have a life together. If I have to drop everything here and come to London, that's what I'm going to do. I'll be on the next plane out of Dallas. Don't you dare get on a plane and start across the Atlantic Ocean. You're only going to miss me."

"No, no, no," David insisted as loudly as he could. "Don't come. I don't want you to come here. You win; I'll stay here. Mrs. Watson will take care of me. You don't need to worry about me. Just promise that you won't come."

"You promise me that you won't come, David," Caroline insisted.

"I promise," David said. "I promise I won't come if you'll stay there and let Monique take care of you."

"Okay," Caroline agreed, "but I'm calling back this afternoon, and you better be there, or I'll get on a plane. You better believe me, David; I mean what I'm saying."

"I'll be here," David whispered. "Caroline, please. Take care of yourself."

The next voice that Caroline heard was Mrs. Watson. "Mrs. Randolph, I'll take care of Mr. Randolph. You know I will. You stay where you are and take care of your family, and I'll take care of Mr. Randolph. I'll call you if there is anything that you need to know."

"Thank you, Mrs. Watson," Caroline said. "I'll call this afternoon to see how he's doing, but please call me if he gets worse or if he tries to leave the house."

"Yes ma'am, I will," Mrs. Watson promised.

"Good-bye, Mrs. Watson," Caroline said, then put the phone down. She looked up at Monique, who was nodding. "Thank you, Monique. I think we've done it. I should be at his side, though. He's very sick."

"This is one of them times when you got to let other people take care of things and let them take care of you," Monique said firmly. "That Miz Watson, she know how to take care of Mr. Randolph, and he got a doctor and medicine and everything he need. He just need to stay still."

Caroline nodded her agreement.

"You got to let me take care of you, Miz Caroline, and together we got to take care of Miz Marian—and Miz Judith." Monique's voice broke when she said the name of her beloved Miz Judith.

Tears sprang to Caroline's eyes, but she nodded her head in agreement.

Two days later Caroline was sitting in a crowded church waiting for Judith's funeral to begin. She had walked through the preceding forty-eight hours in a daze. David had continued to be too ill to travel, and between Mrs. Watson's insistence and Caroline's threat that she would come to London, they had managed to keep him in bed where he could regain his health.

Caroline had spent hours at the funeral home with her mother watching over the body of Judith and receiving the many grieved friends and relatives who came to pay their respects. As often as she possibly could, Marian had sent Caroline home with Monique to rest, but Caroline had been too depressed to do more than lie in her bed. She had slept very little. Now, finally, the time had come for the formal recognition of her grandmother's death. Dressed in black, she sat next to her mother and waited for the music and eulogies to begin.

Caroline would have preferred to stare straight ahead, for she had had almost two days of constant human sympathy, and she did not want to meet anyone's pity-filled eyes. She could not keep her gaze straight ahead, however, for to do so meant to look unceasingly at the open coffin of her grandmother. There lay Judith in her finest clothes with every hair in place, with her makeup on, wearing her favorite jewels. For a ninety-two-year-old woman, she was remarkably beautiful. Anyone but Caroline would have thought she looked wonderful, but to Caroline, the body that lay in front of her was a travesty of the true Judith, for it contained no liveliness. It was a mockery of Judith's life and character, a lie to her typical facial expressions and behavior. It was like a mannequin: serene, at peace, but utterly dead. Judith had never been at peace, and no one knew it better than Caroline. Judith had never been at peace; she had always been full of vim, a vigorous personality who had taken control of every room she had ever entered. Her face had never been serene. It had always been a screen across which flashed every volatile emotion.

Caroline averted her eyes from the open coffin and risked the sympathetic eyes of others in the church. She looked at the windows of the beautiful, old church where her grandmother had held membership all of her married life. Beginning at the window closest to the altar, she saw a depiction of the birth of Christ. There was the mother of God, and Joseph, the manger with the baby Jesus, the angels hovering over the scene, the shepherds in front. It was a dazzlingly beautiful, massive display of color, but it had nothing to do with Judith. Caroline was startled when she realized that she had never heard her grandmother speak of Christmas in any way other than as a family holiday. Caroline wondered, what was Christmas to Grandmother? Was there ever any spiritual connection in her mind, and why am I even thinking about such a thing now?

Disturbed in a way she did not understand, Caroline moved her eyes to the next window. That window depicted a scene from the Bible that Caroline remembered from sermons. The window portrayed Jesus standing in the water with John the Baptist. A dove hovered over the head of Jesus. Caroline remembered that God had spoken at that time in history and had said something about this person, this Jesus, being His Son. She wondered, did Grandmother believe that?. She began to feel overheated and short of breath as tension grew in her. To ease the discomfort she didn't understand, she listened to the music that had just begun; a soloist with a beautiful soprano voice had stood and was singing a hymn which Caroline recognized. Caroline's feelings of tension grew into frightening confusion as the words of the hymn spoke of living in this world knowing that this life would end and that one would go on to live with God. Grandmother never spoke of such things, Caroline thought, and she always ridiculed Mother for being religious. What *did* she believe? Caroline looked back at the dead body of Judith and remembered, Grandmother attended church regularly. In fact, I attended this church with her on many occasions. Is that enough to—to—Caroline cut off her thoughts, tremendously grateful that the first eulogy was beginning. An expensively dressed, silver-haired woman stood before the congregation. She spoke of her memories of Judith and Judith's leadership in the society of the city.

"Judith Bradford Hamilton was the very heart of this city's cultural life," she said. "I remember her well from her first year in Dallas. She came here as a young bride, and what a marvelous addition to this city she has been! For over seventy years Judith Hamilton has created an atmosphere of elegance and grand cultivation of beauty in our beloved city. Her efforts made it possible for all of us to live with such happiness, such joy. Following the glorious tradition of the Bradfords of Charleston, South Carolina, her illustrious family, she became the *grande dame* of all the arts. What a wonderful legacy she has left us. We owe tribute to her for the birth of our ballet, the tremendous growth of our symphony, the introduction of opera, the preservation of our fine old homes. She has been a magnet, drawing to her presence all those who could add refinement—and thus happiness—to our lives."

Caroline listened to the first sentences of the eulogy with a sense of comfort, for the words were true, and they sounded good. She began to feel confirmed once more in what she had always thought, that Judith had lived a fine life and had contributed much. Caroline felt that she had been the luckiest of all the benefactors, for she herself had been the golden girl Judith had lavished the most attention on. She cast her eyes down from the speaker's face to the open coffin, but seeing the face of her grandmother so rigid hurt too much. She lowered her eyes to her own hands which lay in her lap in a pose she had been taught to maintain in the finishing school she had attended. As she looked down at her lap, she realized quite suddenly that she was looking at the spot in her body which housed life at that very moment. A streak of revelation tore through her mind as she looked at her own lap covered in the black cloth of her dress. New life was within her, but she had covered it in black as if it were dead. Her eyes darted back to the coffin. There lay Judith's body, dead, never to breath again, never to speak, never to affect or influence anyone or anything; but it lay beautifully clad in pastel silk. My baby! Caroline almost cried out the words. I carry life that Grandmother wanted me to kill. She looked down at her lap again and thought, there is life here, growing, becoming. She glanced back at the coffin. In spite of the jewels, in spite of the silk, in spite of the makeup and the perfect hair, there was only death. Caroline wanted to get up and run, as fast as she could and as far away as possible, from the confusion of the combination of the church windows with their undeniable spiritual messages, the music which promised heaven, the dead body of her grandmother, and her own black-covered body which was itself alive and contained another life.

Her distress must have been evident, because Marian reached over and took her hand and held it firmly in her own. Caroline glanced at her mother's face and saw the quiet certainty of her mother's thoughts and compared them to the chaos of her own mind. Her mother sat there in a simple black dress, wearing very little makeup, obviously grieving that her mother had died but apparently suffering under no confusion. Caroline looked at her own lap again, and when she thought of her own unborn child safe in her womb for the moment, she thought of the children in the cardboard box. Love is what Mother's life is, she thought, helping the helpless. Grandmother has actually left very little: a stronger symphony, a ballet company for the city, opera for the few who can afford to enjoy it. When Mother dies, she will leave behind people who have been fed and housed and enabled to lift themselves from poverty.

Caroline was grateful when the first speaker sat down and her uncle, James Bradford Hamilton, stood up to eulogize his mother. Surely, Caroline thought, Uncle James' comments will help me relax. He spoke eloquently about Judith's strong dedication to her family, how Judith struggled all her life to guarantee that her descendants would continue on this earth to enrich it. Caroline grew uneasy again. There stood her uncle, James Bradford Hamilton, named after Judith's grandfather, James Bradford of Charleston, the man Judith had eulogized throughout her entire life. Uncle James was describing Judith's strong, loving family feelings, but to Caroline's right sat Marian, Judith's only daughter, who had been practically cast off by Judith. All of her life Caroline had been aware of the fact that Judith had embraced her son because he had followed her values and had taken the path that she had chosen for him, the path of social prestige and wealth. She was equally aware that Judith had rejected her daughter, Marian, Caroline's mother, because she would not continue in the path that Judith had insisted on. Marian had gone to all the schools that Judith had chosen, had made her debut, had married the man whom Judith had approved, and had borne children to continue the dynasty, just as Judith had insisted. But even though Marian had done all those things, when Marian broke from the usual social path of her class and gave her life instead to the service of others, her mother had turned on her. Caroline cringed as she listened to her uncle; she felt ashamed of the lie he told, and once again she lowered her eyes and stared at her hands. Once again she thought of the life that she held within her. She drew her breath in sharply as the painful thought raced through her mind that Judith had encouraged, indeed, almost commanded her to abort her child rather than risk losing the social connection and the financial position that David guaranteed. Caroline began to weep softly. Others, no doubt, saw her as weeping because her grandmother had died, but it was not Judith's death that caused Caroline's tears. It was the sudden revelation that there was something dreadfully wrong with Judith's values, and that she, Caroline, had embraced them unthinkingly.

The minister rose to give the final eulogy for Judith Bradford Hamilton. He spoke at length of her many contributions to the church, and Caroline listened carefully as he enumerated the many things that her grandmother had done for this particular church. He referred to the grand organ that she had donated. He mentioned the magnificent rose window at the back of the church; the light that shone through that rose window was illuminating Judith's face as he spoke, but that light could not comfort Caroline. The pastor continued by stating his belief that Judith was a woman of faith; and that her faith had led her to give so much to her church. Caroline's heart sank as the minister began to talk of Judith's great faith; and Caroline frantically struggled to remember a time when she had heard Judith speak of any religious convictions. She turned her eyes to the first window on the right, with the idea that she would count the pieces of the stained glass to block out what her ears were recording—the amazing dichotomy between what had been true of her grandmother and what these people were saying, especially what the minister was saying at that very moment about Judith's great faith.

When Caroline looked at the first window to the right, she saw that it was a large portrayal of the crucifixion of Christ. She froze, unable to move her eyes away from the scene of the Savior of the world hanging on the cross, asking only that people believe who He was in order to gain their salvation. The minister's words infiltrated her brain as he turned to her and the other bereaved members of her family and said, "Fear not. You will see Judith Hamilton again. You will see your beloved mother and grandmother again, for you will meet in heaven. I have no doubt of it, her faith was so strong."

Caroline jerked her eyes from the scene of the crucifixion and stared at the body of her dead grandmother as total panic rose in her. Quite suddenly and mercifully she knew nothing but blackness.

When Caroline once again became conscious of light, she realized she was in a strange room, lying on something hard. She blinked her eyes as she heard a comforting voice call her, "Caroline? Caroline? It's Mother. I'm here." A cold cloth was pressed against her forehead, and someone picked up her left arm and pressed her wrist.

"She's coming to," she heard a male voice say.

"Caroline, do you hear me?" her mother's voice asked. Caroline was finally able to focus, and she saw her mother's face and that of Dr. Cooke, who was holding her wrist and taking her pulse. Her mother looked dreadfully disturbed.

"You frightened us, but you're just fine. You're okay. You fainted," Marian said.

Dr. Cooke put Caroline's hand down across her waist and patted her on the shoulder. "That's right, Caroline, you're going to be just fine. You fainted, probably because of the stress and your condition. Now I want you to go home and rest. We have to think of that baby of yours, you know."

Suddenly the thought of the funeral came back to Caroline, and she tried to sit up. "Oh, no!" she cried out. Marian pushed her back gently. "Oh, Mother, what have I done?"

"Nothing worth worrying about," Marian insisted.

"The funeral! Is it over?"

"It is by now, dear."

"I must get up," Caroline said.

"You must not get up," Marian countered, "except to go home and go to bed and rest. Monique is here, and she's going to go with you."

"But what about the graveside service and that throng of people who will be over at Grandmother's house. We have to serve them food and—"

"*We* don't have to do a thing," Marian broke in. "There are plenty of members of this family to handle the remainder of what has to be done. Your grandmother had two children and a whole bevy of grandchildren. Only one of those people is pregnant, and you are that one, and you are not going to strain yourself any further."

"But I couldn't possibly not go with Grandmother to the graveside service."

"Caroline, your grandmother left us over two days ago. All that has happened since then or will happen this afternoon is for those of us who are left, and you have had enough. You are going home. The only question is whether or not I must go with you to force you to do it, or whether you will cooperate and allow me to go to the graveside and receive those who will come to your grandmother's house after the service."

Caroline sat up before answering. She felt like a dismal failure;

she had reached the end of her abilities. "I'll go home, Mother, although I feel like I'm deserting you."

"That's nonsense," Marian said calmly. "I have your father and all the members of the family with me. The worst thing you could do is to come to the cemetery and force me to worry about you."

"Then I'll go home and rest," Caroline agreed.

Her mother gave her a hug. "Dr. Cooke is going to take you home, Caroline, rather than coming to the cemetery, and Monique will go with you; and once you're settled in bed, I want you to have a good sleep. Call me when you wake up, and we'll go on from there."

Caroline looked at her mother's calm face and asked, "Can we go on?"

"Of course we can, Caroline. We can go on if we accept that the past is over and that we must live through the present and make the best we can of it. The future depends on our living in the present and getting through these difficult days."

Caroline nodded, and the doctor helped her stand.

"You'll take care of her, won't you, doctor?" Marian asked him.

"Of course, Marian."

"And you won't leave her until you're sure she's all right?"

"I won't leave her," he promised.

Marian gave Caroline a quick hug and a kiss on the cheek. "I'll be praying for you, dear," she said as she hurried out of the room.

Caroline allowed Dr. Cooke to take her and Monique back to her home. Monique helped her undress, and she climbed into bed. The doctor stayed a half hour, watching her and chatting amiably. When he was sure she was in no danger, he left.

"Can I get you anything else?" Monique asked as soon as she had seen the doctor out.

"No, Monique. Just let me rest and perhaps sleep. I'll call you if I need you."

Monique came and pulled up the covers around Caroline's chin, even though it was comfortably warm in the room; then with tears in her eyes she turned around and walked out of the room. Caroline understood that Monique had turned her attention to caring for her, since she could no longer care for Judith.

Caroline lay in bed for a long time, trying not to think about anything that was happening at the graveside. Her eyes lighted on a large photograph on the wall. It was a picture of Judith and her descendants standing on the front steps of Judith's mansion. Only two things remain of Grandmother, Caroline thought. One of them is her children, but they were never well-nurtured. They were never accepted for what they were, and Mother particularly suffered for not mimicking Grandmother's beliefs and values. The only other thing left is that grand house of hers and all the social life in this city that occurred because of her. Her life always seemed so full to me, but now it seems that it was actually empty. She sighed, literally too exhausted to think any further. She turned over on her side, buried her face in her pillow and fell into a nightmare.

Caroline heard a loud sound. It ripped and tore through her mind, wood splintering, bricks crumbling, glass shattering. Finally there was a crashing noise that vibrated the very floor on which she crouched in darkness. She screamed and ran, but her flight was soon stopped by the trunk of a large tree. She reached into the branches of the tree, but drew her hands back. With horror in her soul she looked down at blood flowing freely from her left hand. She sobbed, "I don't want this. Make it go away. Please, please, make it go away." She rubbed her hand on her skirt; but when she looked at it again, it was still bleeding. "Oh, what am I going to do?" she cried. A loud, mocking laugh engulfed her. She looked across the trunk of the tree, and there in the midst of the branches stood a looming, dark, faceless figure. It wafted back and forth in the wind. It reached out a long arm that ended in a pointed finger, pointed at her, and the huge, dark figure jeered at her with its scornful laugh. Caroline was terrified, then suddenly angry. "No!" she screamed. "You won't do it. I won't allow you to do it." With strength beyond that of a human being she reached down and pulled a large limb from the tree. She leapt on top of the tree, raised the limb in her right arm and swung viciously at the black figure. The laughter stopped instantly, and the figure dissolved into smoke as Caroline stood holding the limb.

The tree disintegrated under her feet and became ground covered in several inches of snow. Stretched before her eyes as far as she could see were large, cardboard boxes opening toward her. In each box she saw the faces of children staring out at her, their eyes full of fear and despair. The snow fell around Caroline and heaped itself on top of the boxes. Slowly but surely the boxes began to cave in, one at a time. Each time enough snow accumulated on the top of a box, it collapsed, and children screamed for help. Caroline rushed to the first box that collapsed on the children inside and dug frantically at the snow. "No!" she screamed. "No, you won't die. I won't let you die." Her hands were bloody in the snow, but she grasped the cardboard and tried to rip it open, determined to reach the children and pull them to freedom and safety. With all her might she worked and cried, "I must help them!"

Then she heard the laughter, the mocking laughter. She swung her head to the right, and there was the dark figure, looming over the box she was trying to open. Its laughter rose again as it raised its arm and pointed its finger at the box, which was fast becoming the grave of the children. "No!" Caroline screamed. "You can't have them." She reached to her side and picked up the limb from the tree and swung it at the dark figure. She hit the dark, looming figure, and the laughter stopped, as the figure disappeared in a cloud of smoke.

She turned back to the box and discovered that it had become an oxygen tent. She could see through it, and there lay David. Her ears were filled with the sound of his struggle for breath. Each breath was an agony of effort for David and an agony of terror for Caroline. "I must do something. I must help him!" she cried. She flung herself on the floor of the hospital and put her elbow on the edge of the bed and leaned as close to David's face as the oxygen tent would allow. She willed him with all her heart and mind to breathe, in and out, in and out, to breathe the precious oxygen that would save his life. He was fighting for every breath, and Caroline clasped her hands in hope, but then she heard a mocking laugh. She darted her eyes to the other side of the bed, and there loomed up the shadowy, dark figure. The laughter increased in volume, and the figure raised its arm and pointed its finger at David. Its jeering laughter shook the walls of the hospital room. Caroline's fury rose. "You won't have him!" she screamed. She reached down, picked up the limb from the tree and raced around the bed. She struck the figure. The laughter stopped as the figure disappeared into a wisp of smoke. She turned back to the oxygen tent. "I saved him!" she shouted, but when she looked down, David was not there.

The oxygen tent had become a cradle. Caroline could not see

inside it, but she heard an infant crying, a sad, mournful cry. A shudder permeated Caroline, and her body shook at the sound of the dying infant. She moved closer to the cradle, desperate to see the face of the child. "Who are you, baby? Who are you?" she asked. "I'll save you. Who are you?" The baby's cry became fainter. "No, don't die! I'll save you." The sound of mocking laughter exploded in the room, and the black figure arose on the other side of the cradle. The laughter became so loud that it shook the cradle and covered the baby's dying cries as the dark figure raised its arm and pointed its finger at the baby. Caroline was consumed with anger. She reached to her side and picked up the limb and struck the dark figure. The laughter stopped, and the figure dwindled into smoke. "I have won," she exalted. "I can save this life."

She looked down at the cradle, but it was no longer a cradle. It had become an open coffin. Caroline could not see into the coffin; she saw only her own reflection in the shining walnut of the side of the coffin. She gasped with horror. "No!" she screamed. "No death! I have saved the baby. I have saved David. I have saved the children. No death!" She struggled to reach the edge of the coffin, but when she began to move, she realized that she was on her hands and knees and that she must crawl to the coffin. "Who is it?" she cried. "Who is in there? No one is dead. I have saved them all." She crawled to the side of the coffin, put her fingers on the open edge of it and pulled herself up. When she looked down into the coffin, she saw the dead figure of her grandmother. "No!" she cried. "I will not allow it." She was answered by the mocking laughter of the enormous dark figure that rose all around her. It had grown large enough to fill the room. It raised its right arm and pointed its finger at Judith and laughed. Caroline gathered her strength for one more battle. She reached down and picked up the limb from the tree. She stood, full of fury, raised the limb above her head and swung with all her might at the looming dark figure. This time, the limb went straight through the figure and hit the edge of the coffin. Caroline was stunned. She stopped and stared as the scornful laughter increased and the dark figure approached the coffin still pointing its finger at Judith. "No!" Caroline cried. "You can't have her." She raised the heavy limb one more time and struck again at the figure, but the limb could not make it disappear. It did not dissolve into a wisp of smoke.

Instead, it re-formed itself, like a black blanket, laughing with the pleasure of sadistic mockery. It covered Judith, and Caroline could no longer see her grandmother. "No!" she screamed.

Caroline sat bolt upright in the bed. She was dripping wet with perspiration. Her heart was racing wildly. "I couldn't stop him," she cried. "I couldn't stop him."

She flung the covers of the bed back, leapt to her feet and whirled wildly in the darkened room. "Who can stop him?" she begged. "Please, help me. Who can stop him?"

The more she turned, the more completely she awoke, until finally she staggered back to hold on to the bedpost, her head dizzy. She was finally completely awake.

"It was a nightmare," she told herself, but her heart continued to pound. "Who can stop him?" she whispered urgently. "It was only a nightmare," she insisted. "But who can stop him?" she asked again. She flung herself on her knees at the side of the bed. "Dear God, I can't stop him. Please, Jesus, help me!"

In a flash a memory soared through her mind. It was Christmas Eve, six years earlier after she had rejected Taylor's proposal. She was with the family she didn't know at the little church off the highway. They were all smiling at her. They handed her a candle, and she lit it from the flame of the large nativity candle in front of the baby Jesus. The congregation gathered around the Christ child and lifted their voices in tribute to the newborn King. The memory faded, and Caroline glanced around the room and found she was not in the little church, but in her own bedroom.

Her heartbeat had slowed, and her mind felt as if it were emerging from a mass of cobwebs but not yet free. She walked to the bathroom and threw cold water on her face, drenching the front of her gown. The coolness felt wonderful. She raised her head and looked at her dripping wet face in the mirror. "Why did I think of that?" she asked herself.

She reached for a soft towel to dry her face and the thought of David, sick in London, flashed through her mind. "Dear God," she prayed aloud. "No, please. Don't let David die, too. I must call him. I must know how he is. I've been asleep since early afternoon. I must call him."

She left the bathroom hastily, but she stopped halfway across the room as she realized that it was 5:30 in the morning in London. "Too early to call," she said. "I must wait. I'll call Mother." She jerked up the phone and began to punch out the numbers, but suddenly she remembered the exhausted face of her mother at the church, and she put the phone down. "No, I mustn't bother Mother now. While I've slept, she's gone through the graveside service and the reception at Grandmother's house. Surely she's resting now. I mustn't disturb her. I must get a grip on myself. My imagination is running wild."

Caroline moved to a chaise lounge, sat down and put her legs up on the lounge. "I'll sit here and calm myself down," she spoke firmly to herself. "I'll think of positive things." She tried to clear her mind of the difficulties of the last few days as well as the night-mare she had just endured, but every frightening event of the dream seemed to crouch just at the edge of her mind, ready to spring back onto the stage of her imagination. She listened. The house was quiet. "Monique is here," she whispered to comfort herself, "but she must have gone to bed."

Caroline rose from the chaise lounge and walked determinedly toward the door. "I must move," she told herself. "Only move-ment can chase away the thoughts." She stepped out into the hall and listened. The house was quiet and dark; she couldn't hear a sound. It's like a tomb, the thought flashed through her mind, and she shuddered. "Monique is here somewhere," she told her-self aloud. "This is childish. I must take control of myself. Surely I don't need to run to an old woman for comfort." She walked down the hall and descended the staircase. When she reached the bottom, she stopped and listened. A strange tingling began in the back of her neck. The house was deadly quiet, and Caroline felt absolutely alone in the world. She heard the slightest sound, or imagined it, and whirled around, expecting to confront the dark figure from her nightmare; but there was nothing there, except eerie shadows cast by the moon through the window on the stair-case. She hugged the banister to steady herself, then gasped, "Light. I must have light. Too much darkness. There's been too much darkness." She flung herself toward the light switch. When she flipped the switch, the hall was flooded with golden light. She whirled around and examined every corner. There was no one there.

Caroline began to weep. She was a frightened child who had

endured the horrors of watching death without the hope of eternity. "Dear God, dear God," she prayed, but she could say no more. She hugged herself with her own arms as she shook. "I must calm down, I must," she mumbled.

As soon as she could walk, she stumbled toward the comfort of her study, turning on every light as she went. Once her study was well-lighted and she had gazed at the furniture for a moment, she was able to steady her nerves. "I know this," she told herself the obvious. "I know this place. This is my house. This is my study. Yes, this is my desk. Here is my loveseat in front of the fireplace." She stopped and stared at the fireplace. "I'm chilly. How strange. I was so hot, but now I'm icy cold." She went to the fireplace, which was laid for a fire, reached for a match and lit the crumpled paper under the logs to start the fire. She stood before the opening of the fireplace, waiting for the kindling and the logs to catch fire and watching the paper curl up at the edges and disappear. She was hypnotized as piece after piece of old newspaper curled and darkened toward the center and fell into blackened pieces.

Her mind leapt back to the moment she entered her grandmother's room and found her on the floor burning papers. "Why, Grandmother, why?" Caroline asked. "Why did you risk your life to do something so insane? What difference did it make? So silly, to upset yourself over papers." The kindling now caught fire and began to crackle, and Caroline felt a bit of comfort in the sound. She turned her cold back to the fire and looked across the room at her desk.

"What possessed you, Grandmother, to kill yourself over a bunch of old papers?" Caroline shook her head sadly. "It's not at all like something you would do. Not at all."

She stared blankly at her desk and then her eyes focused on the needlepoint-covered box she had left there. Suddenly she became alert; her muscles tensed as she stared at the box. "No, it isn't like Grandmother at all. It isn't like her to do such a thing."

Caroline walked toward the desk, determined to look at whatever papers remained in the needlepoint-covered box. "There must have been a reason," she said, "a compelling reason." She reached for the box and walked back and sat down on the loveseat. "I've never seen her lose control before, but she was definitely out of control those moments before she died, and the change had something to do with what was in this box."

A log suddenly rolled forward and threatened to send sparks onto the Persian rug of the room. Caroline jumped from the loveseat, grabbed the poker, and pushed the log back into place. Satisfied that the fire was contained, she turned to go back to the loveseat, but her glance fell on the table next to it. There she saw James Bradford's vest, with the note she had found in it tucked in the pocket. She looked from the vest to the needlepoint-covered box.

"You wanted to burn the vest too, Grandmother," she said, "didn't you? Or was it just the note you wanted destroyed? Grandmother, what was it that caused you to do these things? What was it? I have to know," she concluded firmly. "I have to know. It's more than mere curiosity. Somehow the fingers of this ancient darkness have reached into my own life. I must know, or I can never get free."

Chapter 10

Caroline dumped the few remaining papers from the needlepoint-covered box into her lap and began to investigate them. There were not very many papers left, perhaps fifteen pieces of old parchment with spidery handwriting in ink that had faded to a light-brown color. "I'll read every word of these," she said. "Oh, I hope Grandmother didn't burn the ones I need!"

She reached over, pulled the lamp closer, and began to read. The first was a letter from a government official to James Bradford regarding the economy of South Carolina and praising Bradford for his speech to the state House of Representatives. Caroline saw no relevance to her investigation, so she set the letter aside after reading every word. She picked up another paper; it was some sort of commendation to James Bradford from the Confederate government, dated 1862. Caroline continued to search among the few pieces of paper. Next she found a letter. She looked at the signature. It was from James Bradford, written to Mary, his wife. Caroline read every word, but she found nothing in it that was not commonplace. She picked up a marriage license. It recorded the fact that a Mary Caroline Bradford had married Robert Montgomery. There was nothing interesting or suspicious about that piece. She put it in the stack with those she had already examined. The next document was a deed of purchase of land in South Carolina signed by James Bradford. She found a second letter, and her heart leapt with excitement when she saw that it was addressed to Judith. Quickly she turned the paper over and noted that it was from James Bradford.

"This must be it," she told herself excitedly as she went back to the beginning.

"Dear Judith, my beloved granddaughter, how I miss your sparkling presence."

Caroline read through the entire letter and discovered only a letter from a doting grandfather to his granddaughter Judith, who was away from Charleston visiting friends. "This is just a letter to

Grandmother from her grandfather," Caroline muttered in exasperation. She looked at the date. "She must have been very young, and he must have been very elderly. But there's nothing of substance here." She put it on the stack with the other papers she had reviewed and picked up the next paper.

A wave of discouragement flowed over her. "Grandmother must have burned what I need," Caroline sighed and looked down at the next document. "Great," she said aloud. "Another marriage certificate. That tells me nothing." She glanced at it briefly. "Mary Caroline Bradford married to John Kendall." She placed it on the stack of papers and picked up the next, which was a contract of some kind. She began to read the contract, which had something to do with restoring the Bradford plantation house; however, she stopped in the middle of the contract when it suddenly occurred to her that both marriage certificates she had examined were for Mary Caroline Bradford. "Wait a minute," she said quietly. She went back through the papers she had read and pulled out the marriage certificates. "Mary Caroline Bradford. Both marriage certificates say Mary Caroline Bradford married someone. Okay. One says she married John Kendall; one says she married Robert Montgomery. There's nothing strange about that. She probably lost her first husband and remarried. Who was Mary Caroline Bradford? Let's see. There's only been one other Caroline in the Bradford family other than me. Right, Grandmother told me. Mary Caroline was her mother. I was named for Grandmother's mother, my great-grandmother. She was Mary Caroline Bradford, James Bradford's daughter. Grandmother's link to the Bradfords. She was certainly proud of that. She spent her whole life perpetuating the Bradford legacy, as she called it; but she never told me that her mother was married twice. Obviously she was. Her first husband probably died of one of those fevers that were so common at that time, or perhaps in an accident, and she remarried and gave birth to Grandmother. Let's see." Caroline picked up the first marriage certificate. "Yes, here it is. Mary Caroline Bradford married John Kendall, Grandmother's father, on March 21st, 1890. Grandmother wasn't born until 1900, and she was the oldest of her brothers and sisters. That's odd. Women in the nineteenth century had a baby every year or so. Mary Caroline must have lost some babies, perhaps by miscarriage or infant deaths. Grandmother never mentioned any of that, but maybe she didn't even know about it. After all, they didn't talk about things like that in those days. So Mary Caroline married John Kendall after her first husband, Robert Montgomery, had died. Let's see, she married him in March—wait a minute—March 1, 1890? How could she have married John Kendall twenty days after she had married Robert Montgomery? Even if he did die, she wouldn't have married that quickly, especially in the 19th century. Why, they grieved for at least a year before they did anything. Oh, this is all so confusing. And what difference does it make anyway? There must be something else in these few remaining papers."

Caroline put the marriage certificates to the side and picked up the remaining three papers. She looked at them quickly, but two of them contained nothing except praise for some action James Bradford had taken for the state of South Carolina. One was another letter to Judith. Caroline put all the papers together and stared at the fire. "There's nothing worth dying over in these papers," she told the flames. "In fact, there's nothing even very interesting, just this strange thing about my great-grandmother marrying twice so quickly. Who was Robert Montgomery?"

Caroline rose from the loveseat and went to a bookcase built in at the side of the fireplace. "I have a family genealogy here somewhere." She began examining the spines of the books. Finally she pulled out a dark green volume with gold lettering. "Here it is." She sat back down on the loveseat and began to study the family tree she found in the beginning of the book. "Okay. James Bradford, *the* James Bradford, the man Grandmother worshipped. Here he is, born 1840, married Mary Kathleen Fitzgerald. Okay. And, of course, their daughter was Mary Caroline. She married John Kendall in 1890. No, wait a minute. Where's Robert Montgomery? She married him first. I have the marriage certificate right here, but according to the Bradford genealogy she didn't marry a man named Robert Montgomery at all. Well, who was Robert Montgomery? Wait a minute."

She looked across the page at another family tree. "Here's the family tree of Mary Kathleen Fitzgerald, the wife of James Bradford. She had a cousin named Diana, who married a Thomas Montgomery, and they had a son named Robert Montgomery. There's Robert Montgomery, born 1869."

Caroline looked back across the page at the Bradford

family tree. "Mary Caroline Bradford, born 1872. So this Robert Montgomery was a second cousin of hers, about three years older, but they never married, or it would be in the family tree." Caroline put the book down on her lap and picked up the two marriage certificates. "Or would it?" She looked at the certificate that said quite clearly that Mary Caroline, her great-grandmother, had married Robert Montgomery on March 1, 1890. "This certainly looks authentic." She picked up the second marriage certificate. "Quite clearly, this says that Mary Caroline Bradford married John Kendall, March 21, 1890. If both of these marriage certificates are correct, but the genealogy doesn't—"

Time stood still for Caroline as she stared at the two marriage certificates. All other aspects of her world seemed to fade away. She looked at them side by side in her hands, and a pervasive uneasiness rose inside of her. "Something is horribly wrong," she said. She raised her eyes and her glance fell on the vest of James Bradford. She thought of the note: "He knows nothing. Meet me at midnight." Caroline turned her eyes to the fire, and for a flashing moment she saw the figure of her grandmother, the normally composed, elegant Judith, scrambling on the floor, tearing pieces of paper and throwing them into the fire.

"Deceit." The word came unbidden from Caroline's lips. "Deceit." Caroline listened to her own voice. "Deceit," she heard for the third time.

"There's been some horrible lie," Caroline whispered, "and Grandmother has known about it all these years, and she was trying to destroy all evidence of it. But what difference does it make? That vest goes back to Civil War days. These marriage certificates are dated 1890. Over a hundred years ago. Who cares? Why should I care now? This has nothing to do with me. What if there is some dark secret in the Bradford family? So what?"

Caroline reached over and picked up the vest and caressed the embroidered silk with her fingers. She saw her grandmother's frantic face and felt her grandmother's hands clutching at her blouse as she demanded, "Did you bring the vest?"

"Grandmother wanted to burn it," Caroline whispered. "She wanted to burn this vest." Caroline reached into the pocket of the vest and took out the note and opened it. "He knows nothing. Meet me at midnight."

"She wanted to burn it because she knew this dark secret,

whatever it is. She must have sensed that she was dying, and she wanted to destroy the evidence of something about her family that had haunted her. The great Bradfords, yet there is some darkness in the family history." Caroline shivered in spite of the warmth of the fire and felt an oppressive weariness suddenly descend on her. "Grandmother always talked about her family as if they were the most perfect people who ever lived. She was so proud of being a Bradford."

A little voice in Caroline's head whispered, "But she never returned to Charleston. Deceit, Caroline, deceit."

Caroline dropped the vest as if it were poisonous and ran her fingers through her hair and rubbed her forehead in her distress. "Grandmother lied," she concluded. "She lied about her ancestry. She lied about her family. I don't know how, precisely, but there's some grand lie here."

She remembered words from the first eulogy of her grandmother's funeral that very morning. "How fortunate Dallas has been to have gained Judith Hamilton," the society woman had said.

"But why did Grandmother leave Charleston?" Caroline whispered.

"Family was the most important thing to my mother," Caroline's uncle, James Bradford Hamilton, had said. "The ongoing of the Bradfords, from whom she was descended, was a prime motivator in her life."

"Yet she wanted me to abort my child," Caroline said.

"Fear not," the minister had proclaimed. "You will see Judith Hamilton again, for you will meet in heaven. I have no doubt of it. Her faith was so strong."

"She never mentioned God to me, not once," Caroline stood up abruptly and spoke directly to the flames in the fireplace. "Lies, they were all lies. Everything I heard at the funeral was one big lie, and what is this?" She pointed down at the papers on the loveseat. "Evidence of more lies? No, it can't be true. Grandmother's life was the map for my life. She was my mentor. I have always done what she said I should do. I have believed what she believed. It can't all be lies. I'm just overwrought. I'm tired. There's this dreadful depression weighing me down. I'm worried. I can't think about this now. I won't think about this now."

Caroline angrily picked up the fire screen and put it in front of the fireplace. "I'm going back to bed," she announced, as if by saying those words, she could stop the overflowing of the Pandora's box she had opened. She started toward the door but stopped and looked over her shoulder at the papers and the vest on the loveseat. Without consciously willing to do so, she walked back across the room, picked up the two marriage certificates, the vest and the note, and left the room.

Upstairs once again she put those items in a drawer and then went back to bed. She fell into a dreamless sleep.

It was just past dawn when Caroline awoke again. She slipped into her robe and walked to the window. She stared out at the sky, grateful that it was light, as if somehow that fact alone would make life better. A few minutes later she found Monique in the kitchen. Monique's eyes were full of the leaden darkness of grief, but she bustled a little to take care of Caroline.

"I'll make you some tea, Miz Caroline," she announced. "Is you hungry?"

"Yes, Monique, I think I am. Perhaps just some toast."

"What you need is some hot cereal," Monique announced firmly. "I's gonna make you some oatmeal."

"Okay," Caroline agreed listlessly. She watched for a few moments as Monique worked in the kitchen, but her mind was on the marriage certificates she had found the night before. Perhaps Monique knows why there are two marriage certificates for Grandmother's mother, Caroline thought. She was Grandmother's servant, but they were very close, and it was Monique's mother who came with Grandmother from Charleston when she married.

"Monique," she called quietly.

"This oatmeal be ready in just a minute, Miz Caroline," Monique said as she gave the pot another stir. "But your tea's about ready to pour now." She hurried toward the breakfast room table with a tray and set it down before Caroline.

Caroline reached out and poured a cup of the steaming liquid. "Monique?" she said as she reached out to stop the woman from returning to the kitchen. "Do you know anything about my great-grandmother, Mary Caroline?"

"No, Miz Caroline," Monique said briskly. She walked to the stove to stir the oatmeal, and Caroline sipped her tea.

"I think she was married twice," Caroline called after her.

"I don't know nothin about it," Monique said definitely as she scraped the oatmeal into a bowl, placed it and a pitcher of cream on a tray, and carried it to Caroline. "I wasn't even born then."

"But your mother must have told you some of the family history," Caroline insisted.

"She didn't tell me nothing," Monique said abruptly. "Now you best eat that oatmeal and drink your tea, Miz Caroline. I gots some work to do." Monique left the room and went out into the main hall.

She definitely knows something, Caroline thought. She drank her tea and dutifully ate the oatmeal, although she had no appetite now, as all of her strange fears from the night before returned. When she had finished the light breakfast, she went into her study to look at the papers again. The needlepoint-covered box was not on the loveseat where she had left it. Caroline went back to the main hall, called Monique and returned to her study.

When Monique appeared, Caroline asked, "Monique, where's the needlepoint-covered box? Did you put it away?"

"Yes, Miz Caroline, I put it away."

"Well, where did you put it, Monique?" Monique stared at the floor. "Monique, where did you put the box?" Caroline asked again. A crackling sound broke the silence between them, and Caroline realized for the first time that there was a small fire in the fireplace. She looked at it for a moment and then looked back at Monique. "Where is the box, Monique?" she asked sharply.

"I done what you promised Miz Judith you would do," Monique answered, then turned and left the room.

Caroline walked to the fireplace and saw that only one corner of the box had escaped the flames. The contents had been burned.

"So the conspiracy of silence is to continue," Caroline whispered. She looked down at the smoldering logs and saw the dark smoke rise and waver in a mass before it ascended into the chimney. The image brought forth the nightmarish figure of her dreams, and she shuddered and turned away. Her mind was so full of conflicting concerns and unanswered questions. She wandered over to her desk and aimlessly turned the pages of a book that lay there. When she was once again able to concentrate, she looked down at the book under her fingertips and saw that her hand rested on the chronologies of the Bradford family and the Fitzgerald family. Once again she ran her finger down the Bradford family tree. Mary

Caroline Bradford married John Kendall. There was no Robert Montgomery except the son of Mary's cousin, Diana, whom Caroline had found listed on the Fitzgerald family tree. Caroline traced her finger down the Bradford generations from Mary Fitzgerald Bradford to her daughter, Mary Caroline, to her three children, Judith, John and Mary Kathleen. Her eyes rested on the name of her great-aunt, Mary Kathleen.

She is still alive, Caroline thought, living in Charleston. For years I've dutifully sent Christmas cards to her, but I've never met her. Whatever Grandmother knew, her sister, Kathleen, must have known. And Mother might know. After all, she spent an extended time in Charleston with Great Aunt Kathleen when I was in my early teens. Come to think of it, she was always flying off to Charleston. How furious that made Grandmother. I remember how Mother quaked when Grandmother condemned her for going to Charleston, but Mother went back; and each time she came home, Grandmother's fury had less effect on her.

Caroline sat down quickly on the chair in front of the desk as the weighted realization fell on her mind. Each time she came back from Charleston, Mother was more like what she is now, the peaceful, productive woman I know. So different from the way she was when I was a child—a confused, weak creature whom Grandmother controlled. When did Mother's split with Grandmother occur? I don't know exactly. Sometime in my mid teens, but definitely after her trips to Charleston. Mother learned something there, and it made her a different person, one my grandmother laughed at, one I didn't understand. I still don't understand her, but I do know that somehow she became so strong she didn't need our approval. In Charleston Mother learned something life changing; perhaps she knows what I need to know. I feel that I can't take one step forward in my life until I know whether my life has been built upon deceit, deceit perpetrated by Grandmother. I must talk to Mother, but first I must call and see if David needs me.

Caroline stood up, walked around the room and shook her head to clear it. When she felt she could concentrate sufficiently, she picked up the telephone and dialed their townhouse in London. Mrs. Watson answered the phone.

"Mrs. Watson, how is Mr. Randolph?" Caroline asked anxiously.

"Oh, Mrs. Randolph," Mrs. Watson cried across the line. "His fever broke late last night, and he's been sleeping like a baby ever since. I was so afraid for him. I prayed and prayed. The doctor was here for several hours. He wanted to move him to the hospital but was afraid to move him at all. Then finally, thanks be to God, his fever broke. Oh, it was wondrous to see, Mrs. Randolph. I got right down on my knees and thanked God."

Caroline's eyes filled with stinging tears as she recalled the portion of her nightmare when she beat off the figure of death who hovered around David's bed. An image of herself on her knees begging God to help her flashed through her mind.

"Mrs. Randolph, are you there?" Mrs. Watson asked.

"Yes," Caroline managed to answer. "Yes, Mrs. Watson, thank God David is safe. You say he is asleep now?"

"He was about an hour ago. Let me go check on him."

"Don't wake him up," Caroline cautioned.

"No, ma'am. He must sleep if he can, but he may be awake. Let me check and see."

Caroline held onto the telephone with one hand and reached for a handful of tissues with the other. She cried quietly into the tissues, allowing them to catch the grateful tears. When she heard the click of a phone being picked up, she stifled her crying and called, "Hello, hello?"

"Caroline." A weak male voice came across the wires.

"David," Caroline cried. "Oh David, are you all right? Mrs. Watson said you were in terrible danger, but your fever broke. How do you feel?"

"Weak," David said hoarsely, "but it looks like you're going to be stuck with me a little longer."

"Oh, darling, I feel so dreadful that I wasn't there. I feel so guilty and so useless."

"No," David insisted, then paused to cough quietly. "I didn't want you to come. You've had a heavy enough burden to carry."

"I didn't carry it very well," Caroline confessed. "I couldn't— oh, David, I failed Mother horribly."

"No, you didn't," David insisted. "I'm sure you did everything you could."

"But you don't know," Caroline cried out her anguish. "You don't know what I did."

"I'm sure you did everything perfectly, darling." He was obviously exerting himself as much as he could.

"I didn't," Caroline cried. "Oh David, I fainted during the funeral and couldn't go to the graveside or receive the guests afterwards."

"Thank God you didn't try to come over here," he said. "Caroline, you must not blame yourself for this. I know you, and I know that you exhausted yourself through the long days before the funeral. I'll bet you never left the side of your grandmother's body, did you?"

"Not for long," Caroline agreed.

"Darling, listen to me. I can't talk long. You've been through terrible shocks, the storm and then your grandmother's sudden death, then the preparations for the funeral. There's no disgrace in breaking down during the service. You were closer to Judith than anyone. You were the one most entitled to grief, but I know you well, and I am certain you never allowed yourself any space for grief. You took care of everything and everybody, didn't you?"

"I tried to," Caroline said.

"I'm sure you did more than try, darling. I'm sure you did take care of everybody, everybody but yourself. I should have been there with you."

"But, David, you couldn't possibly have come. Look what's happened. Your fever has been high, you've practically been in the hospital. Thank God you didn't come."

"Well, I will come as soon as I can get out of this bed," David said strongly.

"No, you must not do that. You must take the proper time to recuperate. Don't come, David. I'll come there."

"No, you won't, Caroline," David said as firmly as he could.

"But I should have been there to take care of you."

"You should be taking care of yourself, Caroline. Now I have never ordered you around in any way, as you know, but I am telling you now that I forbid you to exhaust yourself by getting on a plane to London to care for me. I am on the road to recovery. I have Mrs. Watson here day and night. The doctor says I'll be able to sit up in a day or two, and I will regain my strength as quickly as I can and come home to you. I want you to promise me you will take care of yourself."

"But David—"

"No arguing, Caroline. I am your husband, and I am older than you, and this time I'm putting my foot down. I do not want you coming to London. I will come home as soon as I am able."

"But not before you're able," Caroline exclaimed. "Oh David, please don't rush it."

"I shall be quite sensible, darling, I promise. Now I want you to rest today. Allow yourself to feel. Talk to someone who can help you, and we'll talk again this evening." He broke off because he started coughing.

"Oh David, you mustn't talk any more," Caroline insisted. "Your cough sounds horrible."

"It's better than it was," he choked out the words, "but I must go. I'll give you back to Mrs. Watson."

Caroline waited as he gave the phone to the housekeeper. "Mrs. Watson," Caroline cried, "Is he okay?"

"He's just fine, Mrs. Randolph. He's weak; he needs rest and good food and to continue taking medication, but he is just fine. Thanks be to God he is going to get well, and if you don't mind my saying so, ma'am, Mr. Randolph is right. You must take care of yourself. You have been through an ordeal too. I'll take care of Mr. Randolph, and in no time the two of you will be reunited."

"Yes, Mrs. Watson, you're right, but please, please don't leave him."

"I wouldn't think of leaving Mr. Randolph, and you know it."

"Thank you, Mrs. Watson. Some day I will figure out a way to thank you properly. Right now, just know that I am so grateful you're there."

"And I shall stay here, ma'am."

"Good-bye, Mrs. Watson," Caroline said and put the phone down.

Caroline covered her face with her hands; she was full of despair as she wondered, how did this all happen? David has been close to death; Grandmother is dead, and I'm sitting here carrying David's child, unable to tell him what I have done. Did all these horrible things happen because I deceived David? No, that makes no sense. Why would Grandmother die because I tricked David into a pregnancy? Grandmother. Something is so horribly wrong there, but what has it got to do with me? I can't shake the feeling that there is some kind of evil in the past that is strangling my life. And I must find out what it is and expose it to the light before it ruins my life. There must have been deceit in Grandmother's life, and I have adopted her values. What if those values are false? What if they are based on lies? I cannot walk blithely along through my life making decisions based on a set of values that are false. But it's so totally confusing. Maybe Mother can shed some light on it. I see now that there must have been a reason why she turned away from Grandmother's way of life.

Caroline picked up the phone and dialed her mother's home. The maid answered the phone. When Caroline asked where her mother was, the maid told her that Marian had gone to the cemetery, to the grave site of Judith, and that she had insisted on going alone.

When Caroline arrived at the cemetery, she found Marian standing by a mound of freshly-turned soil that was heaped with wilting flowers. Caroline approached her quietly; Marian saw her coming and held out her hand to her daughter. When Caroline reached her side, Marian put her arm around Caroline's shoulders and said, "How are you, dear? I hope you slept."

"I did, Mother, and I'm fine. I woke up about 9:30 last night, but I didn't call you. I was afraid you were asleep. I was hoping you were asleep by then."

"I was, dear, very soundly asleep."

"I'm so sorry I couldn't help you yesterday. I shall never forgive myself for—"

"Hush, Caroline. You stayed with me for two solid days at the funeral home. You did everything your body would allow you to do, and then you did me the favor of having the common sense to go home and take care of yourself and your child. Don't you understand that that's much more important to me?"

"If you say so," Caroline agreed quietly. She stared down at the mound of dirt. It had rained during the night; the flowers had been beaten down by the water, and the dirt had turned to mud. "I can't believe Grandmother is really here," Caroline mumbled as tears sprang to her eyes.

"She isn't," Marian said firmly. "Only her body is here."

Caroline nodded and said nothing for a few moments. Then in spite of her efforts not to ask the question, she asked, "Where is she, Mother?"

"I don't know," Marian said, as she turned to look Caroline in the face. "I don't know where your grandmother is, and that fact frightens me and makes me truly grieve. The minister said she was in heaven; but you don't get to heaven, Caroline, by giving money to a church, by buying an organ and a rose window."

"You're talking about—about beliefs, aren't you, Mother?" Caroline worded the question carefully.

"I'm talking about Jesus Christ, Caroline. I realize it makes you uncomfortable when I mention His name, but the truth is the truth. All our bodies come to this," Marian pointed to the mud, "but our souls are eternal, and we spend our eternity in heaven or hell. It is belief in Jesus that makes heaven open its doors to us."

"What did Grandmother believe, about God—about Jesus—I mean?"

"I don't know," Marian said. "It's a terrible thing. She was my mother, and I knew her over sixty years, but I don't know what she believed about God or about His Son."

Marian began to weep. The tears flowed down her cheeks, and Caroline took her in her arms. "Oh, Mother, I'm sure she's fine."

"I'm not sure," Marian sobbed. "I tried to talk to her many times—oh, so many times!"

And you tried to talk to me, too, Caroline thought, but she didn't say that. Instead she asked, "What did Grandmother say?" although she could easily imagine her Grandmother's response.

"Pretty much always the same thing. 'I don't have time for that nonsense.' Something like that. So I tried to show her; I tried to live a life of faith so she would re-examine all the beliefs she had turned away from so long ago. I thought my own life might convince her when my words always seemed to fail."

Caroline felt panic and confusion. I don't know what I believe either, she thought. I don't understand any of this. I don't understand the future, and I don't understand how the past, the past Grandmother tried to burn all record of, has reached into the present and left an evil stain; but I can't ask Mother, not now, not for a long time. She's too upset. But I don't have time. Perhaps I'm just being selfish, but I feel compelled to untangle my life *now*. What am I going to do? Normally I would run to Grandmother, and she would have an answer, and I would just accept it as fact. But I'm not sure I could believe her now, even if she were here to advise me. Her death, the way she died, has convinced me that there was something wrong, deep down, about Grandmother's beliefs about life. I have to know why she was like she was, where she was right and where she was wrong, because I have become a carbon copy of her. Whatever is in the past I must uncover it. No matter how ugly it is. I must go to Charleston. Mother went to Great Aunt Kathleen; I must go see her, too. Even if Mother has made this journey before me, I see now that I must make my own pilgrimage.

Chapter 11

Two days later Caroline opened an exquisitely ornamented wrought-iron gate into the secluded garden of a Charleston, South Carolina house. She had a compelling feeling that she was opening a door into a new understanding of life. She paused with her hand on the gate and looked around. A magnificent, Charleston-style house with a two-storied, double verandah facing the sea dominated the land, but it had strong competition from a glorious garden surrounding it. Caroline's eyes were drawn to a very large and venerable, old live oak, which at some places in the garden draped its dark, massive arms down to the ground itself. It was the season of azaleas, and the garden was a visual delight of rose, pink and white blossoms cascading over hundreds of shrubs. Several hundred years of history seemed to evaporate as Caroline passed through the gate; she was walking into another age.

The garden was silent, except for natural noises, the sound of a light, gentle breeze, a single songbird rejoicing in the beauty of the moment. The adrenaline flow that had pushed Caroline so hard for days tapered off. Her anxiety level dropped, and her pulse actually slowed. Gentleness possessed her and erased from her memory her carefully calculated plans for her stay in Charleston.

"Would you be so kind as to hold this bowl of water for me, my dear?" A voice with an unmistakable Charleston accent quietly asked from a corner of the garden to the left of Caroline. She turned in surprise and saw an elderly lady standing in the midst of a corner rose garden eagerly holding out a glass bowl of water to her. Caroline snapped out of her passive response to the garden, exerted her self-control, and walked toward the lady to give the help that she had requested.

"Of course," she said as she drew close to the elderly lady.

"You see, my dear, a rose should always have water brought to it. Many people cut a rose and take it into the house and put it in water, but that approach never produces the best results. It is essential that water never cease to flow up the stem of a rose, and with just the slightest care, one can see to it that the rose will always have the water it needs. Thus, the rose will last twice as long, become a magnificent explosion of color, and be able to become the delightful creation that God meant it to be."

Caroline nodded as she examined the woman's face. The lady had beautiful silver hair. It was swept up on top of her head with a delicate grace. Caroline judged her to be about 85 years of age, but in spite of the wrinkles on her face, her skin had a translucent whiteness that was remarkably beautiful, and her blue-gray eyes were very clear.

"Now the way we accomplish keeping water flowing through the stem of the rose up to its magnificent bud is that we quickly cut the rose from the bush, and we dip the end of it into this bowl of water"—the lady demonstrated as she spoke. "From this point on we must be diligently cautious to work only under the water. We insert our clippers, cut off about half an inch of stem, hold the stem under the water for a few seconds, and then we quickly take this particular rose stem and drop it into the vase of water that is waiting right here on the table." Caroline held the bowl of water as the lady did precisely what she said.

"Roses are not a bit different from people, my dear," the lady continued. "Any time a person's nutrients, whether physical, emotional, or spiritual are interrupted, there is bound to be damage to that person. If we are each and every one of us to become the flower that God intended us to be, we must work very hard not to interrupt the flow of nutrients that He has given us."

Caroline said only, "Yes, ma'am."

The elderly lady turned and clipped another rose, moved it immediately to the bowl of water that Caroline held, clipped a half an inch off the stem while it was still under water, held the stem in the water for a few seconds, then immediately plunged it into the vase. "There, I think that's just about all we can use in this vase," she announced. She put her clippers down on the table and took the bowl of water from Caroline. Then she turned and looked Caroline directly in the eyes. "I'm so glad to meet you at last, Caroline," she said simply.

Caroline was startled that the lady knew her. "I beg your pardon," she said.

"I said, my dear, that I am so glad to meet you at last. I am your Great Aunt Kathleen."

"Oh," Caroline said very ungracefully. "Oh dear—ah—well, I'm very glad to meet you too, Great Aunt Kathleen. But how did you know who I am?"

"Well, my dear, I am neither blind nor senile, at least not yet, and I do have your wedding picture on my piano."

"On your piano?" Caroline asked in a bewildered tone.

"Yes, of course, my dear. That's where I keep the pictures of all the people that are on my mind."

"On your mind? Am I on your mind?"

"Why, how could you not be on my mind, my dear?" Great Aunt Kathleen picked up the vase of roses. "Considering the needs that you have now, I would naturally want to be saying a little prayer for you now and then. Would you mind getting the bowl of water and the clippers for me, my dear? Then we can go into the house and settle on the piazza with a nice cup of tea and get acquainted. I have waited a long time for this moment, and I must confess that I am rather excited by it."

"Yes, of course." Caroline snapped to attention and picked up the bowl and the clippers. "But, Great Aunt Kathleen, how did you know that I was having difficulties? Did Mother call you?"

"Oh, no. Of course, she called me when my sister died. I am so sorry I was not able to attend her funeral, but I have not spoken to your mother in several days, and she did not mention you."

"Then how did you know that I have some things on my mind?" Caroline tried to phrase it lightly.

"I don't know, my dear. I have just felt for the last three or four weeks that you were quite bothered by something. Well, let us get that cup of tea and get you settled in your room. I have it all ready for you."

"My room?" Caroline gasped.

"Why yes, my dear. I had the maid prepare it about a week ago."

"But that was before Grandmother died, before Mother even called you."

"Yes, I suppose it was."

"Why would you have a room prepared for me a week ago?" Caroline demanded more forcefully than she thought was polite.

"I knew you were coming," Great Aunt Kathleen smiled sweetly. "And, please, don't ask me how I knew. I just did, and the room is all ready and here you are. Obviously whatever drove me to know you were coming was correct. But then it always has been. I can't think why I should be the least bit surprised anymore."

"You must be psychic or something," Caroline exclaimed.

"Oh no, oh heavens no! I don't believe in any of that stuff. I just think the good Lord tells me what I need to know, and apparently I needed to know that you were coming. I don't move around quite as fast as I used to, so He gave me a bit of notice, you see. He might have told me last evening or yesterday, but He is a very gracious God, and He takes into account my age, and so He seems to have given me a week's notice. Come along, my dear. Be careful not to slosh the water on your pretty outfit. We'll have these roses nicely arranged and placed on the table in the piazza in no time, and then we shall have a steaming cup of tea and a nice visit. Just follow me." Great Aunt Kathleen started toward the house but soon stopped abruptly and exclaimed, "Oh look, Caroline! Look there at the alyssum. Isn't that beautiful? That's what you smell. So sweet, just getting started, of course. That plant will be a brightening force in this garden for the entire summer, and the fragrance will almost be more than one can bear at times. And aren't the azaleas absolutely magnificent this year? I declare, I cannot bear to cut them back, but they are about to take over the paths. I do so love azaleas," she continued as she began walking once more down the winding path toward the house. Suddenly she stopped again and turned back toward Caroline. "They are so incredibly beautiful, but only for a short time. They remind me of the fleetingness of a lot of things I cherish. Perhaps it is better to consider something like that old oak over there, or maybe even the sky itself. Yes, the sky is best, I think. It leads one's thoughts to more eternal things, of course. Oh my, let us get that cup of tea. I have been working in this garden for hours, and I declare I certainly deserve a cup. Oh good, here comes Betsy. She will fuss at me; get ready for it, but her bark is a great deal worse than her bite, my dear. Yes, Betsy, I am coming in. I know. Here, take the vase of roses, and take this bowl of water from Caroline."

"Miz Kathleen, you shouldn't oughta be out in the sun that long, and you know—"

"Betsy, I would like you to meet my great niece, Caroline Forrest Randolph."

"I's glad to meet you," Betsy said as she took the bowl of water from Caroline. "We's been waitin' for you any day now."

"Caroline," Great Aunt Kathleen said, "this is Betsy. As you will quickly discover, she is the true proprietor of this house and runs it with an iron fist."

"I don't do no such thing, Miz Kathleen," Betsy replied indignantly, as Caroline looked over the stocky, brown-skinned woman with the gray hair that was pulled tightly away from her face and wound into a ball on the top of her head. "I just tries my best to take care of you, that's what I does."

"Whatever you say, Betsy. I always do what you tell me," Great Aunt Kathleen winked at Caroline.

"Hmm!" said Betsy.

"Betsy," Great Aunt Kathleen ignored Betsy's response, "I'll take Miss Caroline upstairs and show her her bedroom and allow her to freshen up, and then we shall have some tea on the upper piazza."

"Why can't you have your tea down here, Miz Kathleen?"

"Because I prefer to have it on the upper piazza, Betsy." Great Aunt Kathleen walked past Betsy, who now held the vase of roses in one hand and a bowl of water in the other.

"But Miz Kathleen," Betsy rushed behind her. "The doctor say you needs to stay off them stairs."

"One can't stay off of stairs, Betsy, when one lives in a three-story house. Besides, I want Caroline to see the view from the upstairs piazza."

"But you's just gonna have to come back down them stairs for supper, and then you'll have to go back up them stairs to go to bed."

"Well, of course I shall," Great Aunt Kathleen turned and smiled sweetly at Betsy.

"You's gonna die on them stairs if you don't die out in that garden," Betsy declared.

Great Aunt Kathleen looked at Caroline and said wryly, "This is generally when Betsy puts her hands on her hips, but since I have conveniently taken control of her hands, she can't do what she usually does. Follow me, Caroline, I'll show you to your room upstairs, since Betsy feels the stairs are too much for her."

"Hmm," said Betsy.

"Tea on the upstairs piazza," Great Aunt Kathleen announced again. Then she began a slow ascent up an awesome staircase that wound in a serpentine movement and seemed to be suspended in air. Caroline followed, glad that Great Aunt Kathleen couldn't move quickly up the stairs, for she was able to admire the incredible craftsmanship of the suspended staircase.

"You'll soon get accustomed, my dear, to the construction of Charleston houses. Typical Charleston houses have nothing to look at on one side, except, of course, the sky and the tops of trees, as you can see. The houses all face to one side. The piazzas are on the side toward the sea to capture the sea breeze, so naturally enough, that is where one puts one's garden."

"Great Aunt Kathleen," Caroline stopped her, because the older lady seemed to be out of breath. "How on earth does this staircase stay up? There seems to be nothing holding it up."

"Oh, I can't explain that, my dear. It was built a long time ago and has withstood the War Between the States and a very massive earthquake, so I think we can trust it for a few more years anyway. And by the way, Caroline, it is very cumbersome for you to keep calling me Great Aunt Kathleen. Why don't we just drop the 'great'? I am not feeling particularly old anyway. Why don't you just call me Aunt Kathleen?"

Caroline smiled at her, as the dignified lady turned and continued her slow ascent to the second floor.

"Now, here we are. In an historic Charleston house, this is the floor where the majority of the social action occurs. As you can see, there is a hall beginning here at the staircase that goes straight out to the second floor piazza." Caroline followed her great aunt slowly as she was given a tour. "And over to the left we have the drawing room. This is the formal drawing room. And to the right we have a matching formal drawing room. Naturally, there are two drawing rooms because there were many large functions such as balls and receptions held in this house in the past; a great deal of room was needed for the guests. The windows, as you see, go down to the floor so they can be opened and one can walk out of them onto the piazza. The piazza is something of an outdoor living room, outdoor parlor, in Charleston. Now, down this hall there are a number of bedrooms, and, of course, there's a floor above us with quite a few bedrooms; but I'm afraid the third floor is something I haven't seen in a year or two now. I have enough difficulty with Betsy and her fussing about my coming up this far. Fortunately, we have two large bedrooms on this floor, one for me and one for my special guest."

"Now this first bedroom is mine," she ushered Caroline into a large, high-ceilinged room. "I had it painted sunshine yellow when I came here as a bride, and it has not been changed in over sixty years, although the paint has been refurbished occasionally, of course. I am assured by a number of people in Charleston that sunshine yellow is not an appropriate color for the age of the house, but it is an appropriate color for me. Now, let us go down the hall a little further, my dear, and we have my second most favorite bedroom in the house, and that is my blue room. I painted it the color of the sea. I think it will just fit you because it reminds me a great deal of the color of your eyes." She opened a large, paneled door and ushered Caroline into a beautiful blue room, the space of which was monopolized by a large canopy bed with a white crocheted spread. Over the top there was draped an heirloom, hand-tied, fishnet canopy.

Aunt Kathleen walked across the highly-polished, heart of pine floors and opened up French doors onto the piazza. "The lovely thing about the two bedrooms on this floor, my dear, is the ability one has to go outside any time and gaze at the flowers, or revel in the sunshine, or perhaps even dream in the moonlight." Caroline followed her out onto the piazza, then across the width of the piazza to the railing. "Oh!" she exclaimed when she saw the view of the harbor.

"It's magical, isn't it, my dear?" Great Aunt Kathleen sighed happily.

"Magical, that's the perfect word to describe it," Caroline agreed.

"No matter where you look from this piazza, Caroline, you see beauty, whether you're looking out to sea, where the sky meets the water, or whether you're looking straight down into the garden at the flowers with their faces all turned up to smile back at you."

Caroline was awe-struck by what she saw. "I can see why the Bradfords loved Charleston," she murmured.

"Yes, and you are a Bradford, my dear, and you've waited far too long to come home."

"I think you're right," Caroline agreed. "But there's something that puzzles me. Grandmother always described Charleston as being exquisitely beautiful, and now that I'm here, I see that she was absolutely right. It is beautiful, but I keep wondering, if Grandmother loved Charleston so much, why didn't she return after her marriage? She never came back, did she?"

"No, my dear. Your grandmother never came back to Charleston after her marriage. She made Texas her home, and from all the accounts I have heard, she made a marvelous job of it."

"Yes," Caroline said, with a certain hesitancy in her voice. "In some ways she was quite successful."

"You must miss Judith a great deal, my dear. I understand you were very close to her."

"We were very close," Caroline agreed, as she ran her hand along the railing of the piazza. "We were very much alike, I think. I can't imagine how I shall do without her advice in so many areas of my life. She was a very dominant force; she shaped me."

"Yes," Aunt Kathleen said quietly. "Judith was dominant, wherever she was. She had a very strong personality and quite decided opinions, as you no doubt know."

"Opinions I was very comfortable with," Caroline said wistfully.

"Are you still comfortable with them?"

"I don't know." Tears filled Caroline's eyes as she spoke.

"Well, we have plenty of time to talk about that later, or whatever it is you've come to talk about. You've come home, my dear. I know you are Texas born and bred, but there is Bradford blood flowing in your body, and Bradford blood always seeks this place at some point. I shall leave you now to freshen up. You know your way around the house a bit; make yourself totally at home. I shall go tidy up myself and sit on the piazza and wait for Betsy to bring up the tea."

When Caroline joined Aunt Kathleen on the piazza, she walked immediately to the railing and stared out toward the harbor. A few clouds had gathered, light airy clouds that were just beginning to catch the light from the west, creating the slightest beginnings of what promised to be a sensational sunset.

"It's going to be a lovely end of the day," Aunt Kathleen commented from her wicker chair. "I believe God is going to put on quite a show with His sunset this evening. You wait and see if I am not right. Betsy will have the perfect excuse to suggest that we dine here instead of downstairs in the dining room in a proper fashion."

Caroline laughed softly. "I'm sure she has your best interests at heart, Aunt Kathleen."

"Oh, she does, she does, my dear. She's taken care of me for a long, long time, and I don't know what I would do without her, but I cannot give up living just because she is concerned."

Caroline turned back and looked at the beautiful, elderly lady who was surrounded by the grandeur of the old house and the many flowering plants that she nurtured on the piazza. "And will you let her persuade you to have supper here?" Caroline asked lightly. "I can't think of a better place to dine."

"Oh, of course I shall let her persuade me, my dear—but not too easily. That would not be nearly as much fun for either one of us, would it?"

"No, I suppose not," Caroline agreed.

"Come sit here, my dear. I hear Betsy trudging up the stairs with the tea tray. I do believe she comes up those stairs much more slowly than I do, although she will not admit it. I tried bringing in a younger woman to help her. You can imagine what kind of furor that caused." Caroline settled comfortably on a wicker settee as she laughed. "You haven't mentioned David. I suppose business kept him in Texas."

"No, he's in London. He came down with pneumonia right after Grandmother—" Caroline stopped to choke back her tears.

"After Judith passed away," Aunt Kathleen hurried to finish Caroline's sentence. "How awful for you! How torn you must have felt." Caroline could only nod. Aunt Kathleen continued speaking to give Caroline time to recover. "He must be better now, or you would not be here, I am sure."

"Yes, he's much better," Caroline murmured. "The doctor is letting him sit up. Oh, I should be in London, but he wouldn't let me come!"

"I am sure he is fine, my dear, but you look very tired. We shall have our tea and a quiet supper and put you to bed early. Here comes Betsy now."

Betsy walked through the French doors with the tea tray and put it down on a table in front of Aunt Kathleen. Aunt Kathleen lifted the teapot and began to pour the first cup of tea. Betsy wandered over to the railing and exclaimed, "Sure is gonna be a beautiful sunset, Miz Kathleen."

"Oh really?" Aunt Kathleen refused to look out and sounded as nonchalant as she could.

"Yes ma'am. The Lord, He gonna paint quite a picture tonight."

"Well, He's very good at that, isn't He, Betsy? Caroline, do you take milk and sugar, or would you prefer lemon?"

"Milk and sugar," Caroline said as she tried not to laugh.

"You knows what I think, Miz Kathleen?"

"No, Betsy, I am sure I could not imagine what you are thinking," Aunt Kathleen said as she poured a little milk into Caroline's cup, added a teaspoon of sugar and slowly stirred the steaming tea.

Betsy turned away from the railing and bustled over to the tea table. "I thinks you oughta have supper right up here on the piazza, so Miz Caroline can get the full beauty of the harbor and the Lord's grand sunset. That's what I think."

Kathleen handed Caroline her cup of tea, slowly reached for the creamer and poured some milk into the bottom of another cup before she looked up at Betsy. "What was that, Betsy?" There was a twinkle in her eyes, but she maintained a very sober expression on her face.

"The harbor, Miz Kathleen, the sunset. It gonna be beautiful tonight. This be where you oughta have supper for Miz Caroline's first night in Charleston."

Aunt Kathleen lifted the teapot and filled her teacup. "What a remarkable idea," she said quietly. "Oh, I don't think so, Betsy. We really should entertain Caroline properly, especially on her first evening here. I think you should set out supper in the dining room below."

"But Miz Kathleen, that dining room, well, it be too low; it don't show off the view of the harbor."

Aunt Kathleen put a spoonful of sugar in her tea and stirred it slowly. "I suppose that is true enough, Betsy," she said noncommittally.

"And it won't be no trouble at all for me to fix up a nice table up here on the piazza, with a fine linen cloth and our very best china and silver."

"Well," Aunt Kathleen paused as if she were considering the matter for the first time. "I would not want the food to get cold, and it is such a long way up here from the kitchen."

"Oh, I can see to that," Betsy insisted. "I'll keep everything nice and warm. You don't need to worry about nothing. Sides, it might be raining tomorrow. Miz Caroline could enjoy the dining room tomorrow while it be raining."

"Have you heard the weather forecast?" Aunt Kathleen looked

Betsy in the face, showing no hint of her purpose.

"Well, no ma'am," Betsy admitted, "but it gonna be a full moon tonight, and a full moon can mean showers tomorrow."

"Oh, the moon," Aunt Kathleen said more eagerly. "Yes, of course, Betsy, I had forgotten the moon. You have convinced me. Caroline must see the moon from the piazza, and supper will be the perfect time to see it."

Betsy smiled widely. "I'll start gettin' things ready," she hurried off, and Caroline was finally able to giggle.

"I don't think either one of you is fooling the other," Caroline said.

"No, my dear, I doubt that anyone is fooling anyone," Aunt Kathleen laughed softly. "But two old women have to have a little something to have fun over."

"I really would like to have supper up here, Aunt Kathleen, whether you had to climb stairs or not."

"Of course you would, my dear. Anyone would. It really is going to be quite beautiful tonight. But you did not come to Charleston to watch the moon rise or to watch the sunset, or even to look at our magnificent harbor and gardens. You must be almost thirty-five years old, I believe. So if you have waited thirty-five years to come, why have you come now? Has it something to do with Judith's death?"

"In a way," Caroline admitted; then she sipped her tea. "To be perfectly honest, Aunt Kathleen, I'm not sure why I'm here. I'm looking for answers to questions."

"I shall be most happy to answer any questions I can, my dear. What are your questions?"

"That's the difficulty," Caroline said. "I don't know the questions."

"I see," Aunt Kathleen murmured. "Perhaps if you are here a few days, you will discover what the questions are. They must be somewhere inside of you, my dear, to have made you come so far."

"There is one question I do know, Aunt Kathleen. It's really a small, historical thing, but in the oddest way I have a sense that it's important. It's about the family."

"Well, I shall do my best to answer it."

"It's about my great grandmother, your mother, the Caroline I was named for."

"Oh, I do remember so well when you were named Caroline. I

thought Judith would have an absolute fit. Marian, thankfully, stuck to her decision, however, but what question could you possibly want to ask about my mother?"

"Well, it's a very peculiar thing. I don't know what Mother told you about Grandmother's death, but she died trying to burn some family papers, and a few of them remained. When I was looking through them, I found two certificates of marriage for Caroline Bradford, one to a man named Montgomery and one to a man named Kendall; and there was less than a month's time between those two marriages," Caroline laughed nervously. "I feel perfectly silly talking about this. It was such a long time ago, and I can't imagine why it's so important to me."

Aunt Kathleen said nothing for a few moments, and Caroline thought that perhaps the subject made her great aunt uncomfortable for some reason. "If you don't want to talk about it, Aunt Kathleen, it really isn't all that important."

"Oh, it is important, Caroline. It is very important. The lives that were affected by those two marriages were real. Your great grandmother, Caroline, suffered great pain, but she also experienced an ecstatic joy and a deep peace. I was not there to see it all, of course, because I had not been born, but I often heard Mother talk of it; and she kept the most beautiful diary about the journey that she took during those years, as well as the journey her mother, Mary, had taken before her. It is really quite a remarkable story, my dear, one that I think will surprise you, lift you up, and I believe, teach you something. Indeed, it may teach you the very thing you came here to learn."

"But what is that?" Caroline asked quickly.

"I don't know," Aunt Kathleen responded. "I can only tell you the story, and you can only listen; but if you listen with both your spirit and your ears, I think that you will know when you hear the answer you came for. Can I pour you another cup of tea, my dear?"

"Yes, please." Caroline rose from her seat, walked to the railing and looked out at the harbor. The sky was becoming a beautiful, impressionistic landscape of pastel shades. The garden below had fallen into shadow, but the white azaleas popped out of that shadow with amazing clarity, like spots of pure light. A gentle breeze was blowing across the piazza, and it carried the scents of the ocean and the fragrances of all the flowers of the neighborhood. Caroline had the strangest perception that reality had opened its hidden, golden doors—just barely opened them—and that she was about to peer into a place she very much needed to see. She turned and looked at her great aunt, who was watching her.

"I feel very strange," she said to Aunt Kathleen. "I feel as if I am lifted up by supportive arms, as if I am about to see into something I need to see, and that I am being supported as I look, supported by the kindliest, most loving presence."

Her great aunt only responded with a knowing smile.

"Aunt Kathleen, have you ever felt that you were in just the right place at just the right time, and somehow there was a different glimpse of reality coming your way?" Caroline asked eagerly.

"A special gift from heaven," Aunt Kathleen murmured.

"Yes, something like that."

"Oh yes, my dear, life does have those times in it. They are frequently quite brief. They seem to be giving us a reflection of another world that exists along side of ours, and it is a world of great beauty and peace and understanding."

"Well, I feel like that now," Caroline exclaimed. "I feel like that, as I stand here on this piazza looking out at the sea and the sky."

"They are beautiful," Aunt Kathleen agreed, "but it is not they that move us into this other realm. It is the Creator of the sky and the sea."

"I have discovered recently," Caroline admitted, "that I don't know much about that Creator."

"Perhaps that is why you came to Charleston, my dear. Perhaps that is at least one of the questions that you hope to have answered here, although I warn you, you will never have questions about God answered completely or even to your satisfaction. Do you want to talk about the first Caroline now, or are you too tired from your trip?"

"Oh, I'm not too tired," Caroline spoke eagerly, then remembered her great aunt's age, "but you have been gardening. Perhaps you're too tired."

"I am never too tired to speak of Mother's wonderful journey, my dear. We shall have to begin, however, much, much earlier than those two marriage certificates that you found. In fact, we shall have to begin long before Mother was born."

"Oh, Aunt Kathleen. I didn't tell you the other thing that stimulated me to come and talk to you. There was a great storm that passed over my house in Texas, and a tree fell through the drawing room window and ripped a shadowbox off the wall that contained James Bradford's vest."

"Yes," Aunt Kathleen nodded. "I know the vest you mean. It belonged to my grandfather."

"Yes, it did. That's the one," Caroline's voice rose with excitement. "Well, you see I was left alone in the house after the shattering experience of the storm; and just to keep my mind off of things, I took a close look at that vest, and I found a small piece of paper caught between the lining and the outside of the vest. I did something that, perhaps, I shouldn't have done. I opened a seam in the pocket, and I found the paper, and I read it."

"What did it say, my dear?"

"It was in a fine, spidery handwriting, and it was obviously very old because the ink had turned brown, but all it said was, 'He knows nothing. Meet me at midnight.'" Caroline laughed nervously. "It's silly, isn't it, such a non-specific, general kind of communication, and yet it struck me as being so meaningful to my life. I think I may be going a little crazy."

"I don't think so, my dear," Aunt Kathleen responded gravely. "Indeed, that vest is where we need to begin the story of my mother, the story I believe you came here to hear, because her story begins with James Bradford, who was her father and who wore that vest."

"Tell me, please tell me," Caroline leaned forward toward her great aunt, feeling absolutely positive her own life was caught up in this story of so long ago.

Aunt Kathleen's eyes took on a faraway expression as she stared past Caroline at the horizon where the water and sky met. When she spoke, it was obvious that through her own imagination she had transported herself back in time. She told her story as if she were seeing it happen before her eyes.

In 1868 James Bradford dipped the oars of a small boat into the murky river water and strained his shoulders forward as he worked to skim the boat across the water toward the opposite shore. The full moon moved out from behind a cloud and sent a shaft of light down and across the ivory silk vest he was wearing. Five more times James Bradford thrust the oars down into the water and pulled back with all his might.

When he gained the shore, he leapt out of the boat lightly and dragged it up onto the sand. For a moment he stood straight and stared across the water at the land that had been owned by his family for generations. The moon showered its light across the front of the ivory silk vest and displayed the intricate embroidery of tendrils of vines and tiny flowers that had been the height of fashion for a man of wealth before the War Between the States. Now, three years after the War, a man was fortunate, indeed, to have such a garment to wear. So much had been destroyed by the War. James reached into his pocket and pulled out the large-faced gold watch that had been so precious to him that he had risked burying it before he had marched off to fight the Yankees. He flipped open the lid and noted that it was almost midnight. Abruptly he turned and began walking up a path that no one else would have been able to see in the darkness, a path he obviously knew well.

In a short time he came to a shed, a small wooden structure that had at one time before the War been an overseer's office, a place from which the plantation's overseer could direct the slaves as they tended and harvested the rice crop that made the plantation's owner so wealthy. The shack looked like it had been deserted for years, but James walked in confidently, and even though it was pitch dark inside, he walked straight to a small table. He reached for a candlestick, struck a match and produced a dim light in the shack. Eerie shadows danced along the four walls as the candle flame flickered in the slight breeze that inevitably slipped past the loose boards of the walls. James paced around the room, and every time he turned toward the candle the gleam in his eyes became quite evident. He was a handsome man, tall, broad shouldered, with dark hair, a dark beard and light brown eyes. Agitation was evident in all his movements as he paced the shack several times before stopping next to the table, pulling out his watch, and checking the time again. It was now 12:15. "Will she come?" he questioned aloud. He reached inside his vest pocket, and when he could not immediately find what he sought, he uttered an oath of exasperation, plunged his fingers more deeply into the pocket. This time his fingers went through the pocket's lining and grabbed a small piece of paper He pulled it out, unfolded it, and leaned close to the candle to read it. "He knows nothing. Meet me at midnight." James sighed heavily and thrust the note back into the pocket of his vest.

"She should have been mine," he spoke angrily to the walls. "What right does Montgomery have to her? Thomas Montgomery! He's nothing but a gouty old fool, old enough to be her father and more, too old to fight the Yankees, too old to fight for his own land, but not too old to steal a soldier's beloved. How I hate him!"

He walked to the door, opened it, stepped out and peered into the moonlit woods in the direction away from the river. Silently he demanded of himself, if Thomas Montgomery is a fool, what on earth does that make me? I loved Diana for years, and I knew her, knew her well. Only a fool would leave such a woman and go off to war without marrying her first. She never deceived me. I knew she wasn't capable of faithfulness. I knew I should have married her before I left. Then she would be mine now, and we would not be meeting in the shame of darkness. But if I had married her before the war and then left, she would have betrayed me with some other man. I know my Diana. What I don't know is how such a woman could possess my heart all these years. She is beautiful, incredibly beautiful, it's true, but there is more to it than that. She has such power to possess—yes, possess is the right word. She has been able to possess me, somehow. So here I am like a schoolboy walking the floor, waiting out the time, minute by minute, until she can get away from that husband of hers and meet me in the dark. What kind of man am I?

He struck the door frame with his fist as he turned to re-enter the shack. What kind of man allows a woman to control his feelings so completely that he violates his own ethics? The minute the word 'ethics' entered his mind, the face of his wife appeared in his mind's eye, and his thoughts turned to her. My dear, sweet Mary. She was glad enough to marry me after the War, but what madness made me marry her? What madness made me marry Diana's cousin? Was it anger, cold fury that Diana had married another? Oh yes, when I returned from the War, there were weepings and wailings from Diana—her regrets that she had not waited longer. She said, of course, that she had presumed I was dead, so she had taken an old man to her bed because she could not stand the thought of any other young man but me. But she would not leave Thomas Montgomery. Diana is a great one for propriety on the outside, in the public eye. So I knew I could never marry her, not for years and years until that fool Montgomery was dead. With unforgivable impetuosity I turned around and sought a woman who at least looked like Diana, and that, of course, was Mary. There she was, a younger, more innocent version of Diana, the same auburn hair, the same creamy skin, the same blue-gray eyes, but oh what a different kind of woman she was! How very different, I was soon to learn.

James broke off his thoughts of the past and strode to the candle on the table to look at his watch once again. It was almost one o'clock. Anxiety tightened his chest as he demanded silently, where is she? Then he drew in his breath quickly. Could he have caught her? No. He was so drunk by the time dinner was over, he must have passed out. Diana says he drinks himself to sleep every night; besides, it has been hours since Mary and I left the dinner party at their house, drove home, and went to bed ourselves. Sweet Mary, with such an easy conscience she falls asleep, just like a child, totally trusting. I should have thought the War would have taught her about the ugliness of life, but she is still so innocent, so pure. She expects nothing from me and gets even less. Diana, Diana, where are you? He stomped to the door again and stared out into the tangled woods. I hate to think of her on that path. If only she would bring her maid, but she will trust no one. I cannot stand this. I am going to go look for her.

He started down the path just as the moon slid behind a bank of clouds and plunged the path into inky darkness. He uttered an oath as he was forced to stop by the blackness, but the increased darkness made him able to spot a tiny light in the woods. He drew in his breath quickly. "Diana," he whispered. In spite of the difficulties he began to walk hurriedly down the darkened path, and in a few moments he met her. She stumbled into his arms and began to sob; her hair and clothing were all disheveled.

"It's one o'clock," he exclaimed, as if that would calm her. "What happened? Where have you been?"

"Oh, James," she cried. "I could not get away. He did not drink himself into a stupor after you and the other guests left. He always sits on the verandah and drinks until he passes out. Then I have his man put him to bed. But not tonight." She sobbed more furiously.

"Not here, my love." James tried to control his temper which was boiling over. "Hold your lantern carefully," he directed as he swept Diana into his arms.

As quickly as he could, he carried her up the path, through the door of the shack and placed her on a makeshift bed. He took the lantern from her hand and put it on the floor. He hated himself for asking, but he could not contain his words.

"He did not touch you, did he?" he demanded.

"No, no," Diana shook her tear-stained face. "He was too drunk for anything but shouting."

"What has *he* got to shout about?"

"He's furious because I have given him nothing but daughters."

James' mind exploded at the thought of another man touching his Diana. How he wanted to kill him! "The fool has no right to touch you at all," James shouted. "Sons, daughters—what does it matter? He has no right to either one from you."

"James! Lower your voice, and remember he is my husband. He wants an heir; he plans to have one too. Thank God he was too drunk tonight to do anything but pace around my bedroom, a decanter of whisky in his hands. He ranted about the dynasty of sons he wants. He even threatened to divorce me if I do not have a son."

"He cannot do that; he cannot divorce you on those grounds, I only wish he could divorce you!"

"What?" Diana's sobs ceased instantly. She sat bolt upright. "A divorce? Never! I thought you loved me."

"I do love you," James insisted hotly. "That is exactly why I wish he could divorce you. Then we could be married."

"What kind of life would that be? I would lose my position in society."

"I don't care a whit for your position in society," James raised his voice. "If you were divorced, you could be mine, really mine."

"I can see no logic in exchanging one misery for another," Diana insisted. "If I could not hold up my head in society, I would just as soon be dead."

"What is more important to you," James demanded, "your position in society or being mine?"

Diana changed her tone instantly and threw her arms around his neck. "Oh my darling, darling James. I am yours now. I always will be. Even when I am old and gray and you desire me no more"—she began kissing his face and neck fervently.

"That time will never come—never!" James exclaimed as he pulled away from her long enough to blow out the lantern. Then he took her in his arms.

"I can't believe this," Caroline exclaimed to Great Aunt Kathleen. "Did Grandmother know about this?"

"Of course she did, my dear," Aunt Kathleen replied. "After all, James Bradford was her grandfather, just as he was mine."

"But she never told me a word of this."

"That is not surprising, is it?"

"But how could Grandmother have worshipped such a man?" Caroline jumped to her feet, paced away from Aunt Kathleen, then abruptly turned and walked back toward her. "What selfishness! What deplorable values! How could Grandmother have worshipped him all these years?"

"He had wealth and position, Caroline, and I regret to say that in Judith's eyes, those were the things that counted."

"Oh yes, I know all that," Caroline waved her hand in the air as if to dismiss Aunt Kathleen's words. "I heard it often enough from Grandmother. She was always talking about the great Bradford legacy, her wonderful grandfather, a man of wealth, power, and prestige, the incredible blue blood that ran in her veins and also in mine. I can't tell you how often she exhorted me to live up to the great Bradford legacy. Some legacy!"

"Oh, but there *is* a great Bradford legacy." Aunt Kathleen rose from her chair, took Caroline by the shoulders and stared with burning eagerness into Caroline's eyes. "You must believe that, Caroline. There *is* a great Bradford legacy, but it is not the legacy of James Bradford. That is a counterfeit of the true legacy."

"A counterfeit?" Caroline questioned.

"Yes," Aunt Kathleen explained. "The genuine Bradford legacy comes down to us from Mary Bradford and her daughter, Caroline

Bradford Kendall, my mother. Oh, have no doubt of it, Caroline. There is a great Bradford legacy."

"But Grandmother never mentioned her mother or her grandmother. She only talked about her grandfather, James Bradford."

"She never mentioned our mother or our grandmother because she was ashamed of them. You see, my dear, Judith, your grandmother, had no appreciation for the finest things of life, the inner qualities of people. She cared only for outward appearances. I know it is not right to speak ill of the dead, but Judith had over ninety years to rectify her mistakes and give you a balanced view of this family. Obviously she chose to tell you only about the counterfeit legacy of our grandfather, and that legacy is worthless in this world and in the next."

"Will you tell me about Mary Bradford and about your mother?"

"Of course I will, my dear. But we must pause for a few moments, for I hear some steps on the staircase, and I suspect that Betsy is beginning to bring supper up to us."

"But you will tell me, Aunt Kathleen, you promise?"

"I promise, my dear," Aunt Kathleen put her arm around Caroline and led her over to the banister where they stood together admiring the sunset. "I promise to tell you anything you want or need to know, just as soon as we have you well nourished. I want you to know the truth."

Chapter 12

Caroline put her fork down on the translucent, elegant dinner plate. "I can't eat another bite, Aunt Kathleen. I'm absolutely stuffed, and I'm far too excited."

"Oh, but you must have some dessert and perhaps a cup of tea? I'm sure that Betsy has some cake and cookies around. She always keeps those things available."

"I don't care for anything, really, but of course if you want some—"

"Oh no, my dear," Aunt Kathleen sighed. "I am afraid my doctor does not allow me more than two cups of tea a day, and I have already exceeded my limit. Why don't we move over to the wicker settee and enjoy the last bit of dusk before night falls?" Aunt Kathleen rose from the chair at the small table where she and Caroline had dined. "Oh, there is the moon, Caroline. Just look!" She turned and pointed. "What a splendid evening it is, a perfect time for the telling of old tales." She took Caroline's hand, squeezed it, and they walked back to the comfort of the wicker settee.

"Now," she said, after she had seated herself, "let's see, where did I leave off?"

"James Bradford had just met Diana in a shack in the woods."

"Oh yes, of course," Aunt Kathleen agreed. "Well, as you have no doubt understood, that was a regular occurrence; they had met often, but to go on with the story."

Three weeks later James and Mary Bradford were sitting in their pew at the local church, which the wealthy plantation owners had built and had attended for generations. James was staring quietly ahead at the altar and did not see Diana enter the building until she walked down the aisle clinging to the arm of her husband.

Instantly James tightened his spine and clenched his jaw. His anger was intensified by a change in Diana's behavior toward her husband that was perceptible only to James. Diana had not simply put her hand through her husband's bent arm, in the traditional way of a lady. Instead, she was walking with her body pressed as close to his as possible. She smiled adoringly into the eyes of the older man, and once she had entered their pew, she snuggled close to her husband and peered up into his face with a flirtatious sparkle in her eyes. James felt his face grow hot, and he knew that he must be blushing, so he tore his eyes away from Diana, picked up the prayer book, opened it and stared blindly at the words in front of him. His anger was joined by anxiety.

The service became an agony for James. He had no particular personal beliefs. Church services were no more than social occasions to him, and there were very few social occasions left in South Carolina after the War. This service was a particular agony as he fought with himself to keep from staring at Diana. Every little glimpse he allowed himself increased his anxiety, for he saw endless little gestures and looks on her face that suggested that something had happened in her relationship with her husband, something James felt sure would exclude him.

The service finally ended, and various couples gathered on the grassy area outside the small church. James and Mary greeted their neighbors and slowly worked their way toward Mary's cousin, Diana, and her husband, Thomas Montgomery. Typically, the two couples shared Sunday dinner with each other after church services if it were possible to do so. For the previous three Sundays, various circumstances had prevented their meal and afternoon together, so Mary was excited at the thought of hostessing her cousin Diana and Thomas Montgomery, as well as several of their neighbors. Plantations had not yet recovered from the effects of war, so entertaining was greatly simplified. The elegance of the past was gone; shortages were quite evident, but nevertheless, most Southern ladies did their best to maintain a sense of dignity by entertaining as best they could. Thus, after Mary had dispensed a note of invitation to the Montgomerys, she had worked hard all week to gather together the best available foods, and to set the most elegant table possible for the afternoon.

James flushed again as he and Mary approached Diana, who

refused to look him in the eyes. This cannot go on, he thought. The afternoon will be endless. I cannot bear it; I must get her alone as soon as possible.

His opportunity came when Mary struck up a conversation with Thomas and some neighbors. James stepped forward and asked Diana to accompany him to the cemetery to visit the graves of some of their friends who had died in the War. Much to his amazement, Diana accepted his suggestion and left her husband's side, but only after giving his arm a squeeze and flashing him a bright smile. James rigidly held out his arm for Diana to place her hand through, and they walked away quite properly to the cemetery at the side of the church.

When he was sure that they were out of earshot, he demanded, "What is going on?"

Diana simply smiled up at him and said, "Smile."

James was startled by her response but did the best he could to comply. They moved to the first grave, and James quit smiling and stared blindly at the simple, wooden marker. "Diana, surely I am not required to smile as I stare at the graves of my childhood friends. What is going on?"

"It's quite simple, James," Diana spoke firmly. "I am expecting a child."

"What?" James demanded as he turned to her in alarm.

"Please remain composed and continue to look at the graves." She pushed him a little further along the walk. "You can hardly be surprised, James. After all, these things do happen."

"But you told me that he had not touched you since the birth of your daughter a year ago," James spit the words out bitterly.

"And so he had not," Diana said quietly, "until several weeks ago."

"You let him—you went to bed with him and—" James sputtered furiously.

"Yes," Diana stopped him with a single word.

That one word was sufficient for James to take action. He hurried Diana further along the path toward an area of trees where he could stop the pretense of being a bereaved man looking at the graves of his fallen comrades, jerked her around and stared wildly at her. "Why?" he demanded. "Why did you let that fool touch you?"

"I am carrying your child," Diana said calmly. "What else could I do?"

"What else? I will tell you what else! We will be married and stop this outrage now. I love you. I want to marry you."

"I know you do, but I refuse to marry you."

"You do not know what you are saying," James insisted. "How could you possibly respond to the coming of our child in that way? We love each other. This is *our* child. We have a right to be married."

"James, why be emotional about this?"

"Emotional!" James raised his voice. "How can I be anything but emotional?"

"Be quiet!" Diana commanded. "Someone will hear you. These things have been happening for centuries. I am going to have a child. It is your child. There is no reason why my husband must know that. I am certainly not going to tear up my life and yours by making some absurd confession to a man I do not even love."

"I have taken appropriate action," Diana said flatly, "and now it is time for you to do your part."

"Which is what?" James demanded between clenched teeth.

"I want you to leave the county; I want you to leave the state, in fact. I want you to go away, stay gone a month. Go away on business. Make up some excuse, any excuse will do. You just simply cannot be anywhere near here for the next month."

"So you can trick Thomas into thinking he is the father of this child."

"What I do in regard to Thomas is my concern."

"This child is my concern, Diana. This is my child."

"I readily admit that to you, James, but I have no intention of ever admitting it to anyone else. I have made it plain from the beginning that I love you, but I do not intend to give up my position in society and be a total outcast because fate has arranged our lives in a way that prevents us from marrying."

"Diana, I absolutely refuse—"

"No, you will not refuse," Diana interrupted him. "You will do as I ask because you love me and because no one will believe you if you try to say anything different from what I say. You will hurt Mary, and ultimately you will ruin both of our lives as well as the life of our child." She touched his arm lightly. "It is only a temporary problem, James. By this time next year it will all be over, and our relationship need not change."

"What kind of man do you think I am, Diana?"

"I know what kind of man you are, James, just as you know what kind of woman I am. Let us not be hypocritical with each other, at least. I tell you, our relationship need not change."

"Oh, it will change someday, Diana," James insisted, "if for no other reason, it will change because Mary will find out. That is why I say you should let Thomas divorce you now and marry me."

"You may have to worry about Thomas finding out, but for heaven's sake, don't spend any time worrying about my little cousin. She sees only what she wants to see."

"What on earth does that mean?"

"Oh, it is something from Aunt Verity's influence. She used to tell us all the time something from the Bible about looking at only the beautiful things, the uplifting things—that kind of silliness. I never paid any attention to it. I always just make things the way I want them to be, and then they are good. But Mary actually believed that stuff, and so she just sees what she wants to see, concentrates on things that she considers beautiful and positive and hopeful. She will never be suspicious, James; she will never figure out what we are doing. Don't worry about little Mary, believe me. I know her, and she is totally naive." James stared at the ground, hating himself and feeling the kind of defeat he had not felt since the end of the War.

"This is the best way," Diana insisted. "Women have been handling things this way for centuries. James, you are not a sheltered man; you are a man of the world, and you know that plenty of husbands are running around claiming sons that are not theirs."

"I know," James said quietly, "but this is my child. You are the woman I love."

"If I am the woman you love and if you care for your child, you will keep us both safe by doing as I ask. Now, we must get back to the others before they become suspicious." She turned and pulled him back along the path, but he glared angrily at her as they walked. Before they left the cemetery, Diana said sharply, "James, take control of yourself. You must act normally. Do you want your child to be known as a bastard?"

The word 'bastard' stung through his brain and startled him. He looked down at Diana's face, but before he could respond, she smiled at him in a sedate, socially appropriate way. "Smile, James," she said under her breath. He couldn't smile, but at least he quit frowning.

When they returned to the churchyard, Mary slipped her arm into his and said sweetly, "We must get home, dearest; our guests will be arriving." Without a word he escorted her to the carriage and helped her into it. He avoided her eyes and was totally silent on the ride home from the church; Mary kept looking at him with concern in her eyes. When they drove up in front of the house, he jumped down from the carriage and turned to help her down. As soon as her feet were on the ground, he tried to turn toward the house, but she put her hand on his arm and stopped him.

"James, dearest," she said softly and with great tenderness. "I know it must be a frightfully painful experience for you to walk through that cemetery and see the graves of your boyhood friends. It must bring up horrible memories. I only wish, dearest, I could do something to help you." He struggled to keep his face expressionless. She reached up and caressed his beard with her gloved hand. "Life must go on. We must go on. It is no good looking at the past, pondering what we have lost. We must look toward the future. If there is anything I can do to help you, dearest, anything, just ask me." The sweetness of her tone and the sympathetic tears in her eyes made James hate himself. He could not strangle out a single word, so he put his arm around her shoulders and escorted her to the house without a word.

Mary hastened to check preparations for the dinner guests who would be quickly arriving. James had no more than five minutes alone to try to calm himself; then their guests, including Diana and Thomas, arrived. He was quiet throughout the afternoon, doing only the minimal amount that was required of a host. Things were so changed from the dinners he had attended before the War, and he hated their present circumstances. There were only a few household servants, who were now free, the few beloved family servants who had never abandoned their posts. Mary did much more actual physical labor than any hostess did before the War, but she did it with a quiet joy, not with mere resignation. In contrast, her cousin Diana remained the ante-bellum belle, bringing laughter into the room and little flirtations, all of which were directed toward her husband, but doing nothing to help Mary serve the guests.

The afternoon seemed endless to James, but finally dusk came, and the guests began to leave. James helped Diana into the Montgomery carriage while Thomas thanked Mary once again for the meal and the afternoon. Diana managed to give James a special smile and to whisper, "Don't worry, darling. Things will all work out in time, and we'll be back together again."

James felt that he was touching her for the last time. He stepped back and watched Thomas ascend slowly into the carriage and settle next to his beautiful wife. That man is odious, James thought, I hate him. How could she let him touch her? I will not have it! It took all of James' control not to jerk the man back out of the carriage and throw him to the ground, leap into the carriage, and leave with Diana. With great effort he turned and walked back to the front verandah to stand by Mary as she waved good-bye to their guests.

"It was lovely to have guests again," Mary murmured. James made no reply, so she glanced up and noticed the tight set of his jaw and the scowl in his eyes. Not knowing what else to say, she said gently, "It has been a long day. Perhaps we should go to bed early." James did not appear to hear her, so she murmured, "I am quite tired. I believe I will go to bed," and with a soft swish of her skirts she left his side.

James walked halfway down the drive, staring at the road that had taken Diana away. After he had ambled quite some distance from the house, he pulled himself up short and muttered, "You idiot! You must take control of yourself. Quit acting like a lovesick schoolboy. This is absurd." With great resolution he turned back toward the house and began to walk steadily up the hill. In the upstairs window he saw the warm glow of lantern light and assumed that Mary was preparing for bed. How many nights have I lain beside her, he thought, as if she were no relation to me? He stopped and stared at the warm glow in the window, and there was a strange ache in his chest. But I cannot take my body where my heart refuses to go. He sighed as he saw Mary's silhouette in the window. She had walked close to the window as if she were looking out. Then she sat in a chair by the window with her head hanging forward. James wondered, is she ill? Is she depressed? Why is she sitting there with her head down? How strange and how awful. I don't know my own wife well enough to know what she typically does this time of the evening. I've never noticed.

Still James could not bring himself to go upstairs to Mary. Instead he sat out on the verandah until he was certain she would be asleep. He felt guilty for not going to check on her to see if she was ill, but he could not bring himself to go to Mary when it was Diana who filled his mind.

He sat for hours and tried to sort through his feelings about losing Diana for a short period of time during the course of this pregnancy, or perhaps even losing her for good to death when the baby came, or losing her to Thomas, who could give her the luxuries of life that she craved. Every time he thought of the pregnancy a volcano of conflicting emotions surged up in him. There was the hot lava of anger that this child should exist and separate him from the object of his desire. He discovered that he resented the child more than he resented Thomas. He also felt great grief that this was his child; it might very well be his son, his heir, and he could not claim him without destroying Diana's life, his own life, and the life of the child. He raged at fate, the fate that had taken him off to war. He raged at Diana for her faithlessness in not waiting for him to return, and ultimately he raged at himself for entangling his life in this way. The rage kept him from sleeping, but it had a positive side. It also kept him from feeling the guilt that was hiding behind the rage, particularly the guilt he felt about Mary, a good woman whom he knew he had used as no more than camouflage.

The house was totally quiet, and James judged by the position of the moon that it must be two o'clock in the morning. Still he could not sleep, so he left the verandah and began to walk down the drive toward the gates of the plantation. He had no destination in mind, just the need to walk, the need to block his thoughts. When he reached the bottom of the hill, he turned and looked back at the house. The whiteness of the house shone in the moonlight, but all the windows were dark. It looks quite normal from here in this lighting, he thought bitterly. The peeling paint, the damage done by Yankee soldiers is so easily healed by moonlight. Here was another source of pain rising in him, a pain that he had to suppress. The loss of the War was a personal loss for him, a blow to his ego as well as the destruction of his property and the termination of his lifestyle. James Bradford did not like to lose anything.

Suddenly he saw something stirring on the front verandah. He squinted his eyes to see better, but it was not until the figure descended the steps and started down the walk to the drive that he could discern that it was a human being, a woman in light, flowing garments. She paused at the beginning of the drive and looked down the hill, then started resolutely toward him. He knew it was Mary. A kind of sob rose from his chest and escaped his lips, much to his surprise, as he recognized the depth of her concern for him. He tightened his muscles, regained control of himself and began to stride back up the drive toward his wife, his wife whom he would not claim. When she came closer to him, she ran slowly toward him until she threw herself into his arms.

"Are you all right, dearest?" she inquired desperately.

James had meant to be totally controlled and tell her she should be in bed, but instead he clasped her to his chest and held her while a shiver went through his whole body.

"You must come to bed," Mary insisted. "You will be ill."

James could not trust himself to speak for fear that he might break down and reveal something that would hurt her. Fortunately she picked the most obvious explanation for his behavior, the most obvious to her understanding.

"James, dearest, you have been working far too hard. You came back from the war exhausted and sick, but rather than rest, you plunged right into putting this plantation back in order." Her voice was soft and kind, even though she tried to put as much starch into it as she could. "Now I am going to insist that you take some time off. You have not been sleeping well, and today you have not been well at all." James just nodded, and Mary continued, "There is no need for us to talk any more tonight. We must simply get you to bed and allow you to rest."

He permitted her to lead him up the drive, into the house and up to their bedroom. Gently she pushed him down on the bed, and he lay there and stared at the canopy as she pulled off his boots with great effort. He was exhausted, but mostly he was unable to speak about his dilemma. She covered him with a light quilt and blew out the lantern. Then she sat on the edge of the bed and stroked his hair. Much to his amazement, a great peace overtook him, and he felt himself drifting into sleep.

When he awoke, he knew it was late in the morning because the sun was so bright. Mary was not present. He arose from the bed, looked down at his disheveled clothes, and went into his dressing room. After he had washed and dressed, he went down-stairs. Mary met him at the foot of the stairs with an anxious look on her face. "You look better," she said, "but far too tired. Perhaps you should go sit on the porch, and I will bring you some breakfast."

"It must be closer to noon," James said.

"Nevertheless, you need a hearty breakfast," Mary insisted as she gently nudged him toward the front door.

In the sunlight of the late morning, James knew what he must do. He knew that Diana would take whatever measures she deemed necessary to protect her marriage and her position in society. He could do nothing but go away as she had demanded. There was business that he needed to conduct, but the occupation of Charleston by the federal troops made it difficult to conduct business there. He would go to Savannah; that trip should keep him away a sufficient amount of time for Diana's purposes.

When Mary came out the front door, she was carrying a break-fast tray, which she put on a table next to him. She sat down and stirred some cream into his coffee. As she handed the cup to him, she said, "James, I know it is not my place to tell you what to do. You are my husband. But I am going to have to insist that you take a rest, and I do not believe that you can rest while you are here at the plantation. You are going to have to take a trip so that you can get your mind off the problems here."

James was startled by her words; she was making it so easy for him to deceive her. If he had not known it was impossible, he would have believed she had overheard his conversation with Diana in the cemetery. He swallowed some of the coffee and finally met her gaze. "I was just thinking the same thing," he said, "or nearly the same thing. There is some business I need to conduct. I will need to go to Savannah to do it."

"Oh James, not business. You do not need business. You need recreation."

James smiled at her earnest, loving expression. "This will not be taxing business, Mary, and it will be a change from the problems of the plantation."

"Then you must go," Mary insisted.

"Yes, I must." James lowered his eyes and drank more of the coffee.

Mary rose and walked to the edge of the verandah and stared

out at the plantation. "You must go soon," she said quietly. "I am sure I can take care of things here at the plantation while you are gone."

James said nothing.

"The important thing," she continued without looking back at him, "is for you to regain your health and your—your—peace of mind." She broke off her words, and for the first time James realized that she was quite upset at the thought of his leaving.

Good heavens, he thought, she actually wants to be with me. What have I ever given her? Just the respectability of being a married woman, nothing more.

"I am sure I can get your clothing ready this afternoon," Mary broke into his thoughts, "and you will be able—"

"Mary," James finally spoke.

"Yes, dearest," she answered but did not turn to look at him.

He saw her reach her hand up to her face, and he realized that she was wiping tears away.

"I want you to come with me," he said boldly, although it was a lie.

"You do?" Mary wheeled around to stare at him.

"Yes," he said it more firmly than the first time. "I want you to come with me."

Her eyes filled with tears again, and he hurried on, driven by his guilt. "We were never able to take a wedding trip, since we married so quickly after the War. We did not have the time or the money or even the possibility of travel, but things are better now."

James stood resolutely and walked across the verandah toward his wife. He placed his hand lightly on her cheek, and she lowered her eyes and gazed at the floor. "Would you consider coming to Savannah with me, Mary?" he asked gently.

A smile quickly flashed across her face as she lifted it and once again looked into his eyes. "Oh, James, are you truly serious? Do you really want me to come?"

He was startled by the little-girl eagerness that quivered through her whole body. A great stab of grief ran through him as he realized how outcast she must have felt, whether she understood the reasons or not. He smiled at her and put as much eagerness into his voice as he could create. "Yes, Mary. The trip would be so much better for me if you would just consider coming. I know it is a great deal of trouble, but I would be lonely without you." He bit his tongue; he could not say anymore; he knew he was lying.

She smiled eagerly into his face. "James, I would go anywhere with you, and I do not care how difficult the trip is. I will get my things together this very afternoon, and we can leave early in the morning."

"Wait a minute; we really do not have to leave that quickly." Images flashed through his mind of the amount of time it took for ladies to prepare clothing and pack trunks, but those images were quickly replaced by a more realistic picture as he remembered that Mary had few items of clothing to pack. It was not the days before the War, after all.

"Truly, it will not take me long to get ready," she persisted.

"Let us take two or three days to prepare and plan this trip," James said quietly. "After all, there is more to consider than clothing. I must decide where we will stay and make arrangements for the time that we will spend in Savannah."

"Oh, but could we not stay with Aunt Verity," Mary suggested. "She would be so hurt, James, if we did not stay with her. Of course, if you do not want to—"

"If I am going to take my wife on a wedding trip," James tried to smile as he put more energy into his voice, "I am certainly not going to spend my time with Aunt Verity or any other aunt."

Mary ducked her head as a blush spread across her face. "It would be nice to spend some time alone," she murmured, and James remembered how little intimacy there had been in their marriage. "Perhaps," she continued, "we could do both. Aunt Verity would be hurt if we did not spend some time with her, and it is my childhood home," she lifted her eyes to his face. "I would so love to spend some time in the serenity of that old house."

"It may not be the way you remember it," James cautioned. "You have not been there since before the War."

"I know," she nodded her head, "but my memories are still there, and in a situation like this where war has changed everything, it is the memories that count. Do you not agree?"

"Yes, it is the memories that count." He looked over her shoulder and down the drive as his mind floated back over the past and inevitably turned to Diana. He remembered Diana before the War; he remembered the years of longing for Diana during the War and the nights he had spent with her since the War.

Mary watched him anxiously for a moment and set her face

resolutely, a fact that he did not notice. When she spoke, however, her voice was gentle. "James, dearest, we must make new memories. What we do now is what we will have to remember later. It is tempting to think only of things the way they were, but we must not lose ourselves in the past. We must make new memories."

He was shocked by her words; he had never considered Mary a deep thinker; indeed, he had never considered any woman able to think. "Perhaps a week in a hotel in Savannah, if we can find a room," he said, "and then we will spend some weeks with your aunt."

"Oh, that would be perfect!" she exclaimed. She threw her arms around his neck and gave him a quick hug. "I best get about the business of putting things in order here and getting our clothing ready."

"And I had best be sure that we have a carriage that can make it as far as Savannah," James said wryly.

Mary started toward the door, but she stopped and turned back toward him. "James, dearest, I cannot tell you how much this means to me. The thought of having you all to myself is worth going anywhere, so any accommodation you arrange will be fine with me."

James felt a lump rise in his throat, and he could not speak. He just nodded as he tried to meet her gaze steadily. She whisked around and hurried through the door, her mind full of the preparations that were ahead.

Once she was out of sight, James turned around and slammed his fist against one of the pillars of the verandah.

For James, the carriage trip to Savannah was both a rocky physical and emotional journey. The roads themselves were rutted, muddy quagmires that seemed determined to keep him in South Carolina. His heart and mind longed to stay home; their anguish was worse than the quagmire of the roads, for they pulled at him like quicksand. He hated leaving his beloved plantation which he was returning back to life. To him, his land was a long-neglected invalid, and he was its only advocate. Also, leaving Bradford Plantation meant losing his close proximity to Diana. His arms ached to hold her as he simultaneously cursed her for forcing him to leave.

Mary's gratitude, eagerness and excitement, however, were a

whole new experience for James. He was accustomed to the
demanding, but bewitching Diana who expected as her self-evi-
dent right to be adored and showered with all the privileges that
life had to offer. Mary, on the other hand, seemed to take every
positive happening, whether it was a kind word from him or a
beautiful tree along the way, as a special blessing that had been
granted to her. Mentally, James beat himself because he knew that
at least some of the starvation for good things in Mary's soul was
the result of his emotional abandonment of her in the year they
had been married. He remembered their wedding night, but there
were few other nights with Mary that he could actually recall. He
consoled himself with the thought that at least he could give her
more of himself during this trip.

They found Savannah in very good shape, because the city had
surrendered to the Yankees rather than be burned like Atlanta.
Hotel rooms were available, but expensive, and James had little
ready cash.

He did his very best to spend most of his time with Mary, acting the part of the new bridegroom. Much to his surprise, it gave
him a special thrill to see excitement shining in her eyes and serenity radiating from her face. He discovered that she was very beautiful, and it stunned him when he realized that he had never
noticed. She did not have the fire in her eyes that Diana had. She
had none of the flirtatious sexual allure of Diana, but there was a
childlike simplicity and trust and an ever-present excitement over
all the gifts of nature that enchanted him. Mary's voice began to
affect him like the sound of a small, sweet songbird. He wondered, why have I never noticed that special lilt every time she
speaks? Why is it that here in Savannah the sound of her voice
instantly raises my spirits? It never did before. Why did I never see
the eagerness, the joy in small things, in her blue-gray eyes? Why
is it only now, a year after she became my wife, that I recognize
that the very touch of her hand brings peace? James asked himself
such questions daily. The contrast between the tempestuous,
passionate Diana and the gentle, loving Mary was ever-present in
his mind, and he discovered that he loved them both. That thought
made him feel better and worse at the same time. It was surely
good to discover that he loved his wife, that he could love his wife,
but it was surely bad to discover that he still loved Diana, and that

she occupied at least half of his thoughts.

After the expenses of three days in the hotel, James became worried about cash, but Mary seemed to sense the problem. She came to him in their room and asked pleadingly, "James, dearest, I know that you wanted to spend an entire week in the hotel, but I have visited Aunt Verity, and if it would not disappoint you too much, it would please me greatly to be able to go home." Tears stung James' eyes, but he forced them back; he recognized that Mary had made it possible for him to remove them from the hotel without admitting that he did not have the money to keep them there. She had protected his pride.

"Are you sure that is what you want?" he asked. "There are great advantages to staying here in the hotel. I am sure that Aunt Verity has few, if any, servants."

"Yes, I know that, dearest, but I do so much want to go home, if you do not mind." He agreed, silently grateful for Mary's perception and love, and with the greatest of ease they made the transition from the expensive hotel to the waiting arms of Mary's Aunt Verity, a woman whom James had not seen in many years.

Aunt Verity met them just inside the door of her house. The years of the War had crippled her legs, and she now walked with great effort using a cane, but those years had not taken the snap out of her blue eyes. Mary went immediately to her aunt and threw her arms around her, and Aunt Verity's delight in seeing the niece whom she had raised was quite obvious. When Mary turned to re-introduce Aunt Verity to James, Aunt Verity's loving tone changed considerably.

"Oh yes, James Bradford. I remember you well." She walked forward and held out her hand for him to kiss, which he dutifully did.

When he raised his eyes from her white hand, she studied his face, then said, "I see that you have not changed. It is a pity that you have not, but there is still time," she added, as she turned her back on him and put her arms around Mary again. Mary flushed a bright red and helped her aunt into the parlor and settled her on a settee. James followed awkwardly, feeling like a schoolboy who had been taken down several levels by a schoolmaster who could see right through him.

"I regret to say," Aunt Verity began, after everyone one was seated, "that I have only one servant left in this large house, but you are most welcome." She turned and took Mary's hands in hers. "Most welcome, my dear. Welcome to stay as long as you possibly can." She turned and looked across the tea table at James. "And you, too, of course," she added curtly. "My one servant was with me before the War and remained faithful. She is free now, of course, but too old to make changes, much like I am. So we get along pretty well here with things in the house scaled down to a level she can handle."

"I shall be glad to help in any way that I can, Aunt Verity," Mary assured her earnestly.

James said nothing, certain that at this moment that anything he said would be unwelcome.

"You most certainly will not," Aunt Verity said sharply. "You are to be a guest here and are to be entertained as lavishly as we possibly can manage. I understand that you have slaved away on that Bradford Plantation, trying to put it back together, but while you are here in Savannah, you are not to lift a finger." She turned and stared at James as if she were commanding him to say something.

He did. "You are quite right, Aunt Verity. Mary has worked far too hard."

"That is obvious from her hands," Aunt Verity rebuked him as she gently stroked one of Mary's hands.

"Perhaps I can employ a woman to help out while we are here," James suggested.

"No doubt you can," Aunt Verity said briskly. "And no doubt you can take that same said woman back to your plantation with you so that Mary need not work so hard."

"Well," Mary broke in breathlessly. "Perhaps we should get settled, Aunt Verity."

"Perhaps, my dear, we should have some tea first. You and I— while your husband settles the trunks." Again Aunt Verity turned and stared at James.

James took his cue and gladly escaped outside to the carriage where he and the driver unloaded the trunks and brought them into the front hall. Aunt Verity's old servant, a woman named Blossom, led them upstairs with the trunks and showed James where to leave them.

James took his time. He had no keen desire to return to the sharp looks and curt tones of Aunt Verity. He knew that she had raised Mary after the death of her parents and had given Diana a temporary home after her mother died. Thus, Aunt Verity knew the personalities of Mary and Diana well. He also knew that she was well aware of the fact that he had loved Diana since they were in their teens. He began to wonder if it was, in fact, a good idea to stay with Mary's Aunt Verity, but his financial resources really gave him no other option.

His thoughts were cut short when Mary entered the room and sighed with great contentment. "Oh, it has not changed a bit, James." She walked over to where he stood by the window and looked down over the garden. "It is the same dear garden," she sighed again.

"Much in need of weeding," James added.

"Well, yes," Mary agreed. "It is quite a bit more disheveled than it used to be, but it was once Aunt Verity's pride and joy. No doubt she cannot care for it now."

"I believe your Aunt Verity could handle anything," James said wryly.

Mary took his arm and snuggled close to him. "Please don't mind Aunt Verity, dearest. She will learn to love you. It is impossible not to love you," she added.

He smiled down at her and pulled her closer to his side and wrapped his arms around her. "I can see that I have the love of two of the Fitzgerald ladies to gain here in Savannah," he said gallantly.

"Oh, you do not need to gain my love, dearest," Mary cried. "I have loved you for years."

James laughed quietly. "Thank God for that. It is going to take some effort to win the love of Aunt Verity."

"It will not be as hard as you think."

"No," James agreed. "I suspect it is merely a matter of treating you well. You were always her favorite, were you not?"

"I am sure Aunt Verity had no favorites," Mary insisted.

"And I am sure she did," James countered.

"Well," Mary admitted slowly. "She and Diana were not temperamentally suited to each other."

"What a tactful way you have of putting that, my dear," James said. "Is that why Diana went off to live with her father?"

"Yes," Mary said quietly. "It was easy for me to adopt Aunt Verity as my mother because my parents died soon after I was born.

I never really knew them. I never knew any mother but Aunt Verity. Diana, on the other hand, had a father living. He stayed away so much when she was a child that she did not know him really; however, she could not accept Aunt Verity as a substitute mother. I suppose it was inevitable that she would eventually go to her father. Of course, I stayed with Aunt Verity."

"So when did you go to Charleston?" James was appalled with himself that he had to ask such a question of his own wife.

"Several years into the War, when Diana married Thomas. I wanted to go to their wedding, of course, but I wanted to return to Savannah to be with Aunt Verity. She was positive I would be safer on a plantation outside the fortified city of Charleston than I would be in Savannah. In those days one never really knew where safety would be."

"Why didn't she come with you?" James asked.

"Aunt Verity would never leave Savannah. If the Yankees had burned Savannah, they would have had to burn her in her own house. She would never have left it, but she forced me to go to what she thought was safety."

"And in the end," James added, "Savannah turned out to be the safest place to be."

"Yes," Mary added sadly, "but there was no way to return, until now."

"What a mess our lives have been," James declared bitterly.

"Oh, you must not say such things," Mary insisted with more spunk than he had ever seen in her. "Especially not here, especially not standing at this window in my beloved childhood bedroom staring down at my favorite garden in the world."

James smiled at the energy in her voice. "Your garden, my dear, is an absolute mess," he said with a teasing laugh.

"Well, it will not stay that way," she insisted briskly. "A week's worth of sunny mornings and some work, and I shall put it back in order."

"We had better get you some gardening gloves first thing," James replied. "I do not think my constitution can stand many more of Aunt Verity's remarks about the condition of your hands."

He took her hands into his and looked at them on both sides. "They should be lily white and as smooth as marble," he sighed.

"There are much more important things than my hands, dearest. We have survived; the plantation is coming back to life. We have managed to remain a family. Those are the things that count, not hands."

"Just the same," James insisted, "I want to see your hands come back to the condition of their youth. While we are here in Savannah, it is a good time to begin. So one of our first shopping expeditions will have to be for gloves."

"I am sure Aunt Verity has a house full of gloves," Mary laughed. "I cannot remember even seeing my hands when I was growing up, they were so covered with gloves."

"I will get a servant," James promised her. "I do not want you doing any work while you are here, unless it is something you really enjoy, like the garden. And I do not want you doing anything strenuous out there. This city is overrun with free men and women who would be willing to work for a day or for a month. They need the money." James sighed. "No one born in the South has any money, it seems; only those who have moved in."

"Let's not think about that," Mary pleaded. "Let's enjoy what we do have, a time of rest and peace, the sunshine, a time to be together. There may be weeds in the garden, James dearest, but there are also flowers, and the weeds can be uprooted, so that the flowers can multiply and bloom."

He smiled down at her and murmured, "My little optimist."

She shook her head gently and replied, "Your little realist."

Again he was surprised by the depth of thought he perceived behind her words. "I believe I have married more than a pretty face," he said gallantly. "I believe I may have married a philosopher in disguise."

"Is it impossible that the two could go together?" she asked.

He shook his head and laughed softly.

Chapter 13

The first weeks at Aunt Verity's were a golden, idyllic time for Mary. As she enjoyed the genteel company of her Aunt Verity and restored the flowers of the enchanting Savannah garden she had loved as a child, she felt that the war had never come and ripped away her gentle cloister of graciousness. In the evenings she had James' attention, the love she had yearned for for over a year. Finally she felt like a bride; finally she was cherished by her beloved bridegroom, and all the fantasies a young lady has about her first weeks of marriage were being realized.

Aunt Verity seemed to enjoy the weeks also. She obviously adored Mary, and while she could not actively participate in the work on the garden, nothing prevented her from sitting on a garden bench and watching her beautiful flowers emerge from the overgrowth that had begun to strangle them. James had hired a young boy of about twelve named Sammy to do the more strenuous work, and anyone could see the special place in his heart that Mary had already captured. Every time she spoke to him, her gentle requests brought a shining light to his eyes.

James found the weeks to be a time of conflicting thoughts and emotions. Much to his surprise he made some business connections that he felt would prosper his plantation; however, emotionally he felt like a soldier fighting on both sides of a raging battle. Diana was never far from his thoughts, and a consuming flash of passion shot through him whenever her face came to his mind. However, there were moments when he did not think of Diana; when he acted out his part of husband to Mary, Diana disappeared entirely. He found that he was capable of a tenderness that he had never experienced before. He felt more and more protective of Mary, and even though she was always quiet-spoken and very gentle in action, he found that there was a great depth of passion in her. It was a passion born of a strong love for him, a kind of passion he had never experienced, for Diana's love was always self-serving. Furthermore, James had never known a woman who thought as deeply as Mary did, a woman whose mind was full of spiritual and philosophical reflection; indeed, he had never known women were capable of such thought. Much to his amazement he found that he actually enjoyed talking to Mary, sharing his own thoughts with her. She was a woman who was more than a play thing; she could and would share the burdens of life with him.

The only shadow in the week for James was his growing certainty that Aunt Verity had a definite dislike for him. That dislike, he felt sure, was based on her knowledge of his former engagement to Diana and her suspicions that if he could love a woman like Diana, it was not likely that he could truly love Mary as she deserved. James' hours in Aunt Verity's company made him quite anxious, because he felt sure that she was just waiting for the right time to say what was on her mind, and indeed his judgment was correct.

One early afternoon he returned to Aunt Verity's house and found her inside standing by the window watching Mary as she worked in the garden. All week James had carefully avoided being left alone with Aunt Verity, but he had inadvertently entered the parlor too quickly, thinking that Mary was there. Now there was no escape.

"I have something to say to you," Aunt Verity said, without turning around. "As you can see, Mary is not here. She is outside in the garden. I trust we may talk in confidence for a few moments."

James tightened his muscles, but tried to appear totally at ease. "Well certainly, Aunt Verity." He strolled over to her side.

She looked at his face briefly and then turned back to the window. "What do you see outside, James Bradford?"

"I see your garden emerging under the hands of my lovely wife, Mary. It is truly a magnificent garden; obviously it has been carefully designed and—"

"We shall not spend these few moments together talking about my garden, James Bradford," Aunt Verity cut him off. "I have something quite specific to say to you, and I may not get another moment as good as this one."

James said nothing but stood silently at attention by her side. As usual Aunt Verity had reduced him to feeling that he was no more than a tardy schoolboy.

"I shall be brief," Aunt Verity continued. "Have you ever

noticed the difference between the evening star and the moon, James Bradford?"

James was startled, "I beg your pardon?"

Aunt Verity turned and stared coldly into his eyes. "Have you ever noticed the difference between the evening star and the moon, James Bradford?" she repeated.

"I do not believe I have made any particular observations on the subject, ma'am," James replied, still bewildered.

"I did not think that you had, so I shall make them for you."

"Very well," James stammered, "but would you like to sit down?" He was hoping to gain a few moments to gather his wits and regain his own composure.

"I am quite comfortable, thank you," Aunt Verity replied coolly. "As I said, I shall be brief. Since you do not know the difference between the evening star and the moon, James Bradford, I shall tell you the difference. The evening star is always constant. Every evening of your life you will be able to go outside and look into the darkness of the heavens and see the evening star where you expect it to be, shining its small but totally reliable light. In contrast, the moon will be ever changing. It will change its location frequently. It will change its shape. It will change the amount of light that it gives out, shifting from unbelievable brightness that lights a man's way through the terrors of the night, to darkness that leaves a man stumbling and staggering, overwhelmed with anxiety. Yes, James Bradford, the moon is ever changing, ever moving, quite unreliable."

James stared down at her as he felt perspiration breaking out on his forehead. He pretended he did not know what she was referring to.

"When can one best see the evening star?" Aunt Verity glared at him now.

"I am afraid, ma'am, that I have given that question little thought."

"Now is a good time to give it thought, sir." Aunt Verity had no intention of allowing him to escape.

"Well," James tried to smile. "Let me see. Your question was— when is the best time to see the evening star?" He started to turn away from her because her angry eyes were more than he could tolerate, but she stuck out her cane and blocked his way.

"When can one best see the evening star, James Bradford?" she demanded.

Silently he admitted his defeat. He looked straight into her eyes, her eyes of fury that compelled him to answer, and replied, "When there is no moon visible."

"That is correct," Aunt Verity said. "The best time to see the evening star is when the moon is not visible in the sky. The changeable, undependable, sometimes exciting, sometimes dark moon. When that moon, which so tramples human reason and makes men nothing but puppets of their emotions, is not visible in the sky, it is easiest to see the evening star."

"I understand, ma'am," James said, as his face flushed red.

"I believe you do," Aunt Verity said quietly. "And I also believe that your time here in Savannah has greatly improved your night vision."

James made no response.

Aunt Verity turned her face back to the window where she saw that Mary had stood up and was waving at her. She waved back, turned to James, looked him in the face again and asked, "Will you join the evening star and me in the garden for tea?"

"It will be my pleasure," James said haltingly. Aunt Verity walked in front of him and left the room. James stood for a moment and watched as Mary waved at him. He waved back, stepped away from the window, took his handkerchief out of his pocket and wiped his brow. He was not at all certain what Aunt Verity might or might not know about his actions of the past year. If she knew anything about his relationship with Diana, she could only have learned it from one person, and he could not bear to think that Mary knew. He sat down on the settee for a moment to regain his composure and thought about the images that Aunt Verity had used. Diana is like the moon, he thought. How well named she is. Sometimes she is a full moon flashing a bright beacon, calling me to her side, to her bed; sometimes when it suits her convenience, pushing me away, as if there is no light in her at all. Perhaps a man is better off to live with the steadiness of the evening star. If only the evening star were as exciting as the moon! He thought about that for a moment and went back to the window and looked down into the garden. There he saw Mary helping Aunt Verity to a garden bench and seating her with the greatest of care. He watched as Mary arranged a shawl around

Aunt Verity's shoulders. Perhaps, James thought, if a man prefers the passion of the moon to the constancy of the evening star, the fault lies with the man, not with the star.

Three evenings later Mary took a twilight walk in the garden which she had spent so many hours refurbishing. She was enjoying the night scents of the flowers and reflecting on the happy changes in her marriage. She walked all the way to the far end of the garden, to the brick wall, and then turned to come back to the house. As she turned, she heard a strange sound, something like a low moan just on the other side of the garden gate. Frightened, she stopped instantly, held her breath, and listened. The garden was surrounded by a brick wall, but through the wrought iron gate she heard an unmistakable sound. It was the moan of desperate suffering. She trembled with fear, but forced herself to act. The War had left its marks on her, but they were not just marks of fear; they were also marks of courage. She walked cautiously back to the wrought iron gate and called out softly, "Who is there?"

She heard another moan and then a plaintive voice call, "Miz Mary, Miz Mary." In its misery the voice was unrecognizable, but Mary knew someone needed her, so she opened the gate and raced through. On the back side of the wall she found Sammy lying face down on the ground. She rushed to his side, knelt, and turned him over. It was obvious that he was very ill, too ill to speak. Quickly she put her hand to his forehead and was not surprised to discover he had a burning fever. "Lie still," she insisted. "I'll get help." She raced back through the gate toward the house, calling for James. Having heard the frantic quality of her voice, he came running immediately, and Aunt Verity was not too far behind him.

"What is the matter?" he demanded.

"Sammy is outside the garden gate. He is very ill."

"So?" James asked.

"So we must take care of him. We must have a doctor. We must get him into the house. He is very sick, James."

"He is not our responsibility," James said. "He does not belong to us."

"He does not belong to anyone," Mary said impatiently, "not to anyone on this earth. He has no master; he has no parents."

"He has taken care of himself for years now," James insisted. "He is not our responsibility. He does not belong to us."

For the first time since James had met Mary, he saw anger flash in her eyes. "He belongs to God," she proclaimed. "I shall nurse him in the alley if you do not help me bring him inside."

"What is wrong with him, dear?" Aunt Verity demanded.

"I do not know, Aunt Verity. He has a very high fever."

"In that case, dear, perhaps you had better have James put him in the garden shed until a doctor can look at him."

"But Aunt Verity, he is very ill."

"I know, dear, but remember, even if he were a family member, we would isolate him in his present condition. He is undoubtedly contagious."

"And I do not want you nursing him," James insisted.

Mary turned on her heel and started back out the door.

"Mary!" James called after her sternly.

"Do not waste your breath," Aunt Verity said. "She has nursed every sick kitten, puppy and child she has ever found. How could you be married to her for over a year and not know that?"

"What am I to do?" James demanded. "Lock her in the bedroom?"

"It never worked when she was a child," Aunt Verity said calmly. "Go get the boy and put him in the garden shed, and I shall send for the doctor."

James hastened after Mary. When he found her in the alley, bent over Sammy, he pulled her away. "Go make a bed in the garden shed," he ordered. "I shall bring him in there."

"But, James," Mary started to argue, "not the shed."

"Your Aunt is correct, Mary. Even a family member would be quarantined until we know what is wrong. Go make a bed in the shed. Aunt Verity has sent for the doctor."

Mary nodded and ran to the house for blankets.

An hour later Sammy was settled as comfortably as possible in the garden shed. The doctor had come and made a diagnosis of a respiratory infection and suggested that they stay away from the boy.

Mary adamantly refused. "He will die without nursing," she insisted.

"Most likely he will die anyway, ma'am," the doctor said with little feeling. "And if you try to nurse him, you may die along with him."

"Sammy's life is in God's hands," Mary replied, "and so is mine.

Have you no medication you can leave?"

"I can leave you the usual things we have, but these infections have to go through their normal course, and there is not really much you can do but make him as comfortable as possible. He will either survive the fever, or he will not. In the meantime, you are only exposing yourself to needless danger for a child you do not even know."

"Leave the medication," Mary ordered.

The doctor sighed, opened his bag, and handed her a bottle of liquid. "The old servant woman in the house knows what herbs to use," he said. "I really do not have much more to offer."

"You will come back in the morning," Mary insisted.

When the doctor said nothing and looked at James, Mary exclaimed, "James, please!"

"If it is a matter of your fee," James began.

"It is not a matter of my fee," the doctor responded haughtily. "I doubt the boy will be alive, but I shall be back." He turned and left.

"Stay here with him, James," Mary pleaded. "I am going to the house for a basin of cold water."

"Mary, you are not going to nurse this boy." James barred the way out of the shed. "You must listen to reason. The doctor has said without hesitation that whatever this boy has is contagious. There is no reason for you to put yourself in this danger."

"He will die without nursing," Mary insisted.

"He will most likely die anyway," countered James.

"Can you in good conscience leave this boy out here to die alone?" Mary demanded.

James looked back at the boy, who was moaning softly. "Yes, yes I can, and furthermore, Mary, I can stop you, physically if necessary, from coming near this boy again."

Mary lifted her chin and looked James in the eyes. He expected to see anger, rebellion, scorn in her eyes—anything but what he saw. Her eyes were full of pity, and there was no doubt that her pity was for James, not for the boy. "You can stop me," she said quietly, "but you will not."

She turned and left, and in a few moments she was back with the equipment she needed for her night-long vigil. James left her in the garden shed and went back to the house, where Aunt Verity was waiting for him at the door.

"What shall I do?" he asked Aunt Verity. "She will not listen to reason."

"She listens to a higher voice, James."

"What on earth does that mean?"

"She listens to God. Surely you have noticed."

"But what should I do, Aunt Verity?"

Aunt Verity asked him a simple but painful question, "What would you do if she were Diana?"

She turned and started slowly up the stairs. James stared out into the garden, overwhelmed by conflicting emotions. The question made no rational sense to him. Diana would never have endangered herself by spending the night caring for a sick boy, but Mary was doing just that, and he loved her for her charity. But he loved Diana too. Suddenly love was more confusing than ever. He slammed his fist against the wall and hurried out the door to the garden shed.

When he walked in, he found Mary on her knees, bathing the young boy with cold water, trying to break his fever. Mary looked up at him and asked, "James, will you go back to the kitchen and get the herb tea that the cook is brewing and bring it to me?"

"I do not want you here, Mary," James said abruptly; then he almost felt like he would choke. "I do not want you to die."

"The tea, James, I need the tea."

He left the shed and hurried back across the yard. When he returned, he helped Mary raise Sammy's head, and slowly she spooned the tea into the boy's mouth. She worked over him for hours. James spent part of the time in the shed watching her and part of the time outside in the clear sky, staring at the moon, which was no more than a sliver, and the bright evening star.

Mary did her best for Sammy, and James lived in an agony of indecision. About two o'clock in the morning he marched firmly into the kitchen, woke up the cook, and ordered her to prepare a bath for Miss Mary. The cook asked no questions; she simply stoked the fire, added wood, and started boiling water. James went back to the shed, took off his jacket and pulled Mary to her feet.

"I have watched you for two or three hours now. I know what to do for the boy. The cook is boiling water; I want you to go inside, strip yourself of these clothes in the hallway and take the hot bath that she is preparing for you now."

"Someone must nurse this child," Mary insisted as tears ran down her cheeks.

"I know that, dearest, I know. I will nurse him. I will do everything that you have done and anything more you want done, if you will just go and protect yourself. I will treat this boy as if he were my own child. I swear it."

Mary's tears stopped flowing, and she wiped her cheeks dry with her fingers. She peered deeply into James' eyes, as if she were trying to communicate a great truth to him, but she said nothing. Instead, a mysterious smile suddenly radiated her face. Ducking her head so James could not see her eyes, she left the shed. James stood there, stunned, for several moments. He had the most profound conviction that Mary had told him something with that smile, and he thought he knew what her message was. Sammy moaned in his delirium, and James turned to the boy and began to pour more spoonfuls of tea into the boy's mouth and to wash his head and limbs with cold water. For hours he worked over the boy, but he really did not see the brown-skinned figure in front of him. James kept seeing that smile on Mary's face.

When dawn finally came, the boy was sleeping peacefully. True to his word, the doctor came back, looked at the young boy, and nodded his head affirmatively. "He will make it," the doctor said coldly. "There will be another young freeman in Georgia with no job and no future."

James tried to pay the doctor, but he waved the money away and said, "Just keep him warm and well nourished. It will probably take a week to ten days for him to regain some strength. Just let him sleep now, and bring him some broth later."

After the doctor left, James went to the kitchen and ordered the cook to boil more water for his bath so that he could bathe away the germs and change clothes. When he had done so, he went upstairs to look for Mary. He found her curled up in the window seat overlooking the garden. She had watched as long as she could and then had fallen asleep. He picked her up in his arms and took her to the bed and laid her on it. Gently he pulled a coverlet over her and reached down to stroke her hair. She opened her eyes and peered at him drowsily.

"The boy is fine," he said. "His fever has broken. The doctor says he will be fine."

"Thank God," Mary whispered.

James knew that he should let her drift back into sleep, but he could not resist the temptation. "Mary," he called her back from sleep.

"Yes, dearest," she whispered.

"Is it true?" James asked softly.

"Yes, dearest," Mary smiled at him. "We are going to have a child."

"That is wonderful," he whispered hoarsely. "Go to sleep now. You must rest."

She was exhausted, so the moment she closed her eyes, she was asleep. James rose from the side of the bed, went out into the hall and closed the door behind him. He stood there, leaning against the doorjamb, and wept.

James' heart pounded violently as he and Mary rode to the home of Diana and Thomas for a reunion dinner after their trip to Savannah. Mary chatted easily and happily about the future and all the beautiful aspects of nature that she saw along the way. James maintained a stony silence because his mind was in a state of chaos, a state reflected by his rapid heartbeat. For financial reasons he had brought Mary home from Savannah much sooner than he had wished. Not only was there not enough money to stay in Savannah, but since James was the only one who could properly run the plantation, he had to be back in South Carolina as soon as possible. He had brought Mary home far too early, as far as Aunt Verity was concerned. She had had strong words to say to James in private about the delicacy of Mary's condition and the dangers of allowing Mary to travel as this stage of her pregnancy. Through all of her words, James had had a sense that she was talking about things that she was not expressing, that she was concerned about his relationship with Diana and the possibility of Mary's being hurt. Aunt Verity had a way of saying what she wanted to say without saying it directly, and James had received her message. He, too, was worried about Mary's condition, but these were not the days before the War when the plantation ran smoothly with an overseer and slaves. He had to go back. So he arranged a trip by train to keep Mary off the rough roads as much as possible. Now the day had arrived when he would once again come face to face with Diana, and he was not at all certain how he would react and what he would ultimately do about their relationship.

The carriage finally pulled up to the verandah of Diana's home, and she and Thomas hurried out of their front door and down the steps to welcome them home. James gravely shook hands with Thomas, who slapped him on the back in an amiable way that was uncharacteristic of him. Diana kissed James on the cheek and spoke the appropriate words of a cousin by marriage. He tried not to meet her eyes. It did not seem to him that his heart could beat any faster, but the touch of her hand on his arm and the brush of her lips across his cheek increased his pulse even more. To steady himself, he turned his eyes to Mary, who was smiling happily. She put her arm through his, and he escorted her up the stairs and into the house.

As soon as Diana had seated her guests in the parlor, Mary began to give her the latest news about their Aunt Verity, but Diana interrupted her and exclaimed, "Oh, Mary! I have news of my own that is much more exciting than any news of dreadful Aunt Verity."

"Diana," Mary reproached her softly. "Aunt Verity has been our guardian angel since we were little girls."

"Yes, well, of course," Diana said quickly. "I am sorry, I should not have called Aunt Verity 'dreadful,' but you know how she moralizes. At any rate, I have the most wonderful news and cannot wait to share it with you and with dear James." She looked over at James and smiled sweetly at him.

James felt his chest grow tight, and he clenched his jaw in expectation of what Diana was about to say.

"Well, what is this news?" Mary asked curiously. "I can tell you are very excited."

"Oh, I am," Diana agreed gaily. "You see, I am going to have a baby."

"How wonderful!" Mary exclaimed, as she clutched her cousin's hand. "I—"

"And I am positive it is going to be a boy," Diana interrupted. "It absolutely is a boy, an heir to the Montgomery fortune." She smiled at her husband.

"Well, of course, any baby would be a welcome addition to the family," Mary suggested. "Your little girls are so special. Where are they anyway?" She suddenly realized they were not in the room.

"I made them stay upstairs with Mammy. They are always so underfoot at social occasions."

"But Diana," Mary lowered her voice. "They are never under foot at family occasions, and I certainly want to see them."

"But I want to talk about the coming baby," Diana smiled widely, "not the girls. This baby is going to be the son and heir to the Montgomery fortune."

"What is left of it," Thomas said, "after the Yankees came through."

Diana stood and walked to her husband's side. "Oh, I am positive, my darling Thomas, that you will rebuild everything and make even more money than you did before the War." She looked up at him and fluttered her eyelashes as she smiled alluringly.

James felt a surge of nausea as he watched her. He dragged his eyes away from Diana's manipulations of her husband and looked back at Mary, who was watching her cousin. Mary's face was covered with a peaceful compassion. She rose from the settee, walked to the other side of Thomas, put her arm through his and said, "I am sure we will all recover as much prosperity as we need and more. We shall just have to be patient and work hard."

Thomas obviously enjoyed the comfort and support of two women, so he began to grumble, "If it had not been for those damn Yankees—"

"Oh, let us not talk about that," Diana exclaimed. "There is too much to be happy about in the present." She walked across the room, took James' hand and pulled him to his feet. It was the first time their eyes met. "Do you not agree, James, dear?" she asked sweetly. Her voice was that of a cousin, but her eyes were that of Diana, the lover he knew.

"Yes," James stammered.

"Then let us all have a small toast to the present and the future," Diana pulled James across the room to Mary and Thomas.

"Thomas, pour some sherry for all four of us, and we shall have a toast."

Thomas did as she suggested, and when he had poured the sherry into the glasses and handed them around the group, Mary said shyly, "There is something I should like to include in the toast."

James waited for her to go on and make her announcement about her coming child, but instead she turned her eyes to his face. He felt a vast confusion about what was expected of him, and his face flushed, a fact that embarrassed him greatly. When he said nothing, Mary prodded him quietly, "James, dear, would you make the announcement?"

James' brain suddenly clicked into action, and he raised his glass and said, "I wish to toast Mary and the coming of our child."

Diana gasped, but quickly recovered herself and exclaimed, "Oh, Mary! Are you expecting a child too?"

"Yes," Mary beamed proudly. "It is some months off, but I shall need those months to get ready. Cousin, you and I are both going to be mothers within a month or two of each other."

"Marvelous," announced Thomas proudly.

"Yes, marvelous," Diana repeated his comment in a much weaker tone. Swiftly her eyes moved to James' eyes and then back to her cousin, as she recovered her usual gay tone. "Oh, this really is marvelous, darling." She threw her arms around her cousin. "What fun we shall have, gathering baby things and planning the futures of our sons."

"Oh, but I am not at all sure that my child will be a boy," Mary interrupted, as she laughed quietly.

"But you must hope so," Diana insisted. "It is so very important to provide James with an heir."

"I just want to provide James with a child to love," Mary responded. "A healthy child, whether a boy or a girl, will complete my happiness."

"Yes, of course," Diana agreed. "You can afford to feel that way about the first one."

"To the future," Thomas raised his glass.

"Yes," James agreed. "To the future."

The four clicked their glasses gently. Thomas and James gulped their sherry down in one swallow, while Diana and Mary watched in amazement. Then Diana laughed, tilted her glass back and gulped the sherry down in one swallow, too.

"Diana," cried Mary.

"Oh I know Aunt Verity would have a hissy fit," Diana laughed again. "But what do I care about Aunt Verity?"

Mary looked uncomfortable but said no more.

"Are you not going to finish the toast, Mary?" Thomas asked.

"Yes, of course," she responded demurely, raised the sherry glass to her mouth and barely moistened her lips with the liquid.

"I am starving," Diana announced.

"Of course you are, my dear," Thomas agreed. "You are

always starving when you are expecting a child."

"A son," Diana corrected him before she went off in search of the cook.

Dinner was speedily served at an elegantly-laid table. The food included many delicacies James could not afford. Throughout the entire leisurely, early afternoon meal, Diana plied Mary with question after question about their trip to Savannah. It was obvious to James that she didn't listen to a single one of Mary's responses; instead she kept exchanging meaningful glances with him. When the meal was concluded, Diana suggested that Thomas escort Mary out on the verandah where tea would be served. Thomas gaily took up the task, and Mary serenely accepted the arm that he offered her. Diana had managed things so smoothly that she was left in the dining room with James for just a moment.

James knew it was the meeting he had dreaded and felt confusion about for weeks. Diana moved quickly to his side and looked up at him with passion ablaze in her eyes.

"Meet me tonight," she commanded. "I long for your arms. It seems like you have been gone a year."

"I cannot," James suddenly made the decision he had been struggling with.

"Of course you can," Diana insisted.

"Mary is not sleeping as well now. It will not be possible to get away," James stammered.

"That is the lamest excuse I have ever heard," Diana countered. "Get her to drink a glass of sherry, for heaven's sake. That should make her fall asleep immediately."

"You know that Mary does not drink," James replied coldly. "She will not even swallow enough sherry to make a proper toast."

"I know that I want you, James," Diana locked eyes with him. "And I shall be waiting for you at midnight."

She turned toward the door of the dining room.

"I will not come," he said staunchly.

She stopped at the door and looked over her shoulder at him.

"We will see," she answered confidently.

James had never experienced such self hatred as he felt that night at midnight when he opened the door into the overseer's shack. He had told himself as he rowed across the river that he was only coming to break off the relationship with Diana, but in his heart he knew that he would not do it. Diana was there before him, and she rushed into his arms, scantily clad, as soon as he came into the door. The results were inevitable, and as much as he hated to admit it, very satisfying.

Weeks passed, and James witnessed endless gatherings where Diana and Mary chatted happily about their coming babies. He watched as Mary sat on the verandah with great peace in her eyes and sewed, preparing for her own child, but he continued to meet Diana whenever it was possible. A great self-imposed misery surrounded him like a choking, blinding ground fog; it was the result of self-hatred and self-repugnance. Every day that passed, he loved Mary more, yet he chose to be captive to the desire he felt for Diana. James Bradford was a strong-willed man, and he knew it. He did not delude himself by viewing himself as a helpless captive of Diana's beauty or his own passion. He acknowledged to himself that he was choosing his actions, that he was selfish. When he tried to discuss his feelings with Diana, she adamantly denied that there was a problem. She saw no reason why their relationship could not and should not go on. After all, she told James flatly, she wanted him and he wanted her. What else was there to consider? Other than discretion, of course. Her only regret was that their affair would have to be discontinued soon because of her growing pregnancy; she would never risk the life of the baby who might be the Montgomery heir and thus solidify her position in society. James decided that the months apart from Diana which would be required by her advancing pregnancy and the birth of her child would surely be the time to stop his selfish behavior, to make the choice to break off the relationship. He further convinced himself that the arrival of Mary's child, his child, would strengthen his resolve, but in the meantime he continued to meet Diana, and he continued to hate himself. To avoid his feelings he worked longer and longer hours, until he drove himself close to physical exhaustion. Mary often verbalized her concerned for him.

Several months after his return from Savannah, James was sneaking back to the house around two o'clock in the morning, after having met Diana. As he approached the bottom of the hill and looked up at his stately house, he saw a woman in a dressing gown on the front verandah; he knew that it was Mary, looking for him, worrying about him.

He hastened up the hill, hurriedly putting together an

explanation of why he was out roaming at two o'clock in the morning. As he approached the house, she suddenly saw him and raced down the stairs. Helpless horror gripped him as he watched his sweet Mary fall on the bottom stair and land face forward on the ground. He ran to her side, threw himself on his knees and gathered her in his arms. She was unconscious, and her beautiful face was covered with blood. Quickly he picked her up and carried her into the house as he called for help from the servants. By the time he had placed her on the bed and lighted the candles, several black women had appeared in answer to his calls. Mary regained consciousness quickly, but as she did, she placed her hands across her abdomen and groaned, and James' worst fear became reality as Mary cried out, "Oh James, the baby!"

By dawn it was all over. The injuries to Mary's face were dreadful to look at, but James knew that they were superficial and would heal. The injuries to her mind frightened him considerably; she had lost her child and was in a grave state of depression. He sat by her bedside as the sun rose, and he felt many emotions, but by far, self-hatred was the strongest. As he looked down at Mary's tortured face and watched as she writhed in her sleep, he made his final decision about Diana.

Diana arrived about 11 o'clock the next morning, having heard the news about Mary. She stood by Mary's bed and watched her sleep. James still sat by Mary's side, holding her hand.

"I am sorry, James," Diana said softly. "Truly I am, but she will recover from this. Women lose babies all the time and go on to have other babies."

"Mary is not like other women," James said, without taking his eyes off of his wife's face.

"She is more delicate than many," Diana admitted, "but she is not a broken doll, James. I tell you there will be more children. I can understand your being concerned, but this really is just a passing problem."

James dragged his eyes away from Mary's face and stared up at Diana. "Mary is not a mere doll at all, Diana. I shall be forever cursed for not recognizing that fact and treating her with the respect she deserves. I want to talk to you, privately," he said.

"Of course," Diana agreed lightly as she turned to leave the room.

James ordered the servant sitting outside in the hall to go in and sit with his wife, and then he took Diana out on the front verandah. He pointed to the step where Mary had fallen.

"She fell here," he said to Diana, "about two o'clock this morning."

"Try not to think about the details, James. What is the point?" Diana asked impatiently.

James turned on her savagely. "The point is obvious. Mary was waiting for me when I returned from the shack. She thought I was awake and wandering the plantation grounds because I was worried about this land, but you and I know the truth. I was awake because I was holding her cousin in my arms and making love to her."

"James, really," Diana hissed at him. "Stop this at once. Someone might hear you. Think what could happen."

"A great deal has already happened." James raised his voice again.

Diana took his arm and pulled him off the verandah and down the drive. "I am well aware that my cousin lost her child because she fell on the bottom step of the verandah."

"And you are also aware that she would not have been out on the verandah if it had not been for our behavior."

"Of course I am," Diana said flippantly, "but these things happen. You and I have a right to our happiness. Things were stolen from us, James." She turned and glared up into his eyes as she spoke. "We should have been married. We should have had a home of our own. The children I have borne should have—"

"'Should have' does not count, Diana," James interrupted her. "Or if it does, you and I should be saying things like, 'we should have been true to our marriage vows; we should have protected Mary's feelings; we should have behaved differently.'"

"You are upset now," Diana tried to soothe him, "but you will calm down and see things in a better light."

"I hope I will calm down," James said evenly, "but I hope I will never forget the way I feel now, and I want you to know that our relationship is ended."

"James, you are merely overwrought for the moment. There is an understandable remorse working in you. I agree with you that it would be best for us to discontinue seeing each other for a while. Mary will need more of your attention, and you will have to be more careful not to get caught if she is going to continue wandering around looking for you."

"Diana," James tried to interrupt her.

"And then there is the matter of my advancing pregnancy. I cannot risk losing this child, so we shall have to discontinue our relationship for a while anyway."

"I am not talking about temporarily discontinuing our relationship," James insisted. "I am talking about ending the relationship. As far as I am concerned, our relationship is terminated, Diana."

Diana's beautiful face hardened as she stared up at him for several moments. When she spoke, her voice was icy. "Very well, James, you really have become rather boring lately. I shall spend the next few months taking care of myself and my unborn son. After he is born, I shall no longer have to worry about Thomas' contentment with me as a wife. My future will be secure because I shall have given him an heir."

"The heir you think you are going to give Thomas is my child. If it is a boy, it is my son."

"Thomas does not know that," Diana sneered coldly. "And you will never tell him, will you?" she taunted James.

James' face grew white with fury, but he said nothing.

"Thanks for the son," Diana said airily. "Now go back and hold the hand of your boring, but honest, wife."

She walked down the drive to her carriage and ordered her driver to help her into it. James stood like a stone without raising his head while she drove past.

"This is the great James Bradford that Grandmother spoke of constantly?" Caroline demanded. "Why, she made him sound like he was half god, half king."

"Yes, I suspect she did, my dear," Aunt Kathleen responded quietly. "She preferred to see it that way, and of course it is easier to see things the way one wants to see them, when one lives in Texas and the truths are all in South Carolina."

"But she lied to me," Caroline raised her voice angrily. "You have no idea how much she talked about her grandfather, how much she talked about his noble behavior, his honorable life, all his marvelous accomplishments."

"You must not judge too hastily, my dear. I have not finished his story," Aunt Kathleen warned. "He was a young man; certainly he made many mistakes. One might be able to forgive him a certain percentage of those mistakes, considering his confusion after the War. It was a terrible time for everyone. It really is very difficult to judge such things."

"I don't have any difficulty judging him," Caroline persisted. "He carried on an affair, an adulterous affair, with Diana and married her cousin to cover up his sins. What's so hard to judge? And the results are obvious—the death of a child, the misery of Mary. Poor Mary! She sounds like she was a much more worthy person than James or Diana or all the rest of them put together."

"She was very special," Aunt Kathleen murmured. "And she continued to be special, my dear. She was physically delicate, but there was a celestial light in her. I remember it well, although I certainly did not understand it at the time."

"You remember it well?"

"Of course, my dear. James Bradford was my grandfather, too, and Mary was my grandmother."

"Yes, I guess that's true," Caroline stammered. "It's difficult to keep up with the generations."

"You must remember, my dear, that Grandfather, James Bradford, did not cease living when Grandmother, Mary, lost her first child. And Mary did not cease living. It was a dreadful time for both of them, but it was a time for righting things." Aunt Kathleen paused, then added, "not that anything stayed righted."

"He didn't go back to Diana?" Caroline demanded.

"Oh no," Aunt Kathleen shook her head. "He seems to have been thoroughly cured of his feelings for Diana."

"There must have been other children, or obviously you and Grandmother wouldn't exist."

"Several years after Mary lost her child and after Diana had given birth to her son, Mary had a daughter, and that daughter was Caroline, the first Caroline in the family, and the woman for whom you were named, and, of course, that Caroline was my mother."

"What was her life like?" Caroline asked eagerly.

"It was a good life, a carefree childhood. She was called Carrie and was adored by both her parents. James Bradford restored the plantation, regained some of his wealth, and became quite a public servant. Really, on the whole, I would say that he gave more years to positive service in the community than any other member of our family."

"He was probably acting from guilt," Caroline commented acidly.

"No doubt that was one element of it," Aunt Kathleen agreed, "but after his affair with Diana ended, he and Mary, my grandparents, managed to make a very good marriage."

"Why do you think Grandmother never told me about any of the early part of James Bradford's life?"

"Obviously she did not want you to know that he was not perfect," Aunt Kathleen said, "and I am sorry to say that the result of his actions as a young man bore tremendously painful fruit to this family when his daughter, Carrie, was in her teens and was of a marriageable age. I think it most likely that Judith never told you about James Bradford's early mistakes because she did not want to tell you about the difficulties that they caused our mother, Carrie. After all, my dear, you must remember that the public never knew the things that I have told you so far about James Bradford and Diana. Indeed, their actions might not have even been known in the family except for what was to come some eighteen years later, when Carrie fell in love. I am sure it is the story of our mother, Carrie, that Judith never wanted you to know, because it is her story that Judith was most ashamed of, even though what happened was not Mother's fault."

"I don't have the slightest idea what you're talking about," Caroline responded.

"Of course not," Aunt Kathleen replied. "There are people here in Charleston who would remember, but very few of them are still alive, and certainly no one in Texas would have known, and Judith would never have told anyone."

"Will you tell me the story of your mother, Aunt Kathleen? For some reason, I feel that I must know it."

"Yes, my dear," Aunt Kathleen rose slowly from her seat. "I shall be proud to tell you the story that Judith was so ashamed of. You see, your great-grandmother, Carrie, was a woman of strength and remarkable values, and I am proud of her, just as proud of her as Judith was ashamed. I would not want you to go through the remainder of your life without knowing the story of your great-grandmother, but I am afraid, my dear, that I am an old woman and it is growing late. I must rest, but you have given me good reason to wake up in the morning. I want you to know the truth. Indeed, I suspect you need to know about those who came before you and the struggles of their lives." She walked over to Caroline and gave her a gentle hug.

"Thank you, Aunt Kathleen," Caroline whispered and kissed her gently on the cheek. "I'm so glad to be here."

"And I'm glad you've come," Aunt Kathleen said. "We shall have a splendid time. Good night, my dear."

"Good night, Aunt Kathleen," Caroline called as her great-aunt walked across the piazza and back into the house.

Caroline stayed out on the piazza for some time, comparing what she had just heard about James Bradford with the glowing stories that her grandmother had told her. When she had finished her comparison, she was left with many questions. If Grandmother lied to me about James Bradford, she wondered, what else has she lied to me about? Or if it wasn't exactly a lie, if it is a matter of values, different values, then have I been coaxed into adopting the wrong set of values?

I loved David when I married him, and I still do. Oh, so very much! But what if he had not been rich? Would I have ignored him, never given him a second thought? I don't know. How dreadful to think I might have missed loving David because of the values Grandmother taught me. Caroline rose and walked to the railing. She stared at the full moon and at the purity of its white light on the sea. I am so horribly self-centered, she thought, and so superficial. It's true Grandmother taught me to be selfish when I was a child, but I am thirty-four years old now. I am not a child; I can't go on through life valuing only my own enjoyment, measuring everything in terms of protecting the bubble of happiness that David and I have. There is a needy world out there. Think of those poor children living in a cardboard box! And think of their mother struggling against killing odds to feed them. How she must love them! And what about my own child? I chose to be pregnant on a whim, without even sharing the decision with David. But I am pregnant. It's a fact. My baby exists just like those children in the cardboard box. What kind of hypocrite am I to condemn society for abandoning those children, yet think of killing my child for convenience's sake? And how dare I judge James Bradford's behavior or Grandmother's?

Chapter 14

For the first time in well over a week, Caroline awoke without regret that she was alive. Grief over the death of Judith and anxiety about her future with David were still lurking in the shadows of her mind, but they had been shoved into the corners by an expanding light of expectancy. She was on the road to where she needed to go, and although she could not name the destination point yet, she eagerly embraced the journey ahead, whether it would be filled with pain or joy.

A patch of bright sunlight played on the wide pine floors, flashing on the patina of the often-waxed boards, then disappearing for an instant, before skipping back into the room. Clouds, Caroline thought, it must be partly cloudy today. No, the shadows come and go too quickly. Wait, I know. It's the leaves of the oaks that make the sun come and go. The sun is playing tag with the leaves, and I am lucky enough to see the reflection of their game on the floor. Oh dear! I'm beginning to sound like Aunt Kathleen. Caroline laughed and was surprised to hear her own laugh again. But maybe that's not such a bad thing, she quickly decided. She watched the dancing light on the floor a few minutes more as she became aware of the sounds of songbirds. This place has healing power, she concluded—healing power. I wonder where it comes from.

The sound of a human voice began to drift into the room. Someone's singing in the garden, Caroline realized. It must be Aunt Kathleen. She smiled, sat up, and stretched. For a moment she dangled her feet off the side of the high bed, swinging them in the sunshine, watching the shadows she could make. Once again the singing voice drifted into the room, and Caroline slipped off the bed and reached for her robe. Out on the piazza, she was able to hear the voice more distinctly, and she could see Aunt Kathleen sitting in the midst of her rose garden, a book open on her lap. Eagerly Caroline hurried back through her room, and out into the hall to descend the staircase. When her bare feet touched the sun-warmed boards of the lower piazza, she smiled, and when they touched the old brick walk, with its cool, soft mosses in each crack, she laughed aloud and exclaimed, "What a perfect welcome to a new day!"

She stood still a moment, her toes digging into the velvety moss while her ears strained to hear the words of Aunt Kathleen's song.

"'And He walks with me and He talks with me and He tells me I am His own. And the joy we share as we tarry there, no other has ever known.'" Aunt Kathleen finished her song and began humming to herself as Caroline walked down the path toward her.

"Oh, Caroline! Good morning," Aunt Kathleen beckoned to her to join her. "I hope you slept well, and I hope I did not wake you up with my singing."

"It was lovely," Caroline said as she leaned over to kiss Aunt Kathleen's cheek. "What was it?"

"My favorite of all hymns. It's called 'In the Garden,' and that is pretty much what it is about. The lyrics speak of coming to the garden early in the morning to meet Jesus 'while the dew is still on the roses.' Isn't that a marvelous thought, Caroline? You must use that hymn sometime for your own morning devotional."

Caroline hesitated before responding, "I don't have morning devotionals."

"Why not?"

"I guess I never thought of including God in my morning," Caroline answered.

"But you cannot exclude Him, not in the morning or at any other time of the day. It cannot be done; it is impossible. He is here, whether you include Him or not. He made everything and everyone. He made you. He is in you and around you. You cannot create a vacuum that keeps God out."

"I don't exactly exclude God, Aunt Kathleen; I just run my own life."

"Oh, I am afraid I could never do that. If I ran my own life, I would make such a mess of it. Oh my! Look at that yellow rose." Aunt Kathleen stood to caress a bloom and leaned over to smell it.

I have made a mess of my life, Caroline thought, and I didn't even know it until a week ago. "I haven't done such a good job of running my life, Aunt Kathleen," Caroline confessed aloud.

"You are still alive, my dear. Today is a new day, a fresh start. That is what my mother always said to me. 'God gives us a fresh start every minute of our lives. What we do with that start is up to us.' That is what Mother always said. I like to think of that in the morning."

"I need a fresh start, Aunt Kathleen."

"Then start fresh, Caroline, this minute."

"But I need more information."

"Yes, you do, and recognizing that fact is a fresh start in itself."

"Will you tell me about your mother?"

"Of course, my dear, but let's have some breakfast on the upper piazza first. I want to see the sea."

"But Betsy—"

"—will have a wonderful time fussing at me about the stairs. We would not want to take that away from her, would we?"

"My grandmother was ill for a very long time after losing her first baby," Aunt Kathleen began her reminiscing as soon as they had finished eating. "Diana, on the other hand, gave birth easily to a son, who was named Robert Montgomery. I often wondered what my grandfather, James Bradford, must have felt, but I never dared ask him. I do know that he is listed on the baptismal certificate as the godfather of Diana's child."

"You must be joking! Was Mary the godmother?" Caroline asked incredulously.

"No," Aunt Kathleen responded. "She is not listed as the godmother. She was too ill to participate in the baptism."

"How strange it must have been," Caroline said, "for him to stand there and watch his own son be baptized with the name of another man. I can't understand how any man could do that."

"Things have changed, my dear. You know that, of course, but perhaps you cannot really appreciate the scope of the changes. In that day and time, indeed in most of my lifetime, people did almost anything to avoid social embarrassment, and the codes were very rigid. To have claimed his son would have meant ruin for James Bradford and for Diana and, of course, for Mary too, in spite of her innocence."

"You sound as if you have some sort of sympathy for him," Caroline said.

"No, I do not have any sympathy for my grandfather; however, I do have some understanding of what a great crisis in one's life can lead one to do. Whenever I think of him, I try to remember that his affair with Diana and his consequent treatment of my grand-mother came quickly after the horrors of the War Between the States. It is not difficult for me to imagine a young, Southern man claiming any piece of life that was left in the South, especially a beloved relationship that he believed belonged to him."

"But he didn't just have an affair with Diana," Caroline argued. "He married her cousin; he married Mary. Didn't he consider her feelings at all?"

"He was wrong, my dear; there is no justification for what he did. I am not trying to justify him. I am simply putting him into the historical context of his time, and as much as I can, into the context of his own understanding of life when he was in his twen-ties. Some could argue that Mary would never have had a chance to be a wife and mother had it not been for my grandfather, but certainly she did not deserve the treatment that she received. I cannot defend James Bradford. I can only try to understand him."

"Is it necessary for you to understand him?" Caroline asked.

"Yes, it is always necessary for us to understand," Aunt Kathleen answered. "Understanding someone and someone's actions is not the same as excusing them, my dear. But understanding is the beginning of forgiving, and without forgiveness one's life would be a constantly erupting volcano of anger at the various injuries that have been done to one. It is essential to forgive, so it is essen-tial to understand."

"You speak so strongly on the subject of forgiving your grand-father," Caroline commented. "Was he that much a part of your life?"

"No, not really, not directly, but you see, my dear, as I told you last evening, what James Bradford and Diana Montgomery did so many years ago eventually hurt Judith, your grandmother, and me. Once one starts to deceive, the consequences of that deceit go on for years. I know such a statement is a truism, almost a cliché, and consequently the kind of thing we have a tendency to ignore, but the fact of the matter is, it is true. The sins of the father are visited on the sons—and the daughters."

"That's never seemed very fair to me," Caroline commented.

"Don't you think it is simply a matter of the realities of social interaction? What a person does, male or female, affects that person's children; and those children who are emotionally or socially harmed, they pass that harm on to their own children. It seems to me to be no more than an inevitable movement through the generations. I think that is what happened in our family."

"How did James Bradford's actions affect you and Grandmother?" Caroline asked eagerly.

"As I said, my dear, Diana easily gave birth to her son, James Bradford's son, and he was named Robert Montgomery. Mary, my grandmother, eventually recovered her health. It was a full three years before she was able to give birth, but she did give birth to my mother, who was named Caroline, but was always called Carrie. The families of Mary and Diana lived on adjoining plantations and attended the same church, so the children grew up together, and while there must have been some difficult moments for James Bradford and Diana Montgomery, the two families seemed to have interacted in a normal fashion. Both families prospered financially, as they were both able to bring their plantations back to life and to expand their business interests into other fields. James Bradford became one of the first state politicians after the federal troops left South Carolina and a true government was formed in the state. Diana never gave birth to another child. Most likely that would have been her choice, I think. At any rate, in 1879, when Robert was ten years old, he was sent to a military boarding school for most of each year. In 1885, when Robert was sixteen, it was time for him to go off to college. I know that seems very young by modern standards, but it was typical of the time. He wanted to study law eventually, so he chose to go to William and Mary. Two years later, when Robert was eighteen, he hurried back from Virginia as quickly as possible because Thomas Montgomery was gravely ill. Thomas died, and Robert Montgomery became heir to his estate, just as Diana had planned that he would.

"When Robert returned, he was quite handsome and sophisticated, having been away to college in another state for several years. During that time, Carrie had turned into a very beautiful young woman. She was still quite young, only fifteen, not ready yet for society, but she was a remarkable young woman, especially for that day and time. Ladies were not expected to think about anything except running their households, mothering and being good hostesses, but Carrie was different. She was a deep thinker."

"What made her so different?" Caroline asked.

"Carrie, my mother, was a great lover of books. My

grandmother, Mary, was the kind of woman who believed that a child should be an individual, and so she allowed Carrie, to explore her interests, even though they were most unorthodox for young ladies. My mother loved words, and rather than forbid her the books that meant so much to her, my grandmother Mary encouraged her. I know it sounds like such a natural thing to you. It is hard for you to understand how very independent an action this was for my grandmother to take. To allow her daughter, in the 1870's and 1880's, to be an intellectual was absolutely bizarre because it was accepted as a fact that such a young woman would never catch a husband. My grandmother, Mary, however, was much more interested in nurturing the spirit of her daughter rather than insuring that she would become a social success. My grandmother was a remarkable woman, and she had been taught much by the suffering of her own childhood and of the war years."

"And the suffering of her marriage, I would think," Caroline added.

"Yes, I am sure you are right, my dear. She always made it very clear to me that when Carrie was born, she considered her a gift from heaven. She would have considered any child a gift from heaven, but she had lost her first and waited so long, with a great fear that she might be left barren. When Carrie was born, grandmother was ecstatic."

"It sounds like you had a wonderful grandmother. I wish I could have known her. I wish I could have known your mother, too."

"Yes, it is a pity. Of course there was no way that you could have known my grandmother, and you were so very tiny when my mother died, you could not have known her either even if Judith had allowed Marian to bring you to Charleston."

"Did Carrie know I was born?" Caroline asked eagerly.

"Oh yes, my dear. She knew you were born, and she knew that you had been named after her by Marian. It was a great pleasure to her."

"I wonder why Mother named me Caroline. All my life Grandmother has made it clear that she did not agree with Mother's choice."

"I think that Marian began to assert her own personality when you were born. She did not visit Charleston until some years later, but she began to correspond regularly, and I was so glad she did.

You see, my mother was quite enfeebled and bed-ridden, but she could see perfectly well, and Marian very kindly sent a beautiful portrait of you to my mother. I think it was the very first portrait that was made of you, in your christening gown. Mother loved looking at that picture. I have a distinct memory of her, propped up in bed here at the house, looking at your picture, with her copy of Robert Browning in her lap."

"Which room was she in?"

"Why, in the blue room, my dear, where you are staying. It was her idea to paint it that color. She loved the sky on a sunny day, especially a sunny, winter day, and she wanted that room to be sky blue so she could lie in her bed and feel that she was floating above the earth. Well, I must be absolutely wearing you out with all this reminiscing—" Aunt Kathleen started to stand. "I am sure you have a whole agenda of places you want to visit, and if you do not, I certainly want to help you work one out. There are so many things to see here."

"Please don't stop," Caroline begged, "unless, of course, you're tired."

"Oh no, my dear, I am not tired, but I do need to move around. You see, if I am going to continue to go up and down those stairs, I have to keep these old bones well oiled, and that means a gentle walk every morning, if possible. But if you wish to come along, my dear, if you do not think it will be a great bore for you, I shall be delighted to continue talking."

"I'd love to," Caroline rose and gave her Aunt Kathleen a small hug.

"Well, then, we had best both get dressed," Aunt Kathleen laughed happily. "This may be 1996, but Charleston would still be most perturbed if we strolled the sidewalks in our dressing gowns."

"I'm sure," Caroline agreed, "and I must call London to see how David is."

"Of course, my dear. There is no need to rush. Just meet me in the garden when you are ready."

Just as the two women were about to leave the garden through the wrought iron gate, Aunt Kathleen exclaimed, "Oh dear! I forgot my straw hat. Would you run get it? It is just inside the entry there. It is ridiculous, of course, but one cannot get away from certain habits such as protecting one's complexion. Oh, and get yourself one too. You must protect that beautiful skin of yours. By the way, have you seen a picture of Mother?"

"No, I don't think I have," Caroline responded. "It's very strange. I would have thought Grandmother would have had one, now that I think about it, but she didn't."

"It is not so strange really. I am afraid that Judith and Mother were not always compatible, but you certainly need to see a picture of Mother. You need to see a picture of the first Caroline. When you get my hat, step inside the dining room and look at the portrait over the sideboard. That is Mother, the first Caroline in the family, the woman you were named for."

"I will," Caroline agreed, as she eagerly rushed off toward the house. She picked up the two straw hats and hurried into the dining room. She had not previously been in that room, so it took her a moment to take in the arrangement of the furniture, but when her eyes lighted on the sideboard, she looked slowly upward. There was a large portrait of a beautiful woman, dressed in the fashion of the 1880's. Caroline stared in amazement when she saw it, and for some reason she did not understand, her eyes burned with tears as she murmured, "It's almost like looking into a mirror." There before her was the portrait of another auburn-haired, creamy-skinned woman, dressed in a royal blue, silk ball gown. Caroline walked closer to the portrait and studied the eyes of this woman who was her great grandmother. Her eyes are different, Caroline thought. They are the same color as mine, but there is great depth in those eyes that I have never seen in my own. Perhaps what Aunt Kathleen has told me about her early life explains the difference. Great Grandmother was an intellectual, a seeker after truth, and she dared to be an intellectual at a time when it was unthinkable for women. Perhaps that explains the depth I see in her eyes. How amazing that we should look so much alike; no wonder Aunt Kathleen wanted me to see this portrait. Oh my goodness, Aunt Kathleen! She suddenly remembered the elderly lady she had left in the garden, and she turned and rushed outside toward her Aunt.

Aunt Kathleen laughed as she saw her coming. "Did you see someone you know?" she asked brightly.

"I certainly did; the likeness is surprising."

"'Surprising' is definitely the right word. You are almost a carbon copy of your great grandmother. In fact, you gave me quite a start when you showed up at the gate yesterday. I knew it was you, of course, because of your modern clothing, but for a moment I thought Mother had returned. Most uncanny and delightful."

"We do look alike," Caroline agreed, "except for our eyes. They're the same color, but her eyes are very different somehow, very deep. That thoughtfulness I see in them must have been the result of studying all the books she loved."

"I think it was more than that, my dear," Aunt Kathleen took the straw hat Caroline was holding for her and put it on. "How is your David?"

"Much, much better. He can actually talk without coughing."

"I am glad to hear it, very glad. Well, now you can stop worrying about him, and I am sure he is glad to know you are in Charleston, away from your recent troubles in Texas."

"Actually, I didn't tell him," Caroline admitted. "I'm not even sure why. I just didn't."

"I see," was all Aunt Kathleen said on that subject. "Well, now, put your hat on, and let us go for a slow stroll through this beautiful, old neighborhood, and I shall tell you why Mother's eyes have the depth you see there."

They walked through the beautiful, wrought-iron gate and turned on to an old street that was arched over with grand live oaks. They began their amble down the brick sidewalk into a world of incredible grace and beauty. Caroline thought that she had seen the best that the past had to offer in her travels with David in America and abroad, but this place was special. It seemed to be serenely old and vibrantly young at the same time.

"Well, my dear," Aunt Kathleen began, "as I told you, Robert Montgomery returned from college because his father was ill, and within a few days his father died. He was heir to a great estate but still a very young man, only eighteen, and your grandmother, Carrie, his second cousin, was just beginning to bloom into a great beauty. She was fifteen, but as I have said, she already had great depth of thought and feeling, much more than most women would have obtained in a lifetime during that era. She liked to wander off by herself to special places, and the day after Thomas Montgomery's funeral, she decided the house was an oppressive place to be, so she picked up a volume that she loved and wandered away to one of her favorite places of solitude. Little did she know that this wandering of hers would drastically change her life."

Carrie Bradford held her full skirts and petticoats close to her legs and ducked her head low as she scrambled under the wild, tangled wisteria that climbed over the small dogwood trees. She was moving through her own private entrance into a special world of color, light and peace that she had found when she was a child. For her escape from the grief of the Bradford household after her uncle's funeral, she had chosen one of her favorite natural spots, a place she called God's aquarium. After she had struggled through the overgrowth of wisteria and the branches of the dogwoods, she came out into an open space, and before her she could clearly see the Ashley River. She climbed a low, rocky hill until she reached a large rock ledge that jutted out over the water. In the millions of years that had preceded her life, the river had created the ledge she stood on, and the wind had whittled out a perfect seat on top of the rock. Sometime during that geological time frame an oak seed had dropped on the rock and managed to take root, and by the time Carrie arrived in history, that oak tree was ancient and able to spread its protective arms far out over the water.

Carrie placed her book at the foot of the oak tree and walked to the edge of the rock ledge and knelt. She put her hands down on the rock, leaned over the edge and peered into the clear, deep water. "God's aquarium," she whispered, as she stared down at the beautiful fish which glided through the water. For over five years now, this had been Carrie's favorite spot on the plantation. She had never told anyone about it for fear some fisherman would come here and catch her special fish. She knew it wasn't likely, but she liked to think that the same fish were there every time she came, a peaceful family, well provided for, and protected. Just the sight of them was soothing. After watching them for a few moments, she sat back and looked out across the water. She was in love with the reflection of the large oak on the placid, clear surface of the river and exhilarated by the flecks of sunlight that filtered through the leaves of the oak to dance on the water. Further down the river, away from the oak, the water was a shimmer of bright blue, which changed to gray-blue whenever a cloud passed overhead. She was mesmerized by the scene: the softly flowing water, the changing light, the slightest breeze that fluttered a few leaves overhead. She sat quietly for many minutes before she returned to the trunk of the old oak and picked up her volume to read.

She read for half an hour, glancing up now and then to see how the light had changed on the water and on the shore opposite her. When she returned her eyes to the pages she was reading, she heard a thrashing in the underbrush some distance away from her. Many times she had been at this favorite spot of hers and heard people come close, but she had learned over the years that if she remained totally quiet, no one ever came this far. It was too difficult a journey. One had to know the way or else be willing to thrust aside a great tangle of vines and branches. She felt confident that once again today her special place would not be discovered. She listened as the thrashing came closer, but experience had taught her well not to be alarmed. She expected that if anything appeared, it would be one of the large plantation dogs who sometimes visited her and enjoyed her special place with her. A smile covered her face as she remembered the eagerness of these dogs whenever they discovered a comrade sitting on the ledge. The thrashing came closer, and she waited for the animal to appear, to see her, and to wag its tail wildly, but instead the noise in the brush stopped, and she heard a sudden outburst of sobbing. Carrie was startled and filled with compassion. Whoever was there, so close to her and yet not knowing of her presence, was releasing the floodgates of emotion that for some reason had been dammed for a long time. The sobs continued, and Carrie agonized over what action to take. Should she sit quietly and allow this person to spend her or his grief in the solitude that she or he had obviously sought, or should she go to this person and try to console her or him?

Who can it be, she wondered, and why such grief, such misery? Oh, I cannot bear to hear it. Carrie knew of few reasons for such misery, other than death, so she quickly associated this person's suffering with the recent death of Thomas Montgomery, and in the instant that she made that association, she guessed that the sobbing person was Robert, the bereaved son of Thomas Montgomery and her second cousin. Again she debated with herself whether she should leave him unembarrassed to grieve alone or whether she should go to him to console him. She wrung her hands and put her book aside and prayed that God would give him peace, but he cried on.

Finally she could stand it no longer. She jumped abruptly to her feet and walked briskly toward the undergrowth that she knew must be the location Robert had chosen to release his feelings. He was only a few feet away, and Carrie had only to walk down off of the ledge and push aside a tangle of vines and limbs to find him. He was startled to see her, and quickly he wiped his sleeve across his face to dry it of the rain of tears.

"Carrie," he called out in shock, and his voice cracked as he said the single word.

"Oh, Robert," was all she said as she came to his side and knelt down by him.

"I thought I was alone," his voice was still broken, as he tried to speak over the lump in his throat.

"It does not matter," she insisted.

"Oh, but it does. It matters to me. I did not want anyone to know, certainly not—certainly not—"

"Not a girl," Carrie finished the sentence for him, but there was gentleness in her tone, not bitterness.

"I am eighteen years old. I should not be acting this way."

"Of course you should," Carrie insisted. "What kind of unfeeling beast would you be if you felt nothing over your father's death?"

"But I am a man," Robert insisted.

"A man can have feelings," Carrie protested. "A man should have feelings. Other men have allowed themselves to have feelings. Why shouldn't you?"

"It is not right. I need to be strong. It is not manly to break down this way, but every time I look at our house, and realize that he is under the ground and I shall see him no more, I feel a great trembling come over me, and I cannot speak for fear I shall sob and embarrass myself and humiliate my family. That house, the house of my youth, the house of so many happy years with my father, it brings me to sobs now." In despair and embarrassment he covered his face with his hands.

Carrie looked at him and struggled to think of words to help him. Even at fifteen she was too wise to expect to remove his grief, but oh, how she wanted to give him permission to grieve. It is coming home to the house and knowing that his father will never be there again, she thought. He will never hear his father's voice again or feel his arm around his shoulders. What a shocking thing! He is suffering the same torments that Tennyson wrote about in his poetry. She murmured the lines that she had memorized: "'Dark house by which once more I stand, here in the long unlovely street, doors where my heart was used to beat so quickly, waiting for a hand, a hand that can be clasped no more.'"

Robert raised his head and stared at her through tear-filled eyes.

"'Behold me, for I cannot sleep, and like a guilty thing I creep at earliest morning to the door. He is not here, but far away the noise of life begins again, and ghastly through the drizzling rain on the bald street breaks the blank day.'"

"What?" Robert asked. "What did you say?"

"Oh, it was just some verses I memorized," Carrie rubbed her forehead thoughtfully. "I was reminded of them by what you were saying."

"Verses?" Robert repeated in an expressionless voice.

"Yes," Carrie's voice was more energized than his. "Yes, verses. Those were the lines that Tennyson wrote when he lost his dear friend. You see, it was difficult for him to return to the house where he had spent so many happy hours with his friend."

"I am confused, Carrie," Robert turned his face away and wiped his eyes with his sleeve. "I do not seem to be able to understand what you are saying."

"I only wanted to say that men are allowed to grieve," Carrie reached out and patted his hand. "It is true that you are a man, Robert, but you are allowed to grieve over the loss of a loved one. If Tennyson could grieve so much that he wrote poetry about it, what is so shameful about your grief?"

"Tennyson?" Robert turned to look at her. "You were actually quoting Tennyson?"

"Of course," she replied, "he is one of my favorite poets."

"I did not know you read poetry, Carrie. I did not know any girl read poetry."

"I suppose very few do," Carrie shrugged her shoulders, "but I love it, and it seems to me that sometimes it makes life easier to live."

Robert nodded.

"Come with me, Robert," Carrie said suddenly. "I want to show you a special place, my special place, a place I have never shared with anyone, but it is so beautiful, so calming, so serene, I want to share it with you."

Robert preferred to stay where he was and send Carrie away, but he hated to be rude. He looked at her thoughtfully. She was turning into a beautiful woman, but he still remembered her as the little girl she had been when he had last seen her.

"Come with me," Carrie insisted as she stood and began to pull at Robert's arm.

Reluctantly he stood and followed her through a few feet of underbrush and climbed up onto the ledge of rock until they had reached her special spot.

"Just look at it!" Carrie exclaimed. "Is it not magnificent?"

Robert viewed the river and the other shore; it was beautiful, but the weight of grief that pressed on his heart made it impossible for him to match Carrie's enthusiasm.

"And look," Carrie said, as she pointed down into the water. "I call this God's aquarium."

"Where did you learn a word like aquarium?"

"In my reading, of course," Carrie retorted gently.

"Ah, yes."

"Doesn't this spot give you a sense of eternity, Robert?" Carrie asked quietly.

"Yes, it does."

"I suppose that is the only consolation I can offer you, the eternity that you will spend with your father. When I look around this place and think of how many years it has been here, I begin to understand a little bit about how long eternity is, and how long we will be with God and with those we love. You do believe in eternity, don't you, Robert?"

"I suppose so," he said without conviction. "I guess I have never given it much thought. I want to believe in eternity, especially the day after putting my father in the ground," Robert choked up and could not go on for a moment, "but I find the only image in my mind is a hole in the ground and dirt slowly covering up my father. How can I believe in eternity, Carrie, when I remember that hole in the ground and six feet of earth on top of my father?"

"'Strong Son of God, immortal Love,'" Carrie quoted, "'whom we who have not seen thy face, by faith and faith alone embrace, believing where we cannot prove'—"

"Those are only lines of poetry, Carrie," Robert interrupted her.

"But what are lines of poetry? They are the experiences of another man, a man like you, a man who lost someone he loved and felt so deeply that he had to write out his feelings. Ultimately Tennyson said of God, 'Thou will not leave us in the dust. Thou madest man, he knows not why, he thinks he was not made to die, and thou hast made him, thou art just.'"

"Very pretty, Carrie," Robert reached out and patted her slight shoulder. "Thank you for trying to help."

"Oh, I know they are just words I have memorized. I know how young I am; I know I have not lost anyone close to me." She looked down into the water. "I know I have no comfort to offer you, not the kind you need."

There was silence between them for quite a while; then Robert spoke, "Perhaps you do have the comfort I need, for you have offered me the comfort of knowing there is someone who cares for me and can accept me the way I am, even though I am not being the way I am supposed to be." He turned and placed his hand under Carrie's chin and lifted her face until he could look her in the eyes. "Thank you, Carrie, for your concern."

Shyness overcame her, and she looked away. He let go of her chin and glanced behind him and saw the book at the foot of the tree. "Is this your Tennyson?" He changed his tone, making it as light as he possibly could.

"Oh, no," she turned to walk toward the volume, picked it up and stroked it gently on its leather-bound cover. "This is my Browning."

"Your Browning," he smiled. "You are a remarkable girl, Carrie."

Carrie ducked her head, and at just that moment a shaft of sunlight pierced the leaves overhead and cast its light on the mass of auburn hair that trailed down her back.

Robert returned to William and Mary College the next day to continue the semester. As he traveled the long miles away from his roots and the pain he had suffered because of his father's death, he continued to grieve. His mind, however, was often drawn back to a young girl as she stood on a ledge of rock that overlooked the Ashley River with the sun streaming through her auburn hair. His first week back at William and Mary College was hectic, as he studied day and night to catch up on the work he had missed, but he found it a great comfort to work so hard on intellectual subjects. He also found it comforting to remember his afternoon with Carrie. She popped into his mind at most unexpected times, and the vision of her loveliness and her hopefulness lifted his spirits.

About ten days after he had returned to school, he took note paper from his desk to write her a short letter. He had meant to write only a formal thank you for her sympathy, but before he closed his note of gratitude, he found himself writing a few lines from Wordsworth which he had loved enough to memorize. They seemed to Robert to describe perfectly his desires for her future. He closed his letter with: "Therefore let the moon shine on thee in thy solitary walk, and let the misty mountain winds be free to blow against thee." In Robert's conscious mind these lines were in no way associated with romance; they were simply lines that reminded him of her and of their time together overlooking the place she fondly called God's aquarium.

When Carrie silently read the note from Robert, she felt a strange stirring inside of her, and her face felt warm. Indeed she flushed so openly that Mary, her mother, looked at her anxiously and asked, "It is not bad news, is it?"

"Oh no," Carrie replied hastily as she put the note back into its envelope. "It is only a short letter of gratitude from Robert for the sympathy I extended to him." Mary looked a little confused and on the verge of asking further questions, so Carrie chose that moment to go outside to attend to her roses.

Many months passed before Carrie saw Robert again, but in that time they continued to exchange letters, and the letters grew longer. Carrie's pleasure increased with every letter she received from Robert, for he seemed to be most accepting of her unique personality, to applaud her interest in a quiet, intellectual life. She felt free to write to him about the books that she read, to quote from them lines of poetry or statements of prose that seemed meaningful to her. In his return letters, he began to share his own reflections on the passages which she had so carefully copied out of her books and included in her letters. In time, Carrie grew more bold; she no longer simply copied out meaningful passages for Robert to read; she began to send Robert her own reflections on literary passages. He responded with his reflections on her reflections, and before long, she found herself commenting on life itself in her letters. He never chided her; he never seemed amused.

He seemed to accept as a commonplace reality the fact that she, a fifteen-year-old female, had reflections on life that were worth stating and deserved his attention and response.

It was a full year before Robert returned to South Carolina. He knew as he took the train south that he would go to Carrie's father and ask for her hand in marriage. He was only nineteen, and she was only sixteen, but he was heir to a great fortune. He reasoned that if he told James Bradford that he was willing to wait to marry Carrie until they were both a little older and he had finished his schooling, that he could convince James Bradford to accept him as his future son-in-law.

As soon as Robert had greeted his mother sufficiently, he sent a note to Carrie asking her to meet him the next afternoon at the place Carrie called God's aquarium, the ledge of rock hanging over the Ashley River. He could not bear the thought of meeting her in a social situation; when he first saw her again, he wanted to be alone with her.

The next afternoon, as he started the hike that would take him to the ledge, he tried to picture how a year might have changed Carrie's appearance. They had corresponded so many times that he believed he knew her mind well, better than most men know their wives the day they marry. Somehow the many miles that had separated them and the carefully chosen thoughts of their letters had opened doors of honesty between them that might have remained closed in a social setting. Robert, however, was a young man with all the passionate feelings appropriate to his age. He was eager to see the blossoming beauty of Carrie that he was certain had occurred in the year since they had been together. It is funny, he thought to himself as he walked along, when I think of her, I always think of her hair, her beautiful auburn hair with the sun shining through it. I suppose now that she is sixteen she will wear her hair pinned up, but I hope that this first time that I see her, her auburn curls will still be flowing over her shoulders.

He arrived on the ledge early, stood and stared down through the clear water at the fish. How good it is to be home, he thought, to stand once again on land that has nurtured me. How wonderful to see the constancy of the river, the incredible fertility of the soil, the special light that can only be found here in the low country of South Carolina.

He heard Carrie coming long before he was able to see her, and when he finally did see her, she was bent nearly double as she worked her way through the underbrush. His heart leapt with joy because her hair was free and hanging around her head. When she had finally made it through the underbrush, she stood up, raised her head, and her beautiful auburn hair flowed around her face like a halo. Robert laughed aloud, ran to her and grabbed both of her hands.

Suddenly they were both struck with shyness. It was strange to be together in person. They had shared their thoughts so intimately in writing, but being able to see, hear, and touch each other was another world suddenly flung open to them. Robert finally broke the silence, "You brought no book," he teased.

"I brought only myself," she laughed shyly.

"You are more than enough," he assured her as he stared down into her beautiful face.

The intense feeling that Carrie saw in his eyes startled and frightened her a bit. "How is God's aquarium?" she asked awkwardly.

"Still full of God's fish," Robert answered. "Come see." He gently pulled her up the slight incline onto the ledge, and together they walked over to the edge of it and looked down into the clear water.

"Thank God this place never changes," commented Carrie.

"I suppose I would not really know. This is only the second time I have seen it physically, but I have seen it in my mind's eye every day for a year, always trying to imagine how the seasons have changed it—and you," Robert admitted.

Carrie flushed and stared down at the fish.

Robert decided to act decisively. He reached out and turned her to face him. "Carrie, I know this is sudden, but I have been thinking about it for months. I want to marry you."

Carrie gasped, but he held up his hand to keep her from speaking. "I know you are very young; I know I am very young. I have another year of school left, so I am talking about the future, but I want to speak to your father immediately. I want us to know in the few weeks that we have together now, that we will be married in the future, and I want to know when I return to school and your precious letters begin to arrive, that they are letters from my fiancee. I love you, Carrie. I have loved you from the moment that you took such compassion on me a year ago, and by doing so, revealed your extraordinary spirit. This year my love has deepened; I have learned to love your mind. It is a rare gift for a husband to know and love his wife's mind. I know I will never find such a relationship again. I may be young, but I am not a fool; what I see in your soul I shall never find in another woman. Your soaring spirit alone makes me love you, but I also see that you are the most beautiful woman in the world."

Carrie shook her head. "Surely not," she demurred.

"Yes, you are," Robert insisted, "and I mean to marry you, Carrie. I mean to ask your father for your hand if you will accept my proposal of marriage. Will you have me as your husband? I know you may want time to consider what I have said; I know you may want to consider other proposals. I would understand if you do, but I hope against hope that—"

Carrie reached up and put her fingers on his lips. "I would never marry anyone but you, Robert. It is strange to fall in love through letters, but I have. I love you, Robert. I never planned to marry at all. I always assumed that no man would allow me to be what I am; no man would allow me to think the thoughts I think, to care about the things I care about. I cannot believe how blessed I am that you want me."

"I am the blessed one," Robert insisted. "I am certainly not indifferent to your beauty, but if you were the homeliest of girls, I could not help but love you for your mind." He laughed suddenly. "This is a strange proposal, is it not? We should be in a parlor, both of us elegantly dressed, and I should be down on one knee."

"I like it this way," Carrie insisted. "I have no desire to shock other people's proprieties, but in our private association I think we should disregard the typical, socially-appropriate things and just be what we are."

"I cannot imagine a better basis for marriage," Robert agreed "Oh Carrie! You are so beautiful inside and out."

"And you are so handsome," Carrie added ardently, "and I cannot deny that it pleases me that you are, but we both know that physical things do not last. I wish they would, but the lives of our elders show me that physical beauty does fade."

"What we have will never fade," Robert insisted. "Do you think your father will accept my proposal?"

"He will argue that I am too young," Carrie answered. "He

will argue that you need to finish school. However, we are willing to wait, so those arguments have no power."

"Surely he wants only the most happy marriage for you. I shall convince him that I am the man who can give you that."

"Oh, you must succeed!" Carrie exclaimed. "If I cannot marry you, Robert, I will marry no one."

James Bradford was in his small plantation office about eight o'clock that evening when he heard a knock at the door. He called out, "Come in," expecting to see a member of his family or perhaps one of the workers he employed. He was quite startled to see young Robert Montgomery standing nervously in the doorway. Quickly James' expression changed to one of pleasure as he stood and eagerly walked toward the young man. "Robert, come in, come in. This is a pleasant surprise; I had no idea I would see you so soon after your return from school."

The young man came into the circle of light that a lantern cast around James' desk, and James motioned to an extra chair next to his desk. As he settled back into his own chair, he reminded himself for the thousandth time since Robert had been born that he must forget that this young man was his son. In spite of the nineteen years that had passed and all of James' efforts to forget, the boy was never far from his mind, and the sight of his face was both very dear and very painful to James. Once again he struggled to play the role of distant relative and close neighbor to the boy.

"Tell me, Robert," he resisted the urge to call him 'son,' "how do you find South Carolina after Williamsburg?"

"It is strange, sir," Robert began carefully, "to move from an intellectual climate, like William and Mary College, back to the realities of agrarian life."

James laughed lightly. "What you really mean to say is, it is difficult for you to leave behind the world of books for the world of making money."

Robert nodded thoughtfully.

"Are you still glad you went to study law instead of going into the military institute?"

"Oh yes, sir, I should have most certainly been a terrible soldier. I think I shall make a tolerable lawyer."

"Well, let us hope there will be no more wars that you would have to fight in anyway," James said. "And as far as being a lawyer is concerned, I suppose what you are learning may be of some help to you when you come back to run your father's plantation, but the basic grind of running a plantation has little to do with either law or the military, I am afraid."

"Don't you like running a plantation?" Robert asked.

"Yes, yes I do," James replied. "It took some getting used to at first, especially coming home after the war and being confronted with the necessity of rebuilding almost everything, but after all these years, I find the life suits me."

"Then why did you go into politics, sir?"

"Well," James laughed, "I guess the quiet life of a plantation owner does not suit me entirely. I confess I like the excitement, the action of the legislature, and I like having the power to change things. After all, I fought for this land, and for years after the War, our rights were completely obliterated, and we were left in a nearly powerless state during the so-called 'reconstruction.' So now, yes, Robert, I admit it; I like being in charge of the future of the people of this state. I like the thought that now that the Yankees are out of here, we can rebuild at least some of what we had before the War."

"There is still great control from the federal government, I understand, sir."

"Oh yes," James acknowledged, "and I suppose that will never go away. Indeed, if I were to attempt to predict the future, I would predict that federal control will only grow, but I give my time to politics in hopes that South Carolina can retain its own individuality as much as possible, as long as possible. It is, after all, the life I know best and the life I love."

"Yes, sir," Robert agreed. "I hear such sentiments expressed in Virginia also."

"Well now," James changed the subject radically. "One more year of college, as I understand it, and you will be ready to begin your reading of law. I suspect you have some plans to do that closer to home; I certainly hope so."

"Oh yes, sir. I will finish my B.A. degree in two more terms. I have already been offered an opportunity to read law in a firm in Charleston."

"So that is your plan?" James asked.

"Yes, sir. Two more terms of school, and then I shall come back home, read law in Charleston and begin to learn to run the plantation that Father has left me."

"I think you will have to make a decision, Robert, about whether or not you will ever practice law, or whether you are only reading law for enough information to protect your own interests. Dare I hope you might have a political career in mind?" A surge of pride ran through James Bradford, and his heart beat a little faster, but he reminded himself that no matter what Robert might accomplish, he could never claim him as his son. The joy of his pride in Robert's possible accomplishments was quickly doused by a melancholy feeling.

"I have not given serious thought to a political career, sir."

"Well, perhaps I am rushing you," James suggested. "You have some weeks of vacation ahead of you. What kind of fun have you got arranged for yourself?"

"I think I shall have a quiet vacation," Robert replied, as he began to wring his hands nervously. "You know, just riding and perhaps a little fishing and a lot of visiting—that sort of thing." The young man shifted in his seat and tensed his jaw. James was startled by the change he saw in Robert's demeanor.

"Is something wrong, Robert?" he asked.

"Oh, no sir, no sir," Robert stammered as he responded. "Nothing is wrong, sir; in fact, everything is right. It is just that well, sir, I—I need to talk to you about something—that is I want to talk to you about something."

"Of course, Robert, anything. You know how fond I am of you. Feel free to discuss anything. You are not in any kind of trouble, I hope?"

"Oh, no sir. Nothing like that. It is, it is—ah—it is really quite a wonderful thing I want to talk to you about, sir, but it does involve you."

"Me?" James chuckled. "Well, Robert, you know that anything I have is yours, so quit squirming in that chair, and let me hear about this project you obviously have in mind. I suspect I am talked into it before I even hear of it."

"I hope so," Robert said grimly, and then suddenly he blurted out his intention. "Sir, I am here to ask you for Carrie's hand in marriage."

James Bradford's face turned as white as a blank sheet of paper, and for the first time in his life he felt so light-headed he was sure he would pass out.

Robert was stunned and frightened by James' reaction. He jumped from his chair and took several steps toward the older man. "Are you all right, sir? Can I get you something?"

"Brandy," James choked out as he waved his hand toward a decanter on a table close to Robert's chair.

Robert turned back, grabbed the decanter, poured a glass of brandy, and gave it to James. He drank the entire glass, as if it were water, while Robert stared in amazement.

"You are unwell, sir. We must discuss this at another time. You must go to bed; perhaps you need to see a doctor."

"No, Robert, I shall be fine in just a moment." James stared into the empty glass, filled with horror at the prospect of such a marriage. He wondered, *what can I tell him?* What reason can I give that he will accept—that Carrie will accept? I must stop this now!

"A little more brandy, I think," he finally said. Robert eagerly grabbed the decanter and refilled James' glass. He stared intently into the man's face and was much relieved to see color returning.

James sipped the second glass of brandy slowly. "Sit down, Robert," he commanded.

"You are feeling better, sir?" Robert asked as he sat down.

"Yes, just a slight indisposition. Nothing to concern you," James said abruptly.

"If you say so, sir, but we could certainly discuss this matter at another time when you are feeling better."

"I think it best to discuss it now," James said firmly. "Actually there is nothing to discuss. I will never give my consent to your marrying Carrie."

"But why not?" Robert blurted out; all of his carefully prepared, logical arguments seemed to have flown away. "I know you like me, sir. You know everything there is to know about me; you know what kind of man I am, what kind of man I shall become. I assure you I love Carrie with all my heart, and I shall do everything and anything in my power to keep her safe and make her happy."

"I do not doubt any of that," James said, "but you are far too young, and Carrie is far too young. You cannot know your own minds. You may be amazed how you will feel in six months or a year—"

"Yes, sir, I have thought of that. What I propose is a long

engagement. Carrie and I want to be married, but we want to be sensible. I would not marry Carrie, as much as I love her, unless I knew I could take care of her the way that you have taken care of her, sir. So I plan to finish school, come back to Charleston to read law, and pass the bar exam before she and I are married."

When James Bradford said nothing, Robert continued, "I have spoken to Carrie, sir, and she is willing to wait; however, we want to have our engagement settled. Then we can prepare for our marriage and look forward to it."

"I understand all of that," James waved his hand in the air impatiently. "It is not a matter of time, Robert. I said that I would never allow you to marry Carrie. You are too closely related."

"But, sir, we are only second cousins." Robert looked down at his boots. "I think, sir, that second cousins surely have no reason not to marry, and the fact that Carrie and I are cousins is the very reason why we would be happy as a wedded couple. The compatibility we have in interests and the way we have been raised—our values, our standards, all the things that make her who she is and make me who I am—all of these things exist because we are cousins. In short, the fact that we are cousins is a strength, and I need not remind you, sir, that many first cousins marry, and Carrie and I are not that closely related."

"And I need not remind you," James said, as he tried to control his emotions, "that such marriages sometimes produce tragic results."

"Yes, sir, I know, but we are second cousins."

"I will not allow Carrie to marry anyone she is related to. I like you, indeed, I love you," James choked on the last words, cleared his throat and managed to speak with total firmness, "but I forbid Carrie to ever marry you. Let us understand that fact here and now. I shall never give my blessing to a marriage between you and Carrie. She must marry someone she is not related to."

"Perhaps you need time to think," Robert said hopefully.

James Bradford stood and pulled himself up to his great height. His shadow loomed over Robert. "I shall say one more time, Robert, and you must hear me: I shall never allow Carrie to marry you. Never. You are, of course, welcome as a visitor in our home, but only if I have your word of honor that this idea of marrying Carrie will never be raised again between us and that you will not raise it with Carrie either."

Robert stood and confronted James. "I cannot promise that, sir. Obviously I must tell Carrie what you said."

"I shall tell Carrie," James said. "You are not to speak of marriage to her again. If you persist in going down this path with my daughter or encouraging her in any way, you will not be welcome on this plantation, and you will not be allowed to communicate with her in any way. I must have your word of honor that you will never again discuss marriage with Carrie."

Robert stared at the floor while a long, angry silence filled the room. Finally he raised his head, squared his shoulders and looked up at James Bradford.

"I cannot give you my word of honor," he said firmly.

James' chest tightened, and he felt that he would strangle, but he pronounced the words he had to pronounce, "Then you may not speak to my daughter again or communicate with her in any way. I shall tell her of our discussion. Whatever days you are here in South Carolina, I expect you not to communicate with my daughter, and once you have gone back to school, I expect you not to write to her."

"I can make no such promise, sir," Robert said quietly, and he turned and left the plantation office.

James Bradford fell back into his chair and held his head in his hand as he muttered, "What shall I do? This is all my fault. This is all the evil result of the stupid passions of my youth." He thought for a moment and then said, "No, I cannot blame it on youth. I was a man. I knew what I was doing. I did not care about the consequences."

James stayed in the plantation office, suffering in his own private hell, a hell he had created, a hell that was now reaching out and hurting those he loved best. It was his intention to avoid Carrie and Mary for the rest of the night and to think of more plausible reasons to object to Robert's proposal, but soon there was a timid knock on the door. James groaned inwardly, for he knew it was his daughter. She opened the door and walked in with the anxiety she obviously felt painted on her face.

"Father?" she questioned.

"I rejected his proposal," James said abruptly.

Carrie began to weep. He rose from his chair and guided her to the chair where young Robert had sat. He knelt beside his daughter, took both of her delicate hands into his large hands and looked into her face. His voice was full of pleading. "My precious Carrie, you must try to understand. I am your father. I cannot allow you to take the risk of marrying your cousin. He is a fine young man, but he is your cousin. If he were not related to you, I would be overjoyed."

"Oh, but Father, we are only second cousins," Carrie cried.

"You are young, Carrie. You do not know."

"I do know," she insisted. "I know there are a few families around who have a child who is not quite right, and people blame that on the close relationship of the mother and the father, but Robert and I are second cousins."

"My dearest child," James said as tenderly as he could, "the risk is far greater than you know. You have no conception of how many children are hidden away. You simply do not know the truth." He listened to his own words and despised himself because the truth she did not know, the truth that was now breaking her heart, was the result of his own past selfish behavior. "You must put all thoughts of marrying Robert aside," he insisted.

"I cannot," she cried.

"You must."

She wept for a few moments, her tears falling into the lace-trimmed handkerchief in her hands.

"What can I say to him, Father?" she asked.

"There will be no occasion for you to say anything, Carrie. I have forbidden him to communicate with you again."

Carrie stared at her father in amazement and then anger. "Why?" she demanded. "What right have you to separate us so totally?"

"It is not my wish," James said quietly, "or my choice. Robert refuses to drop the subject of marriage. I cannot allow him to see you again until he has put this notion of marriage out of his mind. And Carrie, as your father, I must ask you to promise me that you will not be in communication with him, that you will neither receive communication from him nor send him any."

"Oh, Father, I could not do that to Robert," she exclaimed. "I love him too much."

"Surely your duty to me counts for something," he insisted, as he asked himself scornfully, how can I, of all people, call on duty as my right? "You must trust me in this, Carrie. I am older and more experienced than you, but if you are not persuaded by those facts, remember that I am your father; you owe me obedience. Promise me you will not communicate with Robert."

"Father," she reached forward and put her arms around his neck, "I know that the Scriptures command me to honor you, and I shall do so, but I plead with you to allow me to write Robert one letter. If you insist, I will even allow you to read it, but please allow me to write one letter to Robert telling him why I cannot communicate with him."

"He already knows why, Carrie."

"But I want him to know from me that it is not my choice. Please, Father."

"Very well," James agreed, "you may write Robert one letter."

"And I shall give it to you to read first," Carrie said sadly.

"That will not be necessary, Daughter. You have always been a child of honor. I am sure that in your letter you will do justice to that honor."

"Thank you," she said stiffly. She rose and walked toward the door. She stopped before leaving, turned back and looked at her father who still knelt beside the chair she had just left. "I have not given you my word that I shall not pray that you will change your mind," she warned him. "I shall pray day and night that you will come to understand the love that Robert and I have for each other and that your understanding of that love will overcome your fear for us." She turned and left before James could respond.

When James went to his bedroom, he found it empty of his beloved Mary, but she soon entered the room with an expression of concern on her face. "I can do nothing else, Mary," he told her before she spoke. "She will have to get over this. She is young; there is time."

He expected Mary to argue from Carrie's point-of-view, but instead she came to his side and looked directly into his eyes. "You are right, James," she said quietly. "They must never marry."

James felt that his heart had stopped for a moment as he looked into the eyes of his wife. They had a curious veiled quality that he had never seen there before, and the question shot through his mind, *does she know?*

James did not sleep that night; he tossed and turned, finally rose from his bed and went downstairs to his plantation office. The same thoughts played over and over in his mind. *I must* prevent this marriage; at all costs I must prevent this marriage. I must not allow my sins to produce horrible consequences for other people, but what can I do? By dawn a plan had come to him. The best way to prevent the marriage of Carrie and Robert would be to marry Carrie to someone else. I must find a suitor for her, he told himself, and soon—a man of charm, good looks and property, a man whom Carrie would prefer over Robert. As he went about his morning duties, he racked his brain to create a list of eligible bachelors who lived anywhere near Charleston. Finally he settled his mind on Brandon Hildebrandt, a proud man who was not all that he would wish for Carrie, but a man he could be sure would place Carrie at the pinnacle of Charleston society. Yes, he told himself, Brandon Hildebrandt is the man. He is handsome and charming; the ladies all adore him. More important, he is wealthy and powerful.

After the dinner hour he talked privately to Mary about his decision. She immediately exclaimed, "But he is too old for Carrie! Besides I do not think you should rush anything. Carrie must have time to adjust to this grief she is feeling, this loss of hope. You must wait. Perhaps your idea of distracting her from Robert is good, but Carrie should be introduced to many young men. Then she can make her choice intelligently."

"I have no objection to her meeting other men," James agreed, "but I intend for her to marry Brandon Hildebrandt. As for his age, it would be good for Carrie to have a husband older than she. Besides, he is not considerably older; he is no more than thirty."

"But he has been married before," Mary objected.

"Surely that cannot be held against him," James insisted. "His first wife died in childbirth, a sad fate that many young men must endure."

"I do not like it, James. I do not want her rushed."

"There is no need to rush her," James agreed. "Robert will only be here a few weeks, and then he will be back in Virginia. He should not return for another year."

"Then please, dear James, allow Carrie to become an active participant in society. Allow her to meet many young men, so she can choose a man she loves."

"She loves Robert," James countered.

"But she is young," Mary insisted, "and since you have forbidden her to marry Robert and she would never marry without your consent, quite likely she will fall in love with someone else. Would that not be the best way? For her to find the love of her life on her own?"

"Yes, dear, that would be the best way, and let us hope it happens that way."

"I shall do more than hope," Mary said firmly. "I shall pray every morning and every evening that Carrie will fall in love with another worthy man."

"You pray, dear," James said sternly, "and I shall invite Brandon Hildebrandt to visit us."

Chapter 15

A month later the Bradford house was buzzing with activity as Mary and the servants prepared for a special evening. James and Mary were entertaining friends from Charleston, as well as some of James' political colleagues. Carrie tried to be helpful, but she was trapped in a cloud of depression that had hung over her all day. At tea time, she did not join her mother on the verandah, and when Mary came to check on her, she found Carrie, her face covered with tears, sitting next to the window staring out at a clear, bright, sunny afternoon. Mary had no difficulty guessing the reason for Carrie's misery. She sat down on the window seat next to her daughter and took one of Carrie's hands in her own hands. "Give it time, dear," Mary counseled quietly.

"He left today," Carrie said and then burst into a fresh flow of tears and buried her face in her mother's lap. Mary bent over her daughter, stroked Carrie's hair and tried to comfort her.

"I know, dear. I know that these last few weeks have been totally miserable for you. I know you love Robert, and to have had him so close by and yet be unable to see him, well, I know how horrible you must have felt."

"Oh, Mother, you don't know! How could you know?" Carrie exclaimed as she sat up suddenly. There was a flash of anger in her eyes. "And why do you support Father in his totally unreasonable objections to my engagement?"

"Well," Mary sighed patiently, "Let me answer the last question first. I support your father's insistence that you not become engaged to Robert because I think you have been too sheltered and have not met enough men to know what it is that you need and want in a husband. You are very young, Carrie. I realize that some girls marry at sixteen, but you have never been one to participate in society, and so you really do not know very many men. Before making a commitment that must last your entire life, I would much prefer that you have an opportunity to meet many different kinds of men."

"But I love Robert," Carrie protested.

"I know you do, dear. I believe you when you say you love Robert, and I also know what a fine young man he is, but he too is quite young. He has never been socially inclined; in fact, he has been of a reclusive nature all his life. This last year he has no doubt suffered great grief over the death of his father. I am sure that his grief has encouraged him into even greater solitude. He needs to mature and to meet many young women before he chooses a wife."

"But he loves me, Mother!" Carrie exclaimed.

"I know, dear, but making a hasty, premature proposal to you is not in your best interest. You both need to meet many possible mates of differing personalities before deciding. I want you to go out into society next year and make an honest attempt to evaluate the suitors that you find there."

"Do you think, as Father does, that Robert and I are too closely related?" Carrie demanded.

"I do," Mary said firmly.

"But Mother," Carrie argued, "we are only second cousins."

"I can only say I want you to marry outside the family, totally outside the family, and only after you have gone into society and met many suitors."

"Do you think Father will ever change his mind?" Carrie asked sadly.

"I would not set my heart on it, dear. I have seldom seen your father so firmly opposed to anything. Unless you are willing to marry without your family's blessing and support, you cannot marry Robert. You must make your debut into Charleston society."

"I guess you are right, Mother," Carrie sighed. "I am getting nowhere by spending my days crying at this window, but if only you knew how much it hurts. The man I want, the man I love has been so close by, and yet I am not allowed any communication with him, not even conversation."

"Carrie, dear," Mary said softly, "I have never spoken to you about the first years of my marriage to your father. They were very trying years."

"Of course, Mother, I know those years after the War were difficult for everyone."

"Yes, dear, they were. The deprivations were many; federal troops were still here, but I am not referring to such things. The first year or so that I was married to your father, my situation was similar to having Robert a mile away and being unable to speak to him."

"What do you mean, Mother?"

"Well, you see, dear, your father came back from the War expecting to marry your cousin Diana, Robert's mother."

"He did?" Carrie was startled. "I never knew that."

"Yes, he did. They had been very much in love before the War, and he had assumed that if she had survived the War, that she would be waiting for him. Of course, as you know, when he returned, he found that she had married and was the mother of two little girls. James was heart-broken. He had been through dreadful ordeals as a soldier and unspeakable pains as a prisoner of war. His plantation was wrecked. There seemed to be no way for him to go on. He had lost many years of his youth, and the final blow was to discover that Diana had not waited for him."

"Did she not love him?" Carrie asked.

"I am sure she did, in her own way, before the War, and perhaps for a while at the beginning of the War. I do not know how to judge Diana's feelings. There was good reason to believe that James was dead."

"But you would have waited," Carrie insisted.

"Yes, I would have, but you must always remember, dear, it is not wise to measure other people's actions unless you have actually walked in their shoes. It is easy for me to say I would have waited, but I am not Diana, and I was not in her position. At any rate your father did return from the War and discover that he had lost many years of his youth and the woman he loved. Naturally enough he wanted to pick up the pieces of a normal life as quickly as he could. Things were in great disarray; it is very difficult for you to understand how much disruption there was. Marriages occurred quickly. There was a great fever in the young men and the young women of the time to get on with life, to move forward, to establish families to make up for those they had lost. There were so many dead, Carrie, and not just soldiers. Quite often the soldiers who returned came back to face the knowledge that they had lost their parents; they had lost brothers and sisters. Many of them came home to find their wives had died, and their children had died. There was so much death because of the war, because of the deprivations, because of the fevers that could not be fought without medicines, without proper food. It was chaotic."

"And so Father married you," Carrie guessed at what her mother was about to say.

"Yes, dear. I was staying with my cousin Diana and her husband. I was past a marriageable age, but James married me when he could not have Diana."

"That is horrible!" Carrie exclaimed.

"It is horrible under normal circumstances, Carrie, but you must remember the times. Your father did me a great honor by marrying me; he saved me from being an old maid."

"But, Mother, you were beautiful; Father has often talked about how beautiful you were. Surely you would have married when the men came home."

"Oh, Carrie, can you not understand? So many young men did not come home. Look around you. How many old maids do you see in this county? Only a few men returned, Carrie. It was a great privilege to marry James Bradford. He saved me from the humiliation and the emptiness of life as an old maid, and ultimately he gave me you and this wonderful home he has rebuilt."

"But you knew he didn't love you."

"I knew he loved Diana. I knew where his heart was, but she was out of his reach, so he married me. I felt privileged, but it took some time before your father could give me his heart; it took well over a year. That is the period I refer to as similar to this time that you have experienced with Robert, when you have been close to him for these weeks but unable to communicate with him. I do know what that feels like, dear."

"I am sorry, Mother. I did not know."

"Of course you did not, and I did not tell you my history to make you any sadder than you already feel today. I told you to help you understand that others have gone through the feelings that you are having and that they have come out on the other side of difficult times and made good lives. You have life, as long as the good Lord gives it to you, and it is a sin not to use it, Carrie. We all have periods of depression, times when we worry and grieve; those are part of life too, but God expects us to pick ourselves up, with His help, and to go on and make the most out of the life He has given us. I think that you must do that very thing and live this next year, embracing all of the positive possibilities, embracing everything that God brings within the reach of your experience, and a year from now, who knows what your feelings will be. You must live this next year; it is God-given life, and you must live it. And in fairness to yourself, to Robert, and to your father, you must live it with an open-minded, open-handed attitude, and let it be an adventure as you see what will come."

"That's a lot to ask, Mother."

"Of course it is, dear. Life is never simple, never easy, and it is especially a lot to ask from you today, I know, but Robert is gone now. He is on the train, headed north to Virginia. You know that; you also know that this evening we are entertaining some prominent guests. Why not spend the next few hours preparing to help me entertain those guests? Robert will not be among them, but surely there will be someone whom you can enjoy."

"I just do not know, Mother, if I feel like it."

"Your feelings, dear, are the results of your thoughts. I think you must exercise some resolution to control those thoughts. It will not be any easier tomorrow to exercise that resolution, so you might as well jump right in and take control of your feelings now. Would it not be a more enjoyable evening for you to talk books with some gentleman than to sit in this room crying?"

"Yes," Carrie laughed feebly, "if I can find a gentleman who is willing to talk to a young girl about books."

"John Kendall is coming, and even though he is a professor, he has always been eager to chat with you about poetry." Mary patted Carrie's hands as she rose from the seat. "And there are other interesting people coming. If nothing else, you can listen."

"To politics," Carrie groaned.

"Yes, to politics, but even politics is better than tears."

"Yes, Mother." Carrie stood and gave Mary a hug. "Thank you. It breaks my heart to think that your youth was so marred by war. I guess I really have been quite a spoiled child. I have never had to endure anything that difficult."

"And I hope you never shall, dear. But whatever you do have to endure, remember where your strength comes from."

"Father always says, 'remember you are a Bradford,'" Carrie mimicked her father's tone.

"Well, you are a Bradford," Mary laughed, "and I confess your father is overly proud of the name. The Bradfords do have strength, and that same strength is running in you, but I would add something to your father's statement. Remember that before you were a Bradford, you were God's child. That is your true legacy because that is your eternal legacy."

Carrie shook her head and laughed, "I declare, Mother, sometimes I look at you and Father, and I cannot imagine how you have managed to make a happy marriage."

"With a lot of work, dear."

When Carrie began to descend the staircase several hours later to greet the guests who would soon arrive, she was startled by a cold voice, "So this is the great pride of the Bradford family! She exceeds even her reputation for beauty and grace, and I would not have thought that a possible feat."

Carrie stopped and looked down the remainder of the stairs into the dark brown eyes of a handsome, expensively dressed man who was staring at her. By his side stood James Bradford; both men were holding glasses from which they had been drinking.

"Carrie, dear," called James Bradford. "Come on down. I want you to meet Brandon Hildebrandt."

Carrie continued down the staircase, and when she arrived at the bottom, she looked up into the arrogant face of a tall, slender man around thirty. Every aspect of his demeanor suggested he had a high opinion of himself. Carrie instantly disliked him.

"This is my daughter, as you have already guessed," James said to the haughty man. "Carrie, may I present Mr. Brandon Hildebrandt, of Charleston."

Brandon Hildebrandt laughed, made an elaborate bow, took her hand, and kissed it.

"This is a pleasure beyond description," he said coldly as he stared at Carrie's lovely face. "How fortunate you are, James, to be surrounded by beautiful women. Miss Bradford, I look forward to getting to know you."

"Thank you, sir," Carrie said stiffly. She felt sure that she was staring into dangerous water when she looked into his eyes, and she had no intention of being shipwrecked by such a man.

"I hope I may have the pleasure of sitting next to Miss Carrie," Brandon Hildebrandt commented as he turned to James.

"Well of course," James boomed, "but I have to warn you, she loves poetry, so be prepared to listen to recitations."

"Father!" Carrie exclaimed. "I am sure I shall be happy to listen or participate in any conversations around the table."

"Oh, I had hoped we would have our own private conversation," Brandon Hildebrandt looked down at her meaningfully.

"I would not like to be unkind to our other guests by excluding them," Carrie said primly.

Brandon Hildebrandt laughed harshly and turned to James. "She has spirit, James. I like that in a woman."

"Good," James said, and Carrie began to wonder if her father had had too much to drink.

"May I escort you onto the verandah, Miss Bradford?" Brandon Hildebrandt held out his arm to Carrie.

"Thank you, no," Carrie answered icily. "I believe I shall join my mother to help her prepare for our other guests."

"Then I look forward to seeing you at the earliest possible moment," Hildebrandt insisted.

Carrie merely nodded and walked in front of the man toward the dining room door.

As other guests arrived, Carrie stood by her mother and greeted each one in an attempt to be a gracious hostess, as well as to avoid Brandon Hildebrandt.

When they were seated at the table, however, she found that she was seated at Hildebrandt's right. Throughout the dinner, he attempted to draw her into private conversations, but she diverted him and forced him to rejoin the general conversation at the table. On several occasions when she did just that, she noticed that her father looked annoyed.

The evening was not pleasant for Carrie, but she did manage to keep her promise to her mother, that she would attempt to participate in whatever life brought her way. The happiest minutes of the evening were a brief conversation with Professor John Kendall about the merits of Elizabeth Barrett Browning's poetry. He was just beginning to encourage her to read the poems of Christina Rosetti when her father impatiently interrupted their conversation and asked her to play the piano for their guests. She was flushed as she seated herself at the piano, but she managed to perform well in spite of the bold stare of Brandon Hildebrandt.

She was a relieved young woman when the guests had departed and she was able to retire to her room.

James Bradford summoned Carrie to the parlor at mid morning the next day. She was dismayed to find Brandon Hildebrandt standing there. "Carrie," James said lightly, "Mr. Hildebrandt has just ridden over seeking your company on a ride. It is a lovely autumn day, and I am sure the fresh air would do you a great deal of good."

Carrie stared at her father angrily; his intentions were quite obvious to her. "I have other plans for this morning, Father," she said boldly.

"Nothing pressing, I am sure," James' voice lost its lightness and took on a tone of warning. "I want Mr. Hildebrandt to see the plantation, especially the gardens and the area around the river." He turned to Hildebrandt, "Carrie knows all the beautiful spots on this piece of land, Brandon. She will be the very best guide for you."

"I have no doubt of it, sir," Brandon smiled at Carrie, but there was hardness glinting in his eyes.

"But Father," Carrie stammered, "I have no proper chaperone."

"Oh, that has all been taken care of," James waved his hand as he spoke. "I am sending one of the groomsmen along; in fact, the horses will be brought around soon. You go up and change into your riding habit. And after you have shown Mr. Hildebrandt the plantation, you can stop at some special place on the river and have the little picnic lunch I have had prepared for you." He looked out the window before adding, "Such a beautiful day. How I envy the two of you."

"Of course you do," Hildebrandt said. "What man would not envy my opportunity to spend time with your beautiful daughter?"

Wordlessly, Carrie turned and left the room. She stalked up the stairs angrily, and when she had gained the privacy of her own room, she closed the door behind her and allowed her fury to boil over. "Does Father think I am such an idiot that I cannot see what he is doing?" she demanded. She paced across the room to a window, crossed her arms, and continued angrily. "I have no interest in any man except Robert, but if I did wish to spend time with another man, Brandon Hildebrandt is the last man on earth I would choose. He is absolutely arrogant and completely cold hearted; he made that plain last night at dinner. I do not think the man is capable of thinking of anything except his own wealth and social position. What am I to do?"

There was a soft knock on the door. Guessing it was her mother, Carrie called "Come in," and her mother entered and closed the door behind her.

"Mother," Carrie exclaimed as she turned to face her, "Father expects me to go riding with Brandon Hildebrandt."

"I know," Mary said calmly. "Shall I help you into your riding costume?"

"But I do not want to go," Carrie blurted out.

"I know," Mary said again, "but I believe you should."

"But why? I have no interest in this man whatsoever. Father is obviously matchmaking."

"Yes, dear, I am afraid he is. Mr. Hildebrandt is waiting, so let me help you get dressed."

"I cannot bear two hours in that man's presence."

"You are going to have to bear it, Carrie," Mary warned her.

"Why would Father choose that man of all men? He is too conceited and cold, and he is far too old for me."

"Brandon Hildebrandt is around thirty," Mary said quietly. "He has been married before and lost his wife in childbirth a little over a year ago."

"Then he should be grieving and not going riding with a six-teen-year-old girl," Carrie insisted.

"Carrie, you must go riding with Mr. Hildebrandt; your father thinks he is an appropriate suitor. I know he is older than you, but your father sees that as a plus."

"What else does he see as a plus?" Carrie asked acidly.

"Brandon is seeking a wife, and he is a very wealthy man who can take care of you, even better than your father can, for the rest of your life," Mary said evenly. "Your security is a prime consideration for your father."

"What about love?" Carrie demanded.

"I think your father has little concern for love in this matter."

"Well, it is of great concern to me," Carrie exclaimed.

"Of course it is, dear. Now I want you to listen to me carefully. You and I have already discussed this subject, but I am going to warn you again. Unless it is your intention to defy your father and be an outcast to this family, you must spend the next year getting to know other men."

"It would appear that Father has chosen the only other man he wants me to get to know."

"He will choose for you if you do not choose for yourself; there-fore, I suggest that you take this ride with Mr. Hildebrandt, that you explore whether or not there is, in fact, any basis for a friend-ship between the two of you. Whatever you do, do not refuse to comply with the simple wish of your father to take a ride with this man, and then, dear, please take my advice. Make plans immedi-ately to participate actively in the social season of Charleston next winter. During the season you can stay at our Charleston house, and I shall go and stay there also. If we work diligently between now and then, we can prepare an adequate wardrobe for you. I implore you to go to every ball and party that you can possibly attend to show your father that you are willing to consider men other than Robert as your future husband. Carrie, you must do this, and you must do it with an open mind. As I said yesterday, it is best for you and Robert to find out what the world holds for you other than each other, but even if that were not so, dear, you must enter society this year because your father must be persuaded that you are not defying him."

Carrie recognized the seriousness of her mother's warning, nodded her head, swallowed her anger, and began to undress. Her mother helped her put on her riding clothes, and she quickly joined Brandon Hildebrandt in the center hall. She could tell that her father was pleased with her cooperation, and while the morning ride was not the happy occasion it would have been with Robert, Carrie found the patience to be civil to Hildebrandt by reminding herself of her mother's warning. Her heart ached for Robert, and she prayed her father would change his mind. She decided that her mother's advice to participate actively in the social season was her only hope of either convincing her father that her love for Robert was enduring or convincing him to allow her to remain unmarried. Those were the only two options for her life that she felt she could accept.

Seamstresses were employed and brought to the Bradford plan-tation that fall to create a stunning wardrobe for Carrie, and that winter she did her part by acting out the role of the perfect belle of the ball. She attended dinner parties, picnics, operas, symphonies, balls, and outings to the country plantations—everything that the happy belle of the day would gleefully embrace. She had become a stunningly beautiful, seventeen-year-old young lady, and every other belle envied her glowing auburn hair and perfect creamy skin. The men flocked to her side wherever she went, drawn there by her beauty and a unique, charismatic quality she had that they could never define. Unknown to them, Carrie's special spark was the result of her continued, secret intellectual life. She experienced life more deeply than the other young people around her because she never discontinued her reading, and her reflective thinking about life. She began to write a journal in which she recorded her own thoughts about what she saw firsthand in life and what she experience vicariously from the books she was reading. Quite often at parties Carrie had almost a divided personality; in all the outward forms, she was the perfect belle, but her thoughts were her own, and they were not often on the events or people present. This separateness of her mind from the events of the moment appeared to others to be an aloofness that suggested tremendous sophistication and poise. She was, therefore, even more enchanting to men because she appeared to be unobtainable. They never stopped to wonder why she seemed beyond their reach; they only rushed madly to gain this extraordinary young woman as the ornament for their arms at social events and hopefully the ornament for their lives, if they could only persuade her to marry them.

Carrie kept her word to her father and did not communicate with Robert, but her thoughts were never far from him, and she compared every male whom she saw to Robert, always evaluating which would be the better life partner. In her mind, Robert never had any competition.

In the spring when the social season of Charleston had ended, Carrie returned to the plantation, physically exhausted. She was also emotionally exhausted; all her life she had needed time to herself, quiet, unstructured time. She had been a lucky child in that her parents had allowed her, a female, to wander alone in nature, to bury herself in books. It was, consequently, with great relief that Carrie returned to the quietness of plantation life, to the control over her hours that she craved.

Carrie had had less than one week of the solitude she needed when Brandon Hildebrandt arrived. She came back from a walk in the woods and saw his carriage sitting before the house. Steeling herself against her first impulse, which was to turn back to the woods and hide until he was gone, even if it took the rest of the night, she resolutely continued toward the front steps. She had tried to bring herself to like Brandon Hildebrandt, but she still thought him arrogant and cold. He did not seem to value his first marriage or grieve over the loss of his wife and child. Carrie doubted that he was capable of love; she was positive he did not love her. As she entered the front door, her father called out to her, "Carrie, look who is here; come on in."

When she complied with James' request, Brandon Hildebrandt sprang to his feet and rushed to meet her. He took her hand, kissed it and spoke in a formal tone which he no doubt mistook for the sound of true ardency, "This has been the longest week of my life. Always in the past I have been grateful that the social season was ended but not this year."

"Indeed," Carrie answered quietly but did not ask him why.

Nevertheless he proceeded to explain himself. "You see, my dearest Miss Bradford, the end of the social season meant the end of my ability to be in your presence on a regular basis, a fate most painful to me, I assure you."

Carrie smiled demurely, not trusting herself to respond.

"Mr. Hildebrandt is joining us for supper, Carrie," James said as he strode toward the two with a bright, beaming smile on his face. "He and I have been discussing some business and other affairs. Why don't you go upstairs and change from your walking clothes into something more appropriate for our guest and rejoin us before supper?" Carrie knew that she had been dismissed by her father, and from the look on Brandon Hildebrandt's face, she suspected why her father was eager to remove her from the room. She curtsied to Brandon Hildebrandt and left without a word.

After supper that evening, Carrie's suspicions were confirmed when James Bradford contrived to leave her alone in the parlor with Brandon Hildebrandt.

It was obvious from Hildebrandt's approach to the subject that he felt confident that he would be received positively. He took Carrie's hand in both of his and smiled down at her.

"My dearest Miss Bradford," he said formally. "I should like to talk to you about a matter of the greatest seriousness."

Carrie wanted to say something pert or evasive, but she decided that it was preferable to get past the moment, so she asked, "And what might that be, Mr. Hildebrandt?"

"Won't you sit down over here with me, Miss Bradford?"

Brandon Hildebrandt asked as he gestured toward a settee.

"Certainly," Carrie responded with no enthusiasm, but she did seat herself on the settee. Brandon Hildebrandt sat on the very edge of the same settee and once again took both of her hands in his.

"My dear Miss Bradford," he began. "You must be aware of the strong feelings that I have for you."

Carrie remained silent.

"These feelings have grown over the last months until it is impossible for me not to speak of them to you," Hildebrandt continued.

Still Carrie gave him no encouragement in smile or word.

"Your beauty is beyond description, and your demeanor most impressive. In short, Miss Bradford, everything that you are would make you the greatest prize in any man's life." He paused, apparently hoping that Carrie would at least smile.

Instead, she lowered her head and gazed at her lap.

Brandon Hildebrandt no doubt interpreted her action as shyness at such an important moment in her life, but the truth was that she was trying to hide the fact that she was about to laugh. She did not see herself as a prize; she saw herself as a person.

Suddenly Brandon Hildebrandt embarrassed her by kneeling on one knee and saying directly into her face, "Dear Miss Bradford, would you do me the honor of becoming my wife?"

Carrie bit down hard on her tongue to keep from saying something inappropriate. She gathered her wits, formed a solemn expression on her face, and responded with a single word, "No."

He was shocked and immediately stood up and stared down at her. She rose from the seat, looked him in the eyes and said more clearly, "I will not marry you, Brandon Hildebrandt. You do me great honor by asking me, but I do not intend to marry at this time."

"But why not?" Brandon Hildebrandt demanded without ceremony.

Carrie's anger began to rise, but she controlled herself admirably. She thought it none of his business why she chose not to marry, but rather than offend this friend of her father's, she chose her words carefully. "I am not settled in my mind about what my future path should be," she said gently, "and it seems most unfair of me to encourage any gentleman at this time."

"But surely you intend to marry," Brandon Hildebrandt hurried on. "All young women want to marry."

"I am not sure what all young women want to do," Carrie said politely. "I can only say that at this moment I do not know what I want to do."

"Is there another man you prefer?" Hildebrandt demanded.

Carrie's mind flew naturally to the thought of Robert, and she very much wanted to speak the raw truth, but she dared not. She said quite simply, "I have met many young men in the last year. I need time to consider, and there is, after all, no great hurry. I am only seventeen."

"While you are considering," Brandon Hildebrandt said stiffly, "please do remember the many things that I can offer you. My estate is quite sizable, and my name is an honorable one that goes back to the aristocratic circles of Germany."

"So I have heard," Carrie said.

"I am considered a tolerably handsome man, I believe," Brandon Hildebrandt said with a tone of irritation creeping into his voice.

"Indeed you are," Carrie agreed.

"Well then, if I am handsome enough, wealthy, and from an honorable and old family, I find it difficult, Miss Bradford, to understand why you must consider so long and hard."

Carrie was furious with Hildebrandt's trivilization of a relationship as significant as marriage, but she deemed the man unworthy of an argument. Thus, she chose her next words carefully, hoping that she could make her point and close the matter permanently. "You have mentioned, sir, your physical attributes, your fortune, and your good name as reasons why I should marry you. Does it not seem to you that something is missing in your list?"

Brandon Hildebrandt looked surprised and said nothing.

"I refer, sir, to love, of course," Carrie filled in the gap for him. "You have said nothing about loving me. Certainly I would not choose to marry a man who did not love me."

"But I assumed that we could take that for granted," Brandon Hildebrandt said quickly. "Of course I love you, my dear Miss Bradford. Why else would I be asking you to marry me?"

"I do not think that love is something that is taken for granted," Carrie said coldly. "And as for why you might marry me without love, I believe I could name the same attributes you have listed to recommend yourself, namely my appearance, my family's wealth and good name."

"So it is a perfect match," Hildebrandt insisted.

Carrie could see that she was getting nowhere, that Brandon Hildebrandt's concept of grounds for marriage was simply not hers, so she fell back to her original statement. "I am not now prepared to make a decision about my future as a wife," she said firmly, "nor do I expect to be prepared to make that decision for some time. Will you excuse me please?" She turned quickly and swept out of the room.

She hastened upstairs to her own room, closed the door behind her, walked across the room and collapsed on the window seat. From there she could see straight down the driveway and look up into the sky to see the moon and the stars. She thought of Robert and how happy she would be at this moment if she had spent the evening with him. Her heart would have been full of light, full of the delicious joy that only comes from intimate communication with a beloved one. By contrast, tonight had been empty and tortuous. She was grateful that she was as young as she was, for she felt sure that her father would not pressure her to accept Brandon Hildebrandt.

She was surprised to hear an angry knock at her bedroom door very quickly after Brandon Hildebrandt had driven away. Her father did not wait for a word from her but instead strode through the door and demanded, "Why did you refuse his proposal?"

Carrie stared up at James, amazed at the degree of his anger. His face was tense, and he stood with both fists clenched at his sides.

"I do not love him," Carrie said simply. "Why would I accept the proposal of a man I do not love?"

"You will love him, Daughter," James said angrily, "if you will only give him a chance. It is a good marriage, Carrie, one that I have been hoping for quite some time. Brandon Hildebrandt can give you security and position in society. There is certainly nothing wrong with the man, whether you love him or not."

"But the fact remains," Carrie insisted, "that I do not love him, Father."

"Most brides do not love their husbands, Carrie. I should have thought your mother would have discussed this with you."

"Mother has never encouraged me to marry a man whom I did

not love," Carrie said tartly.

"I only hope that you have not offended Brandon Hildebrandt to such a degree that he will not return to offer you his hand in marriage again," James continued in the same angry tone, "and when he does return, Carrie, I expect you to accept his proposal enthusiastically."

"I cannot promise to marry Brandon Hildebrandt, Father. I do not love him and—"

"I shall have your mother discuss this with you," James interrupted her, "but when Brandon Hildebrandt returns—and he will return, Carrie, because I have assured him that you are simply young, inexperienced, and a bit frightened at the thought of marrying—I expect you to accept his proposal."

"I cannot. I do not want to marry him, and I cannot say I do. I cannot tell a lie," Carrie insisted. "Nothing Mother can say will make any difference. There is no reason for Brandon Hildebrandt to hope that I shall ever marry him. I do not love him, and I do not plan to marry a man I do not love."

"What do you know of love?" James demanded roughly. "You are seventeen years old."

"I have had some experience of love, Father," Carrie said quietly, but she dared not mention Robert's name.

James turned and stalked from the room.

Carrie lay awake many hours that night thinking of Robert. Almost a year had passed since she had communicated with him, and she had no way of knowing what his feelings were. Her feelings had not changed, certainly, but she had no guarantee that his had remained the same.

The next day Mary spoke to her. She did not insist that Carrie accept Brandon Hildebrandt's proposal, but she once again assured Carrie that James would never approve of her marriage to Robert and that the pressure to accept some man of fortune and reputation would only increase as time passed. Throughout the following week, James treated Carrie with cold civility, and she was hurt by his behavior; the loving father she had always known seemed to have disappeared. She lived in dread of the day Brandon Hildebrandt would return.

Chapter 16

Carrie's heart began to beat wildly as she saw a lone figure riding up the driveway. "It is Robert!" she cried out "Oh, dear God, thank you. He has come!" She was frozen in place for a few moments as she drank in the sight of him. Just being able to look at his face is a feast for my eyes, Carrie thought, and the fact that he has come must surely mean that he still cares. She turned and ran to the doorway of her bedroom so she could hear whatever might occur in the hallway downstairs. Her breath held and every one of her muscles tensed, she waited for a knock on the door, but no knock came. Instead she heard the quick, loud footsteps of her father as he strode across the entrance hall and opened the door.

"What are you doing here?" he demanded of Robert before he could speak.

"I have come to speak to you about Carrie."

Carrie's heart leapt with happiness and hope. His voice sounds deeper than I remember, she thought, but then it has been a full year since I have seen him. Perhaps he is now better able to persuade Father that we should be married. She ran to the bannister and leaned over.

"There is absolutely no reason for us to discuss Carrie," James said coldly.

"I am hoping," Robert said, "that you have changed your mind about our relationship."

"You have no relationship with my daughter," James said brusquely, "and I intend to keep it that way."

"If only you would discuss the matter, sir," Robert's voice was patient but determined, "I am sure that I can convince you that I am willing and able to comply with any requirements you might place on our relationship."

"I require nothing of you, Robert, except that you stay totally away from Carrie and do not discuss the idea of marriage with her, with me, or with anyone."

"Is that your final word, sir?" Robert asked with surprising composure.

"That is my final word," James insisted.

"Then I bid you good day," Robert said quietly.

When Carrie realized that Robert was leaving, she raced back across the hall and through her bedroom until she was stopped by the window. "If only I could talk to him, touch his hand!" she cried out. She raised her right hand and pressed it against the glass in an attempt to come as close as possible to touching Robert. Sobbing quietly, she watched him ride down the drive. Fervently she wished he would turn, so she could see his face one last time. In her heart she now understood that her father would never allow her to come into Robert's presence again until she was safely married to another man, a man of her father's choosing. "Robert!" she cried "Oh Robert, do not leave me here!" When Robert reached the gate, he turned in the saddle and looked back up at the house. Carrie held her breath, then said, "I am here. Oh, Robert, look up!" As if some winged messenger had carried her words to him, he looked up at her window and saw her. He raised his left hand and flattened it palm forward toward her, as if he, too, were pressing his hand against the windowpane that separated them.

Carrie's spirits sank even lower as she understood the prophetic nature of their gestures. The reality of her future was obvious; there would always be a barrier between her and the man she loved. At times she would be able to see him from afar, but never again would she be able to touch him.

She heard her bedroom door open, and she knew from the sound of the soft tread on the wide pine floors that her mother was entering the room. She had come, undoubtedly, to comfort Carrie.

"He will not come again," Carrie said, without turning. "He is a very proud young man and very strong willed."

"No, dear, he will not come again. I think you are right; he will not come again." Mary put her hands on Carrie's shoulders. "I am sorry. It seems that there is nothing I can do to help you. Perhaps when you are older, you will understand that this is better for you."

"I do not believe that," Carrie said flatly.

Her Mother did not argue with her or say the predictable,

comforting things. Instead she stood behind Carrie and patted her shoulders.

A few moments later they heard the sound of heavy boots on the staircase. "It is your father, dear. Please, Carrie, do not fight with him; he is very angry with Robert."

"I have no reason to argue with Father. He knows my heart; he knows what I want, but he controls my fate. What would be the point of arguing with him?"

"Carrie!" James Bradford announced his arrival in his daughter's room. "Turn around and look at me."

Obediently Carrie turned around and looked at her father. When she raised her eyes to his, only sadness shone forth from them.

"Carrie, I want you to pack your trunks. You are going back to Charleston," James announced.

"Charleston!" Mary exclaimed. "Why James, you must be insane. She just came home from Charleston. She is worn out; the child needs rest."

"I know all of that," James waved his hand impatiently in the air, "but Carrie's precious Robert has changed her plans."

"What do you mean?" Carrie asked in alarm.

"I mean," James said forcefully, "that since he has returned and asked for your hand again, I now know that this situation will never end until you are married to Brandon Hildebrandt."

"I have told you, Father, that I have no intention of marrying Brandon Hildebrandt. I do not love him."

"And I have told you, young lady, that most couples do not love each other when they marry. Love comes later. I have also told you that Brandon Hildebrandt is the best possible match for any young woman in the South, and I intend that he shall be your husband."

"I will not marry him," Carrie insisted.

"You will do as you are told."

"I will not marry a man I do not love. I prefer not to marry at all."

"That is unthinkable," James replied. "My daughter will marry and bear children who will carry on the Bradford legacy. I will not tolerate an old maid in this family; an old maid is always ridiculed and pitied. No Bradford will ever be ridiculed or pitied."

"James, really, must we get into all this now?" Mary tried to break in.

"Yes, we must," James insisted. "It is clear that Robert Montgomery will not leave off his pursuit of Carrie's hand. I had hoped to hold off for another year before pressing Carrie to marry Brandon, but now I have no choice. Pack her trunks, Mary. She is returning to Charleston."

"But why must she return to Charleston?" Mary demanded. "Why can she not stay here at the plantation and rest?"

"I want her in closer quarters until she is married," James said.

"You make me sound like a prisoner," Carrie accused him.

"I do not mean to make you a prisoner, Carrie." James intentionally softened his voice and walked toward his daughter. "I only meant to say that here at the plantation you are less chaperoned. It is your custom to roam these many acres and go to your private places. I cannot trust Robert any longer. He will find you in one of those private places that you have shared before, and he will press you to do something that is against your better judgment."

"I assure you, Father, even though I am young, I cannot be pressed into marriage by either Robert or you."

"You are going to Charleston," James dropped his false conciliatory tone. "In Charleston you will be well chaperoned and have access to all the shops to prepare for your upcoming wedding."

"But I am not going to be married!" Carrie's temper flared.

"You are going to be married, Carrie, to Brandon Hildebrandt. I am going to speak to him now and assure him that you will welcome a union with him before the summer is out."

"You cannot mean to keep Carrie in Charleston through the whole summer, James!" Mary protested.

"Whether she stays through the summer is entirely up to her, Mary. I should think it would take you no more than a month to arrange a suitable wedding. After that she will be Mrs. Brandon Hildebrandt and may go wherever she wishes with her husband's permission."

"I will not marry Brandon Hildebrandt," Carrie insisted. "I will marry no one."

"You will marry Brandon; furthermore, you will go to Charleston and stay there until you do. Mary, it should take you no more than a few days to get her things ready; then both you and she can return to Charleston. Things will be quieter there now, and you will have the comfort of the sea breezes. It will be a good enough place to rest. I want you to leave in three days."

"James, let us reason—" Mary pleaded.

"She must go, and she will," James cut off his wife's words and stared into Carrie's eyes as he spoke.

"Yes, Father," Carrie stared back stonily. "I shall go to Charleston. I shall go back to Charleston tonight, for I have no desire to look on your face again."

"Carrie!" Mary exclaimed. "You do not mean that."

"I do mean it," Carrie insisted. "No father who loved me would force me into a loveless marriage. I shall go to Charleston, Father, but I shall not marry Brandon Hildebrandt or any other eligible bachelor that you bring forth to continue the Bradford line. I shall stay in Charleston for the rest of my life, leaving only when I know you are coming."

"Carrie, stop this at once!" Mary insisted. "You owe your father an apology."

"She can apologize later," James said, "but she is right about one thing. The sooner she goes the better. I want her away from this plantation before Robert knows what is going on, and since our servants are in close league with his, we need to act quickly. Very well, Carrie, you shall go to Charleston as soon as it is dark. Put together the few things you need for the first day or two. Your mother will join you as soon as possible and bring your other clothing. As for me, I am going to visit Brandon Hildebrandt to make arrangements." He turned and stomped out of the room.

"Oh, Carrie," Mary exclaimed. "I begged you not to confront him. He does not mean what he is saying, dear; he is simply in a terrible temper because Robert has defied him and come again. I must go and speak to him at once before he goes to see Mr. Hildebrandt. Do not worry, dear. He will listen to reason as soon as he calms down. The best thing you can do is pack your things, go to Charleston tonight as your father wishes, and let me talk to him for several days. I will dissuade him from this insane idea of his."

"May God help you," Carrie began to cry. "I meant what I said, Mother. I am not going to marry Brandon Hildebrandt. I shall never marry at all. I would rather—" she stopped speaking as she heard the sound of a horse's hoofs. Both she and Mary raced to the window. "It is Father," Carrie cried. "Oh no! He is on the way to see Mr. Hildebrandt. Oh, Mother, what shall I do? Even you cannot dissuade him once he has given his word to Brandon Hildebrandt. He will never back down from his word."

Mary turned and hurried across the room, calling back, "I shall send a servant after him. We must stop him!"

Carrie collapsed in a nearby chair and buried her face in her hands. "Oh, Robert," she cried, "why does it have to be like this? It is so simple, so obvious that we belong together. Why does Father refuse to see that?"

When her mother returned to the room, Carrie stood up abruptly and stared eagerly at her. "I have dispatched a servant to stop your father," Mary said.

"What is the servant to say, Mother? Father will not return just because you send a servant; he will know what you are trying to do."

"I told the servant to tell him that you wanted to go to Charleston for three days to think over the situation and that"—Mary ducked her head, swallowed with difficulty, then lifted her face once again so that she could look Carrie in the eyes. "I told him to tell your father that you would consider marrying Brandon Hildebrandt."

"Mother, you did not!" Carrie cried. "How could you?"

"It is the only way to stop him, Carrie. Do you not see that? I have known your father much longer than you have. Once he sets his mind to a thing, almost nothing can stop him. He needs time to calm down. Now I want you to pack some things, just enough for a day or two. I have ordered a coach; dusk is coming on. As soon as you can get your things together, I want you to go to Charleston and stay at the house. The servants there will take care of you until I can get there. The most important thing is that when your father returns, he must see that you are fulfilling his wishes by preparing to leave for Charleston this evening."

"What am I going to do in Charleston for three days," Carrie demanded, "walk the floor, wondering what my fate is to be?"

"I do not know what the next three days will bring, Carrie, but I pray that we have a chance to calm your father down. I pray that he will turn back and not see Hildebrandt."

"But even if you do calm him down, Mother, what can you hope to accomplish?"

"I can hope to convince him to give you another year. You are, after all, only seventeen, certainly not an old maid yet. I shall try to convince him to give you another year to consider the situation. I shall remind him of something he should already know, which is that if Mr. Hildebrandt cares anything for you, he will be willing to wait a year. It is not such a long time."

"Father has already said it does not matter whether I love Mr. Hildebrandt or whether he loves me."

"That is true, Carrie, but if I can persuade James that it is a matter of Bradford family dignity, that the Bradfords should not rush into the arms of the Hildebrandts, that instead they should be courted by the Hildebrandts, then I may be able to gain you a year. Now, please, dear, let us get your things together. When your father returns, I want him to see that you are complying with his wishes."

Mary and Carrie hastily assembled a meager wardrobe for Carrie and packed it into a bag. When they had finished, they descended the stairs and walked out on to the porch. The carriage stood ready for Carrie.

"Father has not returned," Carrie cried. "Oh, Mother, what does this mean?"

"Hush," Mary said. "I see some dust down at the gate; perhaps it is James."

Carrie held her breath and watched as the dust settled and a horseman emerged. When he was halfway up the drive, she saw that it was the servant and not her father who was returning. Despair began to creep up through the floorboards of the porch and enclose her in a shroud of hopelessness. The servant rode quickly up to the porch, jumped off his horse, and turned to Mary Bradford.

"Did you speak to Mr. Bradford?" Mary demanded.

"Yes, ma'am," the man said. "I catch him on the road."

"Did you give Mr. Bradford my message?"

"Yes ma'am, I say just what you told me to say."

"And what did Mr. Bradford say?" Mary asked as calmly as she could. Carrie felt sure that she already knew the answer.

"He don't say nothing, ma'am. He just turn his horse and go on down the road."

Mary was silent for a moment while the servant stood before her, his hat in his hand. "Does you want me to do anything else, Miz Mary?" the man finally interrupted her thoughts.

"No," she raised her head quickly. "No, thank you, that will be all."

Once the man was out of hearing, it was Carrie who found the courage to express the obvious. "He refused to turn back. He did not believe us."

"Apparently not," Mary agreed. She raised her tear-filled eyes to her daughter's face and asked, "When has deceit ever accomplished anything worth accomplishing?"

Carrie slowly hugged her mother. "You tried, Mother. I love you." Then she hurried down the steps and entered the carriage. The driver took his place, lashed his whip in the air and shouted at the horses. Carrie wiped the tears from her eyes and watched as the landscape she held so dear slowly passed the carriage window; soon they were out of the gate and on the familiar road to Charleston. The trees provided a canopy of dense shade that shut out the weak twilight. In no time at all it was dark outside, and the only lights Carrie could see were those of the tiny lightning bugs that flitted from bush to bush and momentarily shone their bright, but small, beacons of light.

The coach was almost to Charleston, and Carrie had exhausted her tears, wiped her face, and leaned back against the seat in resignation. Whatever pressures are brought to bear upon me, she thought resolutely, I shall never marry Brandon Hildebrandt. I shall be an old maid.

Suddenly she was thrown forward in the carriage and had to brace herself to stay on the seat. She heard the coachman's voice yelling at the horses to stop; then, outside she heard more horses.

"Get down from there," a male voice shouted as soon as the horses had stopped totally.

Carrie was frightened as thoughts of robbers invaded her mind, but she had never heard of a robbery on this road.

"Get down, I said," the male voice insisted again.

Carrie sat perfectly still, afraid even to lean forward to look out the window.

"Now get over by that tree," the voice commanded.

Carrie heard the sound of men walking through the brush. She ventured a peek out the window and saw two men barely visible in the shadows of the tree. One was walking behind the other, shoving him along. She peered intensely into the darkness, and although she could not see precisely what was happening, the movements suggested that the robber was tying the driver to the tree. He turned and started back toward the carriage. Hastily Carrie sat back on the seat so that she could not be seen through the window. She heard the man shout back at the driver, "Do not worry, I will tell someone you are here."

Carrie was biting her lip to keep from screaming when suddenly she heard a familiar voice. "Carrie, Carrie, do not be frightened, it is Robert."

"Robert!" Carrie cried out his name as joy rushed through her and dissolved her fear. She jumped off of the seat and pushed open the carriage door. "Oh, Robert, is it really you?"

Strong arms reached up and took her by the waist. "Everything is going to be all right, darling. Jump down; I will catch you"

"Robert, what are you doing here? What have you done?"

"I am kidnapping you," he said lightly. "Is that not the first step toward an elopement?"

"An elopement?"

"It is not my first choice, Carrie. I would marry you in front of the world, in any church you choose, but your father will have none of that, and I shall not stand back and see us torn apart by any force."

"Oh, Robert," Carrie cried and threw her arms around his neck.

He pushed her back and looked down into her face. "You do want to marry me, don't you, Carrie?"

"Oh yes!" she exclaimed. "Yes!"

"Even if it means your father never speaks to us again?"

"That will be his loss," Carrie answered, "but we shall have our entire lives together."

Robert kissed her quickly, then asked, "Where is your bag?"

"In the carriage." She pointed to the door.

He stepped up, leaned into the carriage, and pulled her bag out. "I hope you have enough here for several days," he said, "because nobody—and I mean nobody—is going to find us until we are married."

"If I had nothing, it would be enough," Carrie laughed.

"Come quickly, darling," he grabbed her hand. "We must get away before someone comes."

When they reached his horse, Robert tied her bag to the back of the saddle, lifted her up, said, "Steady boy, steady," to his horse, and swung up behind her. Then he put his arms around her, took the reins, and left the road to thread his way through the woods. To Carrie it was a totally uncharted path, but she felt no fear, no hesitation. Robert's arms around her were like a cocoon, a safe place she could snuggle and wait to be reborn as Mrs. Robert Montgomery.

Just as the very first rays of morning light were turning the sky gray, someone pounded on the bedroom door of James and Mary Bradford. Mary welcomed the interruption, for she had not slept a moment. Her worries about Carrie's future in the face of James' obstinate nature had kept her from resting. James, on the other hand, had rested peacefully, safe in the knowledge that before he had returned to the house he had arranged that Carrie would marry Brandon Hildebrandt within a month.

"Mr. Bradford, Mr. Bradford," a man's voice called urgently from the other side of the door.

Mary sat up first; she was suddenly overwhelmed with anxiety, for if anyone ever disturbed them, it was one of the women servants, never a man. "James!" she poked her husband hard. "Something is horribly wrong."

"Mr. Bradford," the voice called again, and then there was more pounding on the door.

"What is it?" James yelled as he sat up and swung his feet over the side of the high, canopied bed. "Come in, come in," he commanded. The door opened tentatively, and Mary pulled the bedclothes up over her shoulders as the overseer stuck his head around the door.

"What in tarnation is wrong with you, Teague? It is still dark."

"Yes, sir," the man mumbled, "but I gotta talk to you, sir."

"Whatever it is, it can wait until light," James shouted, even though he was climbing out of the bed to attend to the emergency.

"I don't think it can wait, sir," Teague insisted.

"Get out in the hall," James ordered. "I will be right there."

"What in the name of heaven, James?" Mary's voice quavered.

"Now do not upset yourself, Mary," James waved his hand back at her. "Whatever it is, I will take care of it." He strode across the room, walked out of the door and closed it behind him.

Mary jumped from the bed, grabbed her dressing gown, and quickly slipped her arms into it. She was tying the belt around her waist when she jerked open the door and rushed out into the hall.

"What is it, Teague?" Mary asked quietly. "Is someone ill?"

"You keep quiet," James shook his finger at the man.

"Hush, James," Mary said to her husband for the first time in her life. "What is it, Teague?"

The overseer looked at James and said nothing.

"Answer me this minute!" Mary demanded.

"It is the coachman, ma'am, the one that took Miz Carrie to Charleston."

Mary felt a tingle of terror run up her spine. "Has something happened to Carrie?" she demanded.

"No ma'am," Teague replied. "That is, yes ma'am."

"What is it, Teague?" Mary demanded. "I will not be spared. Tell me this instant what is going on."

"It seems that Carrie did not make it to Charleston," James said angrily.

"Didn't make it?" Mary exclaimed. "What do you mean 'didn't make it.' Is she hurt?"

"She ain't hurt, ma'am," Teague looked at the floor. "Least ways, I don't figure she's hurt."

"You 'don't figure'? What does that mean? Exactly what happened, Teague? Tell me exactly what happened."

"That young fool Robert stopped the coach," James broke in. "He stopped the coach and took Carrie."

Mary stood quietly for a moment, trying to take in this startling news. "That will be all for now, Teague," she heard James tell the man, and the man backed away saying something unintelligible.

Mary turned and went back into the bedroom, lit a lamp and turned to face the door. "What did he tell you, James?" she demanded as soon as her husband had joined her and had shut the door behind him.

"You heard what he told me, Mary." James walked toward her slowly, and for the first time in many years he avoided looking her in the face.

"So Robert has taken Carrie," Mary said. "No doubt he means to elope with her."

"That is what the coachman heard him say," James muttered.

"Dear God, help us!" Mary cried. "Help my child!"

"She is all right, Mary," James insisted. "After all, this is

Robert. He would never hurt her."

Mary turned angrily toward the table where the kerosene lamp glowed. She snatched up the lamp and turned back to her husband. "Look at me!" she commanded. James continued to look at the floor. She stomped her foot. "Look at me!" she shouted. He raised his face, and their eyes met. "Robert has taken Carrie to marry her, James. What are you going to do?"

"I will try to find them, of course, Mary. I will try to stop them." James turned away from her.

"Trying is not good enough," Mary lowered her voice with effort. "Look at me, James Bradford. Your son has eloped with your daughter."

James wheeled around and stared at her, his eyes wide with fear.

"Of course I know. I have always known. What kind of fool do you think I am?" Mary demanded. "You will not *try* to find them. You *will* find them, and you *will* stop them. You know this marriage can never be. You, better than anyone other than Diana, know that of all the men in the world, Carrie cannot marry Robert."

"But Mary, what can I do?"

"Tell the truth, James. For the first time in your life tell the truth, the whole truth. Find them! Tell them the truth!"

"What will they think of me?" he muttered.

"I do not know," she raised her voice again. "I do not care. All I know is that your deceit, the deceit that has stood between us like a dark curtain of mud, has become quicksand that will pull my daughter down into sin. I want her found! I want her told the truth. I want you to stop her!"

"I will, Mary, I promise." He turned and started toward the door. When he put his hand on the door handle, he paused for just an instant and turned back to her. "Will you ever forgive me, Mary?"

"For your affair with Diana, I forgave you long ago, James. For this, I do not know."

"I will find her, Mary. I will stop her."

It took James over a week to find Carrie and Robert in an apartment of rooms which Robert had rented in a less fashionable area of Charleston. When they returned from their evening meal, they found James, standing, waiting for them in the middle of their small, rented parlor.

"Father," Carrie cried and started to run toward him. She stopped halfway and let her arms hang down limp at her side as she appraised his expression. He didn't seem angry. Somehow he looked beaten. "I am sorry I disobeyed you," she said clearly, "but I am not sorry I married Robert. I have never been happier. I hope you can find it in your heart to forgive us for whatever you think we need to be forgiven of."

"It is you who will have to do the forgiving, Carrie," James said quietly.

"Oh, I do forgive you," Carrie took a few steps toward him. "I am sure you never understood the depth of my love for Robert. I am sure you only wanted the best situation in life for me. You simply did not understand. I forgive you, Father, for trying to force me to marry Brandon Hildebrandt. I forgive you for any of the words that—"

James put up his hand to stop her. "Carrie, you must listen to me. The greatest act of forgiveness of your life still lies ahead of you."

Carrie felt a chill. She walked back and put her hand into Robert's. "I am not leaving Robert, Father," she said quietly.

Robert stepped forward, still holding her hand. "Mr. Bradford, Carrie and I are married, legally married, and we plan to stay that way until death parts us. We hope to gain your blessing—if not now, some day—but whether we do or not, we plan to live happy lives and surround ourselves with a family which, with God's help, we shall create."

"That is just what you must not do," James said emphatically.

"I beg your pardon, sir," Robert's tone grew stiffer, "but Carrie is my wife, a fact you will have to accept."

"And the law is the law, Robert, a fact that you will have to accept."

"If you are referring to Carrie's age, she is legally old enough to marry."

"If her age were the only consideration, Robert, I would fall on my knees this moment and praise God."

"Then I cannot think what law it is you refer to, sir."

James took a deep breath, looked at his daughter's worried face and the angry face of Robert; finally he said, "This state does not allow a brother and sister to marry."

"What?" Carrie exclaimed. "A brother and sister. Father, have you gone mad?"

"I wish I had before this moment came, Carrie." He took several steps toward the couple until he stood directly before them. "This is entirely my fault, and I take full responsibility for it. The fact of the matter is," he looked at Robert, "you are my son by Diana Montgomery." Then he looked at Carrie, "As you know, Carrie, you are my daughter by Mary Fitzgerald."

Carrie gasped and came closer to fainting than she ever had in her life.

"And you have waited until now to tell us?" Robert demanded angrily. "What kind of man are you?"

"A man who has made many mistakes, son, and is not inclined to admit them."

"So your immorality, your deceit, and, yes, your pride have brought my beloved Carrie to this place in her life. I should kill you! Father or not, I should kill you!" He grabbed James around the throat, and Carrie thought that they would fall to the floor, Robert was so determined in his struggle.

"Stop it!" she screamed. When she could not separate them with her feeble arms or her cries, she fell to the floor sobbing. Robert let go of his father, crouched down and picked up Carrie in his arms. He carried her to a settee in the room and placed her gently on it. Kneeling beside her, he spoke to her softly and stroked her hair as he endeavored to calm her. James stood helplessly by.

When Carrie was quiet again, Robert looked up at James and asked, "Who knows this? Who knows you are my father?"

"Carrie's mother knows, and of course, your mother knows," James answered.

Robert turned back to Carrie. "Then somehow we can make it right and still spend our lives together," he said.

She stared up at him, her eyes large in her white face, and said, "Oh, Robert, God knows."

"But we did not intend to sin," Robert insisted. "We did not know."

"We know now," she whispered. "We know now."

"I cannot lose you," Robert begged her, "even if I must live with you as a sister."

"I do not know what to do," Carrie shook her head in

confusion. "I need time to think."

"Let me take you home to the plantation," James finally spoke up.

"No," Carrie refused. "I want to go back to our Charleston house."

"I will not let you leave me," Robert insisted. "You are my wife."

"I cannot be your wife," Carrie cried.

"But you cannot just walk out of here and never communicate with me again."

"Oh Robert! Surely you know me better than that. I could never do such a thing." She placed her hand on his cheek and looked intently into his eyes. "I shall go to the most neutral ground I can think of, and that is our Charleston house. You stay here. I know how to contact you."

"I will take you there," Robert said.

"It would be better if I take her," James interjected.

Robert stood up angrily and confronted his father, "Don't you understand that we do not care about your reputation?"

"Do not fight," Carrie raised her voice. "Do not fight," she repeated as she stood up, "or neither one of you will see me again. Robert, I am going to my family's Charleston house. I need to consult with my mother. You know where the house is; you are welcome at any time, but it is best that Father take me there now."

"We could live as brother and sister," Robert pleaded with her. "We could be very happy."

"Yes," Carrie agreed, "that might be an option. I just need time to think. I am so confused."

"It is the shock," James said. "I will take you home, as you asked."

"I warn you," Robert turned on James, "I will not stay away. Not this time."

"I do not expect you to," James said quietly. "Indeed, I realize I have lost any right to expect obedience from either one of you."

"Do not worry, Robert," Carrie stroked his arm. "After I have rested, I will think about what is best for us to do. Many lives are involved here." She hugged him close, then stumbled, as if she could not see, toward the door. Her father caught up with her and tried to support her, but she shoved him away.

Chapter 17

During the entire carriage ride to the Bradford's Charleston house, James poured out a continuous flow of words, sometimes apologizing to Carrie, sometimes imploring her to be reasonable. She ignored him entirely as she turned her face toward the window and thought her own thoughts: such deceit, such incredible deceit that has led me to degradation. Dear God help me! What am I going to do? I can never forgive him.

When they finally arrived at the Charleston house, Carrie leapt from the carriage without assistance and ran through the pouring rain onto the piazza. A footman opened the door, and she raced past him and tore up the stairs to her bedroom, where she slammed the door behind her and locked it. Throwing herself upon the canopy bed, she wept bitterly and long. She ignored the frequent entreaties of James to allow him to come in, to allow a servant to build a fire or to bring her some tea. Instead Carrie burrowed down into the mattresss, curled her body up like a little child and cried.

Her father finally ceased his attempts and admitted to himself that it would be useless to try to talk to her now. He would wait for Mary to arrive.

Carrie had absolutely no idea how to proceed with her life. Her love for Robert was not diminished one bit by learning that he was her half-brother, but every code she had grown up believing in now decreed that she could not be his wife. Yet she had been, for a few short days. She saw herself as hopelessly lost. She could never be Robert's, yet she could never be another man's. She could never accept her father again. Her future seemed blank. She didn't stir from the bed until she heard the sound of carriage wheels on the drive; then she rose from the bed and crept to the window. When she looked down to the drive, her greatest hope, her only hope, was fulfilled, for there was her mother descending from the carriage while a servant held an umbrella over her.

"Mother," Carrie cried softly. She waited tensely until she heard her mother's steps on the stairs, and then when the soft knock sounded on the door, Carrie flew across the room to unlock the door.

Her mother came in and embraced her, then stood back a few steps, her face covered with pain and compassion.

"What am I to do?" Carrie wailed. "I am victimized by my father's sins."

Mary held her daughter close again and said, "We will take things one step at a time. First, we must have a fire in this room and then some hot tea and a bite to eat."

"I could not possibly swallow," Carrie moaned, her face buried in her mother's shoulders. Then she began to sob like a helpless child.

Mary's face was also quickly covered with tears, but she managed to control her own desire to break into sobs and slowly drew her daughter back to the bed where she encouraged her to lie down once again. She went back to the hallway and said sternly to someone, "Send a servant to build a fire in here and bring a tea tray with some sandwiches. Tell Mr. Bradford that we are not to be disturbed." She closed the door when she returned to the room.

Carrie continued to sob into the pillow, and her mother leaned over the bed and stroked her head, making no attempt to talk to her. As she waited for Carrie's emotional storm to pass, Mary prayed that somehow God would enlighten her with a solution that would not break Carrie's heart or ruin her future.

A servant appeared quickly and built a roaring fire; Mary dismissed her with her hand the moment she was finished. In another ten minutes the housekeeper brought a large tray up. Mary motioned for her to set it on the tea table, and again, without saying any word, she motioned for her to leave.

Finally she spoke to Carrie. She took her by the shoulders and turned her over where she could look her in the face. "Carrie, those are all the tears you have time for now. There will be other times that you can cry, but now we must reason together and think what to do."

"I will not speak to Father," Carrie blurted out. "I will never speak to him as long as I live."

"I do not think I blame you for feeling that way," Mary said calmly. "There is no need to speak to your father now. You and

I must discuss what has happened, but first we must protect your health. I want you to get up from this bed, come sit by the fire, and have some hot tea and sandwiches."

"Mother, I just want to die!"

"Carrie," Mary said sharply, "I have never heard you say such a thing, and I never want to hear you say it again."

"But my life is ruined."

"Your life is not ruined, dear, although I confess at the moment I cannot see how things can be worked out, but it is not your choice to live or die. That is up to God, and we must depend on Him to give us the wisdom to know what to do now. But first we must use our common sense, and you are ice cold. You need to sit by the fire and drink hot tea. Now get up." She pulled Carrie out of the bed and helped her walk toward the fire. "Sit there, dear, in that chair, and I shall pour you a cup of tea. I insist that you drink it, all of it."

Carrie did as her mother requested, and the hot liquid seemed to dissolve the lump in her throat that she thought was surely permanent.

"Now we must talk," Mary said, as she handed Carrie a plate with tiny sandwiches on it.

"I cannot eat, Mother."

"You must eat a little."

Carrie looked her mother straight in the eyes and asked, "Mother, how much do you know?"

"I know everything, dear. I know that you chose to elope with Robert. I know that your father came after you and told you that Robert is your half-brother. I know you are here at our Charleston house because you chose to come here. I am grateful to God that even in the midst of this indescribable pain that you have endured, your good sense has brought you here because clearly some action has to be taken before knowledge of your marriage becomes public."

"Do you think I care about my reputation?" Carrie demanded angrily.

"No, dear. Of all the people I know, you would be the last person to be so superficial as to consider only your reputation, but your reputation has to be considered, along with many other things that I view as more important."

"You have no idea how I feel," Carrie said bitterly. "I feel so totally betrayed by father. How could he have done such a thing? How could he have had an affair with cousin Diana? How could he have done such a thing to you? Don't you hate him?"

"No," Mary responded quietly. "I don't hate your father. I wanted to hate him twenty years ago when he spent those hours with my cousin Diana while I waited for him to return to my bed. I wanted to hate him then, but there was a certain sense of justice in me that made it impossible for me to hate James. I was too aware of what he had been through, what we had all been through during the War."

Carrie stared at her mother in amazement. "You have known all along about father's affair with Cousin Diana? You knew that Robert was his son?"

"I knew about his affair with Diana. Certainly I had good reason to suspect that Robert was your father's son, but it was not until I was carrying you in my womb that I knew for certain that James had fathered Robert. He was very eager for your safe birth, and apparently he had been quite devastated when he could not claim Robert as his son. He had a nightmare, a dreadful dream, about Diana taking you away from him after you were born. He said, 'You stole my son, my Robert. I hate you, Diana! Give me my Robert.' He muttered many such things before I could awaken him."

"Why did you stay with him?" Carrie demanded. "How could you live with him after you knew he had betrayed you? How could you stay one hour?"

"You forget, Carrie, that I had you to consider, my precious unborn child. I would have suffered anything to give you life and then to make your life secure and happy. What did my pride matter compared to your life?"

"If only someone had told the truth—at least to Robert and me!"

"That is where I failed you, dear. I should have told you."

"Father should have told me! He was the one who made this horrible mess—not you."

"But he did not tell you, so I should have told you. How I wish I had! But James kept you away from Robert, and Diana sent Robert off to school long before either of you were old enough to care about such things as love and marriage. To my knowledge you were never alone with Robert; I was stunned by his proposal.

All I knew about was your correspondence with Robert."

"We met by accident in the woods after his father died. I shared my secret, special place on the river with him, and we talked. Don't you see, Mother, we were so much alike. We were so instantly comfortable with each other. Now I know why."

"I should have known. Oh Carrie! I thought I was protecting you and Robert. I am so sorry. Please, please forgive me."

"Of course, Mother. I do not blame you. I blame Father."

"Let us leave the past behind for now. Later we can sort out our angers and hopefully forgive. But now we must think of your future—and Robert's future."

"Oh, don't you know? Father has the perfect solution," Carrie said sarcastically.

"He wants you to marry Brandon Hildebrandt," Mary said quietly.

"Well, of course, Mother. All I have to do is to deceive Brandon Hildebrandt and allow you, my father and a few other people to be deceitful, and my life can go on with the greatest of ease, according to my father. Never mind the fact that I happen to be in love with Robert and that he is bitterly hurt by this. Never mind the fact that I am lying to Brandon Hildebrandt to cover up for Father's sins. Those things do not seem to matter to Father at all."

"I cannot defend him. He has been wrong. He was wrong to have an affair with Diana, and I do not agree that his plans to extricate you from this situation are necessarily the right plans, but frankly at the moment I cannot think of any alternative."

"Well I can," Carrie exclaimed. "I want to return to Robert."

"You can never live as Robert's wife, dear."

"I know that," Carrie said sadly. "I know that the law would not forbid it because the law does not know about our kinship, but my conscience would forbid it. Can I not live with Robert in some sort of platonic way?"

"Carrie, I do not think that marriage between you and Robert, a marriage that is only platonic, would ever be comfortable. And I think also that it would not be fair to either one of you. He would never have the opportunity to love a woman totally; he would never have the opportunity to father a family. And over the years, I think, he would grow to resent that. I think the very same is true for you too, dear. You would want a true marriage and a family. A platonic marriage is simply not practical, dear. I think you already know that."

Carrie nodded her head as her tears began to flow again. Her mother rose, handed her a handkerchief and stroked her hair; then she sat back down and poured Carrie another cup of tea. "Tears are natural and appropriate now, dear, but drink this tea and let us try to reason together."

"Mother, I cannot marry Brandon Hildebrandt," Carrie sobbed. "It would be a total lie. I cannot deceive him. Don't you understand that the misery that I feel at this very moment is the result of deceit, that I cannot turn around and be that deceitful myself?"

"I do understand that," Mary said quietly. "I also understand that you do not care about reputation, at least not now, but, Carrie, you will care in the future about your reputation. Robert will care about his. It is very difficult for you to imagine that you would ever be able to love another man, or that Robert would ever love another woman, but I think that he definitely will want to marry, and I suspect that you will want to marry in time. The shadow of this mistaken marriage must not be allowed to harm your future relationships."

"I will not marry Brandon Hildebrandt," Carrie insisted.

"I am not saying that you should, dear. I am not saying that you should do anything immediately except allow your father to annul your marriage to Robert. You know this is the right thing to do, don't you?"

"Yes," Carrie cried, "but it hurts. Oh, Mother, how it hurts! But, yes, it is right. The marriage must end."

"I shall tell your father to gain you an annulment as quietly as possible."

"I am sure he can handle it," Carrie said wearily. "He has a talent for covering up truth."

Mary said nothing.

"Mother, make sure that Father understands that I will not marry Mr. Hildebrandt."

"I shall tell him, dear."

"And, Mother—about Robert," Carrie began to cry again, and she choked on her words, "I cannot see him again. I could not bear it. I simply could not! If I saw him in the pain that I know he is feeling, I would abandon all my principles and live with him. I know I would. But he deserves some kind of communication from me. What should I do?"

"I shall talk to Robert, Carrie, if you like."

"Keep Father away from him!" Carrie insisted.

"I shall see him alone."

"And tell him that I love him; I truly love him, but we cannot be together. It is not right."

"I think he will have come to the same conclusion," Mary assured her, "if not by now, he will soon. First, I shall go speak to your father about the annulment."

It rained for three days after Carrie returned to her family's Charleston house. She slept very little. During the dark hours of the night, she listened to the wind that seemed to be venting some kind of colossal rage against the edge of the continent where Charleston was situated. She clenched her fists around the bedcovers and fought her own battle of rage against the unfairness of life and particularly against her father, who had closed all doors of future happiness for her. During the daylight hours, the rain persisted, and the wind blew it against the French doors that normally would have allowed Carrie access to the piazza. Instead she stood next to the doors and looked out into the gray, weeping skies, out to the sea where the angry wind had whipped up ferocious waves to beat against the shore.

She dug deep into her soul, searching for the softness of forgiveness that she knew she must eventually find there, but she found only the hard bedrock of unreleased anger. She saw no one except her mother.

When she awoke on the fourth morning, the sky seemed a bit lighter. She rose from the bed and walked over to the French doors that faced seaward. The angry storm had retreated out to sea and left only a gray mist hanging high over the city. The slightest band of light was beginning to appear on the horizon.

"A new day is coming," she murmured, "and there will be another and another. I cannot spend my life standing by this door looking out at the world. I am weary, so weary, but I know that more time in bed will not ease that weariness. I must go outside; only the trees and the birds can ease my pain."

Opening the French doors, she stepped out onto the piazza and discovered that the fresh air from the bay smelled wonderful. Carrie walked to the banister of the piazza and stared down at the late spring flowers in the garden below her. The battering wind and heavy rain had damaged them considerably. Poor, beautiful flowers, she thought, your heads are all drooping. A good many of your blossoms will die from this battering, but some will survive, and in the end you will be nurtured somehow by this excess of water. As she continued her thoughts, a flower that she was concentrating on released its beaten petals, and they floated to the path. With the weight of the soggy petals removed, the stem sprang up. Carrie nodded in affirmation to herself. She looked out at the band of light on the horizon which had become yellow and wider. For an instant, a glimpse of the happy dreams that she and Robert had shared flashed through her mind, and she was overwhelmed by grief. She clutched the banister tightly and looked back at the flower stem that had sprung up once its wet blossoms had dropped.

"I must go on," she whispered.

Carrie heard another French door opening. She looked over her shoulder and saw her mother emerging onto the piazza. "Are you all right, dear?" Mary asked as she approached Carrie.

"Yes, Mother, I am all right now."

Mary put her arm around her daughter's shoulder and looked out at the band of light on the horizon. "I am so glad to see the light," she said quietly.

"It does help immensely, does it not?"

"Carrie, dear, I have been thinking."

"So have I, Mother," Carrie interrupted her. "I have been thinking that I cannot spend the rest of my life in a dark room. What I have experienced is like a death. It has been very painful and will continue to hurt, but somehow I must allow God to use it to strengthen me."

"That is right, dear." Mary turned to face Carrie. "Oh, sometimes you do surprise me, especially in your spiritual maturity. It would have taken me months to come to that statement if I had suffered what you have suffered. Indeed, all those years ago, when I was carrying you, I could not come to the understanding that I had to let go of the past and embrace the present. I was not able to do that until you were born. When I first saw your face, I was finally free of the past."

"I have not been able to pray, Mother." Carrie's voice was flat, but her eyes were beseeching her mother for help.

"I know, dear, but I think that God understands, and in some strange way, even the pain in your heart, even the angry thoughts have been prayers."

"I cannot form the words of a prayer, Mother, but if He is listening to my heart, I hope He sees that I do want to go on with courage and to have some purpose to my life. I shall not marry again. I cannot marry again, so my life will not be dedicated to the things a woman normally embraces. Still, I do hope that God gives me something special to do."

"Oh, Carrie, God will give you something special. He is here, and He has heard your words. Now you must put your actions behind them. You must come out of your room, dress, and go out. Even for just a little walk. Yes, now that the clouds are lifting, let us plan a small walk this morning. It will be good for our spirits."

"And it will be good for my reputation," Carrie added.

"That is true, dear, it will be good for your reputation. I know you care nothing about that now, and perhaps you never will, but it is best to protect it. After all, if God should give you something special to do, a good reputation may be one of the necessities to perform His will."

"I never thought of that," Carrie smiled at her mother. "I think I am just tired of being closed up in a room. It just does not fit my nature."

"No, Carrie, it does not," Mary agreed with her.

"In fact, even though you are very angry with your father, I suspect you are going to want to return to the plantation so you can be outside."

"Perhaps in time," Carrie agreed. "Where is Father?"

"I am not sure I know. I assume that he is at the plantation, since he has not been here." Mary turned and walked away rather than discuss James. "Let us both dress," she said, as she reached her own door, "and have breakfast in the dining room. Then we shall go for a short walk."

In an hour's time Carrie and her mother were strolling along the Battery, keeping a steady pace, nodding to those who passed them, but refusing to stop and converse. The sea air felt wonderful to Carrie, and the morning sunshine that had freed itself from the clouds lifted her spirits. In time she and her mother reached a park and stopped at the end of the Battery walk to look out to sea.

"Look how the light shines on the water," Mary exclaimed.

"I can hardly believe we were here all those months this winter and spent so many hours indoors at parties and teas and dances, not to mention at shops and with your dressmaker. Why, I hardly remember seeing the water and the beautiful light on it. Oh, Carrie, look how it dances on those gentle waves." As she pointed at the water, Mary turned to her daughter. She discovered that Carrie had her hand over her mouth and her eyes were full of panic.

"Oh, Mother," Carrie said urgently. "I feel horribly sick. I am going to be sick and right here in public."

"Oh no! She was pregnant!" Caroline stopped at the wrought iron gate into Great Aunt Kathleen's garden, and turned to stare at her great-aunt. "She was pregnant, wasn't she? And with Robert's child?"

"Yes, dear, she was," Aunt Kathleen said.

"Oh why does it always have to be this way?" Caroline burst out angrily. She turned and slammed her fist down on a bar of the gate. "Why is pregnancy always a problem in this life?"

"It is not always a problem," Aunt Kathleen said calmly as she opened the gate and gently urged Caroline into the garden. After she had shut the gate behind them, she turned back to Caroline. "Many pregnancies, in fact most pregnancies, are happy occurrences, even though they carry their discomforts with them."

"That's a fine romantic idea, Aunt Kathleen," Caroline exclaimed, "but in life it's just not true."

"You sound as if you speak from experience, Caroline."

"I do," Caroline blurted out without thinking. "I do speak from experience. Look what pregnancy has done to my life."

"What has it done, Caroline?"

"Why, it's separated me from David in a way I never thought was possible, and my mind is full of confusion."

"Where does this confusion come from, my dear?"

"From everybody's different opinions about this—this baby that I'm carrying."

"You are pregnant now, Caroline?" Aunt Kathleen's face beamed with pleasure. "Oh, Caroline, that is wonderful!"

"No, it's not," Caroline countered, "at least it's not to most people."

"But what is it to you, dear? And to David? That is all that matters."

"Oh, Aunt Kathleen, you just don't know; you just don't know the circumstances."

"Well perhaps we best quit talking about ancient history; after all, Mother has been dead quite a few years. We best talk about the present. What is going on with you, Caroline, and how could anyone think that a child coming into this world is not a wonderful gift from God? Surely David is excited about it."

"David doesn't know," Caroline found herself telling yet another person.

"I think we should go sit down, Caroline, and you had best give me the short version of what is troubling you."

Caroline nodded her agreement and silently followed her Aunt Kathleen through the garden and the house until they reached the upstairs verandah. "Sit beside me, dear," Aunt Kathleen patted the settee, "and tell me precisely what has been going on."

Caroline sank onto the soft upholstery, paused a moment and rushed through her story. "It's very simple, Aunt Kathleen, simple to start and complicated—almost impossible—to end. I wanted to have a child, but when I married David, I promised him that there would be no children because that was the way he wanted it. He had lost his first wife and their child in childbirth, and he was older than I and did not want children in his life. I tricked him into this pregnancy. I stopped taking my birth-control pills because I was foolish enough to think I could persuade him out of his fears. Grandmother thought I was foolish indeed and warned me that I was only threatening my marriage to David—"

"Something that she thought was worth more than all the babies in the world," Aunt Kathleen interjected.

"Yes, of course," Caroline agreed. "You know how Grandmother was. Social position meant so much to her."

"So when she found out that you were pregnant and that David would be upset, what did she tell you?"

"I think you know the answer to that." Caroline could not bring herself to say the words that seemed to be a betrayal of her dead grandmother.

"I am afraid I do, my dear. She wanted you to get rid of

your child to save your marriage."

Caroline nodded. "But Mother saw my pregnancy the same way you do, as a great gift."

"And in the midst of all of this confusion, you have had to go through your grandmother's death."

"Yes, and David's illness in London, which has worried me more than I can ever say."

"So here you are, my dear, sitting on the piazza of the Bradford house in Charleston, South Carolina, faced with the two legacies that the Bradfords have brought down through their history, beginning with James Bradford. You guessed right. Carrie, my mother, was pregnant. Those few days of marriage with Robert had produced a child, but her marriage to Robert was annulled."

"What did she do?" Caroline demanded. "I must know what she did."

"I shall gladly tell you, and quickly. I have already told you, Caroline, that there are two legacies that came down through the Bradford family, and my mother Carrie was the bearer of the legacy from her mother, Mary."

"Her father tried to make her marry Brandon Hildebrandt, didn't he?" Caroline guessed again.

"That is exactly right, dear. As soon as it was clear that Carrie, my mother, was pregnant, all of James Bradford's pride of name and family position, all of his eagerness for fortune, all of his care for the material things of life rose to a feverish pitch in him, and he came to this house where Carrie was staying with her mother. He demanded that she marry Brandon Hildebrandt immediately, within the week."

"Wouldn't such a thing have made this Brandon Hildebrandt terribly suspicious?" Caroline asked.

"You must remember, my dear, that these two were deceitful men, to say the least, and their major interests were materialistic. James Bradford had, long before, given Carrie's hand to Hildebrandt. While he was struggling through the ordeal of Carrie's marriage to Robert, he was telling Hildebrandt that he was persuading Carrie to marry him."

"What did she do?" Caroline asked. "Oh I hope she was wiser than I am."

"I do not know about her personal wisdom at that time, but I do know that she was in touch with her God. Let me tell you about the evening after James came and demanded that she marry Brandon Hildebrandt. There was a dreadful scene, right here in this house, in the drawing room. You can well imagine it, with James demanding that her reputation and the reputation of the family be protected, with his pleading that the joining of the two fortunes would be such a wonderful thing. Carrie withstood his arguments, and Mary supported her, but James had no intention of losing. He stormed out of the house about nine o'clock in the evening, flinging back the threat that he would return in a few hours and that Carrie would marry Hildebrandt or else."

Carrie stood in her room in the Bradfords' Charleston house and watched out the window as her father rode angrily away. The loud clatter of horse hoofs on the cobblestone street seemed to reiterate the fury she had heard from his lips. Once he was out of sight, Carrie heard her mother ascending the staircase and knew that she would soon join her for words of consolation. There was a soft knock on the door, and when Carrie called, "Come in," Mary opened the door and stood just inside the doorway. Wearily she asked her daughter, "Is there anything I can do for you, dear?"

"No, thank you," Carrie said as composedly as she could. "There seems to be nothing that anyone can do for me, Mother."

"God is still here," Mary responded.

"I wonder," Carrie countered. "I wonder if He has not left this house in disgust, never to return."

"That would not be His way, would it?"

"No, it would not," Carrie agreed.

"I think I shall lie down until your father returns. Try to rest now, dear. Things will somehow look better in the morning, I am sure." Mary's words were hopeful, but her tone was not. She closed the door quietly, and Carrie listened as her mother's footsteps receded down the hallway. She continued to stare out the window, across to the Battery and out into Charleston Bay. There was a beautiful, high moon in the sky sending a silver path across the gentle waves of the bay. Carrie watched as that light seemed to move toward the shore, toward her, with each small wave. She found it reassuring that light was approaching her, coming to her, endlessly seeking her.

When the house was completely quiet, she turned from the window, put a light shawl over her head and shoulders and quietly slipped downstairs. In a matter of moments, she had made her escape from the house and stealthily walked through the garden to the wrought-iron gate. It made the slightest grating noise as she opened it, but she quickly slipped out and left it slightly ajar. The moon was still above her, sending its pure white light onto the street before her. Carrie began to walk. She did not know where she was going; she was allowing something inside of her to draw her to the place she needed to be. She trusted that when she arrived at that place, she would recognize it as her destination.

She walked for almost ten minutes before she found herself ascending the steps of St. Mary's Catholic Church. It was not her family's church, but it seemed to welcome her and to wish to comfort her. Softly she opened the heavy, carved door and walked into the dimly lit vestibule. She walked through the vestibule and opened the second set of doors into the sanctuary itself. Standing still for a moment, she looked down the long aisle toward the altar. There was a large, golden box on the altar, which reflected the flickering, red light of the tall votive candle which was placed next to it. Above the altar a large crucifix hung, and on each side of it were lighted lanterns. Carrie sighed with relief as if she had escaped some dreadful place where she could not breathe and had found a rarefied air of freedom and release. Quietly she made her way down the aisle until she stood a few pews back from the front. She knelt on one knee, then slipped into one of the pews, and sat on the edge of the cushion for a moment before kneeling to pray. With her hands on the back of the pew in front of her, she stared at the golden box and the crucifix. In all the evening's events it had not occurred to her to pray, even though she was of a religious inclination. As she concentrated intently on the golden box and the crucifix, she felt a great peace come to her, and she heard herself whisper, "This is what I need. I need to be with Jesus. I need someone larger and more powerful and much wiser than I am to guide me, and of course that is God."

No eloquent words flowed from her lips. Instead she knelt there and said quite simply, "Lord, have mercy; show me what to do; show me Your will, for nothing else *will* do."

After a long period of peace, tears began to well up in her eyes, and her chest tightened as she felt the distress of the day emerging from her body. She reached into her pocket, pulled out a handkerchief and sat back in the pew and cried softly. She cried tears of sadness, of grief, as well as tears of fear. At first she was ashamed. I should be stronger than this, she told herself. I should have more faith. But the tears continued, and they seemed so necessary that she ceased fighting them. There is no one here, she consoled herself, no one to see these tears but God. I cannot shame myself by crying before Him. She allowed the tears to flood from her eyes as she muffled her sobs in her handkerchief.

"Where has my peace gone?" she asked herself frantically. "I need to recover that blessed peace," but her mind was dragged down with depression and her chest was tightened with fear, so she continued to cry.

"My dear Miss Bradford," a male voice spoke quietly from the darkness. Carrie stifled all her sounds and wiped frantically at her face with her handkerchief. "Can I be of any assistance?" the voice was nearer and familiar to her.

"No, thank you," she managed to say without looking up. "I want to be alone, please."

"But I could never leave you in this state," the kind voice moved out of the shadows and became the figure of a man who approached close enough for her to see, but she would not look into his face.

"It is John Kendall," he said quietly as he came nearer, by walking down the pew. "May I sit down? I could never leave after seeing you so unhappy."

Carrie finally raised her eyes and looked at the scholarly man who had always taken time to encourage her in her studies. When she saw John Kendall's gentle face, she knew that he was the only man in Charleston she could bear to speak to. She nodded, and he sat next to her and took one of her hands. "This is unforgivable boldness, I am certain," he hesitated, waiting for her to encourage him. She did not. "But my esteem for you, Miss Bradford, forces me to leap over the bounds of propriety."

"You cannot help me," she said softly. "No one can help me, no one but God."

There was a pause between them; then John Kendall said quietly but with resolve, "God can do anything, of course, but you may have noticed that He most often chooses to work through people. After all, we are His hands and voice. It is through our eyes that He is able to shine compassion and love on the world."

Carrie listened to his words and repeated them in her own mind. He is right, she thought. God will help me, but He will use His people to help me. She turned to look at John Kendall. "I am in terrible trouble, and I need your help."

The moment she spoke the words, she was released from the dreadful emotions she had been feeling.

"Tell me what I can do, dear Miss Bradford, and it will be done. I promise you."

"I do not know what you can do," Carrie answered quietly.

"Then tell me of your circumstances. I am older than you, more experienced in life. Perhaps solutions will come to my mind more easily."

"I must not disgrace my family."

"I hope, Miss Bradford, you feel confident that my integrity would never allow me to reveal anything you told me in confidence."

"I do not know if I can believe in the apparent integrity of men any longer," she said. He bowed his head, and there was quietness between them. Carrie looked down at her lap and saw that he still held her left hand.

He reached over and lifted her chin and turned her face toward him. "Then please believe, dearest Carrie, that my love for you would prevent me from ever betraying you."

Carrie was startled to hear her scholarly friend speak of love to her, but she quickly said, "You would not love me if I told you my circumstances."

"I shall love you no matter what you say," he insisted, "and you must speak, for it is apparent that you need help. Trust me to do my best."

Carrie took a deep breath, stared into John Kendall's eyes and emptied her soul of its pain. "I eloped with Robert Montgomery. We were married. I am with child, but my marriage has been annulled. My father insists I must marry Brandon Hildebrandt. To do so, I must lie to him. Are you sure you want to help a woman in such a predicament? Do you not want to run as far away from me as you can get?"

"No," he spoke firmly and took both her hands in his. "Carrie Bradford, whatever has brought you to this place in your life, I have total confidence that this situation is not of your making.

Somehow you are a victim. You need not tell me the circumstances. I do not need to know another fact to be certain that you are a victim."

"What am I to do?" Carrie cried. "I cannot be married to Robert, the father of my child, but I cannot bring myself to marry Mr. Hildebrandt. I must deceive him in order to do so, and I have nothing but negative feelings toward him. Surely he deserves better than that."

"Brandon Hildebrandt, for all his wealth, is a scoundrel, but that is no matter. What matters, Miss Carrie, is you."

"What matters most is my child. I do not have the luxury of worrying about myself or Mr. Hildebrandt. I must protect my child. Yet it is deceit that has created this nightmare. I do not see how deceit can deliver me, although my father insists that it can."

"Robert Montgomery is a fine young man. You have not told me why you could not remain married to him, nor need you tell me. I agree with you. You must protect your child at all costs, but deceit is not the way. Deceit is not the way that God would choose for you, so there must be another way."

"There is so little time," Carrie exclaimed. "I must make decisions that affect my child's future and my own, and my mind is a muddle. If I do not marry Brandon Hildebrandt, my child will be labeled illegitimate, and I shall be outcast. I care nothing for myself, but I will do anything to save my child."

"If you do marry Hildebrandt, your child may very well be mistreated, and you most certainly will be, for that is the character of the man."

"Then what am I to do?" Carrie implored.

John Kendall stared deeply into her eyes as she earnestly looked at his kindly face. "Could you bring yourself, Miss Carrie, to marry a middle-aged bachelor, a poor professor, who has loved you for two years?"

"Marry you?" Carrie questioned.

"I know I have little to offer," Kendall replied. "My wealth was lost during the War. My body is not young, as you know, but my heart is yours. It always will be, whether you marry me or not. Surely you are aware of the likeness of our minds. We have shared so many wonderful hours together discussing our perceptions of life. Surely you realize that we are compatible. I know you do not love me. I must seem old to you, and certainly I am poor, compared to your father, but I do love you, and I promise to love your child as if it were my own; indeed, it shall be my own."

"Mr. Kendall," Carrie exclaimed. "Why have you not spoken of your feelings before?"

"I have spoken of my feelings, Miss Carrie, to your father."

"Oh," Carrie nodded sadly.

"He asked for my word of honor that I would not speak of my feelings to you."

"Honor," Carrie repeated the word. "Your word of honor. My father asked for your word of honor? Tonight it seems impossible that my father would be allowed to utter the word 'honor.' Is honor not dead now, Mr. Kendall?"

"No, dear Carrie, it is not dead, but it is struggling for life. I love you. In the face of the circumstances that you have outlined, I feel that I can break my word to your father and ask you to marry me, rather than have you forced into a life of great unhappiness."

"You do not know it all, Mr. Kendall, and when you do, you will not want me."

"I shall want you no matter what you say. I shall want you no matter what you reveal to me or choose to remain silent on."

Carrie realized that he was no longer holding both of her hands in the strength of his. She had exerted pressure on his hands too. She was actually grasping his hands. She looked into his eyes and tried to pierce past them into the brain that was the man called John Kendall. "Then know the truth, John Kendall. Robert Montgomery is the man I love. He is the father of my child. I have learned that he is the son of my father. Robert is my half brother, so I must turn away from my love for him."

"Then marry me, Miss Carrie. Marry me immediately."

"You have no reservations?" Carrie asked.

"No reservations," John Kendall insisted. "I take you as you are because I know what you are. You are everything fine, Carrie. You are everything I love. I would count myself a blessed man if I could have you as my wife."

"And my child?" Tears sprang to Carrie's eyes as she thought of her baby.

"Your child will be mine. Will you marry me, Carrie?"

She grasped his hands more firmly, leaned toward him and said, "Yes. Oh yes, Mr. Kendall, I will marry you. And I will be faithful to you every day of my remaining life."

"I have no doubt of it, my dearest." He removed one of his hands from hers and put his arm around her shoulders and pulled her close to him. She rested her weary head on his shoulder. "All will be well, now, Carrie. We shall make a life together," he promised.

Chapter 18

When Carrie retraced her steps back to the Bradford house, John Kendall was by her side, his hand placed gently under her elbow to lend her support. The core of Carrie's mind was at peace as she re-entered the garden she had left less than two hours before. She had not forgotten Robert, and her heart still grieved because it had been necessary to break off their relationship, yet she was certain that she was doing the right thing. How grateful she was to God for John Kendall!

"The house seems to be quiet. Father must still be away," she spoke softly to John. "I am sure Mother is upstairs resting, but Father said he would return tonight. He may be very late."

"We shall wait for him," John said calmly, "if it takes until dawn."

"Then let us go up to the drawing room and perhaps sit out on the piazza." Carrie led the way through the entry hall and up the curving staircase to the second-floor drawing room.

"This is not going to be an easy encounter," she said more to herself than to John. "I hope Father comes soon, so it can be swiftly settled."

"You will not encounter your father alone, Carrie."

"I know, and I am so grateful, but he has his own solutions to my predicament," Carrie reminded John, "and he is the most determined man I have ever known."

"But we have a better solution, Carrie, a solution based on truth, not deceit."

"Yes," Carrie agreed quietly. "Truth."

"Why don't we wait out on the piazza?" John took her arm and walked with her through the French doors onto the second-story verandah. "Here, at least, we can have the freshness of the sea breezes."

"And the purity of that white moon to inspire us." Carrie stared up into the sky for some time before confessing, "I feel so unclean, John. I am not sure I should be allowed to stand under such a moon."

"You must deny that thought this instant," John insisted, "or you will carry it the rest of your life. You have done nothing wrong, Carrie. You have simply walked through the days of your life believing that those you loved were telling you the truth. If there is any tarnish on anyone's soul, it is on your father's, not on yours."

"And yet I love Father still," Carrie said sadly. "I cannot quit loving him."

"Nor should you," John consoled her. "The more you live, Carrie, the more you will understand that life brings many circumstances where we find that we cannot love the sin, but we can and should love the sinner. Your father has made mistakes, committed sins, and those sins are now bearing fruit in your life, but not one of us is free from mistakes, not one of us is free from sin. You can love your father but disavow what he has done."

"Yes," Carrie's voice sounded lighter. "That I can do, and I do love him—even now. Oh, I hope he is not too insistent about his plans for my marriage to Brandon Hildebrandt."

"I think you should prepare yourself for some insistence on his part, dear Carrie. After all, from your father's perspective, marriage to Hildebrandt is the best solution. Your father has always been a man who values money and social prestige. I can offer you neither. In spite of the wrongness of his plans, try to remember that he thinks he is doing the best for his daughter."

"Those are the very words that Mother spoke earlier."

They stood for a moment and stared at the moon, which still sent a path of silver light across the bay. In the quietness of the moment Carrie thought of Robert, somewhere out there in the city, his heart broken by the long-ago actions of his mother, Diana, with James Bradford. How betrayed he must feel, she thought, that his mother's lies have brought him to such a miserable state. How confused he must feel. And how abandoned. At least I have John Kendall to stand by my side. She thought of John's goodness for a moment. There must be no secret between us, she decided, nothing we do not share. So she spoke the question that was in her heart, "John, what should I do about Robert?"

"What do you want to do, Carrie?"

"I know it is right that our marriage be dissolved; it is a wrong union in the sight of God as well as the law. I know that I must think of my child and that God has blessed me mightily by giving me your love. Through you, God has literally lifted me from sinking sand. But poor Robert—what pain and confusion he must feel now! I need to speak to him."

"Of course you do, Carrie."

"You agree?" Carrie was startled by his approval. "You do not mind?"

"I cannot pretend that I do not wish that you had never met Robert Montgomery, Carrie. Naturally I wish you had loved me always—that you loved me now. But I want you to come to me as unfettered as possible under these difficult circumstances. I do not see how you can do that if you do not talk to Robert. Besides, I feel the young man's anguish. To have lost you—how horrible— and his child. Surely he will feel better if he knows that you are not being forced into a deceitful marriage, into a marriage you abhor."

"Then I shall see him. Do you wish to be there?"

"No, Carrie, you need to see him alone. I trust you, but for the sake of your reputation and your child's reputation, have your mother nearby."

"Yes, that is wise."

"And, Carrie, I ask only one favor."

"What is that?"

"Persuade Robert that he must give up his child entirely. I know that will be difficult for him, but it is best for the child. Surely you can see that this is true; surely he will see it too."

Carrie murmured, "Yes, yes it is best," but tears filled her eyes. How hard it is to stop loving Robert, she thought. I have loved him for so long. Now, within the space of a few days I am supposed to lose all intense feeling for him because I am told that he is my half-brother. Yet those few words do not erase the love of years. Oh, Dearest Lord, stay close beside me. Do not allow me to weaken in my resolve to follow Your will. Help me to learn to love this man you have provided to rescue me—

Her prayer was interrupted by the clatter of the hoofs of a horse; she knew that her father was returning. John took her hand, and they waited in silence for James Bradford to arrive, dismount his horse, and enter the lower level of the house. Within moments Carrie heard her father's heavy boots on the staircase as well as her mother's softer tread as she hurried down the hall to meet her husband.

"I must go in," Carrie said quietly.

"I will go with you."

"No, not now. Please let me try to reason with him, John. I so much want him to approve of what I am going to do."

"Whatever you want, Carrie, but remember, even if he does not approve now, he will in time. When he sees that we are content together, even without great wealth, he will approve." Carrie nodded and walked through the French doors into the dimly lit drawing room.

"Carrie, there you are," her father blurted out. He threw his riding gloves down on a chair and turned to his wife, who was entering the room behind him. "I am glad you are still up, Mary. I have gotten things completely settled now." He turned back to Carrie. "I have visited Brandon Hildebrandt and told him of your eagerness to marry quickly now that you have made up your mind to marry him." He turned to his wife abruptly. "Mary, what we need is an elegant but quiet family wedding. I think it would be best to hold it here in this house. Hildebrandt plans to take Carrie to Europe for an extended wedding trip, and by the time they return—"

"No," Carrie said firmly.

James wheeled around to look at his daughter. "What?" he demanded.

"I am not going to marry Brandon Hildebrandt, Father."

"Carrie, I have no intention of arguing with you any more," James exclaimed in an angry voice.

Carrie flinched but replied firmly. "There will be no argument. I have resolved things my own way. I am not going to marry Brandon Hildebrandt."

"Must I reason with you all over again?" James demanded furiously. "You cannot remain married to Robert. You are carrying his child. Your reputation, the future reputation of the Bradford family, and the well-being of your child are all at stake here. You are going to marry Brandon Hildebrandt and be grateful that he will have you."

"I see no reason to marry a man I do not love, a man who does not love me or my child. What he loves, instead, is your property and your name. I have a better alternative."

"You have no alternative whatsoever," her father insisted.

"That is not true, Bradford." John Kendall stepped through the door, and for the first time James Bradford knew of his presence.

"Kendall, what are you doing here? What kind of man would spy on a family discussion?"

"He is not spying," Carrie said. "He is here at my invitation. He is here to help me."

"Help you!" James exclaimed. "One more person in Charleston now knows of your predicament. What help is that?"

Before Carrie could answer, James turned to John Kendall and took a few steps toward him. "I know you, Kendall. I know you to be a man of honor. I do not know why you are here or how you came to be here, but I depend on your honor to forget everything you have heard in the last few moments."

"The last few moments were no revelation to me, James Bradford. I had heard it all before."

"Heard it before?" James stared at the man as incredulity spread across his angry face.

"I told him, Father," Carrie said quietly.

James whirled around and demanded of his daughter. "You told him? Why in the name of—"

"I told him," Carrie interrupted, "because it is time someone in this family started living the truth."

"Carrie and I are going to be married," John Kendall announced, then took several strides into the room where he could face James Bradford. "I found her in the church, crying out the sorrows that she has endured as a result of your behavior. You know that I have asked for her hand previously. You know that my love for her has nothing to do with her money or her name. I love your daughter for herself. When I discovered the predicament she was in, I felt freed from my promise to you not to speak of marriage to her. I have proposed. She has accepted me. We are going to be married."

"This is unthinkable," James insisted. "Do you know she carries another man's child?"

"I know she carries Robert Montgomery's child. I know how she came to be in that situation. I intend to marry her and make the child my own."

"Why should I allow you to marry my daughter and pretend to be the father of her child when Brandon Hildebrandt stands ready to marry her and make her the heiress to a fortune?" James demanded.

"You are not going to *allow* me to marry anyone, Father." Carrie strode quickly to his side and glared up at him.

"I am your father, Carrie. I have certain rights."

"You lost your rights when you fathered Robert Montgomery, when you lied," Carrie retorted. "My life is now a shambles because of your behavior. I will choose what I will do with my life from now on."

"I do love Carrie," John Kendall spoke up. "I have loved her for two years, as you know, James. I shall always love her. I shall always protect her."

"It is unthinkable that you should consider marrying him," James shouted at Carrie, as he pointed at John, "when you could marry Brandon Hildebrandt and be the wealthiest woman in this state."

"I care nothing for Brandon Hildebrandt's money. I shall marry John Kendall."

James was so angry his face was wine-colored. Rather than trust himself to speak directly to his determined daughter, he wheeled around to Mary and commanded, "Say something to your daughter!"

"I shall say something, James." Mary walked quickly to her daughter's side. "Carrie, I have never been so proud of you. You are making the right decision. You have turned away from deceit and chosen the truth. I thank God that such a man as John Kendall stands here ready to help you undo the damage that your father and I have done."

"Mary!" exclaimed James. "How could you say such a thing?"

"Because it is true!" Mary emphasized each word of her short response as she stared angrily into her husband's eyes. "Because it is true. Deceit has not solved the problems that you created as a young man, James. Instead, deceit has created more problems. I foolishly tried to persuade Carrie to continue that deceit, but she is wiser than both of us put together. She has freed herself, James, and I am proud of her." She turned back to Carrie, "I ask you to forgive me for my part in producing your current dilemma, Carrie."

"But, Mother, you did nothing to harm me."

"I buried my head in the sand. I chose to believe that you were safe when I should have done more to protect you. I should not have let you become a victim of the deceit that has surrounded you all your life." She turned back to her husband. "There will be a wedding in this house, James. Carrie is going to marry John Kendall. We shall have a festive, family wedding and do everything we can to give them a happy start in their new life together. The truth has set Carrie free, just as God's Word promises. The truth has set her free."

"Why, Caroline!" Aunt Kathleen exclaimed, as she returned her concentration to the present and focused on her great-niece's face. "You are crying. It is a moving story, but still," she paused and studied Caroline's face. "I cannot help but wonder, are your tears for Carrie or for yourself?"

"Both, I suppose." Caroline wiped her wet face. "Did the truth set her free, Aunt Kathleen? Did she go on and live happily?"

"It took time for my mother to live happily. She told me about the pains of her first years of marriage to my father, but she insisted she lived joyfully from the moment she rejected deceit."

"I don't understand," Caroline shook her head in confusion. "How can someone be joyful if she is not happy?"

"Well, to put it most simply, dear, happiness is a superficial emotion, something that we derive from the everyday circumstances of our lives. If the circumstances of our lives are positive at any given moment, we feel happy. If the circumstances are negative, we feel sad or angry. Joy, on the other hand, is not really related to the circumstances we are in. It is related to being in line with our convictions."

"In line with our convictions?" Caroline asked.

"Yes, dear, like Carrie, my mother, your great-grandmother. She chose to stay in line with her convictions. She did marry John Kendall. In so doing she remained true to her conviction that honesty is better than deceit. They had a simple but beautiful ceremony right here in the drawing room. She knew she was doing the right thing, and she knew that she had been totally honest with John Kendall. So there was joy deep inside of her about the rightness of what she was doing. At the same time, as you might well expect, she felt a veneer of unhappiness because, after all, she could not quit loving Robert Montgomery the minute she was told he was her half-brother. There had been many painful moments in the week leading up to the wedding. So she felt unhappiness, as well as joy."

"What happened to Robert?"

"He returned to Virginia. He agreed with Carrie that her decision was best. He was a young man of conviction himself, so in spite of his unhappiness from losing Carrie, he was able to do the right thing. Eventually he married and had a family. He never returned to live in Charleston; instead, he sold the family plantation."

"I see," Caroline said quietly. She stood and walked away from her great aunt and looked over the banister. She studied the white azaleas popping out among the red ones, and then she gazed at the sea.

"You have not asked about Carrie's child," Aunt Kathleen said gently.

"No," Caroline answered without turning around. "I assume the child was born."

"Yes," Aunt Kathleen said.

"Was it okay? The baby, I mean. Was it normal?"

"Not entirely," Aunt Kathleen answered. "The child was a boy, a very bright, happy little boy, but he had a club foot and was never able to walk normally."

"I've never heard anything about him." Caroline still did not turn to face her great aunt.

"That does not surprise me," Aunt Kathleen said. "Judith would never have spoken of him because of the circumstances of his conception. He only lived to be seven. Then he died of some sort of heart condition that he had apparently been born with."

"So Grandmother had a brother. She never talked about him, I suppose, because he was crippled; that would have been just like her," there was stinging bitterness in Caroline's voice. "Grandmother had no use for imperfection."

"I think Judith would not have spoken of the boy because of the pain she suffered as a result of his existence. Perhaps she could have accepted his crippled condition if there had not been such scandal attached to it."

"Scandal?" Caroline whirled around to face her great aunt. "They were not able to keep everything hushed up?"

"It is rarely possible to keep such a situation private, human nature being what it is. Eventually the coachman who had witnessed Mother's elopement with Robert Montgomery drank too much and talked too much, in spite of all the money that James Bradford gave him, and this community became aware of Carrie's marriage to Robert Montgomery. They never knew, of course, why she did not continue in that marriage and why she married John Kendall so quickly, but they gossiped a great deal and convinced themselves rather easily that the deformity of Carrie's child was due to her sin of marrying two men. Also, since the boy was born too soon after her marriage to John Kendall, they naturally assumed that he was the son of Robert. I am sorry to say that this community ostracized Carrie, my mother, so Carrie and John lived a quiet life. Even the Bradford name and wealth could not make them socially acceptable."

"So the truth did not set her free," Caroline said fiercely.

"Oh, but it did," Aunt Kathleen insisted. "Carrie cared little for what society said. She had a wonderful relationship with John Kendall, and after the death of her son, she gave birth to Judith, to John, Jr. and to me. My mother had her priorities straight, Caroline. She cared about truth and family."

"Did she never reveal what her father had done and the mess it had made in her life?"

"No, she never publicly revealed that."

"But why not? Why should she be scorned by society because of his mistakes? You just said the truth sets you free. Why didn't she tell the truth to society?"

"The truth only sets you free, Caroline, if you are the one who needs to tell the truth. James Bradford never chose to tell the truth. He chose, instead, to live his life of prestige and wealth and let his daughter pay the consequences for the actions of his youth and for his deceit."

"How could my Grandmother have loved such a man?" Caroline demanded. "She absolutely worshiped him, Aunt Kathleen. From the day I was born, I heard nothing from Grandmother except wonderful things about the grandness of James Bradford of Charleston."

"I do not doubt it, my dear. She did adore Grandfather Bradford."

"But how could she?" Tears sprang to Caroline's eyes. "Didn't she know what he had done? Didn't she care about the pain he had caused her own mother?"

"When she was a little girl, she did not know what James Bradford had done. You see, she was the first child born after Carrie's son died, and she was born into a family that was ostracized by society. Furthermore, her parents had little money. On the other hand, she had a grandfather who was famous by this time, famous as a politician and very wealthy. Judith suffered outrageous social rejection, and for a long time she blamed her parents. She thought that if she had money, she would not be snubbed. James Bradford continued obstinately to pretend that the past had not occurred, and he had plenty of money. Judith turned her love toward him and away from her parents. He eagerly lavished his attention and his wealth on Judith from the moment he realized she craved it. Occasionally Mother allowed him to give things to Judith. Unfortunately she took to wealth and power, just like James Bradford always had. They were as alike in character and personality as any two people could be. Every time Mother refused to allow Judith to receive another gift from her grandfather, Judith turned on her mother in fury. The older Judith became, the more she resented the lower position of her own parents, and the more she admired the higher position of her grandfather."

"Where was her grandmother? Where was Mary during all this?"

"Mary was there, trying her best to counter Judith's natural tendency toward materialism, but it is hard to make a child listen to words about values when her grandfather is offering her dresses and every trinket her heart desires."

"I am surprised that Carrie did not keep Judith from seeing her grandfather."

"I am sure she thought about doing that, but Mary, our grandmother, was such a wonderful influence. Mother would have been crazy indeed to keep us away from her, and there was no way for us to see her without seeing Grandfather. Besides, you must realize, Caroline, that Judith's personality was shaped to some degree before she was born. She was quite naturally like James Bradford. I am not sure that keeping her away would have done that much good, and there were other children to consider. I was born when Judith was four, and then our younger brother, John, was born. We reacted very differently to James Bradford. We adored our grandmother, but we were very aware of a superficiality in James Bradford. We were not like him. We did not do what he wanted, and so for the most part he ignored us."

"So the truth set Carrie free when she told John Kendall the truth, but it didn't set my grandmother free, did it? She ended up being the victim of James Bradford, just like her mother was."

"That is where you are wrong, dear. All her life Judith had heard whispers, bits of gossip about our mother. We all had. We knew we lived on the fringe of society, that we were acceptable only because we were related to James Bradford. When Judith was about twelve, she finally heard more than just whispers of gossip. A little girl who was supposedly a friend of hers told her about Mother's two marriages that had occurred so close together. The little girl went so far as to tell Judith that her dead brother was a bastard, and that that was the reason the family was not socially acceptable. In other words, she told Judith that it was Mother's behavior that had caused so much difficulty in Judith's life. Naturally enough, Judith came home furious and screamed terrible things at our mother. Mother told her that there were reasons why she had married twice. She did not deny the truth, but she did not tell her the actual reasons why she had married twice."

"But why didn't she tell her?" Caroline demanded. "Why did she go on protecting her father?"

"How could she possibly tell a small child about the sinful, sexual activities of her grandfather after the Civil War? At what point, Caroline, do you sit down and tell a little girl that her grandfather has done sinful things that have brought shame upon her mother and consequently upon her? And also, you must remember, dear, that my mother, Carrie, was full of love. She would have done nothing to harm anyone. If the scriptures said, 'honor your father and mother,' she did, whether she agreed with their actions or not. If the scriptures said that love is the greatest of all human actions, then my mother loved. She was a true Christian, and there is, after all, precedence in the Christian tradition for One paying the price for the sins of others."

"So she just let Judith blame her?"

"I do not know what Mother would have done when Judith was older. No one will ever know because Grandmother stepped in and told Judith the truth."

"She told Judith that James Bradford had had an affair?"

"Yes. She told Judith the truth, straightforwardly."

"How did Judith—how did my grandmother respond?"

"Just as one might expect. She turned on Grandfather. She would not listen to Mother, who tried for over a year to reason with her, to convince her that only forgiveness would bring her peace. Judith insisted on being sent to a boarding school in Virginia. Finally Mother decided it was best for Judith to get away; she hoped that distance would help Judith to forgive. Mother had no money to send her to such an exclusive school, of course, but Grandfather did; and in hopes of regaining her affections, he paid for her to go to Virginia and attend boarding school in great style for many years. She returned to Charleston only for short holidays. She never forgave Grandfather; instead, she felt that he owed her anything his money could buy. When she was fifteen, she told me that she had met a wealthy Texas girl at the school and that it was her intention to marry that girl's brother when she was old enough to do so. And utilizing Grandfather's prominent name and his money, she did exactly that and became Mrs. Franklin Hamilton of Dallas, Texas."

"The truth did not set Grandmother free, Aunt Kathleen. At least, it doesn't seem to me it set her free."

"Oh, but it did, my dear. You see, the truth sets you free to *choose*. Mother chose her course of action when she knew the truth about her marriage to Robert Montgomery. My father, John Kendall, chose to marry Mother when he knew the truth. When Judith knew the truth, she chose to turn on those who had loved her, to embrace the same values that had harmed her so much, to go out and use people for her own gain, in the same way her grandfather had."

"Yes, you are right," Caroline said sadly, "yes, that is the way she lived her life, and that is exactly what she taught me to do. I never even knew there was another way to approach life until Mother refused to go on living Grandmother's way and started volunteering to help the poor. I thought she was crazy to do that."

"I am sure Marian tried to explain to you why she was making such a radical change in her life."

"She did," Caroline agreed. "She tried over and over, but I liked Grandmother's way of life better."

"You were accustomed to it. One might even say you were educated to it by Judith. And it is much easier to be self-centered."

"Did you learn the truth about James Bradford at the same

time as Grandmother did?"

"I did. I was eight years old. It was difficult for me to understand exactly what had happened, but I did understand that Mother had been put into an impossible situation and that she was totally innocent of any blame. My grandmother made that plain."

"So you chose to stay here?"

"Of course, my dear. I had no reason to hide my head in shame or to run away. My grandfather had made a mistake that he had never admitted to, but my mother, the victim of his mistake, had told the truth. I honored her greatly for her courage, and I adored my father, John Kendall, for loving her."

"Didn't you suffer from the scandal?" Caroline asked.

"At first, but scandal dies, Caroline. If you are the subject of scandal and you give it no room in your mind or your heart, if you pay no attention to it, it dies. People only keep scandal going if they can see they are causing pain and disruption. I have had a wonderful life here in Charleston. By the time I was a teenager, our family was well-accepted, and I was able to marry the man I loved. My brother was quite successful and married well. We have all been very happy here because our happiness has been based on acceptance of the truth, on the fact that human beings make mistakes, but there is forgiveness and the ability to go on, if one chooses to forgive and to go on."

"Do you think Grandmother was happy?" Caroline asked.

"I think you could tell me better than I could tell you, perhaps."

"It's funny, Aunt Kathleen. I always thought she was happy, even though I could see she was very driven to obtain things and to be considered the grande dame of Dallas society. It's true that I never saw her at peace, but I didn't know that anything was lacking. I didn't know that peace was a part of life. I thought life was all about happiness, and Grandmother seemed to be happy because she was able to get anything she wanted and able to control anyone she wanted to control."

"But something opened your eyes."

"Oh, Aunt Kathleen!" Caroline rushed to where her great-aunt sat and knelt beside her chair. "I simply adopted Grandmother's values. I became a carbon copy of her. I thought I was doing everything so right because I felt so happy, and I was marrying into wealth, and I had so many things, but then—"

Caroline stopped.

"But then what?"

"Then I wanted one thing more."

"A baby." Aunt Kathleen said.

"Yes. A baby. I wanted a baby, so I deceived David, and that deceit is threatening to bring my whole life tumbling down. I was even ready to destroy my baby, rather than see my happy, frivolous life of ease come tumbling down. But now I'm so confused."

Aunt Kathleen leaned forward. "Why are you confused, Caroline?"

"I'm confused because before Grandmother died she tried to destroy the past which she had exalted into a god, a god she had taught me to worship. Her last actions shook me to my core. Why would Grandmother try to destroy the god that she had built? That's why I came here, to find the answer to that question, and now you've answered it. The god was not a god. The god was not worthy, and I built my life around it."

"So now you know that your great-great grandfather was not a saint, was not the god that your grandmother said he was."

"But don't you see," Caroline insisted. "If she was wrong about that, if she lied about that, was anything she taught me true?"

"I do not know, dear, but I do know there is great danger in basing your principles on the opinions of another person, whoever that person is. Your values must be based on bedrock ideas that have lasted thousands of years."

"I have based my ideas on the great Bradford legacy, and I find it is nothing but ashes; it doesn't exist, and when it did, it was not grand; it was poison."

"No, Caroline!" Aunt Kathleen took her by the shoulder and shook her. "There are **two** Bradford legacies. Open your eyes! Judith carried one legacy of the Bradfords throughout her life and gave it to you. But here, now, in Charleston, you see the truth. There is another legacy, a legacy of courage, of love, and of truth. That legacy is as much yours as the one that James Bradford and Judith gave to you. You know the truth, Caroline. It has set you free to choose. **Which legacy will you choose?** The remainder of your life depends on this choice, and so does your eternal life."

Caroline gasped, and a sob escaped her lips as she added, "and the life of my baby."

"I thank God that you are here," Aunt Kathleen said quietly.

Caroline began to cry. She put her head in her great-aunt's lap, as her tears became sobs.

"That is enough," Aunt Kathleen said firmly after a few moments. She stroked the auburn hair of the woman who was crying in her lap like a little child. "That is enough now, Caroline. You have told it all; it is all spoken. It is all out in the open. You have spoken the truth. God has sent you here, and He gave you the instinct to know that what your grandmother had told you was wrong. In His own mysterious way, He had her behave the way she did in the final hours of her life so that your curiosity would be piqued to the point that you could not stay away from Charleston. He brought you here to hear the truth, and now you have heard it."

She lifted Caroline's wet face. "You have heard the story of your great-grandmother's courage, the woman you were named for, the woman you look so much like. When she defied her father and married John Kendall, she took great risks to save her unborn child. The question is, will you honor or dishonor her name?"

"I could lose David," Caroline murmured. "I could lose everything."

"You will not lose your child."

"No, I won't. I will save my baby."

"Do you want a man who does not want his own child, however it was conceived?" Aunt Kathleen asked firmly. "Do these things that this man makes possible in your life, this social prominence, this wealth—do you want these things more than your child?"

"Grandmother would have said—"

"Your grandmother is dead. What do you want, Caroline?"

"I want to tell the truth and be free."

"And pay the cost of telling that truth, Caroline, whatever it might be?"

"Yes," Caroline sighed heavily. "I will pay whatever cost comes. I want to tell the truth and be free. I want to protect my child, and I want it to grow up knowing the truth."

"Well, my dear, we must begin by protecting your child now; we must stop discussing these upsetting things. It has all been told now. There is no need to say more. We shall have a light lunch; then I want you to take a nap. You have been through many upsetting ordeals—far too many in your condition. Besides, now that you have made your decision, I suspect that God will send your David around pretty quickly."

"David? Come here? But Aunt Kathleen, he's in London, and he doesn't know I'm here. No one knows I'm here."

Aunt Kathleen reached for Caroline's hand and smiled at her. A confident twinkle appeared in the elderly lady's eyes. "Those are small obstacles for God, Caroline. He is a great God, after all. Never forget it. Look what He has done in your life in the last week."

Chapter 19

David Morgan Randolph swung the wrought-iron gate open and entered the garden of the historic Charleston house with a resolution that was characteristic of his personality. He was a tall, handsome, obviously confident man who proudly stood straight as an arrow in his custom-tailored suit. He strode quickly into the middle of the garden before stopping to examine the large house with its two-storied piazzas facing toward the sea. It was obvious that he was startled by the beauty of the house and the magnificence of the blooming azaleas all around him, but he was a man with a mission. His eyes were tired; his face was strained, but his jaw was set with determination. He glanced hurriedly at the expensive wrist watch he wore and realized that it was still early, perhaps too early to intrude on this gracious home.

"Sir, would you be so kind as to hold this bowl of water for me?" a sweet voice requested from behind him.

Surprised, he turned and found that he was facing a small, delicate, elderly lady, a woman of great elegance. Her silvery white hair was swept up on top of her head and drew one's attention to her beautiful, blue-gray eyes. She was holding a large, crystal bowl of water, which she handed to David when he replied, "Of course."

"I do so appreciate your help," the lady said. "Now, if you will just follow me over here to the roses," as she spoke, she turned and walked gracefully away. Confused by this apparent apparition in what he had assumed was an empty garden, David followed without question.

"There," the lady said when she arrived at a bush of blooming yellow roses. "I think this is a yellow morning. Now, would you hold the bowl a little lower, please? I am not as tall as you are. I shall clip a stem of these magnificent roses," she did so as she spoke, "and plunge it into this bowl of water." She plunged the stem into the water. "Now I shall reach down into the water with the clippers and snip off about a half inch of the stem while it is still under water." She did so. "You understand, I hope," she said gravely, "that it is very important to cut the stem of the rose under water so that there is absolutely no chance that air can get into the stem."

"Yes, ma'am," David Randolph said as kindly as he could. He was beginning to feel quite tired.

The elderly lady clipped quite a number of roses, transferring each stem to the water immediately after clipping it off the the bush, plunging it under the level of the water, clipping a half inch off the stem and leaving the stem under the water, while David held the bowl for her and struggled to be patient. Slowly but surely she gathered quite a number of yellow roses. Finally she clipped the last stem under the water and left it in the bowl. "Are you sure you understand why these roses must be clipped under water?" she asked, as she peered up into his face.

David felt sure that he had been on trans-Atlantic flights far too long and that the combination of the antibiotic treatment he had been taking and the many hours of flight must have deranged his brain in some way. "I—I understand the chemistry of what you have told me," he said rather formally.

"People are just like roses, you know," the elderly lady informed him.

"They are?" David asked, then shook his head as if he were trying to clear cobwebs from it. "I'm afraid I don't really see the connection—ah—ma'am, I was wondering if—"

"Oh, but they are! People are just like roses. You see, if you do not keep a person sustained constantly by physical and spiritual nourishment, as well as by affection and self-esteem, then that person will not unfold and become the beautiful blossom that God created her to be. Now," she gently took his arm, "do not slosh that water on you, but please bring the bowl over to this little, wrought-iron table, if you do not mind." She turned and led the way down a path that was quickly becoming overgrown with the heavy blossoms of the blooming azaleas and roses. He put the crystal bowl down on the wrought-iron table, feeling that he had somehow wandered into a 1996 version of Oz, or some other mystical land.

"Here, for example," the elderly lady continued to instruct him, "look at this rose." She pointed to a single, pink blossom in a bud vase. The blossom had only opened half way before its stem had collapsed right beneath the bud. "It is a sad thing, is it not?" she asked.

"Yes, ma'am."

"Look at it. It reminds me so much of what can happen to a person. Indeed it reminds me of some people I know. You see, I was not a good nurturer of this particular rose. I cut it properly in the garden. I plunged it into the water and took a half inch off the bottom of the stem, and then I took it to a vase of water and immediately plunged it into that life-giving, nurturing water that God gave me for that flower."

"Yes, ma'am," David sighed and clenched his jaw in an effort to remain patient.

"Then I killed this rose!" The elderly lady looked up at him and confessed as dramatically as if she had just confessed to him that she had killed an innocent child. "Yes, I killed this rose because I did not continue to make it possible for this rose to be nurtured. You see, every day or so, I should have clipped the end of that stem off once again—always under water, of course!—so that the nourishment of the water could continuously flow up the stem of the rose. I should have clipped it every day under water and plunged it back into fresh water in the vase. There is really no other way to bring a rosebud into the full-blown beauty that God intended."

David stared at her for a moment, then looked at the rose, with its bowed, half-opened bloom, decided that he had undoubtedly met a crazy woman and began to think of strategies to extricate himself as gracefully as possible.

"The worst of my crimes," the lady continued, "is in the ultimate effect of what I have done." She nodded her head sadly. She picked up the bud vase and held up the single pink rose with its bowed bloom where he could see it. "There is no way that this beautiful, but stunted, rose will ever reproduce, is there?"

"I don't think I understand, ma'am, but I must be going—"

"Oh, but you must understand. You see, since I did not nurture it properly, since I did not give it all the things it needed to come into its full-blown beauty, it is dying. And since it is dying without opening fully, then it has not been able to produce and disburse its seeds."

"Yes, ma'am—I see, ah—what you're saying, of course, and I'm very sorry that this—ah—pink rose of yours has not been able to reproduce."

"I appreciate your sorrow," the elderly lady said gravely. She turned and put the bud vase back on the table. David took one step back away from her, thinking that he would politely edge his way out of the garden. Suddenly she whirled around and stared boldly into his face and asked, "Do you feel the same sorrow that your wife, Caroline, will not be allowed to come to full bloom, David?"

David stopped in his tracks, as frozen as if he had been instantly placed on the North Pole. He stared down at the silver-haired lady and found that he was mesmerized by her blue-gray eyes. "You know Caroline?" he stammered out his question.

"Of course, I know her. I am her Great Aunt Kathleen."

"You are?" David demanded.

"I am."

"Are you sure?" he asked.

"I am positive," the elderly lady smiled. "You look terribly tired, David. Caroline says you have been ill; nevertheless, I have been expecting you. Let us go inside the house and get you some coffee or breakfast or whatever you would like. Caroline is still asleep, I am happy to say. In fact, she slept all afternoon yesterday. I awakened her to give her a bowl of soup at supper time, but she went back to bed after eating." Aunt Kathleen turned and picked up the bowl of yellow roses and handed it to David before he could speak. "I knew yellow was the perfect color for today," she patted him on the arm. "You see, it's going to be a sunny day in this family. Now you follow me. Be careful. Don't slosh the water on your suit, and we shall get you fed and settled in. Later I shall put these roses in a magnificent vase, and we shall place them on the upstairs piazza. Perhaps outside your room."

David gave up trying to understand and did as he was told. Obediently he followed the tiny, elegant lady as she wound her way through the paths of her garden. He carried the crystal bowl of roses, carefully avoiding spilling the water on his suit. She opened the screen door on the lower piazza and waved for him to go in front of her into the main hall. There she took the bowl of roses from him and placed it on the hall table.

David regained his senses enough to ask, "Did you say that Caroline has been asleep since yesterday afternoon?"

"For the most part, yes. Poor thing, she has been through so much, as you know."

"Is she all right?" David asked.

"Well, I think she is fine, for the moment. No doubt she is in better condition than you are, in fact. You look as if you have been living on an airplane."

"I have," David admitted.

"I am sure it was a long, arduous journey, David, but you have done the right thing to come."

"Then Caroline is not all right?" David asked in alarm.

"No, not entirely. That will be up to you. Now, let us take care of your immediate needs. Have you had any breakfast?"

"No, ma'am."

"That is where we shall begin, by nurturing you." She picked up a bell off the sideboard and rang it. "One cannot nurture the soul if one does not nurture the body first," she explained to him.

An elderly black woman appeared in the hallway, as if she had been waiting to hear the bell. "Is he here, Miz Kathleen?"

"He is here, Betsy. David, may I present my housekeeper, Betsy, who gives me a great deal of trouble, but I put up with her anyway. Betsy, this is Mr. David Randolph."

"Miz Caroline's husband," Betsy nodded as she spoke. "Yes sir, I's been expectin' you. I'll get you some coffee quicker than you can swat a fly." Betsy turned and hurried back through the door that David assumed led into the kitchen.

"Come right this way up the stairs," Aunt Kathleen tucked her arm into the crook of his elbow. "It takes me a little while to climb these stairs, and I am always grateful for a gentleman's arm. But I suspect that you do not mind slowing down a bit anyway this morning."

"No, ma'am," David agreed.

When they reached the top of the stairs, she showed him the way out onto the upper piazza which he had seen from below. "The view out here is as stimulating as any cup of coffee, my dear David. Have a seat and tell me about your trip." She sat down on a wicker chair, and he settled himself on the matching wicker loveseat.

"There's not a great deal to tell, ma'am—"

"Do call me Aunt Kathleen," she interrupted him. "I have already told Caroline to drop the 'great.' There is no point in reminding me of my age; my bones are quite capable of doing that in a rather steady fashion."

David smiled at her. She was the most whimsical woman he had ever met. He still felt like he had been delivered into the hands of a benevolent spirit from another century, but at least Caroline was here and was safe, and this blithe, but possibly irrational creature was about to present him with some breakfast. "I tried to call Caroline from London before I flew out yesterday. Even though we had just talked, I was worried about her. I didn't like the way she sounded. When I called her back in Dallas and discovered that she was not home, I called her mother. Marian had begun to worry about her and had decided that Caroline might be here in Charleston; in fact, for some reason she felt rather certain Caroline had come here. I knew something was disturbing Caroline greatly if she would come to Charleston so quickly after her grandmother's death. By the way, please allow me to extend my condolences to you for the loss of your sister."

"Yes, thank you," Aunt Kathleen stared out across the banister for a long moment, "Poor, confused Judith, I hope she is not lost," she finally concluded her thoughts aloud.

David did not know how to respond, but Betsy saved him by hurrying in with a silver tray that held two silver coffee pots and three cups. She put the tray down in front of Aunt Kathleen. "This pot be yours," she said to Aunt Kathleen severely, as she pointed to the smaller vessel.

"Betsy, I have told you many times, I am grown."

"You's grown, but you ain't always smart," Betsy said, turned on her heel and started back toward the door. She paused at the doorway and spoke directly to David, "Don't you let her drink nothin' out of that other pot, Mr. David. I's leaving you in charge." Then she turned and left.

David turned to Aunt Kathleen in amazement and discovered that she was laughing behind the hand she held over her face.

"It is a little game, you see, David dear. This pot contains decaffeinated coffee, whereas yours contains the full-flavored, wicked brew. My doctor has decreed that I shall have no caffeine. I sneak a good amount in the tea I drink, so Betsy comes down on me rather hard about coffee. Here, let me pour you a cup. I am sure that you want the forbidden kind with all its diabolical stimulants."

"That would be wonderful," David agreed as he laughed.

Aunt Kathleen poured a steaming cup of dark liquid. "Sugar or cream?"

"No, thank you. Just black," he answered.

The coffee began the revitalization of David Randolph, and the breakfast that Betsy served completed it. She had just taken the tray of dishes away, and Aunt Kathleen was pointing out a sailing ship in the harbor, when suddenly one of the French doors at the far end of the piazza opened, and Caroline appeared in a blue dressing gown. The ruffles around the neck of the garment framed her rested, beautiful face and then gracefully cascaded down the full length of the garment to the floor.

"David!" she exclaimed the moment she saw him. "Oh, David!" She began to run the distance of the piazza, and David quickly abandoned Aunt Kathleen to meet Caroline halfway. He put his arms around her, swept her off her feet, and kissed her as if he hadn't seen her in months. Aunt Kathleen laughed quietly to herself as she looked at the couple and saw Caroline's bare feet dangling above the floor.

Eventually Caroline remembered Aunt Kathleen and broke herself away from her husband's arms. "Oh, David, have you met Aunt Kathleen?" She pulled him down the piazza toward the elderly lady.

"Of course, he has met me." Aunt Kathleen stood and walked toward them. She put one of Caroline's hands in her left hand and David's hand in her right hand. "We have had a short but lovely chat. Now I think it is time I make some phone calls I need to make. Besides," she turned and looked meaningfully into David's eyes, "you have a pink rose that needs nurturing." She squeezed both their hands, then pulled them close together before walking as quickly as she could into the house.

"A pink rose?" Caroline asked David.

"Don't ask me," David said. "All I know is, I came into that gate down there, met this little, old, silver-haired lady who immediately gave me a lecture on the proper way to cut roses so as to sustain them for the longest possible time." He lowered his voice and whispered, "Is she batty?"

"No," Caroline cried indignantly. Then she looked at David's face and laughed. "No," she said more softly. "She's not batty at all, David. She's smarter than the two of us put together."

"Well, what's all this about cutting roses then?"

Caroline pulled him over to the wicker settee, and they sat down together. "We can talk about that later," she said. "For the moment, just let me look at you, let me *be* with you. You look so tired, David."

"I am," he admitted, "but I'm so glad to be here."

"And I'm so glad you are here, so glad you cared enough to come."

"Did you ever doubt it?" he asked in amazement.

"I've doubted a lot of things in the last week, but let's not talk of that now. You've had your breakfast. Let's take a short walk in the garden, and then I want to see you sleep the morning away."

David slept more than the morning away once Caroline had pressured him to go to bed; he slept the entire day away. Caroline sat on the piazza outside their room, read a novel and peered out over the ocean and down at the beautiful garden while she waited for David to awaken. Occasionally she went in, stood by his bed and looked down at him, concerned that he might be ill again. She also worried incessantly about what he would say when she told him the truth.

Aunt Kathleen calmed her as much as she could, and when Caroline asked for advice about what to say to David, Aunt Kathleen replied simply, "You must go to a smarter source, my dear. Ask God what to say."

"Whatever I say, David will be furious," Caroline insisted.

"Very likely he will be, at first," Aunt Kathleen agreed. "So you best talk to God about that too. After all, He has control of David just as He has control of the entire universe. Of course, I could offer you some words of advice, but your strongest ally in this situation is God Himself."

"But Aunt Kathleen, I don't know how to pray to God—not really."

"Just talk to Him, my dear. Then be quiet and listen to the thoughts in your head."

During the long hours that Caroline had spent alone sitting on the piazza, she found herself often sending quick prayers to God in a way she never had before. She sent her questions and fears up to Him, and He filled her mind with a strong desire to tell the truth.

About four o'clock in the afternoon, Caroline heard David

stirring in the bedroom. She rang the bell for Betsy and ordered a tray of sandwiches and iced tea, then she paced up and down the piazza, wringing her hands nervously and biting her lower lip as she thought of what she had to tell her husband. It seemed like a century passed before he appeared, but when he did walk out onto the piazza, he looked rested and well. She ran to him and threw her arms around his neck, as if she had not seen him that very morning.

"Goodness, Caroline," he exclaimed. "If this is the kind of reception I'm going to receive after a little nap, I think I'll take up the habit of napping every afternoon." He embraced her tightly and kissed her as he ran one hand through her long, auburn hair. "Where's your aunt?" he whispered.

"She's out at a meeting," Caroline replied.

"Good," he said and began to pull her back toward the bedroom.

For a moment the thought flashed through Caroline's mind that making love to her husband would certainly be to her advantage before she told him the truth and faced his anger and possible rejection. "No, David," she said firmly, as she put away the thought of deceitfully manipulating him before getting down to reality. "We need to talk."

He looked down into her serious eyes and replied, "Normally I would argue that point, my lady, but I see from your face that we do need to talk. What are you doing here in Charleston anyway?"

"Come over here and sit down." She pulled him further down the piazza. "Betsy is bringing up a tray of sandwiches and some iced tea. You must be hungry. You haven't eaten since this morning."

"Okay," he agreed, "but don't drag this out, Caroline. I've been very worried about you, and looking at your face now is making me nervous."

"Here, let's sit here," Caroline said as she reached her favorite spot on the piazza and pointed to two chairs that faced each other. "I love to be able to look out over the ocean. There's something so soothing about this harbor, something so clean about the air that blows off of it. It seems to purify me, and what I have to say, David, is my attempt to achieve total purification from—"

Betsy came across the threshold with a tray, and Caroline stopped speaking.

"That looks great," David said to Betsy as she put it down on a tea table in front of him.

"Thank you, Betsy," Caroline smiled nervously as she looked up at the housekeeper. "Would you mind closing the French doors when you leave?"

Betsy looked a little startled for a moment, but then she nodded and left quickly, closing the doors behind her.

"Purification, Caroline?" David asked instantly. "What on earth are you talking about? You sound as if you're taking up holy orders or something. You do intend to remain my wife, don't you?" he laughed nervously.

"Of course I do," Caroline insisted, "if you want me to."

"What are you talking about? What do you mean, 'if I want you to'?"

"I'm going to explain, I promise." Caroline picked up a plate of sandwiches and served some onto a plate for David. "If you'll eat, I'll talk. I have a lot to fill you in on."

"Okay," David said warily as he took the plate from her. "Start talking, Caroline, before I go crazy worrying about you."

"Well, I suppose I should begin with the storm." Caroline sat back in her chair and tried to relax.

"I know about the storm," David said.

"Did you see the house in Dallas before you came here?"

"No," David said between bites. "I never left the airport. I just called your mother, then changed planes and came directly here. The house is okay, isn't it?"

"Oh, yes, the house is fine, really. It's just that it was such a bizarre kind of damage that was done, and it started me along a path of discovery, David."

David swallowed. "Discovery?" he asked, as he picked up a glass of iced tea.

"Yes, you see, that storm was really quite ferocious. It severely damaged houses all around our house, but the odd thing is that there was only one place damaged in our house. A large tree fell through the front window of the drawing room."

"You've told me about the tree before, Caroline," David said impatiently.

"I know, but it really is significant. Please David, just be patient. You see, the thing is that the tree just scratched the inside wall. It pulled a single item off that wall, and that item was the vest of James Bradford. You remember, my great-great grandfather's vest, the one that Grandmother cherished so much."

David nodded.

"Well anyway, I managed to salvage the vest, but the electricity was off, and I spent the entire night alone in the house with just candlelight and a little fire in my study."

"You shouldn't have stayed there," David exclaimed. "What were you thinking?"

"It doesn't matter now, David. As it turned out, I needed to stay there. You see, something remarkable happened. Since there was nothing to do and I was anxious, I couldn't go to sleep, even though they were patrolling the neighborhood. I had to stay awake, but it was difficult to read, so I examined that vest that has been behind glass for so many years, and I found a tiny piece of paper between the lining and the outer shell of the vest."

"Paper?" David asked. "What kind of paper?

"Well, it took me a little while to get it out, but I finally managed, and when I opened it up, it simply said, 'He knows nothing. Meet me at midnight.'"

"You must be making this up, Caroline. It sounds like something out of a romance novel," David scoffed.

"It has changed my life, David."

"A tiny piece of paper that said, 'He knows nothing. Meet me at midnight' has changed your life? Caroline, are you well?"

"I know it sounds bizarre, but please, just finish your sandwich and listen. There was something eerie about the fact that the storm could have damaged the house in so many ways, but it didn't. The only damage was from the tree. It was like that tree had a purpose, and that purpose was to bring that vest to the floor and shatter the glass so that I was required to handle the vest. It seemed like the storm, the loss of electric power and the necessity of staying in the house—they all led me to find that piece of paper. I felt so strongly that that piece of paper was significant to me, was a message, perhaps."

David stared at her with concern but said nothing.

"Anyway, I went to see Grandmother the next day, and when I told her about finding the note in the vest, she became terribly agitated, and when she did, I was even more positive that that note was significant."

"What did she say about the note?" David asked.

"She just demanded that I go get the note and the vest and bring it to her instantly, but then she and Monique seemed to exchange some kind of significant glance. It was obvious that Grandmother forced herself to curb her outburst so she wouldn't create any suspicion in me, and then she calmly asked me to bring the note and the vest the next day."

"And you did," David said.

"I never got a chance to. That night I received the call from Monique about Grandmother—" Caroline stopped abruptly as tears filled her eyes.

"That she was dying, you mean," David said gently.

"She didn't just die, David. It wasn't like that at all. You don't know. I rushed over there. I expected to find her, I don't know, reclining on a couch or unconscious or something, but instead she was sitting on the floor in front of a blazing fire. She was frantically destroying old family documents. She was obsessed, David; I had never seen her like that before. She was absolutely beside herself with fear, and it all seemed to center around destroying all the records of the Bradford past. It made no sense to me because she's always honored her past so much. Anyway, I couldn't calm her down until I promised to destroy every paper. I burned the papers while she watched. I did everything I could to calm her, but—but she died."

David leaned forward and took Caroline's hand. Tears were running down her face as she remembered the agony of her last hour with her grandmother. He handed her a clean napkin to wipe her tears away. "Don't go over all of this now, honey. It's not important. It takes a long time to get past grief. You have to let it out slowly but surely over an extended time. Don't try to force it out now."

"But I have to, David. You have to understand the sequence of events, or you can't understand what I'm going to say. I know this is so sudden, so absurd in a way, to sit here in this beautiful sunshine in this happy, peaceful place and talk about death. But I have to walk back through the last ten days because you have to know everything."

"Go on then," David said. "Just don't put yourself through more than you have to."

"Well, I didn't understand her reaction at all, to want to burn all the things that she had adored for so long. Even the vest, of all things! I promised her I would burn everything. Then she died, and I was so overwhelmed with her death and your illness, I didn't pay any attention to the papers whatsoever. Monique kept pestering me about them. There were a few things left that Grandmother had not been able to burn, and Monique kept bothering me, insisting I burn them, as if she knew what Grandmother had been trying to do. I could think of nothing but the loss of Grandmother and trying to help Mother and getting through the funeral and—oh David! I was so worried about you, absolutely petrified that you would try to come to the states and that the effort would kill you."

David nodded and squeezed her hand.

"So anyway, we had the funeral and, you know, I told you on the phone that I fainted and had to be taken home. Monique went with me. I was okay, but I woke up in the middle of the night, so I went downstairs to look at the papers that were left, and I found something in those papers that I didn't understand. I found two marriage licenses for my great-grandmother, Carrie, the woman I was named for. The licenses were dated only a few days apart, and that struck me as very significant somehow."

"But why should it be significant to you, Caroline?" David asked gently. "I can understand that it's historically interesting. It's a part of your family heritage. Of course, you would be curious about such a thing, but is it really significant to you in your life? Your great-grandmother lived a very long time ago."

"But I knew it was significant to my life. Somehow I just knew. Don't you understand? It was like I had found the thing that Grandmother was trying to destroy, but I didn't understand why it was so important to the present, so important that she would die trying to destroy it. I took the marriage licenses upstairs with me, and when I awoke again, I found that Monique had burned the papers. She wouldn't talk to me about it; she obviously knew a great deal more than she was telling me, and I became more suspicious."

"It is strange," David agreed. "A very peculiar story. I can't imagine Judith destroying one bit of the glorious past of the Bradfords. It doesn't make much sense. Still, I don't see what it has to do with you. Caroline, darling, I think you have been too overwrought and for good reason. The death of your grandmother alone is enough to make your reason a little off balance."

"No, you don't understand, David. I had plenty of reason to be disturbed. These happenings were like arrows in the woods pointing me down a particular path. I had to follow them. I got the genealogy of the family out, and I discovered that the first marriage license of Carrie, my great-grandmother, was to a man who seemed to be her cousin, and then the second one was to a man who, I knew, was my great-grandfather, John Kendall."

"And the fact that your great-grandmother was married twice in a short time has made you come all this way to Charleston?"

"No, it's more than that. I felt driven to learn the truth about my great-grandmother. I felt driven to understand why Grandmother turned on her past after exalting it for all those years. I had to know, David, but there was something else, too, that happened. You see, before Grandmother died, I went home with Mother and spent the second night after the storm with her. She took me down to an old building where she's trying to start a second shelter for homeless women and children. It was a dilapidated, horrible place, and I found three little children living in a cardboard box in the backyard of that building. Oh David, it was horrible! There were old syringes on the ground from drug users and filth beyond description, and these tiny children were living in a cardboard box. The oldest couldn't have been more than five or six years old, and I found out from Mother that they were probably there because they were homeless, because their father had abandoned their mother." Caroline slowed her words down. "I was very disturbed by that."

"You are a tender-hearted person, Caroline. Of course you were disturbed by that. You've never been exposed to such things, but honestly, darling, I don't see any connection between those children and your great great-grandfather's vest and your coming to Charleston."

"I know, I know, just listen, David. After I saw the children and Grandmother died, I sat at the funeral, and I listened to people extol her way of life, and I began to see that it was all a lie. It was all false."

"A lie? Your grandmother was lying?"

"Yes, I knew she had lied to me about some aspect of the Bradfords, but it was more than that. I knew that all her values were lies. Don't you remember? I told you that Mother raised me like Grandmother wanted me to be raised until I was a young teenager. At that time, Mother came to Charleston and stayed several weeks, and when she returned, she dropped everything to do with society and became a volunteer to serve the homeless of Dallas. Mother became the opposite of what Grandmother was, but I had been raised to be like Grandmother, and I chose Grandmother's way. But when I saw those children, and then Grandmother died trying to destroy something about her past, something she didn't want me to know, something she didn't want the world to know—I was so confused that it drove me almost crazy, David, and finally I just got on a plane and came here."

"And have you learned anything since you came here?"

"Yes, oh yes, David, I've learned a great deal! I told Great-Aunt Kathleen all that I've told you, and she told me the story of James Bradford, my great great-grandfather, that hero whom Grandmother spoke of as if he were a god. But he wasn't what Grandmother said he was."

As briefly as possible Caroline told David the story of James Bradford's affair with Diana Montgomery. She told him about the birth of Robert and later the birth of Carrie, and of how they had fallen in love and married and produced a son. She told him that even John Kendall's loving actions had not saved Carrie from being socially ostracized.

"I know it's all very complicated," she said. "The details are many, but the bottom line is very easy to see, David. James Bradford lived his life for himself. He used people for his own purposes, and because of that, he hurt his wife, he hurt his daughter, Carrie, and he hurt his grandchildren, especially Judith, my grandmother. David, when she was twelve years old, she found out the truth about her grandfather. She turned on him, but unfortunately, she did not turn on his values. Instead, she hardened her heart. She became more determined than ever to rise to the top, to own, to control, and that's exactly what she did, and that's exactly what she taught me to do, and I was a willing student."

David sat back in his chair and stared at Caroline for a moment. "You are like your grandmother, Caroline, in many ways. You are beautiful, and you place great value on your beauty. You are confident, composed and graceful. I've always been so proud of you. I've never seen you in a social situation where you weren't the reigning monarch in the room. Those are the sorts of things that I love you for, and now you tell me they are wrong?"

"They are empty, David. There's nothing wrong with being beautiful or socially adept, but I have cared for no one except the small circle of people who support the bubble I have lived in, the bubble of elegance and wealth and ease of life."

"But, Caroline, I count myself lucky to be the man who creates that bubble for you to live in. I count myself lucky to be the man in your life."

"I know, I know you do. I think you were raised the same way I was, with the same values I was raised with, but those values are flawed, David, and that's what I've discovered. You see, when I came here, Aunt Kathleen told me the real story of her grandfather, James Bradford, the story of the deceit in his life and how that deceit has hurt so many of his descendants. She also told me the story of my great-grandmother, Carrie, who refused to be deceitful, who embraced the truth at all costs. I discovered, David, that there are two legacies from the Bradfords. One of them is the legacy of great-great grandfather, James Bradford. His legacy was power, prestige, money. The legacy of my great-grandmother, Carrie, was the legacy of truth and loving concern for others. Unfortunately for me, my grandmother, Judith, carried James Bradford's legacy to me. The more you get to know Aunt Kathleen, you will see that she has carried the opposite legacy."

"And you now want to be like your Great Aunt Kathleen, not like Judith?"

"Yes," Caroline reached across the table and grabbed his hand. "Yes, David, I want to be like my great-grandmother, Carrie. I want to be exactly like her."

"That's what you think your mother has done?"

"Yes. Mother came here, and she found out the truth, and she changed her life, and look how happy she is. When I compare her happiness to the flimsiness of the happiness that Grandmother and I experienced, it amazes me that I could have been blind so long. David, I want to change my whole value system. I want both of us to change our value systems."

"I really don't understand what's wrong with our value system, Caroline. What would you change?"

"We live for ourselves."

"Who should we live for, Caroline?"

"We should live for other people. God has blessed us with so much wealth, so much control and power in this world. We should try to help other people."

"We can certainly do that, Caroline. Of course we can do that. Darling, if you want to do charity work like your mother does, I'll certainly support you. If you'll be happy doing charity work, if it will make you feel better about yourself, I'm all for it. Surely you know I would give you anything to make you happy."

"But it's not for me, David. I don't want to do charity work for me, to make myself happy. I want to do it to help those in need."

"Well, okay. So you do charity work to help other people who are in need. Great. Take on any projects you want to take on. Help your mother, or start something of your own. You can give as many hours of your day as you want to charity. You have no other obligations, except for the social obligations that we have. Just don't let it interfere with our business obligations and our friends and that part of our life—"

"You don't understand at all, David. If I give my life to help other people, of course it's going to interfere with the beautiful bubble we live in. It's going to push the sides of that bubble out. It's going to burst that bubble, but it will be worth it. I will have changed my value system."

"To what, Caroline?"

"I will be living an unselfish life for a change."

"Okay, okay," David acted as if he were pampering a disturbed child. "So you're going to change your value system. You're going to do charity work. No problem."

"I still don't think you understand. I want to think differently. I don't want to just go do charity work. I want to think differently about my life, about myself, about you, about the world I live in. David, I want to stop and ask God what He wants me to do."

"Caroline, what's come over you? What's happened to you? Darling, I think you just need to take a long rest. You've been through a great deal—"

"No, David, I don't need to rest. I need to push through, push through the barrier to reach the place where I'm supposed to be. I have to finish the journey I started the moment that tree fell through the drawing room window. Don't you understand? My life-style, my thoughts, my actions, the way I approach every hour of my life—they've led me down a bad path, a damaging path."

"Nonsense," David exclaimed. "You've never done a bad thing

in your life, Caroline. So what if you worry about your hair, and you decorate your house, and you care about the arts? That doesn't make you a bad person."

"Does lying make me a bad person, David?"

"You've never told a lie in your life, darling. Oh, maybe some little white lies, some little social lies, but nothing really meaningful. Caroline, you are not a deceitful person. Somehow you've identified yourself excessively with your grandmother in the last week, and apparently she did do a lot of lying, but you're not deceitful."

"I am deceitful, David. I have been deceitful. I have lied to you."

"How?" David drew back and relaxed his arms on the chair. "How have you lied to me, Caroline?"

"I am pregnant, David. I am going to have our child."

David stared at her in silence. His face slowly turned a deeper and deeper shade of crimson, as anger rose in him. "You promised me before we married that you would never put me in this situation," he said coldly. "You promised me. We agreed."

Caroline nodded her head. Her eyes were full of tears. "I promised," she whispered.

"Then why did you do it?" David demanded.

"Don't you see?" Caroline cried. "I wanted to! I wanted a baby. I didn't think about anything else. I didn't think about you. I didn't think about my promise. I didn't come to you and reason with you, plead with you. I did exactly what Grandmother taught me to do. I evaluated the situation on the basis of what I wanted, and I wanted a baby, so I tricked you into this pregnancy."

"Are you telling me that Judith agreed to this plan, that she encouraged you to do this?"

"No, no. Of course not. I am telling you that my selfish, deceitful action was the kind of behavior Grandmother had taught me. She didn't know I was going to trick you into a pregnancy. If she had known, she would have helped me to do a better job of it. When she found out, she was furious with me."

"Well, I'm glad to hear that, at least."

"Are you, David? She was furious with me—furious because I had not manipulated you cleverly enough. I had endangered my relationship with you. That's what angered her. I had endangered my marriage to a wealthy, prominent man. She didn't care about my feelings; she didn't care about your feelings, and she certainly didn't care about our child. In fact, she suggested that I have an abortion."

"An abortion!" David exclaimed.

"Yes, an abortion. That was her solution, but I was way ahead of her. The day you came home furious that Suzanne had tricked Scott into a pregnancy, I was already pregnant, and I knew it. I had planned to tell you on our vacation in Greece, but you were so angry with Suzanne and you said you were so glad you could trust me. But you couldn't trust me, David; you just didn't know it. I was pregnant at the time, but because you were so angry at Suzanne, I immediately thought only of saving myself, of saving my fairytale life. Don't you think I thought of aborting our child?"

"I don't know what to think, Caroline."

"Well just listen, please listen. I didn't know what to do after you were so angry. I didn't want to talk to anyone in the family, but I became ill, and Grandmother guessed. She became furious because my marriage to a prominent, wealthy man was more important to her than her great-great grandchild, which I was carrying. That disturbed me, David. It disturbed me a lot. It disturbed me even more when I realized I had been thinking the same way. I had been thinking that this baby, this life inside of me, was expendable if it meant some inconvenience to me or to you or that you would dismiss me from your life. David, I had to face myself in the mirror and realize that I was considering murdering my child rather than losing my life of luxury. At that very time I knew that there was at least one mother in the slums of our city who was living with her children in a cardboard box and was doing everything she could to keep them alive. I didn't like the image of myself I saw in my mirror, David; I didn't like it at all."

"Caroline, you are not a woman living in a slum in a cardboard box. That has nothing to do with you. That has nothing to do with any of this. It sounds to me like you've been listening to your mother too much or something. I don't know what's wrong with you, but how could you do this to me? How could you promise me, solemnly promise me, that we would not have children and then trick me into a pregnancy?"

"I told you how I could do it, David. I was raised with a set of principles that made it very simple to be deceitful. That's what I want to change. I don't want to live that way any longer."

"I don't want to hear about sets of principles," David stood up so quickly that the wicker chair he had been sitting in fell over backwards. "I don't want to hear about your ancestors, good or bad. I don't want to hear about Judith or about the storm. I don't want to hear about any of this. The bottom line is you broke your promise to me. You lied. It doesn't matter what people have been doing in your family since the Civil War. I am only interested in our lives. You lied to me," he shouted, then turned and strode through the French doors, stormed down the hall and the staircase.

Caroline sat and sobbed. Over the banister of the piazza, she could see David stalking across the garden and slamming out of the gate. "Dear God, help me," she cried aloud. "I told him the truth. Now please, please help me."

Aunt Kathleen joined Caroline a few moments later and held her close while she continued sobbing.

"He's gone, Aunt Kathleen. I've lost him."

"There, there," Aunt Kathleen tried to soothe Caroline. "Let us not draw conclusions too quickly. David loves you. You have just given him a piece of news he never wanted to hear, but he will come to his senses. He may not like everything you have done. He may not like everything you propose to do in the future, but he loves you. We must depend on that love to carry him through this crisis."

"But what if he doesn't come back? What if he just keeps going and our life together is over?"

"I do not think your David is that kind of man, Caroline, but if he is, your life with him is not worth having. Now come, dear, I want you to lie down. This has been very difficult for you, I know, and you have a child to protect."

Caroline looked up at her Aunt Kathleen's gentle face.

"Leave it to God," Aunt Kathleen said quietly. "Come now, let us take care of you and leave David to God."

The daylight was fast leaving the sky when David opened the wrought-iron gate and stepped once again into the garden. He took several decisive steps toward the house, then stopped and looked at it. It was a majestic, white structure that at that moment seemed almost pasted against a sky of rose and amber. All around him the garden was aflame with jeweled tones. He had thought he was ready to face Caroline, but now, when he found himself back in this garden, all the definitive words of rejection that he had planned seemed too harsh, too final. The longer he stood there, the more the garden had its softening effect on David until his decisiveness had disappeared entirely. "Great," he muttered, then retreated to his left, down one of the winding paths, unthinkingly following the path wherever it led. He had a vague idea that he would find a bench and sit and re-examine the conclusions he had reached in the hours he had been away. At the end of the path, he found a wrought-iron table with several chairs around it. Absent-mindedly he sat and stared for some moments at drifting petals that were floating down from a white dogwood. The amber color of the sky began to fade. The rose tones grew deeper and were joined with the purple of twilight.

"So you have returned," a quiet voice said somewhere amidst the bushes to his right.

When Great Aunt Kathleen appeared, David was not surprised. He rose from his chair without thinking.

"Do not bother to rise," she said quietly, "although I appreciate the gesture." She had a pair of gardening shears in her hand and began to cut dead blooms off a pink rose bush close to the table.

David did not know what to expect from her or even what she knew. "It's a beautiful sunset," he offered as an opening to a polite conversation.

"Yes, indeed," Aunt Kathleen said, as she busied herself with her shears. "God seems to me to be most impressive at this time of day." She snipped off a long-stemmed, pink rosebud, and holding it in front of her, walked over to the table where David sat. Without looking into his face, she spoke directly to the pink rosebud she had just cut. "I shall not nurture you, Caroline," she said. "You are beautiful just as you are. I want you to stay exactly as you are now. Do not think of opening your petals. I do not want you to come to maturity. If you should come to maturity, you would die. I insist that you deny that you are a rose. I insist that you pretend that you are a rosebud forever." She lay the pink rosebud in front of David on the table.

He stared at it for a long moment. He wanted to agree with her, but anger rose up in him when he thought of Caroline's lie. "She lied to me," he said bluntly to Aunt Kathleen.

"Ah," Aunt Kathleen said slowly. "So your rose has a thorn? Best cast it away from you. A thorn can pierce your skin and cause you pain. Surely you can find another rose that has no thorns."

"You don't understand," David insisted. "It isn't as simple as you make it out to be."

"I know about your first wife, David. I know you lost her. I know you lost your first child. Caroline's lie is not the first thorn you have found in life, but were those first thorns of life so piercing that you decided, unlike other men, you could not heal and must therefore protect yourself by rejecting fatherhood forever? Or is the truth that you had lived alone, selfishly doing exactly as you pleased for so long, that when you met Caroline, you did not want the wonderful ease and delight of your life to be ruffled in any way?"

"She lied to me," David blurted out.

"Yes," Aunt Kathleen agreed. "She was wrong to do that. She was wrong to lie to you. She was wrong to trick you, but you are wrong to allow your fear or your selfishness to control you now."

"She lied to me," David said again. "I don't need to know anymore. She has deceived me. I can't go on living with a woman who deceives me."

"Very well, David Randolph. Wrap yourself in your great cloak of moral indignation. You who have never lied. You who have never used another person for your own purposes. Wrap yourself in your cloak of moral indignation, if you must. Ignore the fact that you married Caroline and entered into a degree of intimacy with her that was meant to produce children, yet you denied her that possibility. Go! Abandon Caroline and your child, if you must, but do not play the saint with me, you hypocrite. You are no saint, David Randolph, you are a coward." Aunt Kathleen leaned across the table until her face was no more than three feet from David's. "You are a coward, David Randolph, a paltry excuse for a man. You are a self-centered coward who will not allow his love for his wife to overcome his fears. Get out of my garden!"

David stared into the elderly, angry face, and Aunt Kathleen's piercing, blue-gray eyes paralyzed him until she drew herself up to her full height and ordered, "Get out of my garden! This is no place for a coward!"

He rose in confusion and fled from her presence as a great sense of shame overcame him.

Aunt Kathleen smiled slightly and picked up the long-stemmed, pink rosebud. "That should do it," she spoke directly to the flower, dropped it into an empty, dry bud vase on the table, turned and walked serenely back to her house.

Before first light the next morning, Aunt Kathleen rose from her bed and sat down next to the French doors. She turned on a small lamp and opened her Bible. She read a psalm of praise to God, one of the many psalms that proclaim God's ability to do wondrous things in the midst of great obstacles. As light began to dawn, she walked out onto the piazza to watch the sun lift itself out of the bay.

In a few moments she heard Caroline's door open, and Caroline joined her on the piazza as she wrapped her blue dressing gown around herself. Her face looked strained, and her eyes were red from crying. Aunt Kathleen put her arm around Caroline's waist and pointed toward the horizon. "Look at that magnificent, new day coming," she said.

Caroline stared at the new sun, but her heart felt anything but light. Then she heard the wrought-iron gate of the garden opening. Her eyes darted to the gate, and there she saw David. "It's David," she said breathlessly.

"Of course it is," Aunt Kathleen gave her a little hug.

"I must go to him," Caroline started to cross in front of Aunt Kathleen, but Aunt Kathleen stopped her.

"No, my dear. Wait here. If he wants you, he will come to you."

Caroline felt that she did not breathe a single breath while she watched David walk determinedly through the garden and heard him come up the stairs and out onto the piazza.

He said nothing. Instead, he took Caroline's hand and started to pull her back into the house. When they reached the threshold, he turned around and held out his other hand to Aunt Kathleen.

"David, are you okay?" Caroline asked meekly.

"I want to talk to you, both of you, in the garden," was all he would say.

Aunt Kathleen took his extended hand, and they descended the staircase slowly, so that Aunt Kathleen could keep up. He walked them through the lower hall, across the lower piazza, and out into the garden. Caroline looked confused and dazed, but

Aunt Kathleen was trying to hide a smile. David did not allow them to stop until he reached a wrought-iron table amidst the roses. There in the middle of the table, the dry bud vase remained where Aunt Kathleen had left it. The pink rosebud in the dry vase had drooped its lovely head.

Without a word and without any ceremony whatever, he picked up a rusty pail of water and put it on the table. He jerked the drooping, pink rosebud out of the bud vase. He filled the bud vase with water from the pail, turned to a pink rosebush, and taking his pocket knife, he cut a long-stemmed rosebud from the bush. He thrust it immediately into the rusty pail of water, cut a half-inch off the bottom of the stem, and quickly transferred the rosebud to the bud vase. Then he turned to Great-Aunt Kathleen. "Well," he demanded, "did I get it right?"

Aunt Kathleen smiled at him and replied, "That rusty bucket is hardly a crystal bowl, but you have gotten the general idea at last, David Randolph."

"What does all of this mean?" Caroline demanded.

David turned and took her in his arms but held her at arm's length so he could see her face. "It means, darling, that we're going to have a baby. It means I'm going to try my very best to nurture you and our child and maybe a few other people too." He pulled her close to him and embraced her with great tenderness. Then in spite of Aunt Kathleen's presence, he leaned over and kissed her firmly and long on the lips.

Aunt Kathleen laughed happily and proclaimed to her garden, "The true legacy of the Bradfords will live on now. Truth! So simple, yet so powerful. Ah, life is grand!"

Seton St. Clare Books
P.O. BOX 8543, WACO, TX 76714-8543

Please send me the following books:

QUANTITY	TITLE		AMOUNT
_____	CELEBRATION!	$12.00	_____
	Mailing & handling	2.00	_____
(Texas residents please add 8% sales tax)			_____
		TOTAL	_____

(PLEASE PRINT CLEARLY)

NAME _____

ADDRESS _____

CITY_____ STATE_____ ZIP_____

- -

Kay Moser grew up surrounded by the magnolias, pines and azaleas of historic Nacogdoches, Texas, a town with a distinctly Southern culture. Her love of literature led her to become an English profesor. She now lives in Waco, Texas, and writes full time. In her spare time she collects heirloom clothing and grows azaleas and roses.